THE SPANISH CAPE MYSTERY

ELLERY QUEEN was a pen name created and shared by two cousins, Frederic Dannay (1905-1982) and Manfred B. Lee (1905-1971), as well as the name of their most famous detective. Born in Brooklyn, they spent forty-two years writing the greatest puzzle mysteries of their time, gaining the duo a reputation as the foremost American authors of the Golden Age "fair play" mystery.

Besides co-writing the Queen novels, Dannay founded *Ellery Queen's Mystery Magazine*, one of the most influential crime publications of all time. Although Dannay outlived his cousin by nine years, he retired the fictional Queen upon Lee's death.

OTTO PENZLER, the creator of American Mystery Classics, is also the founder of the Mysterious Press (1975), a literary crime imprint; MysteriousPress.com (2011), an electronic-book publishing company; Penzler Publishers (2018); and New York City's Mysterious Bookshop (1979). He has won a Raven, the Ellery Queen Award, two Edgars (for the *Encyclopedia of Mystery and Detection*, 1977, and *The Lineup*, 2010), and lifetime achievement awards from NoirCon and *The Strand Magazine*. He has edited more than 70 anthologies and written extensively about mystery fiction. To learn more, visit his website at MysteriousBookshop.com

THE SPANISH CAPE MYSTERY

ELLERY QUEEN

Introduction by
OTTO PENZLER

AMERICAN MYSTERY CLASSICS

Penzler Publishers
New York

Published in 2022 by Penzler Publishers
58 Warren Street, New York, NY 10007
penzlerpublishers.com

Distributed by W. W. Norton

Cover image: Andy Ross
Cover design: Mauricio Diaz

Paperback ISBN 978-1-61316-359-7
Hardcover ISBN 978-1-61316-360-3

Library of Congress Control Number: 2022906675

Printed in the United States of America

9 8 7 6 5 4 3 2 1

INTRODUCTION

ELLERY QUEEN, the author, among many other unique contributions to detective literature, places Ellery Queen, the detective, in awkward situations.

In the brilliant opening to *The Chinese Orange Mystery*, for example, Queen confronts a dead man on whom all his clothes had been reversed, the corpse wearing everything backwards, including his left shoe on his right foot and vice versa.

In *The Spanish Cape Mystery*, there is another sartorial anomaly. This time, the dead body is totally naked, except for his hat, though decorum is maintained when he is largely covered by a black opera cape. The victim, an amoral lothario named John Marco, was evidently someone who needed to be killed, with any number of suspects who had ample motivation to perform the deed.

Clearly, the murder is a problem that needs to be solved so the local police are fortunate that Ellery Queen happens to be in the neighborhood and they enlist his help. The identity of the killer, however, is not the only questions that needs to be answered.

The estate on which the crime was committed is owned by an eccentric Wall Street financier and his beautiful young wife.

Why did she invite a houseful of guests who were complete strangers to her, and why did they accept without question? Why was the businessman's brother kidnapped by a one-eyed giant? Why are all the female guests at the gathering nervous and frightened when the body is identified as Marco's?

And why in the world did the murderer take the time to completely undress the victim?

The Spanish Cape Mystery is the ninth and final book in the series that used geographical names in the title and, as in the previous volumes, Queen's deductions are logical and fairly presented, with his customary challenge to the reader. But this book marks the beginning of the end of his formal tales of observation and deduction with a character that had been patterned after S.S. Van Dine's Philo Vance.

By the time *The Spanish Cape Mystery* was released in 1935, Queen had surpassed Vance as the most popular detective character in America, and the authors saw the writing on the wall, realizing that a more realistic style was what the public wanted. Their next book, *Halfway House* (1936), was the beginning of that transformation.

Often called the Golden Age of the detective novel, the years between the two World Wars produced some of the most iconic names in the history of mystery. In England, the names Agatha Christie and Dorothy L. Sayers continue to resonate to the present day. In America, there is one name that towers above the rest, and that is Ellery Queen.

That famous name was the brainchild of two Brooklyn-born cousins, Frederic Dannay (born Daniel Nathan, he changed his name to Frederic as a tribute to Chopin, with Dannay merely a combination of the first two syllables of his birth name) and Manfred B. Lee (born Manford Lepofsky). They wanted a simple nom de plume and had the brilliant stroke of inspiration to employ Ellery Queen as both their byline and as the name of their protagonist, reckoning that readers might forget one or the other but not both.

Dannay was a copywriter and art director for an advertising agency while Lee was writing publicity and advertising material for a motion picture company when they were attracted by a $7,500 prize offered by *McClure's* magazine in 1928; they were twenty-three years old.

They were informed that their submission, *The Roman Hat Mystery*, had won the contest but, before the book could be published or the prize money handed over, *McClure's* went bankrupt. Its assets were assumed by *Smart Set* magazine, which gave the prize to a different novel that it thought would have greater appeal to women. Frederick A. Stokes decided to publish *The Roman Hat Mystery* anyway, thus beginning one of the most successful mystery series in the history of the genre. Since the contest had required that books be submitted under pseudonyms, the simple but memorable Ellery Queen name, born out of necessity, became an icon.

The success of the novels got them Hollywood offers and they went to write for Columbia, Paramount, and MGM, though they never received any screen credits. The popular medium of radio also called to them and they wrote all the scripts for the successful *Ellery Queen* radio series for nine years from 1939 to 1948. In an innovative approach, they interrupted the narration so that Ellery could ask his guests—well-known personalities—to solve the case as they now had all the necessary clues. The theories of listeners were almost invariably preferred in vain and the program would then proceed, revealing the correct solution. The Queen character was also translated into a comic strip character and several television series starring Richard Hart, Lee Bowman, Hugh Marlowe, George Nader, Lee Philips, and, finally, Jim Hutton.

While Lee had no particular affection for mystery fiction, always hoping to become the Shakespeare of the twentieth century, Dannay had been interested in detective stories since his boyhood. He wanted to produce a magazine of quality mystery stories in all sub-genres and founded *Mystery* in 1933 but it failed after four issues when the publisher went bankrupt. However, after Dannay's long convalescence from a 1940 automobile accident that nearly took his life, he created *Ellery Queen's Mystery Magazine*; the first issue appeared in 1941 and remains the leading mystery fiction magazine in the world to the present day.

Although Dannay and Lee were lifelong collaborators on their novels and short stories, they had very different personalities and frequently disagreed, often vehemently, in what Lee once described as "a marriage made in hell." Dannay was a quiet, scholarly introvert, noted as a perfectionist. Lee was impulsive and assertive, given to explosiveness and earthy language. They remained steadfast in their refusal to divulge their working methodology, claiming that over their many years together they had tried every possible combination of their skills and talent to produce the best work they could. However, upon close examination of their letters and conversations with their friends and family, it eventually became clear that, in almost all instances, it was Dannay who created the extraordinary plots and Lee who brought them to life.

Each resented the other's ability, with Dannay once writing that he was aware that Lee regarded him as nothing more than "a clever contriver." Dannay's ingenious plots, fiendishly detailed with strict adherence to the notion of playing fair with readers, remain unrivalled by any mystery American author. Yet he did not have the literary skill to make characters plausible, settings visual, or dialogue resonant. Lee, on the other hand, with his dreams of writing important fiction, had no ability to invent stories, although he could improve his cousin's creations to make the characters come to life and the plots suspenseful and compelling.

When Queen made his debut in *The Roman Hat Mystery*, he was ostensibly an author but spends precious little time working at his career. He appears to have unlimited time to collect books and help his father, Inspector Richard Queen, solve cases. Although close to his father, the arrogant young man is often condescending to him as he loves to show off his erudition. As the series progresses (and as the public's appetite for Philo Vance diminished), Ellery becomes a far more realistic and likable character.

The Spanish Cape Mystery served as the inspiration for the first motion picture to feature Queen, a cheaply produced film of the same title and released the same year, made by Republic Pictures. Directed by Lewis D. Collins, it starred Donald Cook, Helen Twelvetrees, Berton Churchill, and Frank Sheridan.

"Ellery Queen *is* the American detective story," as Anthony Boucher, the mystery reviewer for the *New York Times*, wrote. Agatha Christie wrote, "A new Ellery Queen book has always been something to look forward to for many years." And Dorothy B. Hughes added, "Ellery Queen is one of the greatest for all time in mystery fiction," and it would be impossible for any reasonable person to disagree.

—OTTO PENZLER

Nudaque veritas.
HORACE. *Carmina*. I. 24. 7.

PERSONS OF THE STORY

THE HOUSEHOLD	GODFREY, WALTER
	GODFREY, STELLA
	GODFREY, ROSA
	KUMMER, DAVID

THE GUESTS	CONSTABLE, LAURA
	CORT, EARLE
	MARCO, JOHN
	MUNN, CECILIA
	MUNN, JOSEPH A.

THE CASUALS	KIDD (Captain)
	PENFIELD, LUCIUS
	STEBBINS, HARRY
	WARING, HOLLIS

THE MENIALS	BURLEIGH
	JORUM
	PITTS
	TILLER

THE INVESTIGATORS	MACKLIN (Judge)
	MOLEY (Inspector)
	QUEEN, ELLERY

THE SCENE

Spanish Cape, a peculiar coastal formation on the North Atlantic seaboard; and environs. The Cape, an outthrust headland of sheer rock about a square mile in area, is connected with the mainland by a narrow tongue of cliff. Although it is only a few hundred yards from a wide motor highway and is flanked by public bathing beaches, it is utterly private and virtually inaccessible.

FOREWORD

In the course of the five years or so during which we have had the pleasure of publishing Mr. Queen's novels, hundreds of inquiries have been addressed to us demanding an explanation both for the mystery surrounding and the identity of the gentleman who has invariably written the forewords to the Queen books. We regret that we cannot satisfy our correspondents. We do not know.

—THE PUBLISHERS.

I KNOW the place very well, having viewed it innumerable times from the water-side in my modest motorboat, and on at least three occasions panoramically from the air, since Spanish Cape lies on the Atlantic coast directly in the path of a great North-to-South airline.

From the sea it looks for all the world like a gigantic chunk of weathered stone chipped out of some Alpine mother-mountain, sliced roughly down its sides, and plumped into the waters of the Atlantic seaboard to soak its feet thousands of miles from its birthplace. When you get up close to it—as close as those devilish sharp rocks encircling its base permit—it becomes a granite for tress monstrous in its grandeur, impregnable, and overpowering as Gibraltar.

From the sea, as may be imagined, Spanish Cape is a grim and rather chilling object.

But from the air you get an almost poetically different impression. There lies far below you, a queerly shaped emerald, dark green and mysterious, imbedded in the wrinkled blue moiré of the sea. It is thickly powdered with trees and underbrush; from the height of a 'plane there are only three details which give relief from the prevailing green. One is the sandwhite little beach of the Cove, with its terrace slightly above (although still below the level of the surrounding cliffs in which it is sunken). Another is the house itself, a sprawling and somewhat fantastic-appearing habitation, a *hacienda* on a grand scale, with stucco facings and patio and Spanish-tile roofs. Yet it is not ugly; merely foreign to the Yankee modernisms about it, like that filling-station which seems so close to it from the air, but which actually is not on Spanish Cape at all, occupying a site on the other side of the public highway.

The third relieving detail is that knife-like sunken road which slashes across the greenery of the Cape, winging straight as an Indian arrow from the public highway down the slender neck of rock connecting the Cape with the mainland, and cutting through the heart of the Cape to the Cove. The sunken road is white from the air and, although I have never set foot on it, I suspect is made of concrete; even at night it glows under the moon.

In common with most of the informed gentry of that stretch of shore I knew that this remarkable rock formation—of course it is the result of millions of years of patiently chewing sea— was the property of Walter Godfrey. Few people knew more, for

Godfrey had always exercised the prerogative of excessive riches and shut himself away from the world. I had never met any one who had actually visited Spanish Cape, which was only Godfrey's summer place, until the dramatic events which shook it—and its owner—out of their traditional isolation; and then, of course, who should the trespasser be but my good friend Ellery Queen!—who seems dogged by a curious destiny.

Much as he struggles against it, Ellery is constantly being either preceded or followed by crimes of a violent nature; to such an extent that a mutual acquaintance, more than half-seriously, once remarked to me: "Every time I ask Queen out to my shack for an evening or a weekend I hold my breath. He attracts murders the way a hound—if he'll pardon the figure—attracts fleas!"

And so he does. And so, in fact, he did on Spanish Cape.

There are many things about the Problem of the Undressed Man—as Ellery himself refers to it—which are fascinating, *outré*, and downright baffling. It is only rarely in real life that a crime of such peculiar quality occurs in a setting of such extraordinary magnificence. The murder of John Marco, occurring as it did after the Kidnaping-of-the-Wrong-Man, plus the almost weird circumstance of Marco's nakedness, made for a robust poser; and, now that it is merely another successful Queenian adventure in deduction, for a piece of prime reading.

As usual, I consider myself fortunate to have the privilege of acting the herald in this tragedy of violent errors; and, if my friend will forgive me, of strewing flowers once again in the path of his remarkable mental triumph over what, for a long, long time, looked like insurmountable odds.

J. J. McC.

NORTHAMPTON
September 1934.

I
THE COLOSSAL ERROR
OF CAPTAIN KIDD

It was to all intents and purposes a sickening blunder. Criminals have made mistakes before, usually as a result of haste or carelessness or mental myopia, and nearly always to their own disservice; ultimately finding themselves, at the very least, contemplating their errors through steel bars and along a dismal vista of years. But this was a mistake for the books.

The whimsically named Captain Kidd did not number among his few virtues, it appeared, the quality of brilliance. He was an unbelievable mountain of a man; and in return for conferring upon him the gift of physical exaggeration it was assumed that his moody creator had penalized him with a paucity of brains. It seemed clear enough at the beginning that the blunder had been Captain Kidd's, a development of his pure stupidity.

The pity of it was that this was one criminal mistake which seemed to work no hardship upon the rascal responsible for it, and still less apparently upon the mysterious person for whom this immense and dull creature was pulling the strings. All its

5

consequences, as was evident, were massed upon the head of its victim.

Now, why fate in the incredible person of Captain Kidd should have chosen poor David Kummer for the sacrifice, every one agreed when it occurred (including Mr. Ellery Queen), was one of those cosmic problems the answer to which is swathed in veils. They could only nod in silent despair at his sister Stella's hysterical requiem: "But David was always such a quiet boy! I remember . . . Once a Gypsy woman read his palm in our town when we were children. And she said that he had a 'dark destiny.' Oh, David!"

But this is a long hard tale, and how Mr. Ellery Queen became involved in it is another. Certainly, as a laboratory microscopist peering at the *phenomena curiosa* of the human mind, he had cause in the end to feel grateful for Captain Kidd's grotesque mistake. For when the light came, as it did after those wild and astonishing days, he saw with etching clarity how essential to his solution the gigantic seaman's error really was. In a sense, the whole fabric of Ellery's thinking came to depend upon it. And yet, in the beginning, it merely muddled things.

The blunder would never have occurred, in all probability, had it not been for David Kummer's dislike of crowds, on the one hand—it was a personal distaste rather than a pathological dread—and his affection for Rosa, his niece, on the other. Both were characteristic of him. Kummer had never cared for people; they either bored or irritated him. And yet, a social anchorite, he was admired and even liked.

At this time he was in his late thirties, a tall strong well-preserved man. He was irrevocably set in his ways and almost as self-sufficient as Walter Godfrey, his famous brother-in-law. For most of the year Kummer maintained a bachelor's eyrie in

Murray Hill; in the summer he resided on Spanish Cape with the Godfreys. His brother-in-law, a bitter cynic, often suspected that it was not so much the proximity of his sister and niece that drew Kummer to the Cape as the peculiar grandeur of the place itself—a rather unfair suspicion. But the two did have something in common: both were solitary, quiet, and in their own way somehow magnificent.

Occasionally Kummer tramped off in boots and disappeared for a week's shooting somewhere, or sailed one of the Godfrey sloops or the big launch along the coast. He had long since mastered the intricacies of the nine-hole golf-course which lay on the western hemisphere of Spanish Cape; he rarely played, calling golf "an old man's game." He might be induced to play a few sets of tennis if the competition were keen enough; but generally his sports were those which permitted solitary enjoyment. Naturally, he possessed an independent income. And he wrote a little, chiefly on outdoor subjects.

He was not a romantic; life had taught him certain hard lessons, he liked to say, and he believed firmly in the realities. A man primarily of action, he was constantly "facing the facts." His life was not complicated by the sex-problem; except for his sister Stella and her daughter Rosa, women meant less than nothing to him. It was whispered in Mrs. Godfrey's circle that he had had an unfortunate love-affair in his early twenties; none of the Godfreys ever discussed it and he, of course, was perennially silent.

So much for David Kummer, the victim, the tall dark athletic man who was hauled by Captain Kidd into oblivion.

Rosa Godfrey was a Kummer, with the slashing black brows of the clan, the strong straight nose, level eyes, and slim tough body; side by side, she and her mother might have been sisters, and Kummer an older brother of both. Intellectually she was serene, like her uncle; she had nothing of Stella's nervous agility or social restlessness or essential shallowness of mind. And there was nothing, of course, between Rosa and her tall uncle—nothing in the malicious sense. Their affection respected the tie of blood; both of them would have been outraged by any other suggestion; besides, their ages were almost twenty years apart. Yet it was not to her mother that Rosa crept when she was in trouble, nor to her father, who pottered quietly about by himself and asked no greater boon than that he be let alone; but to Kummer. It had been that way since her pigtail days. Any other father but Walter Godfrey would have resented this usurpation of his emotional rights; but Walter Godfrey was as much an enigma to his family as to the blatting lambs from whose shearing he had amassed his heavy fortune.

.   .   .   .

The house was full of people; at least it seemed full of people to Kummer. His sister Stella's penchant for the socializing influences had resulted, as he remarked grimly to his silent brother-in-law on Saturday afternoon, in a particularly slimy group of guests.

The season was drawing to a close; its passing had brought an irritating visitation of nondescripts. Marco, of course, had been there, suavely indifferent to black looks from the male relations of his hostess, for many weeks; trust Marco for that. He had been one of Stella Godfrey's less happy inspirations, as her husband grunted on one rare occasion. Handsome John Marco . . . who had not a male friend in the world, was not a man to stand upon the little ceremonies; once invited, he hung on—as Kummer said, "with the bland persistence of a crab-louse." Marco had quite spoiled the better part of the summer even for Walter Godfrey, who normally trotted about his rock-gardens in dirty ancient overalls frankly oblivious to the creatures brought into his house by his wife. The others spoiled what was left of the season: Laura Constable, "fat, frenetic, and forty," as Rosa characterized her with a giggle; the Munns, husband and wife, of whom it was patent that nothing civilized could be said; and blond Earle Cort, an unhappy young man who haunted Spanish Cape on weekends, languishing after Rosa. They were not many, but—with the possible exception of Cort, whom he rather contemptuously liked—to Kummer they constituted a veritable battalion.

It was after a late dinner Saturday night that the big man drew Rosa from the cool patio into the still warm gardens sloping down from the huge Spanish house. In the flagged inner court Stella conversed with her guests; while Cort, entangled in Mrs. Munn's arch web, could only hurl a furiously yearning glance after uncle and niece. It was already dusk, and Marco's really extraordinary profile was silhouetted against the sky as he perched gracefully on the arm of Mrs. Constable's chair, presumably posing for the benefit of all the females within range. But he was always posing, so there was nothing remarkable in that. The chatter in the court, dominated by Marco, was shrill and empty; utterly without distinction, like the cackling of fowl.

Kummer sighed with relief as they strolled down the stone steps. "God, what a crew! I tell you, Rosa, that blessed mother of yours is becoming a problem. With the bugs she brings here, she's becoming positively a menace to decent society. I don't know how Walter stands it. Those howling baboons!" Then he chuckled and took her arm. "My dear, you look very charming tonight."

Rosa was dressed in something white and cool and billowy that swept to the stone. "Thank you, sir. It's really very simple," she said with a grin. "A combination of organdie and the black art of Miss Whitaker. You're the most naïve creature, David—and also the most anti-social. But you do notice. More," she added, the grin fading, "than *most* people."

Kummer lit a bulldog pipe and puffed thankfully, looking at the pink-flecked sky. "Most people?"

Rosa bit her lip, and they reached the bottom of the stairs. With tacit accord they turned toward the beach terrace, deserted at this hour and quite out of sight and hearing of the house above. It was a small cosy place, beautiful in the dusk; there were colored flags underfoot, and white beams formed an open roof overhead. Steps led down to the terrace from the walk, and steps led down from the terrace to the half-moon of beach below. Rosa seated herself rather petulantly in a basketwork chair under a large gay beach umbrella and folded her hands to stare with pursed lips out over the small beach and the waves lapping the sand in the Cove. Through the narrow mouth of the Cove white-bellied sails could be made out, far off, on the swelling blue expanse.

Kummer watched her quietly, smoking his pipe. "What's troubling you, Skeezicks?"

She started. "Troubling me? Troubling me? Why, whatever makes you think—"

"You act," chuckled Kummer, "just about as expertly as you swim, Rosa. I'm afraid you don't shine in either department. If it's that young Hamlet of yours, Earle—"

She sniffed. "Earle! As if he could. Trouble me, I mean. I can't imagine *why* mother's given him the freedom of the house. She must be going off her mind. Having *him* around . . . *I* don't want him. We'd definitely settled all that, you know, David. Oh, I—I suppose I was silly about him once, that time we were engaged—"

"Which time was that?" asked Kummer gravely. "Oh, yes! The eighth, I believe. The first seven times, I suppose, you two were merely playing house. My dear child, you're still the merest infant emotionally—"

"Thanks, grandpa!" she jeered.

"—as is your sullen young swain. I believe strongly in the mating of emotional likes. For the—er—good of the stock. You could do worse than Cort, you know, Rosa, for all his *Weltschmerz*."

"I'd like to know where! And *I'm* not an infant. And he— he's intolerable. Imagine a grown man licking the pumps of that overdressed, underdone, half-baked imitation of a cheap little ex-chorus girl . . . "

"True to type," sighed Kummer. "The feline strain. The best of you are none too good. Skeezicks, my child, be reasonable. If there was any licking done, Mrs. Munn's pretty tongue did it, not Earle's, I'm sure. He looked after you a moment ago like a sick calf. Come, come, Rosa, you're covering up."

"I don't know what you mean," said Rosa, staring out at the sea. It lay below them no longer blue, but purple. The pink flecks in the sky had died to the accompaniment of musical breakers.

"I believe you do," murmured Kummer. "I believe you're on the thin edge of doing something utterly mad, Rosa darling. I assure you it's mad. If the man were any one but Marco I should mind my own business. But under the circumstances . . . "

"Marco?" she faltered, not very convincingly.

Kummer's cynical blue eyes smiled a little. Even in the gathering murk she saw the smile, and lowered her own blue eyes. "I think I warned you, my dear, once before. But I didn't think it would come to this—"

"To what?"

"Rosa." His reproachful tone made her blush a little.

"I—I thought," said Rosa in a muffled voice, "that Mr.—Mr. Marco's paid considerably more attention to—well, to Mrs. Munn, and to Mrs. Constable, and—yes, to mother, too!—than to me, David."

"That," said the big man grimly, "is something else again. At the moment we're discussing a younger, although perhaps not sillier, woman." His eyes narrowed as he bent over her. "Skeezicks, I tell you the man's impossible, a worthless adventurer. No visible source of income. A smelly reputation, from what I heard; I've gone to some trouble to look the fellow up. Oh, I grant you his physical charms—"

"Thank you. Didn't you know, David darling," said Rosa with a sort of breathless malice, "that physically he resembles you a good deal? Perhaps it's a sexual compensation of some sort—"

"Rosa! Don't be obscene. It's scarcely a joking matter to me. Your mother and you are the only women in this universe I care a rap about. I tell you—"

She rose suddenly, still looking at the sea. "Oh, David, I don't want to discuss him!" Her lips trembled.

"But you do, honey." He put his pipe on the table and gripped her shoulders, turning her about so that her blue eyes were very close to his. "I've seen it coming for a long time. If you do what you intend to do—"

"How do you know what I intend to do?" she asked in a low voice.

"I can guess. Knowing Marco's filthy kind . . . "

She grasped his arm. "But, David, I haven't really promised him—"

"You haven't? From the gloating look in his eye I gathered a different impression. I tell you I've heard that the man's a—"

She dropped her hand violently. "It's nonsense what you've heard! John's so good-looking all the men dislike him. Naturally, there would be women in the life of such a handsome man . . . David, please! I shan't listen to another word."

He released her shoulders, looked quietly at her for a moment, and then turned aside, picked up his pipe, knocked out the ashes, and dropped the brier into his pocket. "Since you've my own stubbornness," he murmured, "I've no right to complain, I suppose. You've quite made up your mind, Rosa?"

"Yes!"

Then they both fell silent and turned toward the terrace stairs, moving a little closer together. Some one was coming down the upper path toward the terrace.

.   .   .   .

It was the oddest thing. They could hear heavy steps in the gravel, crunching sounds which held a note of clumsy stealth. Like a giant tiptoeing on broken glass, inhumanly oblivious to pain.

It was almost dark now. Kummer suddenly looked at his wrist-watch. It was thirteen minutes past eight.

Rosa felt her skin crawl and she shivered, quite without knowing why. She shrank back against her uncle, staring into the depths of the shadowy path above them.

"What's the matter?" asked Kummer coolly. "Rosa, you're trembling."

"I don't know. I wish we could—I wonder who it is."

"Probably Jorum making one of his eternal rounds. Sit down, darling. I'm sorry if I've made you nerv—"

From such small beginnings are large endings made. It seemed, too, an ending inspired by coincidence. Kummer was clad in spotless whites; a big man, brunette both as to hair and complexion, clean-shaven, not ill-looking . . . And it was growing dark very fast, the kind of thick black night peculiar to moonless country and seaside.

An inky shape loomed at the head of the terrace stairs. It was monumental and yet composed of shadows. It moved, fluidly. And then it froze still and seemed to search their faces.

A hoarse bass voice said: "Quiet. Both of ye. You're covered," and they saw something small in what might have been a hand.

Kummer said coldly: "Who in hell are you?"

"Never mind who I am." The immense paw never wavered. Rosa was very still, and she could feel the tension of Kummer's body beside her. She groped for his hand in the darkness and pressed it, warningly, pleadingly. His fingers closed over hers with a warm electric strength and she sighed noiselessly, reassured. "Now come on up here," continued the bass voice, "an' make it snappy an' make it quiet."

"Is that really," demanded Rosa, surprised at the steadiness of her voice, "a revolver you're pointing at us?"

"Step!"

"Come on, Rosa," said Kummer softly, and he shifted his hand to grip her bare arm. They marched across the intervening flags and began to mount the stairs. The formless shadow retreated a little before them. Rosa felt like giggling, now that the intangible fear had materialized. It was all so perfectly silly! And on Spanish Cape, of all places. Probably, now that she came to think of it, it was all an inane joke of some one's. No doubt Earle's! It would be just like him, the—the—

Then the giggle turned into a gasp. At arm's length the creature with the bass voice became real. She saw him now, not clearly, but well enough to establish certain horrible truths.

The man—it could only have been a man—stood so tall that by contrast Kummer, who himself measured over six feet, looked a pigmy. He must have been at least six feet eight inches in height. And he was gross, a Chinese wrestler of a man, an inflated Falstaff, with an enormous belly and the shoulders of a Percheron. Really, he was too big and too fat, thought Rosa with a shiver, to be—to be human. The .38 revolver which nestled in the palm of his hand was a child's toy. He was clothed in something roughly sailorish: a pair of dirty tattered dungarees like windblown canvas, a black or dark blue pea-jacket with tarnished brass buttons and the spread of a mainsail, and a cap with a chipped and broken visor.

And, to complete the horror, over the expanse of his globular face there was a handkerchief, a very dark handkerchief; probably a bandanna. It came up to the eyes. Rosa gaped: the man had only one eye. That was all this impossible creature needed—one eye. A black patch over the left . . . Rosa felt suddenly like laughing again. Not a very subtle robber! As if his mask were an insurance of anonymity! A brute over six and a half feet tall, weighing in the neighborhood of three hundred pounds, with only one eye . . . It was ridiculous. He was something out of Gilbert and Sullivan.

"You may as well," said Rosa breathlessly, "take that foul thing off your face. We could describe you—"

"Rosa," said Kummer. She stopped. They heard the giant draw his breath in slowly.

"But you ain't goin' to," said the bass voice. They detected a little uncertainty in it. "You ain't goin' to, lady." There was something bovine, ponderous, and stupid in his vibrating undertones; he was like an ox. "The two o' ye walk on up this here path till ye git to the place where the autos turn in an' go up to the house; see? I'll be walkin' behind ye, an' my shooter's ready."

"If it's robbery you've come for," said Rosa with contempt in her voice, "take my ring and bracelet and be off with you. I'm sure we won't—"

"Ain't trinkets I'm after. Git goin'."

"Look here," said Kummer calmly; his hands were at his sides. "There's no point in dragging the lady into this, whoever you are. If it's I you want, why—"

"You Rosa Godfrey?" demanded the giant.

"Yes," said Rosa, feeling a little frightened once more.

"That's all I want to know," the man rumbled with a sort of thunderous satisfaction. "Then I ain't made no mistake. You and this here fr—"

Kummer's hard fist sank into the fat man's belly. Rosa's nostrils flared and she turned to run. Several astonishing things happened at once. The giant, for all his obesity, had iron under his lard. The blow seemed to make no impression upon him; he neither doubled up nor grunted. Instead, he dropped the gun into one of his pockets almost carelessly, flung an enormous arm about Kummer's neck, jerking him off his feet as if he were a boy, and with the other paw clutched Rosa's shoulder. Rosa opened her mouth to scream and closed it again. David was gasping, choking . . .

The giant said mildly: "None o' your tricks, either o' ye. You goin' to be good, Mr. Marco?"

.   .   .   .

The ground heaved beneath Rosa's feet and the cliff-walls flanking the path whirled before her eyes. Kummer moved a little, his face white under its tan and his legs jerking like the legs of a hanged man.

She saw it at last. It was a plot, a plot directed against John Marco, whom all women loved and all men hated. And poor David! It was the clothes chiefly, no doubt; Marco was wearing whites tonight, too. And both men were of an age, a height, and a build. If this hulking idiot had been provided with a description of Marco, it would have been easy under the circumstances to blunder and seize David Kummer instead. But how did he know where to find them on the sprawling grounds of Spanish Cape? No one had followed them, she was sure. And who had told him how Marco would be dressed? For he must have been told . . . A thousand thoughts raced through her brain. She came to her senses with a feeling that hours had passed.

"Let him go!" she cried. "You've the—*the wrong man*! Let him—"

The giant released her shoulder and clapped his paw, redolent of sour dirt, whisky, and cordage, over her mouth. Then he lowered Kummer to the gravel and hooked the fingers of his other hand into Kummer's collar at the nape. Kummer choked, fighting to regain his breath.

"March," rumbled the giant, and they marched.

Rosa made inarticulate sounds behind the steel hand; once she tried her teeth on it. But the giant merely cuffed her mouth lightly, and she gave up, tears of pain in her eyes. They marched, their captor between them, gripping Kummer's collar on one side and cupping Rosa's mouth on the other. In this way, and in a silence broken only by the assaults of their shoes on the gravel, they made their way awkwardly but rapidly back along the road.

They walked between walls of sheer cliff, towering above them on both sides to form a geometric canyon.

At last they reached the point in the path where it branched off to the left in the wide ascending automobile road. In the shadows of the cliffs just before this branch stood an old sedan, without lights, and already turned around to face the main road leading out of Spanish Cape.

The giant said evenly: "Miss Godfrey, I'm goin' to take my hand off your mouth. Scream, an' I swear I'll shove your teeth down your throat. You open the front door of that there auto. Mr. Marco, when I let go that collar o' yourn, I want ye to jump into the front an' git behind the wheel. I'll climb in the back an' tell ye where to drive to. No noise, either o' ye. Now do as I tell ye."

He released them. Kummer fingered his throat gingerly and essayed a pallid grin. Rosa wiped her lips with a dainty cambric handkerchief and flashed an angry glance at her uncle. But Kummer shook his head the slightest bit, as if in warning.

"I tell you," whispered Rosa desperately, whirling on the giant, "this *isn't* John Marco! It's Mr. Kummer, Mr. David Kummer, my uncle. You've caught the wrong man. Oh, don't you see—"

"Uncle, hey?" said the giant with a low chuckle of admiration. "He ain't Marco, hey? Jump in, girlie; I'd hate to have to mess ye up. Ye've got guts."

"Oh, you stupid *oaf!*" she cried, but she pulled the door open and crawled into the car. Kummer stepped in after her with sagging shoulders; he seemed to have felt a presentiment of his dark destiny even then, and perhaps he was husbanding his strength for a final struggle. That was the impression Rosa, her brain a stew of panic, received. She twisted in the front seat and glared balefully at the giant. He had opened the back door and set his foot upon the running-board.

She realized with a start that the moon had risen, for the gravel road was dimly illuminated now and there were patches of silver light on the striated walls of the cliff looming up to the face of Spanish Cape. And then she saw the giant's foot . . . It was shod in ripped black leather; it was his right foot; and on the inner side there was a hole and a bulge, where a bunion of gargantuan size grew. A foot of such dimensions that she blinked. It was simply incredible that a human being . . . Then the foot vanished as the big man thrust himself through the doorway and crashed down upon the cushions. The screams of the springs made the girl want to laugh. She checked herself with a horrified consciousness of her incipient hysteria.

"Git movin', Mr. Marco," said the bass voice. "Ye'll find the key in the switch, an' I know ye can drive by that yaller roadster o' yourn."

Kummer leaned forward, touched the light-switch, turned the ignition-key, and stepped on the starter. A quiet motor hummed, and he released the hand-brake. "Where to?" he asked in a dry, cracked undertone.

"Straight ahead off the Cape. Right smack through the sunk road here, acrost the neck, straight through the park, an' out onto the main stem. Turn left there an' keep goin'." A note of impatience crept into the heavy voice. "Come on, come on. An' you give one move I don't like an' I'll choke the life out o' ye. You keep still, girlie."

Rosa shut her eyes and sank back as the car trundled off. This was just a bad dream. Soon she would shudder into wakefulness and laugh at the whole preposterous thing. She'd find David and tell him about it, and they would laugh together . . .

Then she felt Kummer's rigid right arm next to hers, and she shivered. Poor David! It was brutal for him, unnecessary, a cruel caprice of fate. And as for her . . . Her skin crawled. She was too sick to encompass all the possibilities.

When she opened her eyes they had left behind them the narrow strip of parkland beyond the neck of the Cape, and were turning left into the main highway. Across the road, directly opposite the entrance to the park-road, were the lights of a filling-station. She could see the white-overalled figure of old Harry Stebbins stooped over the gasoline tank of a car, gas-hose in hand. Good old Harry! If she only dared scream, once . . . And then she felt the hot sour breath of the monster on her neck and heard his warning rumble in her ear and sank back, nauseated.

Kummer drove quietly, almost humbly. But she knew David. Under his black thatch there was a keen brain, and she knew that it must be working furiously. She prayed silently that he would concoct a plan. It would take gray matter to defeat this ogrish creature. Brawn, even Kummer's, would be futile against the man's negligent power.

They skimmed along the concrete highway. There was a good deal of traffic; cars headed for Wayland Amusement Park ten miles up the road. Saturday night . . . Rosa wondered what the others were doing at the house. Mother. John Marco—Was David right? About John? Had she made a hideous mistake after all? But then—It was quite possible, she reflected bitterly, that it would be hours before she and David were missed. People were always wandering off at Spanish Cape, especially David; and of late she herself had been moody . . .

"Turn left here," said the giant.

They both started. Surely something was wrong? They had

travelled barely a mile since turning off the Spanish Cape road. Kummer muttered something beneath his breath, but Rosa could not hear. Turn left—That must be the private road that led down to the Waring shack off the public beach—in sight, almost within reach, of the cliffs of Spanish Cape!

Again they swept through deserted parkland, and all too soon were out on the road in open country. The bathing beach . . . They began to skim along beside a high fence, and the ground turned to sand beside the road. Kummer switched on the headlights; directly in their path stood a little cluster of rather decrepit buildings. He slowed the car.

"Where to, Cyclops?" he said quietly.

"Lay off. Smack up to them there buildings." Then the giant chuckled at Rosa's gasp. "Don't bank on anything, girlie; ain't nobody here. This here Waring owns the place ain't been here pretty near all summer. Shut down tight, she is. Go on, Marco."

"I'm not Marco, you know," said Kummer in the same quiet voice; but he drove on, slowly.

"You, too?" growled the giant in disgust. Rosa sank back in despair.

The car rolled to a stop beside a cottage, unilluminated and obviously deserted. Beyond it lay a small building which looked like a boathouse; and nearby another which might have been a garage. The buildings were quite near the beach. As they got stiffly out of the car they could see the towering black cliffs of Spanish Cape across the moon-flecked water, only a few hundred yards away. But it might have been a few hundred miles away, for all the good it could do them. For the cliffs were perpendicular, and at least fifty feet high, and at their base lay sharp tumbled rocks against which the lashing tides raged. Even here, on Waring's beach, there was no approach to the Cape. The cliff stopped high above the little structures, and there was scarcely a handhold in its entire side, which was only slightly less high than the cliffs in the sea.

Off to the other side, where the public bathing beach lay, there was nothing but paper-littered sand. The sand glistened under the moon.

Rosa saw her uncle casting quick secret glances all about, with what seemed to her desperation. The giant stood slightly behind them, his one eye tolerantly watchful. He acted as if he were in no hurry at all, but permitted them to inspect the deserted premises to their hearts' content. A ramp-like structure led from the boathouse to the water's edge, and half in the surf lay a small powerful-looking cabin cruiser. Several rollers lay scattered about in the sand, and the doors of the boathouse stood open. Apparently, then, the giant had broken into the place, rolled the boat out himself, in readiness for . . . what?

"That's Mr. Waring's boat!" exclaimed the dark girl, staring at it. "You're stealing it, you—you monster?"

"Never mind about the names, lady," said the giant gruffly, almost as if he were offended. "I'll do what I damn want to. Now, Mr. Marco—"

Kummer had turned and was walking slowly toward his captor. Rosa, catching sight of his blue eyes glinting in the moonlight, saw that he had determined to act upon some last desperate plan. Resolution was written all over his hard, clean face. There was no fear in it at all as he stalked the immense figure of the man in sailor's costume, who stood watching him quite expressionlessly.

"I can give you more money than you ever saw in—" began David Kummer in a smooth conversational voice, as without haste he strolled toward the giant.

He never finished; Rosa never learned what he had intended to do. Struck dumb with horror, she could only feel her legs go weak beneath her and marvel dully at the extraordinary monster who had kidnaped them. For, so swiftly that her dazed eye barely followed, the giant lunged forward with upheld fist. The huge club of bone and skin thumped soggily against something, and the next thing she saw was Kummer's face sinking below the fixed level of her stricken eyes. And then he was sprawled on the sand, very still.

Something snapped in the girl's brain and with a scream she flung herself with clawing fingers at the vast back of the giant. He was kneeling calmly by the unconscious man, listening to his breathing. When he felt the weight of her body he merely rose and twitched his shoulders, and she fell off to land in a sobbing heap on the sand. Without a word he picked her up and carried her, weeping and kicking, toward the dark cottage.

The door was locked, or bolted. He tucked her under one arm and with the other heaved against the panels. They gave with a splintering crash; he kicked the broken door open and strode in.

The last thing Rosa saw as her captor toed the door shut behind her was David Kummer's face on the sand before the silent cruiser under the moon.

·   ·   ·   ·   ·   ·   ·

It was a living-room, quite habitable, as she noted with glazed surprise in the ray of the giant's flashlight. She did not know Hollis Waring, had never met him; he was a New York business-man who occasionally spent a week or a few days there. She had often seen him cruising about beyond the Cape (as she told Mr. Ellery Queen later) in the very boat beached outside—a tiny fragile gray man in a linen cap, always alone. She had known vaguely that he had not visited his cottage since the beginning of the summer, long before John Marco had appeared in his yellow roadster with multitudinous luggage; and some one—her father, she vaguely recalled—had mentioned that he had gone to Europe. She had never known that her father and Waring were acquainted; certainly they had never met here at the shore; for that matter they may merely have known of each other through a business connection; her father had so many . . .

The giant set her on the rug before the fireplace. "Sit down in that there chair," he directed in the gentlest of voices. He set the flashlight on a divan nearby so that its powerful beam concentrated on the chair.

Silently, she sat down. On a small table not three feet from her elbow stood a telephone. From the appearance of the instrument she saw that it was a local telephone, on which service had probably not been discontinued. If she could reach it, snatch off the receiver, shriek for help . . . The giant took the telephone and put it down on the floor ten feet away, stretching the cord to its utmost. She wilted in the chair, finally beyond resistance.

"What are you going to—to do with me?" she asked in a dry, small voice.

"Ain't goin' to hurt ye. Don't git scared, girlie. It's jest this here Marco bird I want. Took ye along to keep ye from raisin' an alarm. Ye would, too." As he chuckled admiringly, he took a coil of heavy cord from one of his pockets and began to unwind it. "Sit still now, Miss Godfrey. Be good an' ye'll be all right." And before she could move he had, with his incredible quickness, tied her hands behind her back and to the back of the chair. She tugged and pulled in sudden desperation; the knots only tightened. Then he stooped and bound her ankles to the legs of the chair. She could see the coarse grayish hair beneath his cap, and an ugly depression covered with old scar-tissue at the back of his ruddy neck.

"Why don't you gag me, too?" she demanded bitterly.

"What for?" he chuckled, apparently in good humor. "Screech your head off if ye like, lady; won't no one hear ye. Up we go!"

He lifted her, chair and all, and carried her to another door. Opening it with a kick of one huge foot, he carried her through into a stuffy little bedroom and deposited her and the chair near the bed.

"You're not *leaving* me here?" she cried, appalled. "Why, I'll—I'll starve, I'll suffocate!"

"Now, now, ye'll be all right," he said soothingly. "I'll see to it ye'll be found."

"But David—my uncle—that man outside," she panted. "What are you going to do with *him*?"

He strode to the door to the living-room, making thunder in the small chamber. "Hey?" he growled, without looking back. His back expressed sudden menace.

"What are you going to *do* with him?" shrieked Rosa, frantic with fear.

"Hey?" he said again, and went out. Rosa sank back in the chair to which she was tied, her heart pounding painfully in her throat. Oh, he was stupid, stupid—a hulking, murdering clown. If ever she got out of this—quickly enough—it would be easy to track him down. There could be only one like him in the world; such travesties on the human form, she thought bitterly, do not happen in pairs. And then—if only it wasn't too late—revenge would be sweet . . .

She sat there, a helpless trussed fowl, listening with all the power of her small ears. She could hear the monster plainly enough as he tramped back and forth in the living-room. And then she heard something else: a minute tinkle, crystal-clear. She frowned and bit her lip. What was—The telephone! Yes, she could hear the metallic click of the instrument as he dialed some number. Oh, if only she could—

She tried desperately to rise and succeeded only in achieving a sort of squat, the chair lifting a bit from the floor. How she managed she did not know, but she found herself making painful progress toward the door, one foot after another in a waddle, the chair bumping alone derisively behind her. She made a good deal of noise, but the giant in the next room apparently was too absorbed to hear.

When she reached the door and set her ear against it, trembling more from excitement than exertion, she heard nothing. He couldn't be through already! But then she realized that he must be waiting for the connection. She concentrated all her energies in a single fierce application of will. She *must* hear what he said, if possible find out to whom he talked. She held her breath as the vibrating tones of his voice rumbled through the door. But the first tones came through garbled, indistinguishable. He might have been asking for someone. If he was, she could not make out the name. If it was a name . . . Her head spun with vertigo and she shook it impatiently, biting her lower lip until the pain cleared her brain. Ah!

" . . . job's done. Yeah . . . Got Marco outside now. Had to slug him one . . . Naw! He'll keep. When I slug 'em they stays slugged." Silence. Rosa wished for wings, second sight, anything. Oh, if only she could hear the voice of the man or woman at the other end of the wire! But the giant's bass reached her again. "Miss Godfrey's all right. Got her tied up in the bedroom . . . Ain't hurt. No, I tell ye! Only better see she don't have to stay here too long. *She* ain't done nothin' to ye, has she? . . . Yeah, yeah! . . . out to sea an' then . . . You're the doctor . . . All right, all right! I tell ye he'll keep . . . " For a moment she could hear nothing more than a blurred *vibrato* of hoarse sound. Wouldn't he *ever* mention that murderous creature's name? Anything, anything. Some clue . . . "Okay. Okay! I'm goin' now. Marco won't bother you no more. But don't forgit about the girl. She's got guts, that one." And Rosa, with a sickness in her stomach, heard the crash of the instrument and the giant's slow, stupid, rather good-natured chuckle.

She sank back again, exhausted, closing her eyes. But she opened them again quickly; she had heard the slam of the living-room door. Had he gone out, or had some one come in? But there was only silence, and she knew that the giant had left the cottage. She *must* see . . . She squirmed back, opened the door, and in the same awkward duck-like fashion waddled across the floor of the living-room to the nearest front window. The giant's flashlight was gone and the room was pitch-dark; she bumped into things and once bruised her strapped right arm painfully. At last she reached the window.

The moon was high now, and the white sand of the beach before the cottage and the calm surface of the sea acted like reflectors. The whole beach was smothered in a gentle glow of silver light; visibility was perfect.

She forgot the pain in her arm, the needles stinging in her cramped muscles, the dryness of her throat and lips. The scene outside the window was so perfect, so brilliant, so flat in its lights and shadows, that it might have come from a motion-picture reel. Even the figure of their gigantic captor looked small, as if some invisible director had ordered a long shot. At the moment

Rosa reached the uncurtained window he was stooping over the figure of David Kummer, who lay in precisely the same tumbled, unconscious position as when she had last seen him. She watched the mountainous creature lift Kummer without effort, sling the limp body over his shoulder, and stalk to the beached cruiser. He dumped Kummer into the boat with little ceremony, dug his huge feet into the ramp, set his shoulders against the hull, and shoved . . .

The cruiser began to move, gathering speed as the giant pushed, and finally rode clear in the water, the giant up to his knees in the sea. He grasped the gunwale and clambered overside as nimbly as an ape. A moment later the cruiser's riding lights winked calmly on. And she saw the giant stoop on deck, lift her uncle's still form, and carry it into the cabin. A motor roared then, there was a thrashing of purple-white sea, and the slim craft scudded away from shore.

Rosa watched it until her eyes ached. She never took them off the riding lights. They bobbed and swam—toward the south, away from Spanish Cape. And finally they vanished as if a wave had extinguished them.

And it seemed to the dark girl suddenly in her crushed and dirtied gown, strapped to her chair like a felon, that she was going mad, and that the beach was rising with stealth to smother her, and that the sea formed animate waves with leering, changing faces.

And as she sank back into unconsciousness, through her spinning brain flashed the conviction that she should never see David Kummer again.

II
THE ERROR IS RECTIFIED

THE MORNING was fresh and cool, with the merest suggestion of dampness. But it was the salt dampness of sea-spray, and it stung the nostrils of the two men with an effect of invigoration. The sun was still low in the east and the wind in the sky over the sea was just whipping the gray night-mists away, revealing curlicue patches of white cloud and bluest heaven.

Mr. Ellery Queen, a notorious lover of Nature, filled his lungs behind the wheel of the low-slung, dilapidated Duesenberg; and, since he was also a practical creature, listened to the satisfactory hum of the rubber wheels on the concrete highway. Both were good, and he sighed. The road stretched behind him in a straight line, a lambent gray-white ribbon of clean deserted morning miles.

He glanced at his companion, a silvered old gentleman whose long legs were jackknifed before him and whose sunken gray eyes were deeply imbedded in ruches of wrinkles, like old gems in crumpled velvet. Judge Macklin was seventy-six; but he was sniffing the salt breeze like a puppy drawing its first breath.

"Tired?" yelled Ellery over the roar of the engine.

"I'm fresher than you are," retorted the Judge. "'The sea, the sea, the beautiful sea . . . ' Ellery, I feel positively rejuvenated!"

"The hardy perennial. I was beginning to feel the weight of my own years after that long drive, but this breeze does something to you. We must be nearly there, Judge."

"Not far. Drive on, O Hermes!" And the old gentleman stretched his scraggly neck and began to sing in a powerful baritone that vied with the motor very creditably. The song had something to do with a sailor, and Ellery grinned. The old coot had more stamina than a youngster! Ellery returned his attention to the road and pressed his right foot a little more heavily on the accelerator.

Mr. Ellery Queen's summer had been not unproductive; if anything, it had been overproductive. So much so that he had had little more than a weekend or two at the shore—he loved the sea—and no proper vacation at all. Imprisoned in New York for the best part of the hot season struggling with the ramifications of a peculiarly baffling murder-case[1] which, truth to tell, he had been unable to solve, he found himself after Labor Day yearning after at least one extended fling at sparkling salt-water and comparative nudity before the fall set in. Perhaps, too, he was annoyed by his failure. At any rate, finding his father up to his little ears in work at Centre Street and all of his friends unavailable, he was beginning to resign himself to a solitary vacation somewhere when he heard from Judge Macklin.

Judge Macklin was a lifelong friend of Ellery's father; he had sponsored, in fact, the Inspector's early career in the Police De-

---

1   One of the most extraordinary cases Ellery has ever investigated. The newspapers called it "The Case of the Wounded Tyroleans"; more specific identification may not be given here. It is one of the few problems, to my knowledge, which stalemated Ellery; and it is still an unsolved crime.

J. J. McC.

partment. One of those rare jurists to whom truth is beauty and beauty truth, he had devoted the better part of his crowded life to the administration of justice; in the process acquiring a sense of humor, a modest fortune, and a national reputation. A widower and childless, he had tucked a younger Ellery under his wing, had selected Ellery's university and curriculum, had seen him through the dark years of adolescence when the Inspector was plainly bewildered by the responsibilities of fatherhood, and had contributed a good deal to the development of Ellery's unmistakable flair for the logical verities. At this time, well past the three-score-and-ten mark, the old gentleman had already been retired from the bench for a number of years, spending his leisure in slow peaceful travel. To Ellery he was a comrade and a tonic, for all the disparity in their ages. But after the Judge's retirement from public life they had seen little of each other; their last meeting was over a year old. To hear from "the Solon," as Ellery affectionately called him, so unexpectedly and fortuitously was a distinct pleasure, then; especially since he could not have asked for a more delightful vacation companion.

The Judge had wired Ellery from some improbable place in Tennessee—where (he said) he had perversely been resting his venerable bones during the hot weather and "studying the natives"—to meet him at a midway point so that they might journey the rest of the way to the coast together to take up a joint abode by the sea for a month's vacation. The wire made Ellery whoop for joy, sling some things into a suitcase, grin goodbye to Djuna and his father, and make for his "faithful Rosinante," a Quixotic affair of wheels and gadgets which had once been a famous racing-car. And he was on his way. They had met at the appointed place, embraced, babbled like women for an hour, conferred solemnly on the problem of whether to wait over the night—it was 2.30 in the morning when they met—or push on at once, decided that the occasion called for heroic measures; and despite the fact that neither had slept they paid off an astonished innkeeper at 4.15, jumped into Ellery's Duesenberg, and were off to the accompaniment of the Judge's most robust baritone.

"By the way," demanded Ellery when the important things had been polished off and over a year's conversation made up, "just where is this Arcadia? I'm headed in the general direction, but I'll be blessed if I possess second sight."

"Know where Spanish Cape is?"

"Vaguely. I've heard of it."

"Well," said the Judge, "that's where we're going. Not to Spanish Cape, but to a lovely old dump right near it. About ten miles from Wayland Park and some fifty south of Maartens. It's right off the State highway."

"You're not visiting some one?" asked Ellery in alarm. "With your juvenile enthusiasm, it would be just like you to foist a friend of yours upon some unsuspecting host."

"And serve the rascal right, too," chuckled the Judge. "But no, nothing like that. There's a man I know who owns a cottage near Spanish Cape—only a few feet from the water's edge, quite modest, but comfortable; regular summer affair—and the cottage is our destination."

"Sounds alluring."

"Wait until you see it. I've rented it from him in previous years—didn't make it last summer because I was in Norway—so it came to mind this spring and I wrote him at his New York office. We made the usual deal, and here I am. I've taken the place until the middle of October, so we've a splendid bit of fishing in view."

"Fishing," groaned Ellery. "You're a veritable Mr. Tutt! Always makes me think of broiled human skin and smarting eyes. I haven't brought even an—an anchor. *Do* people fish?"

"They do, and we're going to. I'll make a young Walton out of you yet. There's a perfectly scrumptious cruiser in the boathouse; one of the chief reasons I like the place. Don't worry about gear. I've written my housekeeper in the city, and a whole mess of rods and lines and reels and hooks and things will be here Monday, express."

"I hope," said Ellery gloomily, "there's a trainwreck."

"Buck up! Matter of fact, we're a day early. My arrangements with Waring—"

"With whom?"

"Hollis Waring. Chap who owns the place. I'm not supposed to take possession until Monday, but I imagine it will be all right."

"No chance of bumping into him, is there? I feel an uncommon craving for sequestration, somehow."

"Not likely. He wrote me this spring that he wasn't intending to use the cottage much this summer—that he expected to be in Europe during August and September."

"Know him well?"

"Scarcely at all. In fact, only through correspondence. And then it was about the cottage, three years ago."

"I suppose there's a caretaker on the premises?"

Judge Macklin's gray eyes, which by themselves were extraordinarily youthful, twinkled. "Oh, certainly! And a stiffish butler with sideburns and a man to brush our boots. Genuine Bertram Wooster-and-Jeeves arrangement. My dear young Crœsus, where do you think you're going? It's the merest shack, and unless we can rustle a capable lady somewhere in the vicinity, we'll have to do our own cleaning, marketing, and cooking. I'm a mean hand with the skillet, you know."

Ellery looked doubtful. "I'm afraid my culinary genius is restricted to biscuits made from prepared flour, turgid coffee, and more or less Spanish omelets. You've the key, of course?"

"Waring said he'd leave it," replied the Judge solemnly, "buried one foot deep, located two paces on a diagonal from the northeast corner of the cottage. That man has a sense of humor. My dear boy, this is honest country! In all the time I've spent here the nearest thing to a crime I've encountered was when Harry Stebbins, who has a gas-station and refreshment place on the main road nearby, charged me thirty-five cents for a ham sandwich. Hell, son, nobody locks his doors down this way!"

．　　．　　．　　．　　．　　．　　．

"It won't be long now," remarked the Judge with a sigh of eagerness, straining his eyes through the windshield as they topped a rise in the road.

"And high time, too," shouted Ellery. "I'm beginning to feel hungry. How about victuals? Don't tell me your whimsical landlord left a stock of canned goods there!"

"Lord," moaned the old gentleman, "I'd clean forgotten about that. We'll have to stop in Wye—that's just before you get to Spanish Cape; about two miles north of it—and lay in some provender. There! There it is now, straight ahead. I hope we find a grocer's or market open. It can't be more than seven."

By great good fortune they found a yawning tradesman unloading fresh vegetables before his establishment, and Ellery staggered back to the car under full sail with a princely larder. There was some argument about who should pay; which was settled in short order by the Judge's masterly lecture on the unwritten laws of hospitality. The two men then stowed their provisions in the built-in rumbleseat and continued their journey. This time the Judge sang *Anchors Aweigh*.

In three minutes they were approaching Spanish Cape. Ellery braked the car to a roll while he admired the looming rock. Through some freak of nature it was the only bit of country within sight above sea-level to any considerable degree. It lay placidly in the young sun, a sleeping giant, its plateau-like top out of range except for the fringes, which they could see were covered with trees and bushes.

"Nice, isn't it?" roared the Judge happily. "Here, El, stop the car. Opposite that gas-station there. I want to say hello to my old friend Harry Stebbins—the brigand!"

"I suppose that chunk of inviting rubble," murmured Ellery, steering the Duesenberg off the road onto the gravel before the Grecian-pillared structure with its heraldic red pumps, "isn't public property? Couldn't be. Our millionaires don't permit such things."

"Private as the very devil," laughed Judge Macklin. "Where's Harry? In more ways than one. In the first place, there's only one way to get to it by land, and that's up the branch-road across the highway there." Ellery saw two massive stone pylons flanking the entrance to the branch-road across the way, slashing through the cool-looking trees of the parkland. "Park's only a narrow piece, the branch is fenced on both sides with high barbed wire, and when you get through the park you have to proceed on the neck—just a bit of rock-road wide enough for a couple of cars. Road's on a level, and since Spanish Cape rises, the result is a sunken highway clear through to the sea-end of the Cape. Look at those cliffs! Extend all around the Cape. How would you like to climb 'em? . . . In the second place, the

Cape's owned by Walter Godfrey." He said this in a grim tone of finality, as if the mere name were sufficient explanation.

"Godfrey?" frowned Ellery. "The Wall Street Godfrey?"

"One of the—uh—many wolves of that distinguished thoroughfare," murmured Judge Macklin. "Exclusive, too. There are several human beings on that blessed rock, I understand, but its owner isn't numbered among 'em. In all the time I've spent barely a stone's-throw from the place, I've never set foot on it. Not that I haven't tried to be neighborly!"

"He doesn't believe in the bucolic virtues?"

"Not he. Matter of fact, in one of the chattier exchanges of correspondence between Waring and me, he mentioned the same thing. He's never been anywhere near the Godfrey—er—palace, and he's been a neighbor of Godfrey's for God knows how many years."

"Maybe," grinned Ellery, "you and your landlord aren't hoity-toity enough."

"Oh, no doubt about it. In some quarters an honest judge isn't too welcome. You see—"

"Come, come, there's a story under your whiskers!"

"Haven't any, and nothing of the sort. I simply mean that a man like Godfrey could scarcely have amassed a fortune on the Street in so short a time unless he took liberties with the law. I know nothing about the fellow, but I know enough about human nature to make me suspect various things. From all I hear, he's a queer one. Nice daughter, though. She came sailing along in a canoe one day a couple of summers ago with a blond young man, and we made quite firm friends while the young man scowled . . . Ah, there, Harry, you young dog! And in a bathing suit, too!"

The Judge scrambled from the Duesenberg and ran, beaming, to grasp the hand of a florid, pot-bellied, middle-aged little man in a flaming red bathing-suit and rubber shoes who had just emerged, blinking, from the office of his establishment. He was rubbing his fat red neck with a Turkish towel.

"Judge Macklin!" gasped Stebbins, dropping the towel; then he grinned from ear to ear and pumped the old man's hand vigorously. "Sight for sore eyes, all right. Might 'a' known you'd be up in these parts this time o' year. Where were you last September? And how've you been, sir?"

"Middling, middling, Harry. I was abroad last year. How's Annie?"

Stebbins shook his bullet-head dolefully. "Been ailin' bad, Judge, with her sciatica." Ellery grasped that the unfortunate Annie was the fortunate Mrs. Stebbins.

"Tut, tut; a young woman like her! Send her my regrets and love. Harry, shake hands with Mr. Ellery Queen, a dear friend of mine." Ellery dutifully shook the man's hard, damp hand. "We're spending a month on Waring's place together. By the way, Waring isn't here, is he?"

"Ain't seen him since beginning of summer, Judge."

"I see you've been swimming already. Aren't you ashamed to be seen trotting along the public highways with that pot-belly of yours hanging over your knees, you young reprobate?"

Stebbins grinned sheepishly. "Well, sir, I guess I *am* a sight for sore eyes, at that. But then everybody does it around here, and I like a dip in the early mornin'. Public beach is deserted this time o' day."

"Is that the beach we passed a mile or so back?" demanded Ellery.

"Yes, Mr. Queen. There's another on the other side—right next to Mr. Waring's place, where you're goin'."

"Must be an interesting stretch of road right here," said Ellery reflectively, "of a hot summer's afternoon. With all the pretty girls tripping along in their bathing suits—and considering what bathing suits are this season . . . "

"You young men," groaned the Judge. "As a matter of fact, I remember some of the local prudes complained to the authorities two summers ago about the near-nakedness of the bathers on the road. You see, there's a local ordinance which permits bathers to walk on this stretch of highway in bathing costume. Anything happen, Harry?"

"Not a thing, Judge," chuckled Stebbins. "We still do it within the law."

"It's the envy of oldsters that create such controversies. We can't swim—"

"High time you learned," said Ellery severely. "Then I won't have to act young Rollo and go about fishing you out of oceans and things, as I was forced to do six years ago up in Maine. I should think that in seventy-six years or so a man would learn to comport himself in other media than dry land."

"Talking about fishing," said the Judge hastily, with a blush, "how is it, Harry? They biting?"

"Pretty good, Judge, from all I hear. Ain't got much time, myself, for the rod. Well, well! You're lookin' fine. I see you stocked up on grub. Anytime, ye know—"

"You'll not hook me thirty-five cents for a ham sandwich again in a hurry," said the Judge in a severe tone. "I'll never—"

A small drab-looking automobile came whizzing down the highway very intent on its business, whatever it might be. There was a strip of gilt lettering on the front door of the sedan, but the car was going so fast that they could not make out the legend. To their surprise brakes squealed, the sedan lurched left, and then shot like a dart between the two pylons marking the entrance to Spanish Cape and disappeared under the flanking trees of the park.

"Is that," asked Ellery, "the normal method of driving in this part of our great and glorious country, Mr. Stebbins?"

The filling-station proprietor scratched his head. "Not for ordinary folks, maybe, but them's police."

"Police?" echoed the Judge and Ellery together.

"County police car." Stebbins seemed troubled. "Second one I've seen scoot into the Cape in the last fifteen minutes. Must be somethin' doin'."

They squinted in silence down the shaded road through the park. But they could hear nothing, and the sky was still blue, and the sun was a little higher and growing warmish, and the salt breeze had a hot smell about it.

"Police, eh?" said Judge Macklin reflectively. His fine nostrils were quivering a little.

Ellery tapped his arm in sudden panic. "Now, Judge, for the love of heaven! Is this surcease from care or isn't it? You're not intending to meddle in some one's private affairs, I trust?"

The old man sighed. "I suppose not. I should think, though, that *you* would feel—"

"Naughty, naughty," said Ellery grimly. "Nothing doing. I've just had one taste of work, dear Solon, and I assure you it has been sufficient unto the day. My needs at the moment are purely animal: a swim, a mess of eggs, and then sweet Morpheus. See you again soon, Mr. Stebbins."

"Sure, sure," said Stebbins with a start; he had been staring with grave eyes at the Spanish Cape road. "Glad to've met you, Mr. Queen. You'll be wantin' a housekeeper, won't you, Judge?"

"We certainly shall. Do you know any one?"

"If my Annie were feelin' better—" said Stebbins. "Well, I don't know no one offhand, Judge, but I'll keep my eyes peeled. Maybe Annie will hear o' some one."

"I'm sure she will. See you soon, Harry." And the Judge climbed back into the Duesenberg. They all seemed rather depressed: the Judge was silent, Stebbins uneasy, and Ellery desperately intent upon the usually simple business of starting the car. Then they rolled off, leaving the gray little filling-station man staring.

.   .   .   .

Both men were occupied with uncommunicated thoughts on the short journey from the service station to the leftward branch-road which led to the Waring cottage and the waterfront. Ellery turned off at the Judge's brief direction and they were at once plunged in the cool green depths of the park.

"Well!" said Ellery after a moment. "This is something like. Despite hunger, thirst, and fatigue I'm beginning to enjoy myself."

"Eh?" said the Judge absently. "Oh, yes. This is really a lovely spot, El."

"You don't act," commented Ellery in a dry tone, "as if you appreciated it."

"Nonsense!" The Judge raised his lank form vigorously and peered ahead. "I feel ten years younger already. Keep going, son. We'll be out of the park in a moment, and the road's perfectly straight from that point on."

They emerged into the full glare of the sun, drinking in the beauty of the shimmering beach, the blue of water and sky. The cliffs of Spanish Cape towered, silent and a little forbidding, beyond and to their left.

"Impressive place," murmured Ellery, driving slowly.

"Oh, quite. There you are, El. That group of little buildings ahead. This fence here on the right keeps the rabble away; that's a public bathing beach beyond the fence. Never could understand why Waring built a cottage so close to such a place; although I don't believe we'll be pestered. The people here are well-behaved." He stopped rather abruptly and blinked his wrinkled lids over the wise liquid eyes, sitting up a little and peering ahead. "Ellery," he said in a sharp tone, "is that a car down by the Waring cottage, or am I seeing things?"

"It's a car, right enough," said Ellery, "but I had some vague notion that it might have belonged to Waring and that he left it here for you. Crumby idea, though, I can see that. Queer, isn't it?"

"It could scarcely be Waring's," muttered Judge Macklin. "I'm sure he's in Europe; and besides he has nothing smaller than a Packard. That thing looks like one of Henry Ford's more cosmic errors. Step on it, son!"

The Duesenberg slid very quietly indeed to a stop behind a battered old car at the end of the Waring road, near the cottage. Ellery vaulted to the gravel and strolled over to the parked car, his eyes restless. The Judge got out a little stiffly, his mouth set in a thin line.

They looked over the car together. There was nothing alien inside, either human or inanimate. The key to the ignition protruded from the lock, several others hanging below the dashboard from a small chain.

"Lights are still on," murmured Ellery, but even as they spoke the lights flickered and died. "Hmm. Battery's exhausted. It's been standing here all night, probably. Well, well! A pretty little mystery. Sneak-thieves, d'ye think?" He extended his hand to the front door of the car. The Judge grasped his arm.

"I shouldn't," he said quietly.

"For heaven's sake, why not?"

"One never knows. I'm an incorrigible believer in the efficacy of fingerprints."

"Pshaw! Your imagination's been heated by that scuttling little police car." Nevertheless Ellery refrained from touching the handle. "Well, what are we waiting for? Let's—er—dig up that romantic key Waring buried for you and be about our business. I'm tired."

They circled the car and slowly walked up to the cottage. And stopped short.

The door stood ajar a bit, and about its hinges the wood was freshly splintered. The interior of the house exuded cool silence.

They looked at each other with puzzled, suddenly wary glances. Then Ellery darted noiselessly back to the Duesenberg, rummaged, came up with a heavy wrench, sped back, motioned the Judge aside, sprang at the door, kicked it open, raised the wrench and dashed over the sill.

The old gentleman set his lips and followed with a rush.

He found Ellery just inside the shattered door, glaring at the floor to one side, beneath a front window. Then Ellery swore beneath his breath, raised the wrench again, and plunged off into the bedroom. He reappeared a moment later to vanish into the kitchen.

"No luck," he panted, returning, and hurled the wrench away. "Well, Judge?"

Judge Macklin was on his bony knees on the cement floor. A chair had turned over and a woman lay in the chair, her arms and legs tied to it with tough cord. Her head, it was plain, had struck the cement; there was a trickle of dried blood beneath her right temple, and she was unconscious.

"Well!" said the Judge quietly. "We're in something messy up to our respective necks. Ellery, this is Rosa Godfrey, daughter of that old robber-baron on Spanish Cape!"

．　　．　　．　　．　　．　　．

There were violet shadows under her closed eyes. And her hair had come loose, tumbling about her face like black silk. She looked horribly tired and worn.

"Poor child," murmured Judge Macklin. "Thank heaven, she's breathing normally. Let's get her out of this atrocious harness, Ellery."

They released her with the aid of Ellery's penknife, raised her limp soft body between them, carried her into the bedroom, and deposited her upon the bed. She moaned a little as the Judge bathed her face with water Ellery fetched from the kitchen. The wound on her temple was very slight, a superficial scratch. It was evident that she had been sitting by the window in the chair to which she had been bound, had fainted and relaxed, and the sudden movement had upset the chair so that she had fallen with it to strike her temple against the rough cement floor.

"I admire your robber-baron's taste in daughters," murmured Ellery. "Very beautiful young wench. I approve." He chafed her numb hands with enthusiasm; the cords had bitten deeply.

"Poor child," said the Judge again, and bathed the blood away from her temple. She shivered and moaned once more, her lids fluttering. Ellery went away, found a medicine chest, and returned with a bottle of iodine. At the sting of the antiseptic she gasped and opened her eyes enormously, staring with horror.

"There, there, dear," soothed the Judge, "you needn't be frightened any more. You're with friends. I'm Judge Macklin—

you remember two summers ago? Judge Macklin. Don't exert yourself, child; you've had a wretched experience."

"Judge Macklin!" she panted, trying to sit up. She sank back with a groan, but the horror drained out of her blue eyes. "Oh, thank God. Thank God. Have they—have they found David?"

"David?"

"My uncle. David Kummer! He isn't—don't tell me he's dea . . . " She put the back of her hand to her mouth and stared at them.

"We don't know, my dear," said the Judge gently, patting her other hand. "You see, we've just come; and there you were in the living room tied to a chair. Please rest, Miss Godfrey, and meanwhile we'll notify your father and mother—"

"You don't understand!" she cried, and stopped. "Is this the Waring cottage?"

"Yes," said the old man, astonished.

She looked at the window; the sunlight painted the floor. "And it's morning! I've been here all night. The most dreadful thing's happened." Then she bit her lip and flashed a queer glance at Ellery. "Is it all right—Who is this, Judge Macklin?"

"A very dear young friend of mine," said the Judge hastily. "Allow me to present Mr. Ellery Queen. As a matter of fact, he has something of a reputation as a detective. If anything drastic has happened—"

"Detective," she repeated in a bitter voice. "I'm afraid it's too late for that." She sank back on the pillow and closed her eyes. "But let me tell you what happened, Mr. Queen. Who knows?" She shivered and opened her startling blue eyes again and began to tell the story of the wicked giant.

The two men listened with drawn brows, silent and troubled. She spoke clearly and left nothing out but the substance of her conversation with her uncle on the terrace before the arrival of the giant. And when she had finished they looked at each other, and Ellery sighed, and went out of the room.

When he returned the slim dark girl had swung her feet off the bed and was attempting in an absent way to tidy herself. She had smoothed her crumpled organdie and was fixing her hair. But at Ellery's step she sprang to her feet. "Well, Mr. Queen?"

"There's nothing outside that puts a fresh complexion on anything you've told us, Miss Godfrey," he murmured, offering her a cigaret. She refused, and he lit one himself absently. The Judge did not smoke. "The cruiser is gone and there's no sign of either your uncle or the man who spirited him away. The only clue is that car, which is still outside; and I don't believe we'll get much out of that."

"Probably stolen," muttered the Judge. "He wouldn't have left it if it were traceable to him."

"But he was so—so stupid!" cried Rosa. "He'd be capable of anything!"

"I agree," said Ellery with a sorry smile, "that he can't be very brilliant, if what you've told us is true. Quite a remarkable story, by the way, Miss Godfrey; almost incredible."

"A monster of that size—" The Judge's nostrils were quivering again. "He'll be easy enough to identify. And that patch over one eye—"

"It might be a false one. Although I can't see . . . It's that telephone call he made that's most interesting, Miss Godfrey. You're sure you can't give us a clue to the person he called?"

"Oh, I wish I could," she panted, clenching her fists.

"Hmm. I think it's fairly clear in its broad outline." Ellery took a turn about the room, frowning. "This huge and stupid creature was hired by some one to kidnap your Mr. John Marco, who seems to be a very lucky chap all round. In the absence of a photograph, possibly, Marco was described roughly to your captor; does Marco generally wear whites for dinner, Miss Godfrey?"

"Yes, oh, yes!"

"Then unfortunately your uncle, who, you say, bears a superficial resemblance to Marco in build and size, also dressed in whites last night and innocently became the victim of a mistake in identity. By the way, Miss Godfrey—you'll forgive me, I'm sure—has it been your custom to stroll out with Mr. Marco after dinner—perhaps to the terrace you described?"

Her eyes fell. "Yes."

Ellery regarded her curiously for a moment. "Then you contributed, too. A ghastly tragedy of errors. This man came, blindly faithful to his instructions, refused to believe that your uncle was not Marco, and there you are. The telephone call is immensely important, since it establishes the hireling nature of your assailant. Apparently, too, he was commanded to report from the cottage. This place makes an ideal base of operations, deserted as it is and with a cruiser handy in the boathouse. The giant is quite obviously the merest tool."

"But whom might he have been telephoning?" asked the Judge quietly.

Ellery shrugged. "If we knew that—"

They were all silent, and they were all thinking the same thing. A local telephone, the proximity of the mansion on Spanish Cape . . .

"What," whispered Rosa, "do you think will—will happen to David?"

The Judge averted his face. Ellery said gently: "I see no point in ignoring the self-evident truth, Miss Godfrey. According to your story this big fellow said over the 'phone: 'He won't bother you any more,' or something like that. I referred to the crime before as a kidnaping. I'm afraid I was trying to spare your feelings, Miss Godfrey. What your captor said doesn't sound at all like an abduction. It sounds brutally like—finale."

Rosa choked something down and lowered her eyes; there was a sick look on her white face.

"I'm afraid so, my dear," muttered the Judge.

"However," continued Ellery in a more cheerful voice, "there's no sense in anticipating. Anything may have happened or may still happen; at any rate, the whole affair's a job for your regular police. They're already at Spanish Cape, you know, Miss Godfrey."

"They—are?"

"Two police cars were seen entering the grounds only a short time ago." He looked at his cigaret. "In a way, our stumbling in here may have bungled matters. Whomever the big chap called, that person was apparently intending to see to it that you were released, Miss Godfrey, before any real harm came to you. You said your Goliath mentioned it over the 'phone. Now, I'm afraid, it may be too late." He shook his head. "On second thought, perhaps not. It's possible that the instigator of this nasty business has already discovered his hireling's blunder in nabbing the wrong man. That would make him lie low . . . " He went to one of the windows, opened it, and rather abruptly hurled his cigaret out. "Don't you think, Miss Godfrey, you should notify your mother that you're safe? She must be frantic."

"Oh . . . mother," mumbled Rosa, raising haggard eyes. "I'd—I'd forgotten. Yes. I'll telephone right away."

The Judge stepped in front of her, throwing a warning glance at Ellery. "Let Mr. Queen do it, my dear. You'd better lie down again." She permitted herself to be led back to the bed; her mouth worked jerkily.

Ellery went into the living-room, shutting the door to the bedroom behind him. They heard the clatter of the dial, and his low voice. Neither the old man nor the girl said anything. Then the door opened and Ellery came back, a rather odd expression on his lean face.

"D-Dav—" began Rosa in a strangled voice.

"No, there's no news about your uncle, Miss Godfrey," said Ellery slowly. "Naturally, there's been some anxiety about you and Mr. Kummer. I spoke to a local gentleman named Moley— Inspector Moley of the county detectives, you see." He paused, apparently reluctant to go on.

"No news," she said in an empty tone, staring at the floor.

"Moley?" growled the Judge. "I've met him. Good man. We had quite a chat on professional matters two years ago."

"Your mother is sending a car over at once," continued Ellery, eying the dark girl as if he were weighing something difficult and intangible. "A police car . . . By the way, it seems that one of your guests, Miss Godfrey, has been acting oddly. He appropriated one of your father's cars a few minutes ago and went scooting off Spanish Cape as if all the devils in hell were after him. It was reported to Moley a moment before I called. Two motorcycle officers are after him."

Her forehead was wrinkled, as if she had difficulty in hearing. "He?"

"A young man named Earle Cort."

She started violently, and the Judge looked perturbed. "Earle!"

"Isn't that the young man who was with you in the canoe two years ago, my dear?" muttered the Judge.

"Yes, yes. Earle . . . It isn't possible. Not—He wouldn't—"

"The complications seem to be accumulating," said Ellery. Then he swung about abruptly. "Something a bit more immediate than Mr. Cort's defection and the abduction of Miss Godfrey and Mr. Kummer has occurred, Judge."

The old gentleman's lips tightened. "Do you think—"

"I believe Miss Godfrey should know. She's bound to know in a few moments, anyway."

The dark girl looked up at him in a broken, confused way; she was dazed. "Wh-wh—" Her lips refused to function.

Ellery opened his mouth to speak, and closed it again. They all turned, startled. A high-powered car, to judge by its roar, was hurtling down the road toward the cottage. Before they could move they heard the grind of brakes, the slam of a door, and pounding footsteps on the gravel path. Then a whirlwind burst into the cottage—a tall, powerfully built young man with disheveled blond hair and a smooth skin burned dark brown by the sun. He was in shorts, and the muscles of his thighs and arms were taut.

"Earle!" cried Rosa.

He slammed the door shut behind him, set his half-naked back against it, flung one glance at Rosa as if to make sure that she was intact, and then growled at Ellery: "Well, you brigand, speak up. What in hell's the idea, and where's David Kummer?"

"Earle, don't be silly," snapped Rosa; normal color had returned to her face. "Don't you remember Judge Macklin from two years ago? And this is Mr. Queen, a friend of his. They've taken this cottage and found me here this morning. Earle! Don't stand there like a lump! What's happened?"

The young man glared at them, and the glare turned to shame as a slow red crept down his neck. "I—I beg your pardon," he muttered. "I didn't know—Rosa, you're all right?" He sprang to the bed and knelt by it, seizing her hand.

She snatched it away. "Quite well, thank you. Where were you last night when I needed you, when—when Uncle David and I were kidnaped by a horrible beast with one eye?" She laughed half-hysterically.

"Kidnaped!" he gasped. "Da—I didn't know. I thought—"

Ellery eyed Cort reflectively. "I don't hear the sounds of pursuit, Mr. Cort. I've just spoken with Inspector Moley at Spanish Cape, and he tells me two motorcycle policemen are after you."

The young man stumbled to his feet, still dazed. "I shook 'em off, turned into this side-road . . . They went ahead. But Da—"

"How," asked Judge Macklin softly, "did you know where to find Miss Godfrey, Mr. Cort?"

He sank into a chair, burying his face in his hands. Then he shook his head and looked up. "I'll admit," he said slowly, "this is too much for my feeble brain. I got a telephone-call at the house a few minutes ago from somebody who said that I'd find Rosa here, in the Waring cottage. The police were already there, but I thought I'd—I tried to trace the call. But I couldn't. Then I guess I—I lost my head, and here I am."

Rosa kept her eyes steadfastly averted from the young man's face; she seemed angry about something.

"Hmm," said Ellery. "Was it a bass voice?"

Cort looked miserable. "I don't know. It seemed to be a bad connection. I couldn't get any feeling of sex out of the voice at all. It was a whisper." He turned to regard the dark girl with a queer look of suffering. "Rosa—"

"Well," said Rosa coldly, looking at the wall, "do I have to sit here all day listening to a—listening, or will some one please tell me what's happened at home?"

Ellery answered without removing his eyes from Earle Cort's face. "Cort's caller complicates matters. How many telephones are there in the house, Miss Godfrey?"

"Several. And extensions in every room."

"Ah," said Ellery softly. "Then it's possible that your caller, Mr. Cort, telephoned from the house itself. Because the events of last night—certain events subsequent to your abduction, Miss Godfrey—would seem to indicate that the call your abductor put through was meant for some one in your father's house. It's not certain, of course, but . . . "

"I—I can't believe it," whispered Rosa, paling again.

"Because, you see," muttered Ellery, "your improbable pirate's error seems to have been discovered by his employer almost at once."

"At once? I—"

"And the mistake rectified—perhaps personally." Ellery frowned at another cigaret, and Earle Cort turned his head away. And Ellery said in a rather tight and puzzled voice: "For, you see, John Marco was found sitting on that beach terrace of yours, Miss Godfrey, early this morning . . . dead."

"D-d—"

"Murdered."

III
THE PROBLEM OF THE NAKED
MAN

Inspector Moley proved to be a grizzled veteran of the red-faced, hard-lipped, solidly built variety—the marks of the experienced man-hunter the world over who has come up from the ranks by the free use of fists, a knowledge of the faces and ways of professional criminals, and a certain cool native shrewdness. Such men are often bewildered when crime strays off the path of orthodoxy.

He listened to Rosa's story and Earle Cort's muttered explanation without comment, but Ellery detected the puzzlement between his brows.

"Well, Mr. Queen," he said as the Judge helped Rosa into the police car, Cort scowling behind them in a helpless way, "this business sure looks tough. A little out of my line. I—uh—I've heard of you, and of course the Judge's recommendation is plenty. Would you like to—sort of—help?"

Ellery sighed. "I was hoping . . . We haven't had any sleep, Inspector, and as for food—" He eyed the open rumbleseat of the Duesenberg longingly. "However, Judge Macklin and I might make a—er—a tentative reconnaissance, as it were." And there was something eager in his tone.

There was a county trooper on guard now at the entrance to Spanish Cape off the main road; apparently Cort's temporary escape had evoked martial precautionary measures The car swished through, and no one said anything at all. Rosa sat stiffly, like a woman going to her execution; her eyes were glassy. Cort tormented his fingernails by her side . . . At the bottle-end of the neck of rock stood another trooper. And parked motorcycles dotted the length of the sunken stone road leading into the heart of the Cape.

"That abandoned car," began Ellery in a murmur to Inspector Moley. His eyes were brightly inquisitive.

"A couple of my men are looking her over now," said the detective gloomily. "If there are any prints, they'll find 'em. I'm not puttin' too much hope on prints, though. Doesn't sound like a professional job, for all the smooth way it went off. That big guy . . . " He sucked in his hard lips. "A queer one, all right. He ought to be a cinch to spot. Seems to me I've heard of somebody around here, anyway, that answers to some such description. It'll come back to me in a minute."

Ellery said nothing more. As they turned off the sunken road he could see, farther up the road they were leaving, the entrance to the beach terrace. A swarm of men buzzed there. Then they had rounded the corner and begun to climb toward the house. Its gayly tiled, careless roofs were discernible as gables from the distance.

On either side of the road lay tiny wildernesses of rock-garden, flung about with a subtle lack of plan; they gave off an aroma of mingled sweetnesses which blended pungently with the salt air. A gnarled old man whose skin was the color of the rocks worked stooped over off to the left, with an air of immutable concentration, as if not even violent death might disturb the sanctity of his labors. The whole place was a riot of blooming bushes, colored stones and immaculate shrubs. Then the house loomed ahead—a long low Spanish structure . . . Ellery wondered suddenly if the old man poking about in the rock-gardens might not be Walter Godfrey himself.

"Jorum," said Inspector Moley, noticing his frown.

"And who might Jorum be?"

"Harmless old critter potters around the place; I guess he's about the only friend old Godfrey has in the world. Works as a kind of Good Man Friday to Godfrey's Robinson Crusoe— drives one of the cars sometimes, acts as watchman, helps the boss with his 'tarnal gardening, and so on. The two of 'em are thick as thieves." Inspector Moley's shrewd eyes turned thoughtful. "Couple of things I want to do. First off that call from Hollis Waring's cottage last night. I don't know but what we might be able to trace it—"

"Trace a call on the dial system?" Ellery murmured. "And then, too, young Cort says he was unsuccessful in the matter of *his* call."

"What young Cort says," remarked the Inspector grimly, "don't cut any ice with *me*. Though I've had one of the boys check up on him already, and so far he seems to have told the truth . . . Say, here we are. Chin up, now, Miss Godfrey. You don't want to make your mother feel any worse than she feels already. She's had plenty of grief today."

Rosa smiled a mechanical smile and poked her fingers in her hair.

A cluster of frozen people occupied the inner court. About

them circulated restless, hard-looking men. From the balcony peered several pairs of frightened eyes, apparently of the *genus* domestic. There was not the whisper of human speech. Bright colored furniture stood about; a fountain gushed in the center of the patio; the floor was paved with cheerful flagstones—all glittering and fixed. The whole scene was unreal in the glare of the sun, something out of a crazy painting.

As Rosa jumped out of the police car a tall dark woman of statuesque figure, her eyes reddened, a handkerchief fluttering from a slender wrist, ran blindly into the driveway. The two women fell into each other's arms.

"I'm all right, mother," said Rosa in a low tone. "B-but David—I'm afraid—"

"Rosa, darling. Oh, thank God . . . "

"Now, mother—"

"We've been *frantic* about you . . . It's been such a terrible, terrible day . . . First you and David, then J—Mr. Marco . . . Darling, he's been m-murdered!"

"Mother, please. Control yourself."

"It's simply . . . *Everything's* gone wrong. First it was Pitts this morning—I don't know where she is—then you and David, then Mr. Marco . . . "

"I know, I know, mother. You've said that already."

"But David. Is he—is he—?"

"I don't know, mother. I don't know."

Ellery murmured to Inspector Moley: "Now who, Inspector, is Pitts?"

"Damned if I know. Wait a minute." The Inspector pulled out a notebook and consulted a much-scribbled page. "Oh! She's one of the house-maids. Mrs. Godfrey's personal maid."

"But Mrs. Godfrey just said that she's gone."

Moley shrugged. "She's probably around somewhere. I'm not goin' to worry about a maid right now . . . Just a second till I break this up. I—"

He stopped, and waited. The disheveled young man had taken up his station by the entrance of the patio, and he was glaring at Rosa in a fierce, baffled way, biting his fingernails and devouring the girl with his eyes. Now he jerked his head irritably, changed expression, and with a sullen acquiescence stepped aside.

A small stout gray man in dirty slacks shuffled through the gateway and rather helplessly took Rosa's hand. His head was long and narrow, and tiny in comparison with his bloated little body, giving him a bottom-heavy appearance, like Humpty-Dumpty. He had no chin at all, which made his piratical nose look larger than it was. His eyes small and bad and unwinking, almost ophidian; utterly without color and without feeling . . . In the ensemble he looked like an under-gardener, or a cook's helper. Certainly there was nothing in his appearance to suggest power—except possibly the snaky eyes—or in his demeanor to suggest the builder and destroyer of fortunes. Walter Godfrey held his daughter's hand like any parental pensioner, and ignored his wife utterly.

The chauffeur of the police car drove away and after a moment of awkward silence the three Godfreys slowly went into the patio.

"By God!" whispered Inspector Moley, snapping his fingers.

"What's the matter?" growled Judge Macklin; the old gentleman had not taken his eyes off Godfrey.

"I've got it! Him, I mean. Wait till I get a couple of calls off my chest . . . Right, right, Joe; I'm coming. Hold those reports." He went around the corner of the house quickly. Then his head reappeared. "Go right in and wait for me, Judge. You, too, Mr. Queen. I'll be back in a jiffy." And he vanished again.

Ellery and the Judge strolled rather diffidently into the patio. "I invariably feel awed in the presence of riches," murmured Ellery, "until I remember what Prud'hon said."

"And what did Prud'hon say?"

"*La propriété, c'est le vol.*" The judge grunted. "And then I feel better. Humble as I am, I can still hold my own in the company of—er—thieves. Consequently, we may as well make ourselves at home."

"Always the sophist! I can't forget that there's the smell of death in this air."

"Apparently some of these good folks can't, either. Do you know any of them?"

"Nary a soul," shrugged the old gentleman. "I'm afraid, judging from Godfrey's sour expression—if that disreputable little rascal *is* Godfrey—we're not too welcome."

Rosa got out of her wicker chair rather wearily. "I'm so sorry, Judge. I'm afraid I—I'm a little upset. Mother, father, this is Judge Macklin. He's offered to help. And this is Mr. Ellery Queen, a—a detective. I—*Where* is he?" she cried suddenly in a stricken voice, and she began to weep. Whether she meant David Kummer or John Marco no one knew.

The brown young man winced. He sprang forward and seized her hand. "Rosa—"

"Detective," said Walter Godfrey, hitching his dirty slacks. "Seems to me we have plenty of *those*. Rosa, stop sniffling! It's unmannerly of you. The scoundrel got what he deserved, I daresay, and I hope the benefactor of mankind who polished him off goes scot-free. If you listened to your father more often instead of to—"

"Pleasant chap," muttered Ellery, turning away with the Judge as Stella Godfrey flashed an angry look at her husband and hurried to her daughter. "Observe our young hero. The world's most ubiquitous swain, with an obvious weakness for tears. Can't say I blame him in this case. And wouldn't you say that that human barge over there is the 'frenetic' Mrs. Constable Rosa mentioned?"

Laura Constable, attired in an aching red morning dress, sat in a trance nearby. She did not see the two men, nor Stella Godfrey escorting Rosa into the house, nor Earle Cort biting his lip, nor Walter Godfrey staring malevolently at the detectives hovering over the patio. The woman was indecently stout even in the armor she wore beneath her gown; and her bosom was frightening.

But the size of her body was insignificant beside the magnitude of her terror. It was more than fear on the fat, lumpy, insipid, enameled face; it was pure panic. It could not be explained by the presence of the numerous police, nor even by the proximity of a dead man. Ellery studied her intently. There was an artery jumping in the skin of her fat throat, and a spasmodic nerve in her left eyelid, over bloodshot eyes. She breathed in slow, heavy, labored, almost asthmatic breaths.

"There's a spectacle of raw nature," said the Judge grimly. "I wonder what's bothering her?"

"An inadequate verb . . . And there, I suppose, sit the Munns."

"Towers," murmured Judge Macklin, "of silence. An interesting collection of animals, my son."

The woman was easily identified. Her beautiful face had been pictured in a thousand newspapers and periodicals. Emanating from the grubby soil of a mid-Western hamlet, she had

flashed to a doubtful fame before she was twenty as the win-
ner of numerous beauty contests. For a time she had modeled—
there was a hard blonde loveliness in her face and figure that
photographed superbly. Then she had disappeared, to turn up
in Paris as the wife of a dissolute American millionaire. Two
months later she had secured a lucrative divorce and a motion
picture contract in Hollywood.

This episode in her career was as cursory as it was eventful.
Possessing no special talent, embroiled in three successive scan-
dals, she had quit Hollywood and returned to New York—almost at once securing another contract, this one to appear in a
featured rôle of a Broadway revue. And here, apparently, Cecilia Ball struck her true *métier*; for she hurtled from one revue to
another uninterruptedly and with that skyrocketing velocity of
success possible only to Broadway and Balkan politics. Then she
met Joseph A. Munn.

Munn was something of a character. A far-Westerner who
had punched cattle in his teens for thirty dollars a month, he
had joined Pershing's punitive army in the *Villista* war, found
himself caught up in the maelstrom of the European conflict,
achieved a sergeantcy and two medals in France, and returned
to the United States a penniless hero with three scraps of
shrapnel in his body. That his wounds did not impair a her-
culean vigor was proved by his subsequent history. Almost at
once he quit New York and disappeared by way of a shabby
tramp-liner. For many years he remained invisible. Then suddenly he turned up in New York, a man of forty-odd, black as
a *mestizo*, his hair as strong and curly as ever, with an air of
quiet authority and a fortune of several million dollars. How
he made it no one but his banker knew; but the preponder-
ant rumor placed the source of his wealth in revolution, cat-

tle, and mines. He seemed intimately familiar with the South American continent.

Joe Munn came to New York with an idea that amounted to an obsession: to make up as quickly as possible for his years of hard riding, hard campaigning, and hard association with halfbreed women. It was inevitable that he should stumble over Cecilia Ball. It was in a gaudy nightclub, the party was hilarious and liquorish, the music inciting; Munn got roaring drunk and flung his money about with the incredible carelessness of a maharajah. He was so big and masterful, so different from the pale men she was accustomed to, and moreover had so much more money—as was self-evident—that to Cecilia he became instantly irresistible. At noon the next day Munn awoke in a Connecticut hotel-room to find Cecilia smiling coyly by his side; there was a marriage license on the bureau.

Another man might have stormed and threatened, or consulted a lawyer, according to his nature. Joe Munn laughed and said: "All right, kid, you hooked me; but it was my own fault and I guess you're not so hard to take. Only remember; from now on you're Joe Munn's wife."

"How could I forget it, handsome?" she cooed, snuggling close.

"Oh, I've seen it happen," said Munn with a grim chuckle. "This is going to be one of those closed corporations, see? I don't give a whoop in hell what you were or who you played around with; my own past isn't any too sweet-smelling. I've got scads of dough; more than any one *you'll* meet can give you. And I think I can take care of myself in a clinch. You see our clinches are private, that's all." And he promptly proceeded to prove his point.

Cecilia Munn shivered a little, however, whenever she had cause to remember the look in his hard black eyes.

That had been some months before.

Now the Munns, husband and wife, sat side by side in the patio of Walter Godfrey's *hacienda*—saying nothing, doing nothing, scarcely breathing. It was not difficult to gauge the condition of Cecilia Munn's emotions: she was deathly pale beneath her make-up, her hands were rolled into a hard knot in her lap, and her enormous gray-green eyes were swimming with fear. Her breasts rose and fell in minute, repressed surges. She was frankly scared; as scared in her own way as Laura Constable.

Munn towered by her side, a bull of a man, his black eyes almost closed and roving under the brown lids like restless little rats, missing nothing. His big muscular hands were half-hidden in the pockets of his sport coat. His face was absolutely blank, the face of a gambler in a professional moment. Ellery gathered the impression from some secret place in his mind that the brown Westerner's muscles under his loose stylish clothes were gathered for lightning action. He seemed aware of—and ready for—everything.

"What in tunket are they all afraid of?" murmured Ellery to the Judge as Inspector Moley's powerful figure emerged from a door at the far corner of the patio. "I've never seen a crew in greater funk."

The old gentleman did not reply for a moment. Then he said slowly: "I'm most curious about this man who's been murdered. I should like a look at his face. Was he afraid, too?"

Ellery's glance flickered over the immobile figure of Joe Munn. "I shouldn't wonder," he said softly.

The detective hurried up with long strides. "Something and nothing," he reported in a low voice. "I've checked with the 'phone company. They've a record of a call last night from the Waring cottage."

"Good!" exclaimed the Judge.

"Not so good. That's all. No way of telling who was dialed; the dial system doesn't show, or something. It was a local call, though."

"Ah!"

"Yes, that's something, I admit. It sure looks as if this big man-mountain reported back to somebody in this house. But try and prove it." The Inspector's jaw-muscles bunched. "But I know now what the identity of that big gent is."

"The kidnaper?"

"I knew it would come back to me, and I've already checked up on him." Moley jammed a twisted Italian cheroot into his mouth. "Get this, now—you won't believe it. He's a guy by the name of Captain Kidd!"

"Nonsense," protested Ellery. "That's stretching the proba-bilities to an unconscionable degree. With a patch over one eye? What's the world coming to? Captain Kidd! I'm surprised he hasn't a pegleg."

"Probably the patch," remarked the Judge in a dry tone, "sug-gested the name, my son."

"Seems to be the size of it, sir," grunted the Inspector, drib-bling acrid smoke. "Talking about peglegs, Mr. Queen—one of the things Miss Godfrey told us about him was what brought him to mind. He's got just about the biggest pair of clodhoppers this side o' Poland. Bigger than Carnera's, they say; some of the boys down his way call him 'Tugboat Annie' when they want to get his goat. That scar on his neck she mentioned helped, too. Bullet-hole, I think."

"A veritable gladiator," murmured Ellery.

"And then some. Nobody knows his real handle. Just Captain Kidd. The patch is on the level; he had his eye poked out about ten years ago, I understand, in a fight on the waterfront with some tough little Wop."

"Then he's well-known in these parts?"

"Well enough," said Moley grimly. "Lives alone in a shack on the mudflats down Barham way, and he manages to get along by hiring out as a fishing-guide. He's got a dirty little sloop, or something. Drinks quarts of bug-juice a day and keeps pretty much to himself. Got a rep as a bad customer. He's been a fixture on this stretch of coast for about twenty years, but nobody seems to know much about him."

"Sloop," said Ellery thoughtfully. "Then why did he steal Waring's cruiser, unless it was out of sheer cussedness?"

"Faster. You can go places in that thing. And it's got a cabin. Matter of fact, one of my men reports that he sold his sloop out to another fisherman just Wednesday. Sounds interesting."

"Sold out," repeated the Judge with sudden gravity.

"That's the story. I've sent the alarm out all along the shore, and the Coast Guard are warned to keep their eyes open. Must be something of a dope if he expects to get away with that job he pulled last night. Somebody's playing him heavy for a sucker. With that carcass of his he couldn't any more disguise himself than an elephant in a one-tent circus. Mask!" The Inspector snorted. "He pinched the car, all right. Man who owns it identified it five minutes ago. It was stolen off a side-road where it was parked last night around six. About five miles from here."

"Queer," muttered Ellery. "And yet, at that, it isn't as stupid as it appears on the surface. A man like your piratical Kidd might easily decide to pull one last desperate job and light out. Seems indicated by his sale of the sloop, his only means of livelihood." He slowly lit a cigaret. "He is now in possession of a boat, as you say, that can go places. If he's been paid off in advance he can ditch Kummer's body miles off the coast in the ocean, where it will never be found, and head for anywhere he pleases. Even if you pick him up, where's the well-known and frequently elusive *corpus delicti*? But that seems to me a remote possibility. He's gone, I fear, for something better than good. A birdie tells me, Inspector, that you're in for it."

"Running out on me already?" grinned Moley. "Anyway, it's a question whether *he* murdered Marco last night. By all accounts he hauled Kummer out to sea thinking *he* was Marco. And the guy he reported to by 'phone probably to his surprise saw Marco after Kidd's call, realized Kidd had messed things up and grabbed the wrong man, and bumped Marco last night himself while Kidd was attending to Kummer miles out at sea."

"It's possible," pointed out the Judge, "that Kidd landed late last night somewhere along the coast and 'phoned his employer again, you know. And he *might* have been instructed to return and finish the job."

"Possible, but I'm convinced we're investigating two murder cases, not one. With two separate killers."

"But, Moley; they must be connected!"

"Sure, sure." Inspector blinked. "He's got to land for gas some time, y'see, and then we'll nab him. Kidd, I mean."

"For the cruiser?" Ellery shrugged; "Despite his stupidity, he pulled off his job. I see no reason to believe that in so elementary a precaution as fuel he should have slipped up. He probably has a lot of it cached somewhere in an isolated spot. I shouldn't rely—"

"Well, we'll see. There's a hell of a lot of work to be done. Haven't had a chance even to give the house a thorough looking-over. Come along, gents. I want to show you something pretty."

Ellery removed the cigaret from his mouth and stared hard at the detective. "Pretty?"

"It's a pip. Something you don't see every day, Mr. Queen— even *you* don't." There was a trace of sarcasm in Moley's voice. "This thing ought to be right up your alley."

"Come, come, Inspector, you're being deliberately provoking. Pretty about whom?"

"The stiff."

"Oh! Well," grinned Ellery, "from all I hear he was something of an Adonis."

"You ought to see him now," said the Inspector grimly. "Adonis was a wall-eyed bohunk compared to *him*. I'll bet a lot of gals wouldn't mind peekin', even if he is deader'n a mackerel. It's the screwiest thing I've run across in twenty-five years of looking at dead men."

.   .   .   .

The appalling truth was that John Marco sat, very dead, in a chair at one of the round terrace tables, slumped a little, a black stick still in his right hand and resting almost horizontally on the flagstones, his black crisp curls covered by a black fedora hat a trifle askew, a theatrical-looking black opera cloak draped about his shoulders and caught at the neck by a metal hasp and braided loop—and otherwise naked.

He was not three-quarters naked, not half-naked, not almost naked. Under the cloak he was naked as the day he had been born.

The two men gaped like bumpkins at a country fair. Then Ellery blinked and looked again, to make sure. "By God," he said in such a tone as a connoisseur might employ in awed contemplation of a work of art. Judge Macklin merely stared, incapable of speech.

Inspector Moley stood to one side watching their astonished faces with a sort of unhappy pleasure. "How's that for a new wrinkle, Judge?" he growled. "I'll bet you sat on the bench hearing many a case in which the subject was an undressed woman, but an undressed man—! I don't know what the devil this country's coming to."

"You're not suggesting," began the old gentleman with a grimace of disgust, "that some woman—"

Moley shrugged his powerful shoulders and puffed at his cheroot.

"Bilge," said Ellery, but his tone was unconvincing. He could only stare.

Naked! Beneath the cloak the dead man wore not a scrap of clothing. The blue-white hairless torso gleamed in the morning sun, marble statuary worn smooth and pallid by time; death had left its unmistakable imprint on that firm skin. He had flat angular breasts, and the shoulders were broad and strong, tapering to a small waist. Long flanks, rigid in death, were roundly muscled. The legs were slim and unveined, like the legs of a boy; and he had almost beautiful feet.

"Handsome devil," sighed Ellery, raising his eyes to the dead man's face. It was a faintly Latin face, with rather full lips and the merest suggestion of aquilinity in the nose—a well-shaven, scrubbed and dangerous face, languid and strong and mocking even in death. Of the fear Judge Macklin had speculated upon there was not a trace. "This is the way he was found?"

"Just the way you see him, Mr. Queen," said Moley, "except that the cloak wasn't draped around and over his shoulders as it is now. It fell straight down, covering his body pretty well. We turned the flaps back ourselves and got the shock of our lives . . . Nuts, isn't it? We haven't moved him, though, an inch. Something out of a book, or a lunatic asylum . . . Here comes our county coroner. Hi, Blackie, shake a leg, will you?"

"Curious," muttered Judge Macklin, shifting his lean old body aside as a thin and bony man with a tired face trudged down the terrace steps. "This gentleman, Inspector: was he in the habit of strolling about in what I confess is a very fetching nude, or was last night a special occasion? By the way, it *was* last night, I take it?"

"Looks like it, from the little I've been able to dig out so far, Judge. As for his habits, your guess is as good as mine," said Moley sourly. "If he was, he must have given the gals around here a great big thrill. 'Lo, Blackie. How's this for a godly chore of a Sunday morning?"

The coroner's jaw sagged. "Why, the fellow's naked! Is this the way you found him?" His black bag thudded on the flags as he bent over the corpse, peering incredulously.

"For the tenth time," said the Inspector in a weary voice, "the answer is yes. Get going, Blackie, for the love of Mike. This is a funny business all around and I want as much as you can give me on the spot, pronto."

The three men stepped back and watched the coroner go to work. For a moment none of them said anything.

Then Ellery drawled: "You haven't found his clothes, Inspector?"

His eyes ranged over the terrace. It was not spacious, but what it lacked in size it made up for in color and atmosphere. It invited leisure—an intimate little temple of lazy pleasure. Its open-beamed white roof permitted the rays of the sun to fall on the gay flags underfoot in a striped pattern of light and shadow that was of the very essence of summer.

A clever hand and eye had supervised the decorations; one received the dual impression of sea and Spain. There were beach umbrellas over saucy round tables in a prevailing motif of Spanish reds and yellows; sea-shell ashtrays lay about, and small brass-and-leather-bound chests of cigarets and cigars, and various sets of table games. At the head of the terrace steps, one on each side of the walk, were two huge Spanish oil jars, implanted with flowers; at the bottom, resting on the flagstones, two others. They were magnificently gigantic, something out of the Arabian Nights' Entertainment; almost as tall as a man, and voluptuously fat-bellied. Against the left-hand rock wall, nestling in the shadow of the high cliff, stood a miniature Spanish galleon on a stand (which Ellery discovered later split in two by some alchemy of ingenuity and became a very practical bar). Several pieces of superb colored statuary in marble occupied niches hewn out of the rock walls, and upon the walls themselves a capable hand had molded *bas-relief* sculptures of Spanish historical figures, chiefly maritime, in terra cotta and stucco. Two large searchlights, the sun glittering on their brasswork and prisms, stood sentinel on two of the opposite beams of the openwork roof. They faced straight ahead, piercing the opening between the cliff walls forming the Cove.

Upon the round table at which the naked dead man sat were writing implements—an oddly shaped inkpot, an ornate and delightful quill in a box of fine sand, and a rather elaborate repository for stationery.

"Clothes?" scowled Inspector Moley. "Not yet. That's what makes it so screwy, Mr. Queen. You could say that a guy might come trotting down to this little pocket-sized beach at night, take off his things, and splash around in the ocean for a while to cool off, or something; but what the devil happened to his clothes? And his towel; can't dry off at night without a towel. Don't tell me somebody *swiped* his clothes while he was taking a swim, like the kids do! Anyway, that's the way I was thinking—in dizzy circles—till I found out something."

"He couldn't swim, I suppose;" murmured Ellery.

"Right, right!" Vast disgust was on the red honest face. "Anyway, that swim stuff would be out. He's wearing a cloak and holding a cane. Hell, he was even writing a letter when he was killed!"

"Now that," said Ellery dryly, "sounds like something." They were standing behind the still seated figure now. Marco's dead body faced the little beach squarely, the broad cloaked back to the terrace stairs. He seemed to be brooding out over the coruscating sand, and the tiny curve of blue sea filling the mouth of the Cove. The tide was out, although even as Ellery watched there was an almost imperceptible inward creep of the water. The thirty feet or so of uncovered sand were perfectly smooth, unmarked by the slightest alien impression.

"What d'ye mean—something?" snorted Moley. "Sure it's something. Take a look for yourself."

Ellery poked his head over the dead man's shoulder; the coroner, working from the side, grunted something and he stepped back again. But he had seen clearly enough the evidence of Moley's assertion. Marco's left hand hung straight down, near the table; directly below on the flags, the stiff fingers grotesquely pointing to it, lay a brightly colored quill pen like the one sticking in the sand-box. The nib was discolored with dried black ink. A sheet of stationery on which several lines of script appeared—a creamy sheet with a coronal crest embossed in red and gold at the top, the name *Godfrey* in antique lettering on the little streamer below the crest—lay on the table only a few inches away from the dead man's body. Apparently Marco had been assaulted in the midst of writing, for the last word of his message—obviously an incomplete letter broke off abruptly, and a thick black ink-line trailed off down the sheet, across the intervening stretch of table-top to the very edge. There was a smudge of black ink on the side of the middle finger of the dead man's left hand, as Ellery ascertained by stooping and squinting.

"Looks genuine enough," he remarked, straightening. "But doesn't it strike you as odd, to say the least, that he was writing with only one hand?"

The Inspector stared, and Judge Macklin frowned. "Well, for God's sake," exploded Moley, "how many hands does a man need to write a letter with?"

"I think I know what Mr. Queen means," said the Judge slowly, his fine eyes lighting up. "We don't usually think of a man's needing two hands to write with, but actually it's so. One to write with, and the other to hold the sheet of paper steady."

"Yet Marco," drawled Ellery, nodding his approval at the old gentleman's quick understanding, "was holding his ebony stick with his right hand, to judge from what we see here, at the same time that he wrote with his left. I say it's—er—spinach." He added hastily: "On the surface, on the surface only. There may be an explanation."

The Inspector permitted himself a fleeting grin. "You don't let anything get by, do you, Mr. Queen? Can't say you're wrong, though I didn't think of it myself. But there could be an explanation. He might have had his stick lyin' on the table next to him while he wrote. He heard a sound behind him—maybe he was tense, anyway—his left hand trailed off the page as he grabbed the stick up in his right with some quick idea of defending himself. Before he could do more than grab it he was bopped. And there you are."

"That sounds reasonable enough."

"It must be the answer," went on Moley quietly, "because there just isn't any doubt about this letter. Marco wrote it. If you think this is a phony, forget it. It isn't."

"You're positive?"

"Couldn't be more so. It was one of the first things I checked up on this morning. There are samples of his fist all over the house—he was one of those guys who like to scribble their names wherever they happen to be standing—and this stuff he wrote last night is absolutely on the level. Here, see for yourself—"

"No, no," said Ellery hurriedly, "I'm not impugning your opinion, Inspector. I'm quite ready to take your word for the genuineness of the letter." But then he added with a sigh: "He *was* left-handed?"

"I've checked that, too. He was."

"Then there's really nothing more to be said on that score. I agree it's a puzzler all round. And no, it doesn't seem likely that a man would sit down outdoors in nothing but an opera cloak to write a letter. He must have been wearing clothes. Er—Spanish Cape is a rather extensive chunk of God's country, Inspector. You're *sure* his clothes aren't about?"

"I'm not sure of anything, Mr. Queen," said Moley patiently. "But I've had a squad of men doing nothing but look for them ever since we got here, and they're still missing."

Ellery sucked his lower lip. "And that fringe of jagged rock that circles the base of these cliffs, Inspector?"

"Two minds with but a single thought. Naturally, I worked

on the theory that somebody might have thrown Marco's duds off the cliff somewhere on the Cape into the water; it's twenty feet deep and more even at the foot of the cliffs. Don't ask me *why*. But there's nothing on the rocks, and I'll have the boys drag as soon as I can get some apparatus out here."

"Precisely what," demanded the Judge, "makes both of you attach so much importance to Marco's—for all you know—possibly non-existent attire?"

The Inspector shrugged. "I think Mr. Queen will agree with me that his clothes exist, all right, and that if they do there must have been a damn good reason for the killer's having toted 'em off, or disposed of them."

"Or," murmured Ellery, "as friend Fluellen said so ungrammatically: 'There is occasions and causes why and wherefore in all things.' I beg your pardon, Inspector. I'm sure you said it much more aptly."

Moley stared. "Say . . . Oh. You through, Blackie?"

"Pretty near."

Moley picked the sheet of paper very carefully from the table and held it up for Ellery's inspection. Judge Macklin squinted a little over Ellery's shoulder—he had never worn glasses, and although at seventy-six his eyes were beginning to fail, he would not give in to his infirmity.

A little below and to the right of the crest was written the date and then, in a bold hand, *Sunday 1 a.m.* On the left there appeared, above the salutation, the legend:

> *Lucius Penfield, Esq.,*
> *11 Park Row*
> *New York, N. Y.*

and the salutation read: *Dear Luke.* The message ran:

"It's a hell of a time to be writing a letter, but I have a couple of minutes alone now and while I'm waiting I want to tell you how I am getting on. It's been hard to write lately because I have to be careful. You know the kind of pot I'm sitting on. I don't want it to boil over until I am good and ready; and then let it boil! It won't hurt *me*.

"Things look good and rosy, and it is only a matter of days now that I will be able to make that last sweet clean—"

And that was all. From the tail of the *n* ran the heavy ink-line, slashing down the creamy paper like a knife.

"Now what kind of clean-up—'last' clean-up—was this monkey figuring on?" asked Inspector Moley quietly. "And if that's not something, Mr. Queen, I'm the monkey's uncle!"

"An excellent question—" began Ellery, when an exclamation from the coroner whirled them all around.

For some time he had been regarding the corpse with a puzzled air, as if there were something about the stiff clay he could not understand. But now he had leaned over and removed the braided loop from the metal hasp on the collar of the opera cloak at the dead man's throat, the cloak slipping off the marble shoulders, and then had placed his finger on the dead man's chin and tilted the rigid head far up.

There was a thin deep red line in the flesh of Marco's neck.

"Strangled!" exclaimed the Judge.

"Sure was," said the coroner, studying the wound. "Goes all around his throat. Ragged wound at the nape of the same nature; that's where it must have been knotted. Wire, I'd say from the looks of it. But the wire isn't here. Did you find it, Inspector?"

"Something else to look for," groaned Moley.

"Then Marco was attacked from the rear?" demanded Ellery, twirling his *pince-nez* thoughtfully.

"If you mean the corpse," said the coroner in a rather sour tone, "yes. The strangler stood behind him, slipped the wire around his neck and under the loose collar of the cloak, pulled hard, twisted the wire in a knot at the nape of the neck . . . It couldn't have taken very long." He stooped, picked up the cloak, flung it carelessly over the dead man's body. "Well, I'm through."

"But even so," protested the Inspector, "there isn't the sign of a struggle. He'd at least have twisted back in his seat, made a pass at his assailant, something! But this bird just sat here and took it and never even turned around, from what you say,"

"Didn't let me finish," retorted the bony man. "He was unconscious when he was strangled."

"Unconscious!"

"Here." The coroner lifted the cloak and uncovered Marco's curly black hair. He parted the hair skillfully almost at the very top of the head; a livid bruise showed through on the skin of the skull. Then he let the cloak go. "He was struck squarely on top of the parietal bone with some heavy instrument, not enough to break the bone but sufficient to cause a contusion. That put him to sleep. After that it was a simple enough matter to slip the wire under his collar and strangle him."

"But why didn't the murderer finish the job with his bludgeon?" muttered Judge Macklin.

The coroner sniggered. "Oh, might be lots of reasons. Maybe he didn't like messy corpses. Or maybe he brought the wire along with him and didn't want to waste it. I don't know, but that's what he did."

"Struck him with what?" demanded Ellery. "Have you found anything, Inspector?"

Moley went back to a niche in the rock wall, near one of the big Spanish jars, and picked up a small heavy bust. "He got socked by Columbus," he drawled. "We found this thing on the floor behind the table, and I put it back in that niche there; it was the only empty one, so the bust must have come from there. This stone doesn't take fingerprints, so there's no use looking. At that, we swept up the floor of this terrace before we set foot on it; but we didn't find a damned thing except a lot of sand and dirt blown up here by the wind. Awfully clean folks, these Godfreys, or maybe their servants were brought up right." He replaced the bust.

"And no trace of the wire, eh?"

"Weren't looking for it, but I got a report on every blessed morsel the boys've picked up around the premises that looked promising, and there wasn't any wire. I suppose the killer took it away with him."

"What time did this man die, sir?" asked Ellery abruptly.

The coroner looked surprised, and then surly, and then glanced at Inspector Moley; Moley nodded and the man said: "As closely as I can figure—which isn't always as close as we like to pretend—he died between one and one-thirty a.m. Certainly not before one o'clock this morning. And I think a half-hour's margin is ample."

"He *did* die of strangulation?"

"I said he did, didn't I?" snapped the coroner. "I may be a country yokel, y'understand, but I know my business. Strangled. Died practically at once. That's all. Not another mark on his body. Want an autopsy, Moley?"

"Might as well. You never know."

"All right, but I don't think it's necessary. If you're through with him I'll have the boys cart him away."

"I'm through. Anything else you want to know, Mr. Queen?"

Ellery drawled: "Oh, loads of things, but I'm afraid Mr. Coroner wouldn't be of much assistance. Before you take dead Apollo away . . . " He knelt on the flags suddenly and putting his hand on the dead man's ankle, tugged. But it was rooted to the spot as if it were part of the flag-stories. He looked up.

"*Rigor,*" said the coroner with a sneer. "What do you want?"

"I want," replied Ellery in a patient voice, "to look at his feet."

"His feet? Well, there they are!"

"Inspector, if you and the coroner will raise him, chair and all, please—?"

Moley and the bony man, assisted by a policeman, lifted body and chair. Ellery inclined his head and squinted up at the naked soles of the dead man's feet.

"Clean," he murmured. "Quite clean. I wonder—" He took a pencil from his pocket and with difficulty inserted its length between the great and index toes. He repeated the operation on all the man's toes, and on both feet. "Not even a grain of sand. All right, gentlemen, thank you. I've had enough of your precious Mr. Marco—certainly of his mortal remains." And Ellery rose and dusted off his knees and groped absently for a cigaret and stared out to sea through the opening in the walls of the Cove.

The two men set the body down and the coroner signalled to two white-clad men lolling at the head of the terrace steps.

"Well, my son," said a voice over Ellery's shoulder, and he turned to find Judge Macklin quietly regarding him. "What do you think?"

Ellery shrugged. "Nothing startling. It must be that the murderer undressed him. I thought the soles of his feet might show signs that he had been walking about barefoot while alive, which in a sense might have established that he had undressed himself. But his feet are much cleaner than they would be if he had actually walked about; he certainly wasn't on the beach there in naked feet, for there's no sand between his toes; or for that matter in shoes, either, since there are no prints—" He halted suddenly, staring at the beach with eyes that seemed to be seeing it for the first time.

"What's the matter?"

Before Ellery could reply a gruffly patient male voice broke into speech above their heads. They all looked up. They could see the blue-clad elbow of a policeman; he was standing on the lip of the high cliff overhead, the cliff which looked down upon the terrace and the beach from the side where the house lay.

He was saying: "I'm sorry, ma'am, but ye can't do that. Ye'll have to go back to the house."

They had one glimpse of her face with its unnaturally staring eyes, as she peered over the edge of the abyss gazing fiercely at the defenseless naked body of John Marco being dumped in a crate-like basket by the two white-clad men on the terrace. The marble body had strong black welts on it, where the beams of the terrace roof cast their shadows. It looked like the body of a man lashed to death—a queer illusion that was reflected by the female face glaring down at it.

It was the fat, pale, frenzied face of Mrs. Constable.

IV
THE NOTORIOUS IMPATIENCE
OF TIME AND TIDE

Then she vanished, and Inspector Moley said reflectively: "I wonder what's eating *her*. She looked at him as if she'd never seen a man before."

"That dangerous age," frowned Judge Macklin. "Is she a widow?"

"Just as good as one. From the little I've been able to learn, she's got a sick husband who's been off in Arizona or some other place out West for a year or so. He's in a sanitarium for his health. I don't wonder. Lookin' at that face for fifteen years or so wouldn't make a man *healthy*."

"Then her husband doesn't know the Godfreys?" The old gentleman pursed his lips thoughtfully. "Really an unnecessary question. I got the impression before that she doesn't know them any too well herself."

"Is that so?" said Moley with a queer look. "Well, from what I hear, they don't know Constable at all. Never met him and he's never been in this house. What's that you were saying, Mr. Queen?"

Ellery, who had been listening absently, glanced back; the

two men were trudging away up the gravel road with the basket between them. They plodded under its weight, chattering cheerfully. Then he shrugged and sat down in a comfortable wicker rocker.

"What," he said between puffs on his cigaret, "do you know about the tides here, Inspector Moley?"

"Tides? What d'ye mean? Tides?"

"Merely a hypothetical something in mind at the moment. Specific information might clarify certain, at present, nebulosities, if you follow me."

"I'm not sure I do," said the Inspector with a wry grin. "What's he talking about, Judge?"

Judge Macklin grunted. "I'm blessed if I know. It's a vicious habit of his to say something which sounds as if it might have meaning but which on examination comes to precisely nothing. Come, come, Ellery; this is serious business, not a clambake."

"Thanks for the reminder. I asked a simple question," replied Ellery in a hurt tone. "The tides, man, the tides. Especially the tides in this Cove. I want information about them, the more exact the better."

"Oh," said the Inspector. He scratched his head. "Well, I'll tell you. I don't know much about 'em myself, but I've got a lad on my force who knows this coast like the palm of his hand. Maybe he can tell you—though *what*, I'm damned if I know."

"It might be wise," sighed Ellery, "to send for him."

Moley roared: "Sam! Get Lefty down here, will you?"

"He's off lookin' for them clothes!" yelled some one from the road.

"Hell, yes, I forgot. Locate him right away."

"By the way," demanded the Judge, "who found the body, Inspector? I never did get that straight."

"Thunder, that's right. It was Mrs. Godfrey. Sam," he roared again, "get Mrs. Godfrey down here—alone! Y'see, Judge, we got the flash around half-past six this morning; and we were here in fifteen minutes. Since then it's been nothing but head-aches. I haven't had a chance to talk to any of these folks at all, except Mrs. Godfrey, and she wasn't in any condition to tell a straight story. Might as will clean that out right away."

They waited in silence, brooding out over the sea. After a space Ellery glanced at his wrist-watch. It was a little past ten. And then he looked at the water sparkling in the Cove. It had risen perceptibly and had eaten a good piece of the beach.

They rose at a step on the terrace stairs. The tall dark wom-an was descending with painful slowness, her eyes distended as if she were a victim of goiter. The handkerchief at her wrist was limp and soggy with tears.

"Come on down," said Inspector Moley genially. "It's all right now, Mrs. Godfrey. There's just a few questions—"

She was looking for him, of that they were certain. Her bulging eyes swept from side to side, moved helplessly by a pow-er stronger than herself. And she kept coming down in spurts of slowness, as if both reluctant and eager at the same time.

"He's gone—al—" she began in an unsteady undertone.

"We've taken him away," said the Inspector gravely. "Sit down."

She groped for a chair. And she began slowly to rock, looking meanwhile at the chair in which John Marco had been sitting.

"You told me this morning," began the Inspector, "that it was you who found Marco's body on the terrace. You were wearing a bathing suit. Were you going down to the beach for a swim, Mrs. Godfrey?"

"Yes."

Ellery said gently: "At six-thirty in the morning?"

She looked up at him with an expression of vacant surprise, as if she had just noticed him. "Why, you're Mr.—Mr.—"

"Queen."

"Yes. The detective. Aren't you?" And she began to laugh. Suddenly she covered her face with her hands. "Why can't you all go away," she said with a muffled sob, "and let us alone? What's done is done. He's—dead, that's all. Can you bring him back?"

"Would you," asked Judge Macklin dryly, "*want* to bring him back, Mrs. Godfrey?"

"No, oh, good God, no," she whispered. "Not for anything. It's better, this way. I—I'm glad he's . . . " Then she took her hands from her face and they saw fear in her eyes. "I didn't mean that," she said quickly. "I'm upset—"

"At six-thirty in the morning, Mrs. Godfrey?" murmured Ellery, as if nothing had happened.

"Oh." She shaded her eyes against the sun in a gesture of hopeless weariness. "Yes, that's quite right. I've done it for years. I'm an early riser. I've never been able to understand women who lie in bed until ten and eleven o'clock." She spoke vaguely, her thoughts apparently elsewhere. Then pain and awareness crept into her voice. "My brother and I—"

"Yes, Mrs. Godfrey?" prompted the Inspector eagerly.

"We generally came down together," she whispered. "David is—was—"

"Is, Mrs. Godfrey. Until we learn differently."

"David and I of-often went swimming together before seven. I've always loved the sea and David, of course, w-is athletic; he swims like a fish. We're the only two in our family that way; my husband detests the water, and Rosa has never learned to swim.

She had a bad scare as a child—almost drowned; and refused to learn after that." She spoke dreamily, as if something veiled impelled her to the irrelevant explanation. Her voice broke. "This morning I went down alone—"

"You knew your brother was missing, then," murmured Ellery.

"No, oh, no, I didn't! I knocked at the door of his bedroom but there was no answer, so I thought he'd already gone down to the beach. *I*—I didn't know he hadn't been home all night. I retired early last night with a—" She paused, and a veil came over her eyes. "I wasn't feeling well. Well, earlier than usual. So I didn't know Rosa and David were missing. I went down to the terrace. Then I—I saw him there, sitting at that table in a cloak with his back turned to me. I said: 'Good morning,' or something as inconsequential, but he didn't turn." Her features were convulsed with, horror. "I went past him, looked back at his face—something made me turn . . . " She shuddered and stopped.

"Did you touch anything—anything at all?" asked Ellery sharply.

"Heavens, no!" she cried. "I—I'd sooner have died myself. How could any one—" She shuddered again, her whole body shaking with repulsion. "I screamed. Jorum came running—Jorum is my husband's man-of-all-work . . . I think I fainted. The next thing I knew you gentlemen were here—the police, I mean."

"Well," said the Inspector. There was a large silence. She sat chewing the hem of her wet handkerchief.

Even in grief there was a youth, a springiness, in her body that belied Rosa; it seemed impossible that this woman should have a grown daughter. Ellery studied the curve of her slim waist. "By the way, Mrs. Godfrey. This swimming habit of yours. Does—er—weather deter you?"

"I don't know what you mean," she murmured in dull surprise.

"You come down at six-thirty every morning for a dip, rain or shine?"

"Oh, that." She tossed her head indifferently. "Of course. I love the sea in rainy weather. It's warm and it . . . it prickles your skin."

"The remark of a true hedonist," said Ellery with a smile. "I know precisely how you feel. However, it didn't rain last night so I fancy the whole matter's irrelevant."

Inspector Moley passed his hand over his lips and chin in a peculiar gesture. "Look here, Mrs. Godfrey, there's no sense sparring around. A man's been murdered who's been a house-guest of yours, and people aren't murdered just to put a little spice in a weekend. What do you know about this business?"

"I?"

"You invited Marco here, didn't you? Or did your husband?"

"I . . . did."

"Well?"

She raised her eyes to his; and her eyes were suddenly a perfect blank. "Well, what, Inspector?"

"Well!" Moley was growing angry. "You know what I mean. Who's he been fighting around with? Who might have had a reason for bumping him off?"

She half-rose. "Please, Inspector. This is very stupid. I don't snoop in my guests' affairs."

Moley checked himself, eying her narrowly. "Of course. I didn't mean that you do. But something must have happened up here, Mrs. Godfrey; murder isn't committed out of a clear sky."

"So far as I know, Inspector," she said tonelessly, "nothing has happened. Naturally, I can't know everything."

"Have you had any guests or visitors other than the people staying here now—I mean in the past couple of weeks?"

"No."

"Nobody at all?"

"Nobody at all."

"There's been no quarrel here, with Marco either the subject or otherwise one of the people involved?"

Stella Godfrey lowered her eyes. "No . . . I mean, I haven't heard of any."

"Hmm! And you're sure no one came here to see Marco?"

"As sure as any hostess can be. We don't have unexpected visitors at Spanish Gape, Inspector." There was dignity in her bearing now. "And as for skulkers, Jorum keeps rather close watch. If there'd been someone, I should have heard about it."

"Did Marco receive much mail while he was here?"

"Mail?" She grew thoughtful at that, almost a little relieved, Ellery thought. "Come to think of it, Inspector, not much. You see, when the postman delivers the mail Mrs. Burleigh, my housekeeper, brings it all to me. I sort it, and Mrs. Burleigh distributes it either to the rooms of—of members of the family or to what guests we happen to be having. That's the way I—I know. Mr. Marco"—her voice caught—"received only two or three letters in all the time he's been here."

"And how long," asked Judge Macklin gently, "has he been here, Mrs. Godfrey?"

"All . . . summer."

"Ah, a quasi-permanent guest! You knew him very well, then?" The Judge's eyes pierced hers.

"I beg your pardon?" She blinked rapidly several times. "Quite well. That is, I—we came to know him quite intimately during the past few months. We had met him early this spring in the city."

"How'd you come to invite him?" growled Moley.

Her hands writhed. "He—he happened to mention that he loved the sea, and that he hadn't any definite plans for the summer . . . I—we all liked him very much. He was jolly company, he sang Spanish songs charmingly—"

"Spanish songs? Marco," said Ellery reflectively. "That might be . . . Was he Spanish, Mrs. Godfrey?"

"I—I think so. Remotely."

"Then his nationality and the name of your summer place come under the tolerant head of coincidence. Quite so. You were saying—?"

"Well, he played tennis like an expert—we've several turf courts on the other side of the Cape, you know, as well as a nine-hole golf course . . . He played the piano and an excellent game of bridge. The ideal summer house-guest, you see—"

"Not to mention, of course," smiled Ellery, "his personal attractiveness, a distinct asset in the case of female-heavy weekends. Yes, indeed, it's really a sad case. And so you invited this paragon, Mrs. Godfrey, for the summer. He lived up to his glowing promise?"

Her eyes flashed angrily; then she swallowed hard and lowered them again. "Oh, quite, quite. Rosa—my daughter liked him very much."

"Then it was Miss Godfrey who was really responsible for Marco's presence here, Mrs. Godfrey?"

"I—I didn't say that . . . exactly."

"If I may," murmured the Judge. "Ah—how good a game of

bridge did Mr. Marco play?" The old gentleman played a fiend-
ish game himself.

Mrs. Godfrey raised her eyebrows. "I don't see—Excellent,
as I said, Judge Macklin. He was better than any of us."

The Judge said gently: "You generally play for high stakes?"

"No, indeed. Half a cent sometimes, most times a fifth."

"That would be called high enough in my circle," smiled the
old gentleman. "Marco won consistently, I take it?"

"Well—I *beg* your pardon, Judge!" said Mrs. Godfrey coldly, rising. "Really, that's an unpardonable insinuation. Do you
think I—"

"I'm sorry. Who," asked the Judge inflexibly, "has been his
most consistent victim among those present?"

"Your choice of terms, Judge Macklin, is scarcely in the best
of taste. I've lost a little. Mrs. Munn has lost some—"

"Sit down," snapped Inspector Moley. "We're getting nowhere fast. Sorry, Judge, but this isn't a case of card-killing.
These letters, now, Mrs. Godfrey. Any idea who was writing to
him?"

"Yes, yes, the letters," drawled Ellery. "Extremely important."

"I think I can help you there," replied Mrs. Godfrey in the
same cold tone. But she sat down. "I couldn't help noticing,
you see, when I sorted the mail . . . The ones that came were
from the same source, I think. All the envelopes were of the
business type, with a business imprint in the corners. The same
imprint."

"Not from a certain Lucius Penfield," asked Ellery grimly,
"of 11 Park Row, New York City?"

Her eyes widened in genuine surprise. "Yes, that's the name
and address. I think there were three, not two. About two or
three weeks apart."

The three men exchanged glances. "When'd the last one come?" demanded Moley.

"Four or five days ago. The envelope-imprint said *Attorney-at-Law*, under his name."

"Lawyer!" muttered Judge Macklin. "By George, I might have known. From the address . . . " He stopped short, his lids coming down in a concealing way.

"Surely that's enough for now?" murmured Mrs. Godfrey with difficulty, rising again. "Rosa needs my attention—"

"All right," said the Inspector sourly. "But I'll get to the bottom of this in spite of hell and high water, Mrs. Godfrey. I'm not satisfied with your answers, I'll tell you frankly. I think you're being a very foolish woman. It pays in the end to tell the truth in the beginning . . . Sam! See that Mrs. Godfrey gets back to the house—all right."

Stella Godfrey scanned their faces with brief, anxious, questioning glances; then she compressed her lips, tossed her dark and handsome head, and preceded the Inspector's man up the terrace steps.

They gazed silently after her until she disappeared.

Then Moley said: "She knows a lot more than she pretends to. God, what a pipe this racket would be if only people talked straight!"

"'It pays in the end to tell the truth in the beginning,'" repeated Ellery reflectively. "How's that for homely wisdom, Judge?" He chuckled. "Inspector, that was well if crudely put; it deserves an honored place in Bartlett's. The lady's weakening. A little pressure on the right spot . . . "

.   .   .   .

"This," said Inspector Moley wearily, "is Lefty. Come on

down here, Lefty. Meet Judge Macklin and Mr. Queen. Mr. Queen wants to know something about the tides around here. Find the duds yet?"

Lefty was a wiry little man with the suggestion of a roll in his gait. He had red hair, a red face, red hands, and freckles by the quart. "Not yet, sir. The boys are on the golf course now. And the draggin' crews 'a' just come down from Barham . . . Pleased to meet ye, gentlemen. What was it ye wanted to know about the tides, sir?"

"Very nearly everything," said Ellery. "Sit down, Lefty. Smoke? Now. You've known these waters for a long time?"

"Long enough, sir. I was born not three miles from here."

"Good! How tricky are these tides?"

"Tricky? Don't know's they are, specially, exceptin' in places where conditions freak 'em up a bit. Otherwise," grinned the man, "we get a passable grade o' tide out this way."

"And how about the tides in this Cove, Lefty?"

"Oh." The grin faded. "I get ye, sir. This *is* one of the trick spots. Queer formation of the cliffs here and that narrow openin' play old hob with the chart."

"Can you give me the respective tide-times for any given period?"

Lefty solemnly fished in a roomy pocket and produced a dog-eared pamphlet. "Sure, sir. I once did some work for the Coast Geodetic along in here and I know all about this Cove. What day?"

Ellery looked at his cigaret and drawled: "Last night."

The man riffled the pages. Judge Macklin's eyes narrowed and he directed them inquiringly at Ellery. But Ellery was studying the incoming hem of water, with its frilled edge, in a pleasant reverie.

"Well," said Lefty, "here she is. Yesterday mornin'—"

"Begin with last night, Lefty."

"Well, sir, high tide last night was at twelve-six."

"A little after midnight," said Ellery thoughtfully. "Then the tide begins to go out, so . . . When was the next high tide?"

Lefty grinned again. "She's a-comin' in now, sir. High at a quarter after twelve this afternoon."

"And at what time was it low tide during the night?"

"Six-one this mornin', sir."

"I see. Tell me this, Lefty. How rapidly, as a general rule, do the tides go out in the Cove?"

Lefty scratched his red head. "Depends on the season of the year, Mr. Queen, like every place else. But she goes out fast. Soundings show a funny bottom down here, and the cliffs mess things up. Kind of sucked out, the tide is."

"Ah, then there's a considerable difference between the depths in here at low tide and at high?"

"Sure, sir. That's a shelvin' beach, as you see; drops fast. Some spring tides the high covers the third step down there leadin' from the terrace to the sand. Difference in depth might be as much as nine, ten feet sometimes."

"That seems like a lot of feet."

"Consid'able, sir. More than anywhere along here. But that's nothin' compared to the tidefall up at, say, Eastport, Maine. Goes eighteen feet 'n' more there! And in the Bay of Fundy it's forty-five—granddaddy of 'em all, I guess. Then there's—"

"Peace, peace; I'm convinced. Since you seem omniscient, at least in so far as dynamic oceanography is concerned, suppose you tell us, Lefty," murmured Ellery, "how much of this beach must have been uncovered *at one o'clock or so this morning.*"

For the first time Judge Macklin and Inspector Moley

grasped the end Ellery had in view. The Judge whipped his long legs into a twist and gazed intently at the creeping water.

Lefty pursed his lips and studied the Cove; then his lips moved silently, as if he were computing something. "Well, sir," he said at last, "you have to take a lot of things into consideration. But, figurin' it as close as I can, takin' into account the fact that at this time o' year at high tide there's about two feet of beach left uncovered, I'd say that at one this mornin' there must have been at least eighteen, maybe nineteen feet of beach out of water. I told ye she goes out fast in here. At half-past one maybe more'n thirty. This Cove plays hell with the chart."

Ellery clapped the man's shoulder resoundingly. "Excellent! That's all, Lefty, and many thanks. You've cleared up a pretty point."

"Glad to've been of help, sir. Anything else, Chief?"

Moley shook his head absently and the detective went away. "So what?" demanded Moley after a while.

Ellery rose and went down the terrace steps leading to the beach. But he did not set foot upon the sand. "By the way, Inspector, I'm correct in assuming that there are only two ways of getting to this terrace: by way of the main path up there, and by way of this Cove?"

"Sure! Easy enough to see."

"I like corroboration. Now then—"

"Much as I dislike argument," murmured Judge Macklin, "may I point out that there are cliffs on each side of the terrace, my boy?"

"But they're forty feet or more high here," retorted Ellery. "Are you contending that some one may have jumped forty feet from the top of one of these cliffs onto the terrace or beach, which is even farther below?"

"Not quite. But there are such things as ropes, and to let oneself down—"

"Nothing to tie a rope to up there," snapped Inspector Moley. "No trees or boulders on either side for at least two hundred yards."

"But how," protested the Judge mildly, "about an accomplice to hold the rope?"

"Oh, come," said Ellery with impatience. "It's you who are being the sophist now, dear Solon. Of course I'd thought of such a patent possibility. But why on earth should any one take that devious route in reaching the terrace when there are the path and the stairs? It isn't guarded, you know; and at night the shadows of the cliffs would make it quite dark."

"There's the noise. That's gravel on that path."

"True, but a man would make just as much noise' scraping and bumping down forty feet of striated rock if he were lowered on a rope. And it would be a much more suspicious noise to the intended victim than the mere sounds of footsteps on gravel."

"Not if they were this Captain Kidd's footsteps," chuckled the Judge. "My dear boy, I've no doubt you're perfectly right. I'm merely clarifying an issue which it seems to me requires clarification. You yourself are always preaching that everything must be taken into account."

Ellery grunted, appeased. "Very well, then. There are two avenues of approach to the terrace: the path above, and the Cove below. Now we know that John Marco was alive on this terrace at one o'clock this morning. We know that from his own testimony—he set the time down at the heading of the letter he began to write to this man Penfield. Incidentally, there can't be any doubt about the fact that he did write it at one o'clock *this* morning; he set the date down, too."

"That's right," nodded Moley.

"Now, even assuming his watch was wrong, the error could not have exceeded at the utmost a half-hour, and the probabilities are all against its having been as much as that, if anything at all. The coroner set down the time of death, which was virtually instantaneous, as between one and one-thirty. So far, then, we check all along the line." He paused to gaze over the placid little beach.

"But what of it?" growled the Inspector.

"He's obviously trying to establish the time the murderer came," murmured the Judge. "Go on, Ellery."

"Now if Marco was down here, alive, at one o'clock or so this morning, at what time did his murderer come?" asked Ellery, nodding his approval at the old gentleman. "That's a vital question, naturally. Well, we can make genuine progress toward answering it. For we have Marco's own word for the fact that it was he who came *first*."

"Whoa!" said Moley. "Not so fast. How do you figure that?"

"Why, man, he said so—in practically so many words—in his letter!"

"You'll have to show me," said Moley stubbornly.

Ellery sighed. "Didn't he write that he had a 'few minutes alone'? Obviously he wouldn't have written that had some one been with him. In fact, he stated that he was waiting for somebody. The only argument that would invalidate that would be to establish the falsity of the letter. But you maintain there's no question whatever about the authenticity of the handwriting as Marco's, and I'm quite eager to accept your word for it. Because it helps my argument. If Marco was alone and alive at one o'clock, then his murderer had not yet come." He paused as the Inspector stared. Through the rift in the cliffs the nose of a large rowboat was pushing into sight. It was full of men and peculiar-looking apparatus which trailed over the sides of the boat to disappear in the blue depths of the water. They were dragging the sea-bottom about the cliffs of Spanish Cape, looking for John Marco's clothing.

"Now our tidal expert," continued Ellery, without taking his eyes from the boat, "tells us that at one o'clock this morning something like eighteen feet of beach were above water. But I've just shown that at one o'clock this morning Marco was still alive."

"So what?" said the Inspector after a while.

"Well, *you* saw that beach this morning, Inspector!" exclaimed Ellery, flinging his arm forward. "Even at the time Judge Macklin and I came here, a couple of hours ago, there were from twenty-five to thirty feet of beach exposed. You didn't see any impressions in the sand, did you?"

"Can't say I remember any."

"There weren't. Then there weren't any impressions in the sand last night between one and one-thirty, either! The tide had kept steadily ebbing, receding farther and farther from the terrace. The water, then, had no chance after one o'clock to wash away any footprints which might have been imbedded in that eighteen-foot stretch of sand extending seaward from the foot of the steps down there. Nor did it rain last night; and what wind there was could scarcely have smoothed away any footprints in this sheltered place, protected as it is by forty-foot walls of sheer rock."

"Go on, son, go on," said the Judge quickly.

"Now, observe. Had Marco's murderer come to the terrace by way of the beach down there, he couldn't have avoided leaving prints of some kind in the sand, since I've just shown that he must have arrived after one o'clock—at a time when more than eighteen feet of beach were uncovered. But there are no prints in the sand. *Therefore the murderer of Marco didn't come to the terrace by way of the beach!*"

There was a long silence, broken only by the shouts of the draggers in the boat and the lap of wavelets on the beach.

"So that's what you were driving at." Inspector Moley nodded gloomily. "That's straight arguing, Mr. Queen, but hell! I could have told you the same thing myself without all that folderol. It stood to reason that—"

"It stood to reason that, since there are only two ways to the terrace and the beach way has been eliminated, the murderer must therefore have come by land, by the path there. Certainly, Inspector! That stood to reason after reasoning. It did not merely stand to reason. Nothing stands to reason until it can be demonstrated logically that alternatives do *not* stand to reason." Moley threw his hands into the air. "Yes, Marco's murderer came from the path up there; can't be any doubt about that. It's something to start with."

"Precious little," grumbled Moley. Then he eyed Ellery rather slyly. "You think, then, that the killer came from the house?"

Ellery shrugged. "The path is—the path. The people in that Spanish excrescence are, by the very nature of things, proximate suspects. But the path also leads from the road across the rock-neck, and the road across the rock-neck leads from the road through the park, and the road through the park—"

"Leads from the main highway. Yeah, I know," said Moley disconsolately. "The whole world could have bumped him off, including myself. Nuts and bolts! Let's go on up to the house."

. . . .

As they strolled after the Inspector, who was mumbling to himself, Ellery absently polishing the lenses of his *pince-nez*, Judge Macklin muttered: "For that matter, the murderer *left* the scene of the crime by the path, too. It's quite impossible that he should have been able to hurdle a minimum of eighteen feet of sand. When he killed Marco he didn't go near the water, or we would have found his footprints."

"Oh, that! Quite true. I'm afraid the Inspector's disappointment is justified. There's nothing of a cosmic nature derivative from my monologue a moment ago. But it did need clarification . . . " Ellery sighed. "I can't get the fact of Marco's nudity out of my mind. It's been running through this old brain like a Wagnerian *leit motif.* Judge, there's a subtle point hidden there!"

"Subtlety's what you make it, my son," asserted Judge Macklin, taking long reflective strides. "More probably the answer's of the very essence of simplicity. I confess it's a trying riddle. Why any man or woman should deliberately undress his victim—" He shook his head.

"Hmm. It must have been rather a job, at that," mused Ellery. "Have you ever tried to disrobe an unconscious or sleeping person? I have, and you may take my word for it it's not as easy as it sounds. There are all manner of arms and legs and things that get in the way. Yes, yes, a job. A job that wouldn't have been undertaken, especially at such a time, without a definite and utterly essential end in view. Of course, he could have taken everything off Marco without removing the cloak; cloak has no sleeves to interfere. Or else he took the cloak off, undressed Marco, and then put the cloak back on again. But why undress him at all? For that matter, why undress him and leave the cloak about him? And now that I think of it, even if Marco was gripping the stick while writing, the murderer must have taken it out of Marco's right hand in order to undress him. That means he put it back in Marco's hand again—an inane procedure. But there must have been a reason. Why? For effect? For confusion? I'm beginning to get a headache."

Judge Macklin pursed his lips. "On the surface, admittedly, it doesn't make sense, especially the undressing part; at least it doesn't make normal sense. Ellery, it's a genuine effort for me to keep from thinking of a diseased mind, of abnormal psychology, of perversion."

"If the killer were a woman—" began Ellery dreamily.

"Nonsense," snapped the old gentleman. "You can't believe that!"

"Oh, can't I?" jeered Ellery. "I notice you were thinking along somewhat the same lines yourself. It's not at all outside the realm of possibility. You're a pure old churchman, and all that, but this may be simply a case for a psychopathist. If it is, there's a discarded mistress with a sex-mania in the offing . . . "

"You've a nasty mind," growled the Judge.

"I've a logical mind," retorted Ellery. "At the same time, I'll admit that there are a few facts floating about which don't precisely tenon with the psychopathic theory—chiefly certain omissions on the part of the murderer . . . or murderess, as you prefer." Then he sighed. "Well! What's the dirt on friend Penfield?"

"Eh?" cried the Judge, stopping short.

"Penfield," drawled Ellery. "Surely you remember Penfield, Lucius Penfield, attorney-at-law, 11 Park Row, New York City? It was childishly evident back there that you were emulating Melancholy, sitting 'with eyes upraised, as one inspired.' Suppose you remain true to Will Collins and 'pour through the mellow horn' your 'pensive soul.'"

"Mellow horn your foot! Sometimes you're infuriating," said the Judge grumpily. "Is my face as legible as that? I was once known, *sub rosa*, as the Sphinx. I wasn't melancholy, though; merely gratified at the sudden apprehension of a fugitive memory. I remembered."

"Remembered what?"

"It happened a good many years ago. Ten or more. I was— er—rather prominent in the extra-legal activities of the Bar Association at that time. Frequently there were irritating little matters of house-cleaning. I had the doubtful pleasure of meeting Mr. Lucius Penfield in connection with one particularly odoriferous investigation. Theretofore I had known the gentleman by reputation only. And a smelly one it was."

"Ah!"

"'Faugh' would be more like it," said the Judge dryly.

"He was up on charges brought by an indignant brotherhood of fellow-attorneys. If it's the same Penfield, of course ... Anyway, he was charged with conduct unbecoming a lawyer. Specifically, and less politely, with conspiring to cause witnesses to perjure their testimony; with doling out substantial bribes to rival jurymen; and a number of other activities quite as pleasant."

"What happened?"

"Nothing; the legal fraternity had let indignation run away with better sense, and they didn't have the goods on him. His defense was masterly, as usual. The disbarment proceedings were dropped ... I could orate all day, my son, on the subject of Mr. Lucius Penfield. Memory becomes fresher with each passing instant."

"So John Marco was corresponding with a rotten egg, eh?" muttered Ellery. "And from the familiarity of the salutation, he didn't mind the odor at all. Tell me all you know about Penfield, will you?"

"It may be summed up in a common phrase," said Judge Macklin with a bitter twist of his lips. "Luke Penfield's the biggest scoundrel unhanged!"

V
THE HOUSE OF STRANGE GUESTS

THEY FOUND the patio deserted except for two bored police-men, and followed Inspector Moley across the bright flags to an exotic-looking Moorish archway, which brought them into a small arcade decorated with conventional arabesques and fin-ished off with dados of glazed and painted tile.

"You'd never suspect the nabob, from looking at him, of having a passion for Orientalism," remarked Ellery. "Apparently he instructed his architect to stress the Moorish side of Spanish architecture. Page Freud."

"I sometimes wonder," growled the old gentleman, "how you sleep so soundly of nights—with your mind."

"At the same time," continued Ellery, pausing to inspect a vivid tile in red, yellow, and green, "I wonder if living in a Sar-acenic atmosphere—with a hot Spanish sauce added—doesn't do something to the Nordic mind. At that, it doesn't take much to kindle apparently dead fires. There's a certain type of female Occidental, like Mrs. Constable, for instance, who . . . "

"Come in, come in, gentlemen," said Inspector Moley fret-fully. "There's a lot to do."

They were assembled in a vast Spanish living-room which

might have been transported whole from the country *hacienda* of a mediæval don of Castile. They were all there—Mrs. Constable, her pallor relieved by a faint color, her eyes warily blank now instead of frightened; the Munns, two unsmiling statues; Mrs. Godfrey and her nervous handkerchief; Rosa, her back to an unhappy Earle Cort; and Walter Godfrey, still in dirty slacks, a fat little menial restlessly pacing the brilliant mats on the floor. The shadow of John Marco loomed black and heavy over their heads.

"We'll look at his room right away," continued Moley, his eyes distracted. "Now, folks, listen to me. I've got my duty to perform, I don't give a rap who you people are or how sore you get or how many high muckamucks you call up to make your kicks to. We've got an honest administration in this County and State. And that goes for you, too, Mr. Godfrey." The fat little man looked at Moley with smouldering eyes, but he continued his pacing. "I'm going to get to the bottom of this thing and nobody here's going to stop me. Is that clear?"

Godfrey halted. "No one is trying to stop you," he snapped. "Quit gabbling, man, and get to work!"

"That's what I'm doing right now—working," grinned Moley a little maliciously. "You'd be surprised what hard work it is sometimes to convince people in a murder-case that there won't be any funny business tolerated. You're so anxious, Mr. Godfrey; suppose we start with you. It is true that you didn't have anything to do with the presence here this summer of the deceased, John Marco?"

Godfrey flashed a queer look at the tense face of his wife. "Did Mrs. Godfrey tell you that?" It was almost as if he were surprised.

"Never mind what Mrs. Godfrey told me. Please answer the question."

"It's true, I didn't."

"Did you know Marco socially before Mrs. Godfrey invited him to stay here?"

"I know very few people socially, Inspector," said the millionaire coldly. "I believe Mrs. Godfrey met the man at some function in the city. I was probably introduced to him."

"Have any business dealings with him?"

"I beg your pardon!" Godfrey looked contemptuous.

"You didn't have a deal on with him?" persisted Moley.

"Nonsense. I don't believe I spoke three words to the fellow all summer. I didn't like him and I don't care who knows it. But, since I never interfere in Mrs. Godfrey's social arrangements—"

"Where were you at one o'clock this morning?"

The millionaire's snaky little eyes hardened. "In bed, asleep."

"What time'd you go to bed?"

"At ten-thirty."

Moley barked: "And left your guests still up?"

Godfrey said softly: "They are not my guests, Inspector, but my wife's; suppose we get that clear at once. If you will question these people, I believe you'll find that I have had as little to do with them as was physically possible."

"Walter!" cried Stella Godfrey in an anguished voice; she bit her lip at once. Rosa averted her dark young head; there was sick embarrassment on her face. The Munns looked uncomfortable and the big man muttered something beneath his breath. Only Mrs. Constable did not change expression.

"Then ten-thirty was the last time you saw Marco alive?"

Godfrey stared at him. "You're a fool."

"Hey?" gasped the Inspector.

"If I had seen Marco after ten-thirty, do you think I should admit it?" The millionaire hitched his slacks like a perspiring little laborer and actually smiled. "You're wasting your time, man."

Ellery saw Moley's big hands twitch convulsively and the cords of his thick throat tighten. But he merely turned his head away and demanded, quietly enough: "Who saw Marco last?"

There was an itchy silence. Moley's eyes swept about, searching. "Well, well?" he said patiently. "Don't be bashful. I'm just trying to trace the man's movements last night up to the time he was killed."

Mrs. Godfrey smiled desperately. "We—we played bridge."

"That's better! Who, and at what time?"

"Mrs. Munn and Mr. Cort," said Stella Godfrey in a low voice, "played against Mrs. Constable and Mr. Marco. Mr. Munn and my daughter, and my brother David and I were also to play; but since Rosa and David didn't appear, Mr. Munn and I merely watched. We had separated immediately after dinner for a few moments, and finally we gathered in the patio. Then we went into the living-room—came in here, you see—and began to play at about eight, I should say, or a little after. We broke up near midnight. Perhaps a quarter to twelve, to be more accurate. That's all, Inspector."

"Then what?"

She lowered her eyes. "Why—we just broke up, that's all. Mr. Marco was the first to leave. He—he had seemed a little impatient toward the end of the game, and as soon as the last rubber was played he said good-night to everybody and went upstairs to his room. The others—"

"He went up alone?"

"I think—Yes, he did."

"Is that right, everybody?"

They nodded instantly; with the exception of Walter Godfrey, who had a half-sneer on his ugly little face.

"May I interrupt, Inspector?" Moley shrugged, and Ellery faced them with a friendly smile. "Mrs. Godfrey, were you all in this room constantly between the time the game began and the time it broke up?"

She looked vague. "Oh, I don't think so. I think that at some time during the evening every one was out of the room for a few moments or so. You don't notice those things particularly—"

"Did the original four players play continuously all evening? Was there any change of partners, or players?"

Mrs. Godfrey averted her head slightly. "I—don't recall."

Mrs. Munn's hard, beautiful face came alive suddenly. Her platinum hair radiated a sheen in the sunshine pouring through the windows. "I do! Mrs. Godfrey was asked by Mr. Cort at one time—it must have been around nine o'clock—if she wouldn't like to take his hand. She said no, but suggested that if Mr. Cort didn't want to play any more maybe Mr. Munn did."

"That's right," said Munn quickly. "That's right. Clean forgot about that, Cecilia." His mahogany face was perfectly wooden. "I sat in, and Cort moseyed off somewhere."

"Oh, he did, did he?" said the Inspector. "Where'd you go, Mr. Cort?"

The young man, his ears flaming, set his lips angrily.

"What difference does it make? Marco was still at the table when I left!"

"Where'd you go?"

"Well—if you must know," muttered Cort in a sullen way, "I went off looking for Rosa—for Miss Godfrey." Rosa's back twitched, and she sniffed audibly. "I was worried about her!"

burst out the young man. "She'd gone off with her uncle not long after dinner and hadn't come back. I couldn't understand—"

"I can take care of myself," said Rosa coldly, without turning.

"You took care of yourself last night, all right," retorted Cort with bitterness. "That's a fine way to take care of yourself—"

"I suppose you'd have been the brave hero and—"

"Rosa dear," said Mrs. Godfrey helplessly.

"How long was Mr. Cort away?" asked Ellery gently. No one answered. "How long, Mrs. Munn?"

"Oh, a long time!" shrilled the ex-actress.

"And was Mr. Cort the only one who left the table and remained away—a long time?"

Unaccountably, they all looked at one another and then away. Then Mrs. Munn said again, in her high metallic voice: "He was not. Jo—Mr. Marco left, too."

Dead silence enveloped them. "And what time was that?" asked Ellery in a soft voice.

"A couple of minutes after Mr. Cort left." Her thin white hand strayed to her hair and she smiled with a sort of nervous coquetry. "He asked Mrs. Godfrey to take his hand, and then he excused himself and went out into the patio."

"You have a good memory, haven't you, Mrs. Munn?" grunted Moley.

"Oh, swell—I mean, a *very* good memory. Joe—Mr. Munn always says to me—"

"Where'd you go exactly, Cort?" demanded Moley abruptly.

Something flickered in the young man's hazel eyes. "Oh, I wandered about the grounds. I called for Rosa several times, but there was no answer."

"Did you come back before Marco quit the game?"

"Well . . . "

"I beg your pardon, sir, but I believe I can tell you that," said a soft pleasant male voice from a far doorway, and they turned, startled, toward the sound. A little man dressed in decorously-cut black stood there in a half-bowed attitude that was at once obsequious and self-possessed. He was a colorless midge with tiny hands and feet and a perfectly smooth face that suggested in a vague, elusive way—the bland skin, the faint elongation of the eyes—Oriental blood. But he spoke facile, cultured English and his sober clothes had a London look about them. "Eurasian far back," thought Ellery.

"And who are you?" growled the Inspector.

"Tiller, you get back where you belong!" shouted Walter Godfrey furiously, advancing upon the little man in black with pudgy doubled fists. "Who asked you to volunteer information? Speak when you're spoken to!"

The little man said apologetically: "Of course, Mr. Godfrey," and turned to go; but there was an amused gleam in his eye.

"Here, here, come back here," said Moley hastily. "And I'll thank you, Mr. Godfrey, not to interfere."

"Tiller, I warn you—" snarled the millionaire.

The little man hesitated. Moley said in an even voice: "Come back here, Tiller." Godfrey shrugged suddenly and retreated to a huge armorial chair in a corner of the room. The little man advanced with silent steps. "Just who are you?"

"I am the house valet, sir."

"Mr. Godfrey's, too?"

"No, sir, Mr. Godfrey does not employ the services of a personal valet. Mrs. Godfrey employs me to attend the wants of the gentlemen who visit Spanish Cape."

Moley fixed him with an expectant eye. "All right. Now what were you going to say?"

Earle Cort glared at him for an instant and then turned away, smoothing his blond hair with a nervous brown hand. Mrs. Godfrey fumbled with her handkerchief. The little man said: "I can tell you about Mr. Cort and Mr. Marco last night, sir. You see—"

"Tiller," whispered Stella Godfrey, "you're discharged."

"Yes, Madam."

"Oh, no, he isn't," said Moley. "Not until this murder is cleared up. What about Mr. Cort and Mr. Marco, Tiller?"

The valet cleared his throat and spoke quietly, his almost-almond eyes fixed upon two crossed Saracen swords on the opposite wall. "It is my custom," he began in a quaint way, "to take a breath of air in the evening after my dinner, sir. Generally the gentlemen have all been attended to by that time, and I have an hour or so to myself. Sometimes I drop into Mr. Jorum's cottage for a pipe and chat—"

"The gardener?"

"Quite so, sir. Mr. Jorum has a cottage of his own on the grounds. Last night, while Mrs. Godfrey and her guests were at the bridge table, I walked down to Mr. Jorum's place as usual, sir. We talked for a while and then I wandered off by myself. I thought I might stroll down to the terrace—"

"Why?" asked Moley quickly.

Tiller looked blank. "I beg your pardon? Oh, no special reason, sir. I like it there; it's so restful. I hadn't expected to find any one there. Naturally I know my place, if I may say so, sir . . . "

"But you did find some one there?"

"Yes, sir. Mr. Cort and Mr. Marco."

"What time was this?"

"I should say at about a few minutes past nine, sir."

"Were they talking? Did you hear what they said?"

"Yes, sir. They were—er—quarreling, sir."

"And you listened, damn you," said young Cort bitterly. "A spy!"

"No, sir," murmured Tiller in a distressed voice. "I couldn't help hearing, you and Mr. Marco were speaking so loudly."

"You could have gone away, damn you!"

"I was afraid you might hear—"

"Never mind that," rasped the Inspector. "What were they quarreling about, Tiller?"

"Miss Rosa, sir."

"Rosa!" gasped Mrs. Godfrey. She turned wide, shocked eyes upon her daughter, who went slowly crimson.

"All right, all right," said young Cort thickly. "I suppose it's got to come out, now that that rotten little meddler's spilled the beans. I did lace it into that damned gigolo, good and hot! I told him if ever he laid a hand on Rosa again, I'd—"

"You'd what?" asked Moley softly, as Cort paused.

"I believe," murmured Tiller, "Mr. Cort mentioned something about a sound thrashing."

"Oh." Moley was disappointed. "Marco was annoying Miss Godfrey, then, Cort?"

"Rosa," whispered Mrs. Godfrey, "you never told me—"

"Oh, you're impossible, all of you!" cried Rosa, springing to her feet. "And as for you, Mr. Smart-Alec Cort, don't ever speak to me again! What right did you have to—to quarrel with John . . . yes, *John!* . . . about me? He did not annoy me! Any lib—anything that may have passed between us was with my permission, you may be sure!"

"Rosa," began the young man miserably, "it's just that—"

"Don't *speak* to me!" Her blue eyes flashed anger and defiance, and she held her head with something very like pride. "If you must know, all of you—yes, and you, too, mother!—John had asked me to marry him!"

"Mar—" Mrs. Godfrey gasped. "And you—"

Rosa said more quietly. "I—well, I'd practically accepted. Not in so many words, but . . ."

The most remarkable thing happened. Mrs. Constable moved in her chair and said in a husky voice—the first time she had spoken since early morning: "The devil. The cunning, filthy, heartless devil. I saw it coming. You were blind, Mrs. Godfrey. If I had a daughter—He used all his old tricks . . . " Then she stopped abruptly. Her frozen features had not even twitched.

Something like fear crept into Rosa's eyes. Rosa's mother was staring with a hand over her mouth, staring at the tall dark young woman who was her daughter as if she were seeing her for the first time.

Young Cort's face was gray, but he said with dignity: "I don't believe Miss Godfrey knew quite what she was letting herself in for, Inspector. I may as well tell you, because if I don't, Tiller will—since he seems to have hung about near the terrace long enough to hear the whole messy business.

"Marco told me in the course of our argument what Miss Godfrey has just told you: that he had proposed to her just Friday and that she had virtually accepted him, and that he was so sure of the outcome he had made all his plans. He was going to run off with her next week and be married." He winced a little.

Rosa faltered: "I never—He shouldn't—"

"He said," continued Cort quietly, "that it didn't matter if I told Mr. Godfrey and Mrs. Godfrey and the whole world; they loved each other and nothing would stop them. Besides, he said, Rosa would do anything he suggested. I was a meddling young fool, he said, and an upstart and barely out of diapers. He said a lot of other things not quite so mild. Is that right, Tiller?"

"Quite right, Mr. Cort," murmured Tiller.

"I'd got him downright angry, I guess; I don't think he would have spoken so frankly and lost his temper so easily if he'd been his usual self. He seemed very excited. And I was so mad I ran away; I think I'd have killed him if I stayed another minute."

Rosa tossed her head suddenly and without a word stalked across the room to a door. Moley watched her go without comment.

"Marriage," said Mrs. Constable bitterly. "Generous of him." And she said no more.

"Well!" Inspector Moley hunched his shoulders. "This is a nice kettle of fish. Anyway, Marco and you returned to the game?"

"I don't know about Marco," muttered the young man, his eyes still on the door, "because I just wandered about the grounds, too ripping mad to be seen in polite company. I guess in my dumb way I must have been looking for Rosa. But when I did cool off and go back, about half-past ten, I found Marco in the game again, jolly as you please, as if nothing had happened."

"What did happen, Tiller?" demanded Moley.

Tiller coughed behind a little hand. "Mr. Cort ran off up the path, as he says, sir; I heard him clattering up the steps leading to the house a little later. Mr. Marco remained on the terrace for a few minutes, muttering angrily to himself. Then I saw him— the terrace-light was on, sir—fix his clothing (he was in whites at that time, sir), smooth his hair down, adjust his necktie, sort of try out a smile, turn the lights off, and go away. He went straight to the house, I believe, sir."

"Did he, or didn't he? Did you follow him?"

"I—Yes, sir."

"Remarkable observer, Tiller," smiled Ellery; he had not once taken his gaze from the man's bland little face. "Excellent reporting. By the way, who answers telephone calls here?"

"Generally the under-butler, sir. The switchboard is in one of the inner halls, sir. I believe—"

Moley put his mouth to Ellery's ear and said: "I've had a man talk to the butler already. And the other regular servants. Nobody remembers a call last night about the time Kidd must have rung up. But that doesn't mean anything; either they're lying, or don't remember."

"Or the recipient was waiting for it," said Ellery quietly, "at the switchboard . . . Thank you, Tiller."

"Yes, sir. Thank you, sir." Tiller glanced at him briefly and looked away; but in that cursory inspection he seemed to have seen everything.

"I hope," said Walter Godfrey acidly from his corner, where he sat grotesquely enthroned, like Soglow's Little King, "that you're satisfied with your handiwork, Stella, my dear." And he rose and followed his daughter out of the living-room. What he meant by this cryptic remark no one—least of all Mrs. Godfrey, who sat steeped in mortification and pain—volunteered to explain.

The detective whom Moley had called Sam hurried in from the patio and said something to the Inspector in an undertone. Moley nodded without enthusiasm, threw a meaning look at Ellery and Judge Macklin—who all this time had been standing stiffly by himself in a corner—and stalked out.

There was an instant raising of tension, as if an electric current had been turned off. Joseph B. Munn silently moved his right foot and drew a noiseless deep breath. An almost human expression came into Mrs. Constable's gargoyle face and her heavy shoulders shook. Mrs. Munn raised a minute square of cambric to her hard eyes. Cort made unsteadily for a taboret and poured himself a drink . . . Tiller turned as if to leave.

"If you please, Tiller," said Ellery pleasantly; Tiller halted, and the current was magically turned on again. "An observer of your calibre can ill be spared. We may have use for your talents in the very near future . . . Ladies and gentlemen. If I may intrude my unwelcome personality into this sad discussion. My name is Queen, the gentleman at my left is Judge Macklin, and—"

"Who gave you birds permission to horn in?" growled Joe Munn suddenly, rising to his full hard height. "Isn't one cop enough?"

"I was about to explain," said Ellery patiently, "that Inspector Moley has requested us to act as—er—consultants. In that capacity, it behooves me to ask a few—I trust—pertinent questions. Suppose we begin with you, Mr. Munn, since you seem impatient. At what hour did you turn in last night?"

Munn stared at him coldly for a few seconds before replying. His black eyes were as steady as the sea-washed rocks at the feet of Spanish Cape. He said: "Around eleven thirty."

"I thought the game had broken up at a quarter of twelve?"

"I wasn't playing for the last half-hour. I excused myself and went on up to bed."

"I see," said Ellery quietly. "Then why did you say before, Mrs. Godfrey, that Mr. Marco was the first to retire from the game?"

"Oh, I don't know! I can't remember everything. This is so utterly impossible . . . "

"Quite understandable. But we must get truthful answers,

Mrs. Godfrey; a good deal may depend upon the faithfulness of your collective memories . . . Mr. Munn, when you went upstairs Marco was still in this room playing?"

"That's the ticket."

"Did you see him, or hear him, when he followed you upstairs?"

Munn snapped: "He didn't follow me."

"In a manner of speaking," said Ellery hastily. "Did you?"

"Naw. I told you I went right to bed. Didn't hear nothing."

"And you, Mrs. Munn?"

The beautiful woman cried: "I don't know why we have to answer questions, questions, questions, Joe!" in her shrill voice.

"Shut up, Cecilia," said Munn. "Mrs. Munn came upstairs just as I was crawlin' into bed, Queen. We've been sharing the same room here."

"I see," smiled Ellery. "Now, Mr. Munn, I take it you've known Marco for some time?"

"You can take it, but it won't do you any good. You're all wrong, partner. I never saw that lily-faced guy in my life before we came up here." Munn shrugged his broad shoulders carelessly. "Not much of a loss, I'd say. Down in Rio a gig like him wouldn't last long among white men. Matter of fact," he continued with a hard grin, "I don't cotton to this society stuff at all, now I've sampled it—with all due respect to Mrs. Godfrey. Cecilia and me, we're goin' to beat it the hell out of here first chance we get, aren't we, hon?"

"Hush, Joe!" said Mrs. Munn fiercely, casting an anxious look at Mrs. Godfrey.

"Er—but you did know Mrs. Godfrey, of course?"

The big man shrugged again. "Nope. I just got in from the Argentine four, five months ago; met Mrs. Munn in New York and we got hitched, y'see. Made a pile of jack out there, and I guess jack talks in any man's country. We got an invite to come up here to Spanish Cape, that's all I know. Sounded kind of funny, but hell! I'm not scared of the tony crowd any more the way I used to be."

Mrs. Godfrey's hand came up in a sudden helpless, frightened gesture, as if she were trying to stop Munn or ward off a danger. He looked at her with a sudden narrowing of his bleak eyes. "What's the matter? Did I let out somethin' I wasn't supposed to?"

"Do you mean to say," demanded Ellery softly, leaning forward, "that you had never met, never heard of the Godfreys before you received an invitation to spend a few days at their summer home?"

Munn stroked his big brown chin. "You'll have to ask Mrs. Godfrey that," he said abruptly, and sat down.

"Why—" began Stella Godfrey in a choked voice; her nostrils were pinched and she looked about to faint. "Why—I'm always asking . . . interesting people out here, Mr. Queen. Mr.— Mr. Munn seemed a refreshing personality from what I read about him in the papers, and then I—I'd seen Mrs. Munn when she was Cecilia Ball in several Broadway revues . . . "

"That's right," nodded Mrs. Munn, smiling in a pleased way. "I was in a lot of shows. We show people always get asked to the nice places."

Judge Macklin shambled forward and said quietly: "And you, Mrs. Constable? Of course, you're an old friend of Mrs. Godfrey's?"

The stout woman started and the old panic leaped, newborn, into her eyes. Mrs. Godfrey made a gasping little sound, as if she were dying.

"Y-y-yes," whispered Mrs. Godfrey, her teeth chattering. "Oh, I've known Mrs. Constable—"

"For . . . years," breathed Mrs. Constable in her husky monotone; her gigantic bosom heaved like a sweeping sea.

Ellery and Judge Macklin exchanged meaning glances as Inspector Moley strode in from the patio, his heavy brogans clumping on the polished floor. "Well," he growled below his breath, "nothing doing on Marco's clothes; that's about settled. The boys have dragged the water near the rocks, right under the cliffs, all around the Cape. And they've covered every inch of the grounds and searched the highway and park in the vicinity. No duds. No duds, that's all." He gnawed at his lower lip as if he could not credit the reports of his men. "Why, they've even looked over those two bathing beaches—the public ones—on either side of the Cape. And, of course, the whole stretch of the Waring property. Thought there was a chance on those beaches—never can tell. But except for a lot of papers and lunch-boxes and footprints and such, there wasn't a thing, I can't understand it."

"It's horribly queer," murmured Judge Macklin.

"Only one thing left for us to do." Moley set his stubborn jaw. "They're not goin' to like it in this high-class dump, but I'm going to do it just the same. Those clothes simply must be here somewhere; how do I know they aren't *in the house?*"

"The house? Here?"

"Sure." Moley shrugged. "I'm having the boys search it on the q.t. There's a back entrance and some of 'em are upstairs now, rootin' around in the bedrooms. We've covered this Jorum's shack and the garage and the boat-house and all the outbuildings already. I told 'em to pick up anything that looked promising."

"No other developments?" asked Ellery absently.

"Not a thing. There's still no sign of this Captain Kidd guy and David Kummer; the boat's just disappeared. There's a Coast Guard cutter on the job right now, and a lot of local cops are on the watch. I've just been shooing off a mess of reporters. Place is lousy with 'em. I've had 'em all kicked out . . . About the only lead I've got that looks hot is this Penfield in New York."

"What have you done?"

"Sent one of my best men there to look him up. My man's got authorizations with him and if necessary he'll bring Penfield back."

"Not if I know Penfield," said Judge Macklin grimly. "He's a slippery lawyer, Inspector, with plenty of gray matter. Your man won't bring him back unless he wants to be brought back. At that, he may come along quietly if he thinks it serves his purpose or to avoid a bit of trouble. All you can do is trust in God."

"Oh, hell," groaned Moley. "Let's go up to Marco's room."

·   ·   ·   ·   ·   ·   ·

"After you, Tiller," said Ellery, smiling at the little man. "I think every one else may as well wait here."

"I, sir?" murmured the valet, raising his precise little brows.

"Yes, indeed."

They followed Tiller, who was following the glum Inspector, out of the living-room. Stony faces disappeared behind them. In an adjoining corridor they came to a spacious staircase, at which Tiller nodded, bowed to the Inspector, and led the way upstairs.

"Well?" asked Judge Macklin softly, as they raised and lowered their leaden feet. They both realized at the same instant that they had not slept the night before, and that they were sodden with fatigue. It took excruciating effort to climb the stairs.

Ellery pursed his lips and screwed up his eyes, a little red about the lids from lack of rest. "An extraordinary situation," he muttered. "I think the plot is vaguely legible, however."

"If you mean as it concerns the Munns and Mrs. Constable—"

"What do you make of them?"

"As personalities, not much. Munn, from what Rosa told us this morning and from what I observed just now, is a dangerous type. He's an outdoor man, physically arrogant and quite fearless, besides having lived obviously on familiar terms with violence. But aside from these tangibles he's a mystery. His wife . . . " The Judge sighed. "A common enough type, I'm afraid, but then the potentialities of even the common types are often unpredictable. She's a hard, cheap, mercenary creature who no doubt married Munn as much for his money as for his physical attractiveness. She would be quite capable of conducting an *affair du coeur* under her husband's nose . . . Mrs. Constable is—to me, at least—sheer fog. I can't make her funk out at all."

"No?"

"She's apparently a middle-aged woman of the upper middle classes. No doubt she has a large family, grown and perhaps married, and is a good wife and mother. I should say she's considerably more than forty, despite the testimony of Rosa Godfrey. We really should talk to her, my boy. She's as out of place—"

"And yet she's exactly the kind of American woman," said Ellery quietly, "whom you will find leering at certain well-built, slim-waisted young dandies across a boulevard cafe table in Paris."

"I never thought of that," murmured the Judge. "By George, you're right. Then you think she and Marco—"

"This," said Ellery, "is a strange house, and it has some very strange people in it. The queerest thing about it is the presence of the Munns and Mrs. Constable."

"Then you saw it, too," whispered the old gentleman quickly. "She was lying—they all lied—"

"Of course," shrugged Ellery, pausing to light a cigaret. "A good deal will be explained," he resumed, blowing smoke, "when we find out why Mrs. Godfrey invited three perfect strangers to her summer home." They had reached the head of the staircase and now found themselves in a wide, hushed corridor. "And why," continued Ellery in an odd tone, eying Tiller's perfect little back a few feet ahead as he trotted along on the deep carpet, "three perfect strangers accepted her invitation without, apparently, the slightest question!"

VI
NO MAN IS A HERO

"You might put it down to social ambition—at least the latter part of it," suggested the Judge.

"You might, and then again you mightn't." Ellery stopped short. "What's the matter, Tiller?"

The little man had halted in his tracks before Inspector Moley and clapped a well-manicured hand to his bland brow.

"Well, what's eatin' *you*, for cripe's sake?" growled Moley.

Tiller seemed distressed. "I'm so sorry, sir. I'd quite forgotten."

"Forgotten? Forgotten what?" asked Ellery swiftly, joining them in one stride, the Judge a step behind.

"The note, sir." Tiller lowered his secretive little eyes. "It quite slipped my mind. I'm fearfully sorry, sir."

"Note!" exclaimed Moley. He shook Tiller's trim shoulder with violence. "What note? What the devil are you talking about?"

"If you don't mind, sir," said Tiller between a wince and a smile, and somehow he contrived to wriggle from under the Inspector's heavy hand. "That hurts, sir . . . Why, the note I found in my own room last night, sir, when I returned from my stroll about the grounds."

He backed against the corridor wall, a pigmy looking up apologetically at the three big men standing still before him.

"Now that," said Ellery warmly, "is news. Tiller, you're manna from an otherwise sterile heaven. What note precisely? Certainly a man of your—er—attainments wouldn't have neglected to observe certain minutiæ in which we might conceivably be interested."

"Yes, sir," murmured Tiller. "I did observe certain—er—minutiæ, as you say, sir; and they struck me, if I may presume to say so, sir, as rather odd." He paused to lick his thin lips and peer slyly up at them.

"Come, come, Tiller," said the Judge impatiently, "this note was addressed to you? I assume it had something of importance to say, or something relevant to this nasty business, if you bring the matter up at all."

"Whether it concerned something of importance or relevance, sir," murmured the valet, "I'm sorry I cannot say. For you see, sir, the note was *not* addressed to me. I mention it only because it was addressed to—Mr. John Marco."

"Marco!" burst out the Inspector. "Then how the deuce did it come to be left in your room?"

"I'm sure I don't know, sir. But I'll tell you about it and then you may judge for yourself. It was nine-thirty or so when I returned to the house—I have my quarters on the ground floor, sir, in the servants' wing—and I went directly to my room. I found the note pinned with a common pin to the exterior of the inside breast pocket of my mess jacket, where I could not avoid seeing it. Because you see, sir, at nine-thirty or so every evening

I change into my mess jacket and wait about until the gentle-men who are visiting at the house come upstairs for one thing or another, to serve them drinks if they should so desire. The but-ler, of course, attends to such matters on the ground floor. So, you see—"

"That's a custom here, Tiller?" asked Ellery slowly.

"Yes, sir. I've done it ever since I came here, on Mrs. God-frey's instructions."

"Everybody in the house knows of this custom?"

"Oh, yes, sir. It is my duty to inform all the gentlemen-guests as soon as they arrive."

"And you don't wear your mess jacket before nine-thirty in the evening?"

"No, sir. Until then I am attired as you see me, in dark clothing."

"Hmm. That's interesting . . . Well, go on, Tiller."

Tiller bowed. "Yes, sir. To proceed. I naturally unpinned the note—it was in a sealed envelope—and looked at the legend on the envelope—"

"Legend? Tiller, you're priceless. How did you know there was a note inside? You didn't tear open the envelope, I trust?"

"I felt it," replied Tiller gravely. "It was house stationery, sir—at least, the envelope was. On it was typewritten the words: *For Mr. John Marco. Personal. Important. Deliver Privately TO-NIGHT.* Those are the exact words, sir; I remember perfectly. The word 'tonight' was underscored and in capital letters."

"You've no idea, I suppose," frowned the Judge, "at what time approximately that note was pinned to your mess jacket, Tiller?"

"I believe I have, sir," said the astonishing little man prompt-ly. "Yes, indeed, sir. Some time after Mrs. Godfrey and her guests had had their dinner—a matter of minutes—I had occasion to go to my room and to my wardrobe closet. I happened to brush against my mess jacket in the closet and it flipped open, as you might say, sir, by accident. I'm sure that had the note been there then I should have noticed it."

"What time was dinner over?" growled Moley.

"A bit after seven-thirty, sir; perhaps twenty-five to eight."

"You left your room right after that?"

"Yes, sir, and I wasn't back until nine-thirty, when I found the note."

"The note was placed there, then," muttered Ellery, "roughly between a quarter of eight and nine-thirty. It's too bad we can't determine exactly who wandered away from that bridge-table and when . . . What then, Tiller? What did you do?"

"I took the note, sir, and went looking for Mr. Marco. But when I saw him at play in the living-room—he had just returned, you will remember, sir, from the terrace—I decided to respect the admonition on the envelope and wait until I could see him privately. I hung about in the patio, waiting; and finally, during a game, I fancy, in which he was dummy, Mr. Marco strolled out for a breath of air. I handed him the note at once and he read it. I saw his face change and a very wicked smile come into his eyes. Then he re-read it, and I thought he looked a bit—" Tiller cast about delicately for the word—"a bit puzzled. But he shrugged, flung me a bill, and—er—growled that I was not to mention the note to any one. Then he went back to the game. I returned upstairs to wait on the gentlemen with my portable bar."

"What did he do with the note?" demanded the Inspector.

"He crumpled it and jammed it into one of his coat-pockets, sir."

"That explains his impatience to quit the game, perhaps,"

murmured Ellery. "Remarkable, Tiller! Don't know what we'd do without you."

"Thank you, sir. Very kind of you, I'm sure. Will that be all?"

"Not by a long shot," said Moley grimly. "Trail along with us to Marco's room, Tiller. Something tells me there's more where that came from!"

A plainclothesman had his legs hooked about the feet of a chair tilted against a door at the extreme east end of the corridor.

"Anything doing, Roush?" demanded the Inspector.

The man spat lazily out an open window at the end of the corridor and shook his head. "Dead as hell, Chief. They're keepin' away from here."

"That's sensible," said Moley dryly. "Stand aside, Roush. I want a look at Mr. Marco's boodwawr." He turned the knob and pushed open the door.

The elaborate living-room downstairs should have prepared them. As it was, they stared at what passed for a guest-room at Spanish Cape. It might have been a king's bedchamber. It was done in the best Spanish style, and it possessed an undeniable flavor—the flavor of old things in dark wood and wrought iron and raw color. The bed was a gigantic four-poster surmounted by a royal tester, from which fell drapes of heavy tapestried cloth. The posts, the bed, the secretary, the chairs, the bureau, the tables were hardily carved; a huge affair of chain and wrought iron and glass cunningly shaped like candles furnished the chief overhead illumination. There were two genuine candles, monsters in wax, on the bureau ensconced in beautiful iron holders. A stone fireplace which, from its fire-licked appearance, had seen good round service supported a mantelpiece of gargantuan proportions, hewn out of a single log.

"Old Godfrey does himself proud, doesn't he?" murmured

Ellery, stepping into the room. "And all for what? For a plainly undesirable guest who gets himself separated from his worthless life, with all the attendant annoyances to his host. Inconsiderate of Marco, to say the least. At that, he must have shown to advantage in this magnificent setting. There is something vaguely Spanish about him even in death. Put him in long hose and doublet . . . "

"Put him six feet under would be more like it," grunted Inspector Moley. "Let's not dawdle, Mr. Queen. From what Roush tells me, he's spoken to the maids and they say none of them disturbed this room today. We got here so quickly they didn't have a chance, and Roush has been roostin' by this door since a quarter to seven. So it ought to be about like what it was last night, when Marco came back up here after the bridge-game."

"Unless some one got in here during the night," pointed out Judge Macklin with a worried air. "I wonder now—" He stepped forward and thrust his long neck toward the bed. Its spread had been removed, for it was not in evidence, and the corner of the sheet and the gay monogrammed quilt had been turned down—apparently by a maid the night before, in anticipation of the guest's retirement. But the pillow was large and square and fat and un-crushed, and there was no impression of a human body under the tester. Flung carelessly on the quilt there was a white, slightly rumpled linen suit, a white shirt, an oyster-colored four-in-hand, a suit of two-piece underwear, a crumpled handkerchief, and a pair of white silk socks. All had obviously been worn. On the floor near the bed stood a pair of men's white calfskin shoes. "Is this the costume Marco was wearing all last evening, Tiller?" demanded the old gentleman.

The little valet, who had been standing quietly in the open doorway, now closed the door in Detective Roush's slightly astonished face and advanced to Judge Macklin's side, where he proceeded to peer down at the discarded garments and then at the shoes. He raised his inscrutable eyes and said respectfully: "Yes, sir."

"Anything missing?" demanded Moley.

"No, sir. Except perhaps," continued Tiller soberly, after a moment's silence, "for the contents of the pockets. There was a watch—Elgin, radial dial, sir, white gold, seventeen-jewel— which isn't here. And Mr. Marco's wallet and cigaret-case are missing, too."

Moley eyed him with grudging respect. "Good boy. Any time you want a job doin' detective work, Tiller, you come to me. Well, Mr. Queen, what d'ye think of *that?*"

Ellery picked up the white trousers between two negligent fingers, shrugged and dropped them carelessly on the bed. "What should I think?"

"Well," said the Judge in an exasperated tone, "we find the man stark naked and now we find the clothes he wore last night; what should any one think? I'll confess it's a weird, an obscene conclusion, but I'll be jaspered if it doesn't look as if he went down to the terrace last night with only that blessed cloak over his naked body!"

"Nuts," said Inspector Moley distinctly. "Beg pardon, Judge. But why the devil d'ye think I told the boys to look for his duds on the grounds? Hell, if I thought *that* I'd have searched this room the very first thing!"

"Gentlemen, gentlemen," chuckled Ellery, without removing his gaze from the strewn garments. "Apparently, dear Solon, you haven't thought of the alternative possibility, which is just as grotesque, that Marco's murderer killed him here, undressed him, and then toted his dead body down through a populated house to the terrace! No, no, Judge, it's as the Inspector says. The explanation's much simpler than that, and I fancy Tiller can, as usual, provide it. Eh, Tiller?"

"I believe I can, sir," murmured Tiller modestly, looking at Ellery with bright eyes.

"There you are," drawled Ellery. "Tiller Tells All. I suppose Marco undressed when he returned to this room last night and promptly proceeded to change into a completely new costume?"

Judge Macklin's thin old face fell. "I'm turning obscurantist in my old age. My own fault. That nudity business led me into a trap. Of course that's it."

"Yes, sir," said Tiller, nodding gravely. "You see, sir, I have a cubbyhole of sorts—like a pantry—at the west end of the hall where I stay in the late evening until all the gentlemen retire. It was a quarter to twelve, I should say, when a buzzer—you'll find the button beside the bed, Inspector Moley, sir—summoned me to Mr. Marco's room."

"Just about when he got upstairs after the game," muttered Moley. He was standing by the bed going through the pockets of the discarded white garments; but he found nothing at all.

"Undoubtedly, sir. Mr. Marco was stripping off that white coat when I entered the room. His face was flushed and he seemed impatient. He—er—cursed me roundly for what he called my 'damned shilly-shallying' and directed me to fetch him a whisky-and-soda, double strength, and to lay out certain garments."

"Swore at you, eh?" said the Inspector quietly. "Go on."

"I fetched the whiskey-and-soda, sir, and then while he was—er—tossing it down proceeded to lay out the clothes he had designated."

"And they were?" snapped Ellery. "Please, Tiller, fewer genteelisms. We haven't all week, you know."

"Yes, sir. They were," Tiller pursed his lips and screwed up his eyebrows, "his oxford-gray suit, double-breasted, including waistcoat; black pointed oxfords; white shirt, collar attached; dark gray four-in-hand; a suit of fresh two-piece underclothing; black silk socks; black garters; black braces; a gray silk display kerchief for his breast-pocket; black felt fedora; his heavy ebony stick; and the long black opera-cloak from his full-dress outfit."

"Just a moment, Tiller. I'd meant to ask about that cloak before. Have you any idea why he should have worn it last night? It's rather a quaint costume."

"Indeed it is, sir. But Mr. Marco was a trifle eccentric. His tastes in clothing, sir . . . " Tiller shook his sleek dark little head sadly. "I believe he did mutter something about the evening's being chilly, which was true, sir, when he asked me to lay the cloak out with the other things. And so—"

"He intended going out?"

"Of course I can't say exactly, sir; although I did gather that impression."

"Did he usually redress so late at night?"

"Oh, no, sir; it was quite unusual. At any rate, sir, while I laid out his things he went into the bathroom there and took a shower. When he came out in his slippers' and robe, freshly shaved and combed—"

"Cripe, where did he think he was going at midnight?" exploded Inspector Moley. "That's a hell of a time to be primping!"

"Yes, sir," murmured Tiller. "I wondered myself. But I felt fairly certain that he was preparing to meet a lady, sir. You see—"

"Lady!" exclaimed the Judge. "How do you know that?"

"It was the expression on his face, sir, and a certain anxiety he showed in a very minute wrinkle—oh, most minute, sir—on the collar of the shirt. He always acted that way when he was dressing for—er—some special lady. In fact, he abused me quite—oh, quite—" For once Tiller seemed at a loss for the proper word. A peculiar expression crept into his eyes which vanished almost at once.

Ellery was staring at him. "You didn't care for Mr. Marco, did you, Tiller?"

Tiller smiled deprecatingly, self-possessed once more. "I shouldn't go so far as to say that, sir, but—he was a difficult gentleman. Most difficult. *And*, if anything, overcareful of his appearance, as you might say. He would spend fifteen minutes to a half-hour examining his face in the bathroom mirror, turning it this way and that, sir, as if to see that every pore was clean, and whether the right profile, sir, was really more fetching than the left. And—er—he scented himself."

"Scented himself!" cried the Judge, shocked.

"Devastating, Tiller, simply devastating," remarked Ellery with a smile. "I shouldn't care to have you discourse upon *my* idiosyncrasies. Valet's-eye view—oh, excellent! You were saying that when he came out of the bathroom . . . "

"Woman, hey?" muttered Moley, whose mind seemed on other matters.

"Yes, sir. When he came out of the bathroom after his shower I was removing the contents of his pockets—some change, the watch and wallet and cigaret-case I mentioned, and a few other trifles. Of course, I meant to transfer them to the dark suit. But he pounced upon me immediately after the—er—unpleasant incident of the wrinkled collar, so to speak, and snatched the white coat out of my hands. Called me a 'damned meddler,' if I remember correctly, sir. And he ordered me out of the room, saying angrily that he would dress himself."

"So that's that," began Moley, when Ellery stopped him.

"Perhaps not quite." He regarded the little man thoughtfully. "Did you gather that there was any special reason, Tiller, for his irritation? Did you find something—ah—personal in one of the pockets of the suit?"

Tiller nodded brightly. "Yes, sir. The note."

"Ah! That was his reason for driving you from the room?"

"I fancy so, sir." Tiller sighed. "In fact, I'm almost sure of it. For as I went to the door I saw him tear the note, envelope and all, and hurl it into that fireplace there, where I had kindled a small fire earlier in the evening!"

.   .   .   .

With one accord the three big men bounded to the fireplace, their eyes alight with anticipation. Tiller stood still where he was, respectfully watching. Then, as they flung themselves to their knees and began to scrabble about in the little heap of cold ashes in the grate, he cleared his throat, blinked several times, and moved quietly over to the large wardrobe closet on the farther side of the room. He opened the door and began to poke about inside.

"What a break if—" began Moley in a mutter.

"Careful," cried Ellery. "It's still possible—if they're only partially burned they'll be brittle . . . "

Five minutes later the three brushed off their grimy hands, frowning deeply. There was nothing.

"All burned up," snarled the Inspector. "What a break is right, damn it all—"

"Just a second." Ellery sprang to his feet and looked about quickly. "It doesn't seem to me as if those ashes in the grate are the residue of paper. Certainly not sufficient to account for . . . " He stopped short, eyeing Tiller sharply. The little man was calmly closing the door of the closet. "What the devil are you up to now, Tiller?"

"Why, checking up on Mr. Marco's wardrobe, sir," replied Tiller modestly. "It occurred to me that you might wish to know if anything is missing besides the garments I itemized a few moments ago."

Ellery gaped at him. Then he chuckled: "Tiller, come to my bosom. We could easily be boon companions. And is anything missing?"

"No, sir," said Tiller, almost regretfully.

"You're positive?"

"Quite. You see, sir, I've come to know Mr. Marco's wardrobe very thoroughly indeed. If you'd care to have me look through the bureau—"

"There's an idea. Do." And Ellery turned away to scan the room again, as if he were searching for something, while Tiller—a smile of satisfaction on his bland little face—trotted over to the ornately carved bureau and began to open drawers. Inspector Moley sauntered quietly over to watch him.

A glance passed between Ellery and Judge Macklin, and without a word they began a separate but complementary search of the bedroom. They worked in silence; the only audible sounds came from the opening and shutting of drawers.

"Nothing," reported Tiller sadly at last, shutting the bottom drawer of the bureau. "Nothing that should not be here. And nothing missing. I'm sorry, sir."

"You say that as if it were your fault," drawled Ellery,

moving toward the bathroom, the door of which stood open. "Good idea, though, Tiller—" He disappeared into the bathroom.

"Not even a letter in the damned thing," scowled Moley. "Careful jigger, he must have been. Well, I guess that's all for—"

Ellery's voice, strangely cold, interrupted. They looked around to find him standing, straight and stern, in the bathroom doorway. He was staring at Tiller's expressionless face. "Tiller," he said, flatly and without inflection.

"Yes, sir?" The little man's brows went up inquiringly.

"You lied, didn't you, about not having read the contents of the note you delivered to Mr. Marco?"

Something glittered in Tiller's eyes and the tips of his ears went slowly red. "I beg your pardon, sir?" he said quietly.

Their eyes locked. Then Ellery sighed. "I beg *yours*. But I had to know. You didn't return to this room after Marco sent you away last night?"

"I did not, sir," replied the valet in the same quiet tone.

"You went to bed?"

"I did, sir. I returned to the pantry first to make sure there were no other calls. You see, sir, there were still Mr. Munn and Mr. Cort, and I thought Mr. Kummer. I did not know at the time that Mr. Kummer had been kidnaped. But there was nothing, and so I went downstairs to my own quarters and to bed."

"And what time was it when you left this room at Marco's order?"

"I should say at almost exactly midnight, sir."

Ellery sighed again and jerked his head at Inspector Moley and Judge Macklin. Puzzled, the two men went to him.

"By the way, Tiller, I suppose you saw Mr. Munn, and later Mrs. Munn, go to their rooms on this floor?"

"Mr. Munn, sir, at about eleven-thirty. I did not see Mrs. Munn."

"I see." Ellery stepped aside. "There, gentlemen," he said absently, "is your note."

. . . .

At first all they saw was a litter of shaving things on the rim of the washbowl—a brush encrusted with dry white lather, a safety-razor, a small bottle of green lotion and a can of shaving powder. But Ellery used his thumb and they went in and saw the note lying on the covered toilet-seat.

It was composed of tiny scraps of creamy paper—the same kind of stationery they had seen lying on the round terrace-table. There were many ragged little pieces, all of them wrinkled, most of them charred at the edges, and some—from the gaps in the rectangle—missing. For the scraps had been painstakingly put together, torn edge fitted against torn edge, by some one who obviously had fished them out of the fireplace.

A disorderly pile of other cream-colored scraps lay on the tiled floor beside the toilet-bowl.

"Don't bother with that stuff on the floor," directed Ellery. "It's the fragments of the envelope, pretty badly burned. Read the note."

"Did you put those pieces together?" demanded the Judge.

"I?" Ellery shrugged. "That's precisely how I found them."

The two older men stooped over the bowl. The message, fragmentary though it was, was still startlingly intelligible. There was no date, no salutation. The message had been typewritten, and what remained of it read:

". . . . . et me on ter . . . . ight
at 1 . . . . .k. It's v . . . . ust
see yo . . . . . . .ne. I will . . . . .e, too.
Pl . . . . . . lease don't fa . . . . . .

Rosa."

"Rosa!" gasped the Judge. "That—that's incredible. It can't be—Why, it just isn't physically possible!"

"Screwy," muttered Inspector Moley. "It's all screwy. The whole damn' case is screwy."

"I can't understand—Funny."

"Excruciatingly," remarked Ellery dryly. "At least, Marco must have found it so. For, you see, by obeying its instructions he walked headfirst into the well-known arms of death."

"You think this is a case of cause and effect?" demanded the Judge. "The note led him to his death?"

"That should be easily determined."

"It seems plain enough," frowned the old gentleman. "'Meet me on the terrace tonight at 1 o'clock. It's v . . .'—yes, yes!— 'very important. I must see you'—I suppose—'alone. I will'— let's see, now—'be alone, too,' in all probability. The rest is easy: 'Please, please don't fail me. Rosa.'"

"There's one young lady," said the Inspector grimly, starting for the door, "I want to talk to right away." Then he turned around slowly. "Say, it just hit me. Who the deuce put those torn pieces together? Maybe it *was* Tiller. If—"

"Tiller told the truth," said Ellery, polishing the lenses of his *pince-nez* absently. "I'm sure of that. Besides, had Tiller been the one who put the pieces together, he wouldn't have been so stupid as to leave them where they would be found. He's a very brainy little gentleman. No, no; forget Tiller.

"On the other hand, some one did steal in here after Marco left to keep his fatal rendezvous last night, fished the scraps out of the fireplace—I daresay it was a feeble fire which went out without being noticed by Marco, who seems to have been in a state of considerable excitement—took them into the bathroom here, sorted them, discarded the envelope-fragments as non-essential, and very carefully put together the remaining scraps of the note itself."

"Why in the bathroom?" growled Moley. "That's something else that smells."

Ellery shrugged. "I'm not so sure it's of importance. Probably to ensure privacy during the reconstruction of the note—a precaution against sudden interruption." He took a glassine envelope from his wallet and carefully tucked the pieces of the note into it. "We'll need this, Inspector. Of course, I'm merely borrowing it."

"The signature," muttered Judge Macklin, who seemed lost in his original train of thought, "is also typed. It looks—"

Ellery strode to the bathroom door. "Tiller," he said genially.

The little man was standing precisely where they had left him, in an attitude of respectful attention.

"Yes, sir?"

Ellery sauntered over to him, produced his cigaret-case, snapped it open, and said: "Have one?"

Tiller seemed shocked. "Oh, no, sir, I couldn't!"

"Don't see why, but suit yourself." Ellery put one between his lips. From the doorway the two older men watched in puzzled silence. Tiller materialized a match from somewhere about his person and struck it, holding it deferentially to the tip of Ellery's cigaret. "Thank you. Y'know, Tiller," continued Ellery, puffing with enjoyment, "you've been invaluable in this affair so far. Don't know what we should have done without you."

"Thank you, sir. Justice should be done."

"Quite so. By the way, is there a typewriter in the house?"

Tiller blinked. "I believe so, sir. In the library."

"Is that the only one?"

"Yes, sir. You see, Mr. Godfrey transacts no business at all of the usual sort during the summer; doesn't even maintain a secretary here. The typewriter is very little used."

"Hmm . . . Of course, Tiller, I don't have to point out to you that there are one or two unfortunate elements."

"Indeed, sir?"

"Indeed. For example, the fact that with the exception of that benefactor of mankind—to quote Mr. Godfrey—who polished off Marco, you seem to have been the last to see Marco alive. That's bad. Now, if good fortune were really on our side—"

"But good fortune," said Tiller gently, clasping his tiny hands before him, "is, sir."

"Eh?" Ellery lowered his cigaret sharply.

"You see, sir, I *wasn't* the last to see Mr. Marco alive—I mean, always excepting the murderer, sir." And Tiller coughed and paused, lowering his eyes discreetly.

Moley charged across the room. "You exasperatin' little devil!" he bellowed. "It's like pulling teeth, gettin' anything out of you. Why didn't you spill this before—"

"Please. Inspector," murmured Ellery. "Tiller and I understand each other. These matters of revelation require a certain— ah—delicacy of delivery. Yes, Tiller?"

The little man coughed again, and this time it was a cough of embarrassment. "I scarcely know if I should speak, sir. It's rather a delicate situation for me, you see—as you say—"

"Talk, damn you!" roared the Inspector.

"I was about to leave the pantry after having been ordered out of this room, sir, by Mr. Marco," continued Tiller imperturbably, "when I heard some one coming up the stairs. I saw her—"

"Her, Tiller?" asked Ellery mildly. His eyes warned Moley.

"Yes, sir. I saw her tiptoe up the corridor, sir, toward Mr. Marco's room and go in quickly . . . without knocking."

"Without knocking, eh?" mumbled the Judge. "Then she—whoever she was—was the one who fished that note out of the fireplace!"

"I think not, sir," said Tiller regretfully. "For Mr. Marco had not yet finished dressing. He couldn't have; it was only a minute or so after I'd left him. So he was still in the bedroom. Besides, I heard them arguing—"

"Arguing!"

"Oh, yes, sir. Quite violently."

"I thought," said Ellery softly, "you said your pantry is at the other end of the corridor, Tiller. Were you listening at Marco's door?"

"No, sir. But they were speaking very—loudly at one point. I couldn't help but hear. Then they quieted down."

Moley was biting his lips and striding about, glaring at Tiller's sleek little head as if he wished he had a headsman's ax.

"Well, well, Tiller," said Ellery with a smile of pure *cama-raderie*, "and who was this stealthy nocturnal visitor of Mr. Marco's?"

Tiller licked his lips and looked slyly at the Inspector. Then he drew down the corners of his mouth in a shocked expression. "It was most dreadful, sir. When Mr. Marco was shouting the loudest he called her—I remember the exact words, sir, if you'll pardon me—a 'damned interfering bitch' . . . "

"Who was she?" shrieked Moley, unable to contain himself longer.

"Mrs. Godfrey, sir."

VII
DISSERTATION ON MORALS, MURDERERS, AND MAIDS

"WE PROGRESS," said Mr. Ellery Queen dreamily. "Inspector, we have struck the pay-lode. Thanks again to the omnipresence of Tiller."

"Now what," demanded Judge Macklin with exasperation, "are you talking about? It was Mrs. Godfrey. Marco was rude—"

"And they talk," sighed Ellery, "about the innocence of babes. Dear Solon, you should have spent a few years in the Court of Domestic Relations instead of drowsing away in General Sessions."

"For cripe's sake," said Moley desperately, "what's on your mind, Mr. Queen? I hate to be crossin' you this way all the time, but, man—this is a murder investigation, not a kaffee klatch! Spill it, spill it!"

"Tiller," said Ellery with a glint in his eye, "we've had ample proof that you are an acute observer of the human animal and his gyrations." He flung himself on John Marco's bed and crossed his arms behind his head. "What kind of male swears at a woman?"

"Well, sir," murmured Tiller after a discreet cough, "in fiction it is the—ah—Dashiell Hammett type, sir."

"Ah. Heart of gold beneath hardboiled exterior?"

"Yes, sir. Blasphemy, the use of violence . . . "

"Let's restrict ourselves to life as it is lived, Tiller. By the way, I infer you're an addict of detective fiction."

"Oh, yes, sir! And I've read many of your own, sir, and—"

"Hmm," said Ellery hastily. "Let that pass. In real life, Tiller?"

"I fear," said the valet in a sad murmur, "that there are few hearts of gold in real life, sir. Hard exteriors, certainly. I should say, sir, that there are two general types of woman-abusing men. Confirmed misogynists, sir, and—husbands."

"*Bravo!*" cried Ellery, sitting up in the bed. "And a couple of *bravi*. Did you hear that, Judge? Misogynists and husbands. Very good, Tiller; almost epigrammatic. No, by George, I take that back. It is epigrammatic."

The Judge could not help chuckling. But Inspector Moley threw up his hands, glared at Ellery, and stamped to the door.

"One moment, Inspector," drawled Ellery. "This is not idle conversation." Moley stopped and slowly turned about. "Very good as far as you've gone, Tiller. We are philosophizing with a gentleman by the name of John Marco in mind. The merest analysis will show that he falls neither into the one classification nor the other. From all we have learned about the deceased, he was the very antitype of the chronic misogynist; he loved the ladies dearly. And certainly he was not the husband of the specific lady at whom he swore so graphically last night. And yet swear at her he did. Do you see light?"

"Yes, sir," murmured Tiller, "but it is not for me to—"

"If you mean," growled the Inspector, "that he'd been monkeyin' around with Mrs. Godfrey, why the devil don't you come out and say so in plain English?"

Ellery crawled off the bed and clapped his hands together. "Trust an old shellback of the police to get to the heart of matters!" he chuckled. "Yes, yes, Inspector, that's what I meant. Tiller, there's one other classification: men who have loved and wearied. Men—the tabloids and the poets call them 'lovers'— who have fed at the 'sacred flame' and after a while become bored with the same fare. Sad! Then the Era of Epithets sets in."

Judge Macklin scowled. "You're not suggesting chat Marco and Mrs. Godfrey—"

Ellery sighed. "It's a vicious habit, this business of suggesting, but what can a poor sleuth do? My dear innocent, we can't close our eyes to facts. Mrs. Godfrey stole into Marco's room at midnight. Without knocking. That's not the action of a mere hostess, no matter how possessive she may feel about her Spanish guest-chambers. Shortly after, Marco damned her loudly for a meddling mustn't-say-the-naughty-word. That's not the chit-chat of a mere guest . . . Yes, yes, La Rochefoucauld was right: The more we love a mistress, the nearer we are to hating her. Marco must once have cherished a grand passion for the lovely Stella to have abused her so roundly last night."

"I agree," snapped Moley, "that there must have been somethin' between the two of 'em. But d'ye think *she*—"

"I think with de Staël that love is the history of a woman's life," said Ellery softly, "and an episode in man's. The woman under the circumstances, I daresay, would take its death rather seriously. I may be wrong about that in this case, but—"

Detective Roush opened the door and said with pathetic eagerness: "I think it's chow, Chief."

·   ·   ·   ·   ·   ·   ·

Stella Godfrey appeared in the doorway. They looked at her with the guilty feeling that comes to all who are suddenly confronted with the object of their gossip. Only Tiller was discreetly studying the floor.

She had taken a grip on herself; her face was freshly powdered and her handkerchief crisp. Each of them was wholly masculine, and each of them wondered anew at the eternal mystery of Eve. Here was a woman, superbly constructed, still beautiful, gracious, regal, wealthy, of the highest social caste in her own right. To look at her, a vision of self-possession, it did not seem possible that she was floundering in a morass of ugly fears, that she could have stooped to the age-old folly, that those slim well-bred hands had lately been clenched in violence. There was something essentially immaculate about her, her person, her appearance, her bearing; immaculate and detached.

She said coolly: "Excuse me for interrupting, gentlemen. I've had the cook prepare something. You must be hungry, all of you. If you'll follow Mrs. Burleigh—"

She had thought of food! Judge Macklin swallowed hard and averted his head. Ellery mumbled something that sounded as if it might have come from *Macbeth* and instantly smiled.

"Mrs. Godfrey—" began Moley in a strangled voice.

"Charming and thoughtful of you," said Ellery cheerfully, prodding Moley's ribs. "As a matter of fact, Judge Macklin and I have been uncomfortably aware all morning of the void in our stomachs. We haven't eaten since last night's dinner, you see."

"This is Mrs. Burleigh, my housekeeper," said Stella Godfrey quietly, stepping aside.

A timid voice said: "Yes, Madam," and a starched and ancient little female edged into sight from behind her mistress. "If you'll follow me to the small dining-room, sir, and the other gentlemen—"

"With a will, Mrs. Burleigh, with a will! By the way, you know what's happened?"

"Oh, yes, sir. It's dreadful."

"Indeed it is. I suppose you can't assist us in any way?"

"I, sir?" Mrs. Burleigh's eyes became enormous discs. "Oh no, sir. I knew the gentleman only by sight, sir. How could I—"

"Don't go, Mrs. Godfrey," said Moley suddenly, as the tall dark woman stirred.

"I wasn't going," she said, raising her eyebrows. "I was about to say—"

"I want to talk to you.—No, Mr. Queen, I'm going to have my way about this. Mrs. Godfrey—"

"I think," said Ellery with a grimace, "we'll have to defer our luncheon a bit, Mrs. Burleigh; I detect the inflexible note of authority. You might advise Cookie to keep those comestibles warm." Mrs. Burleigh smiled uncertainly and retreated. "And thank you, Tiller. No telling what we'd have done without you."

The valet bowed. "That will be all, sir?"

"Not unless you've something left up your sleeve."

"I'm afraid not, sir," said Tiller, almost ruefully; and he bowed himself past Mrs. Godfrey and vanished.

The dark woman had frozen suddenly; all but her eyes. They roved the room, shrank from the tumbled male clothing on the bed, the drawers, the closet . . . Inspector Moley looked fiercely at her and she took a slow step backward. He shut the door with a meaning glance at Roush, kicked forward a chair, and motioned her into it.

"What is it now?" she murmured, sitting down. Her lips seemed dry, for she moistened them with the tip of her tongue.

"Mrs. Godfrey," said the Inspector bitterly, "why don't you come clean? Why don't you tell us the truth?"

"Oh." She paused. "I don't know what you mean, Inspector."

"You know well enough what I mean!" Moley paced up and down before her, gesticulating. "Don't you folks realize what you're up against? What the devil does a little personal trouble mean when it's a case of life and death? This is murder, Mrs. Godfrey—murder!" He stopped and grasped the arms of her chair, glaring down at her. "They electrocute people in this State for murder, Mrs. Godfrey. Murder; m-u-r-d-e-r. Do you understand now?"

"I don't know what you mean," repeated Mrs. Godfrey stonily. "Are you trying to frighten me?"

"You don't want to know! Do you people think you can make up a mess of conflicting testimony and get away with it?"

"I've told you the truth," she said in a low tone.

"You've told me a pack of lies!" raged Moley. "You're afraid of the scandal. You're afraid of what your husband will say when—"

"Scandal?" she faltered; and they saw that her defenses were slowly coming down. Already the torment in her mind was becoming visible on her features.

Inspector Moley jerked at his collar. "What were you doing in this room—Marco's room—last night at midnight, Mrs. Godfrey?"

Another rampart crumbled. She stared up at him, mouth open, skin the color of wet ashes. "I—" Her face fell into her palms suddenly and she began to sob.

Ellery, perched on John Marco's bed, sighed noiselessly; he was very hungry and sleepy. Judge Macklin placed his old hands together behind his back and walked to one of the windows. The sea was blue and beautiful, he thought. Some people could be very happy looking at such a sea day after day. It must be striking in winter. The waves crashing against the cliffs below, the song of hissing spray, the whip of wind-driven spume against one's cheeks . . . His eyes narrowed. Below a bent male figure appeared, small from the Judge's eyrie, small and gnarled and busy. It was Jorum, poking about in his eternal gardens. Then Walter Godfrey's tubby figure, a ragged straw hat on his head, materialized from the side. How like a fat, filthy little peon the man looked! thought the Judge . . . Godfrey placed his hand on Jorum's shoulder and his rubbery lips moved; Jorum looked up, smiled briefly, and continued weeding. Judge Macklin felt the kinship between them, a tacit *camaraderie* that puzzled him a little . . . The millionaire dropped to his knees to study a flaming flower. There was something ironic in the spectacle. It appeared, thought the Judge, that Walter Godfrey had consistently paid more attention to the blooms in his gardens than to those in his house. Some one had stolen his rarest flower from under his nose.

The Judge sighed and turned away from the window.

There was a remarkable change in Inspector Moley. He was the picture of fatherly sympathy. "There, there," he was saying in a syrupy bass, patting Stella Godfrey's slim shoulder. "I know it's tough. It's a hard thing to admit, especially to strange men. But Mr. Queen and Judge Macklin and I aren't just people, Mrs. Godfrey; in a way we're not people at all, just the way priests aren't. And *we* know how to keep our mouths shut after confessional, too. Why don't you—? You'll feel better if you tell some one." He continued to pat her shoulder.

Ellery choked over his cigaret. Hypocrite! he thought with a silent chuckle.

She flung her head up. There were tears in the powder on her cheeks and lines of age had miraculously appeared about her eyes and mouth. But the mouth was firm, and her expression was not that of a woman who finds silence utterly intolerable. "Very well," she said in a steady voice, "since you seem to know, I shan't deny it. Yes, I was here—alone with him—last night."

Moley's shoulders twitched eloquently, as if to say: "How's *that* for tactics?" Ellery glanced at his broad back with sad amusement. Moley had not seen the expression in the woman's eyes nor noticed the set of her lips. Stella Godfrey had found a fresh defense somewhere in the dark storeroom of her soul. "*That's* right," murmured the Inspector. "*That's* sensible, Mrs. Godfrey. You can't hope to keep things like that a secret—"

"No," she said coldly. "I suppose not. Tiller, of course? He must have been in his serving pantry. I'd forgotten."

Something in her tone chilled Moley. He took out his handkerchief and rather doubtfully wiped the back of his neck, glancing out of the corner of his eye at Ellery. Ellery shrugged. "Well, what were you doin' there, then?" asked Moley slowly.

"That," she replied in the same cold tons, "is my affair, Inspector."

He said with savagery: "You didn't even knock at the door!" He seemed to realize that he had lost.

"Didn't I? How careless of me."

Moley swallowed hard, trying to curb his rage. "You refuse to tell me why you sneaked into a man's room at midnight?"

"Sneaked, Inspector?"

"You lied, then, when you told me earlier today that you went to bed early! That the last time you saw Marco was when he left the bridge-table downstairs!"

"Of course. One doesn't admit such things, Inspector." Her knuckles were dead with the tightness of her fists.

Moley gulped, jammed a cheroot into his mouth, and struck a match. He was striving to steady himself. "All right. You won't talk about *that*. But you had a fight with him, didn't you?" She was silent. "He called you a dirty name, didn't he?" A sickness came into her eyes, but she merely compressed her lips. "Well, how long did this go on, Mrs. Godfrey? How long were you with him?"

"I left him at ten minutes to one."

"More than three-quarters of an hour, eh?" snarled Moley. He puffed bitter smoke, baffled. She sat quietly on the edge of the chair.

Ellery sighed again. "Er—was Marco fully dressed when you entered this room last night, Mrs. Godfrey?"

This time she had a little difficulty with her tongue. "No. I mean—not fully."

"What was he wearing? You may be reluctant to discuss your personal affairs, Mrs. Godfrey, but this matter of his attire last night is of the most vital importance, and surely you can't have any reason for withholding information about it. His whites—the things he'd been wearing during the evening—they were on the bed, as they are now?"

"Yes." She was staring at her knuckles now. "He had changed into his—his trousers just before I came in, apparently. Dark gray. As we . . . talked, he continued dressing. It was a double-breasted oxford-gray suit, I believe, with gray accessories to match. A white shirt—Oh, I can't remember!"

"Did you notice his hat, stick, and cloak?"

"I—yes. They were on the bed."

"Was he completely dressed when you left him?"

"Well . . . yes. He had just adjusted his necktie and put on his coat."

"Did you leave together?"

"No. I—I went out of the room first and to my own."

"Did you see him leave, by any chance?"

"No." Her features contracted in an involuntary spasm of pain. "After I'd gone to my own rooms—just after—I heard the sound of a door closing. I took it for granted he—he had left his room."

Ellery nodded. "And you didn't open your door and look out to see?"

"No!"

"Hmm. Did he tell you why he had changed into fresh clothes, Mrs. Godfrey? Or where he was going?"

"No!" Her voice had a curious ring. "He did not. But he seemed very impatient. As if he had an appointment . . . with some one."

Inspector Moley snorted. "And you didn't even have the desire to follow him, hey? Oh, no."

"I did not, I say!" She rose suddenly. "I—I shan't be persecuted any longer, gentlemen. As far as I've gone I've told you the truth. I was too—too heart-sick to follow him, even look for him. Why, I simply can't tell you—anybody. I—I went straight to bed, and I never saw him alive again."

The three men weighed the timbre of her voice, calculating its sincerity, what it concealed, the depth of its emotion.

Then the Inspector said: "All right. That's all for now."

She went out with a stiff back, but eagerly. Her whole body expressed relief.

"And that," remarked Ellery, "is that. She's not ready for cracking yet, Inspector. You chose an unpropitious time. That woman hasn't too much intellectual equipment, but there's nothing wrong with her backbone. I tried to warn you."

"This thing'll have me crocked yet," groaned Moley. "The—" For some seconds he expressed himself with violence and fluency, describing the nature, habits, temperament, and antecedents (probable) of John Marco with a comprehensiveness, lucidity, and imagery that shocked Judge Macklin and caused Ellery's eyes to widen with admiration.

"Oh, lovely," said Ellery warmly when Moley perforce paused for breath. "An exquisite object-lesson in invective. And now that you feel better spiritually, Inspector, how about taking advantage of Mrs. Burleigh's invitation and ameliorating the more animal wants?"

．　．　．　．　．　．　．

During luncheon—a princely repast served by an under butler, supervised by frail Mrs. Burleigh very capably, and set in the Saracenic magnificence of the "small" dining-room—Inspector Moley was the personification of gloom. His low spirits did not prevent him from making vast inroads upon the viands, although they influenced the tone of the gathering. He alternated between frowns and swallows, and with each draught of coffee sighed tumultuously. Several minor satellites, evidently recognizing the signs, preserved a tactful silence toward the foot of the board. Only Ellery and the Judge ate with complete absorption in the food, as food. They were hungry men; and before the gnawings of appetite even death must wait.

"'S all very well for you two," grumbled Moley over an Austrian tart. "You're just havin' a good time helping out. If I go floppo on this case it's no cut out of *your* cake. Why the hell do people have to go get themselves bumped off?"

Ellery engulfed the last mouthful, put aside his serviette, and sighed with Bacchic repletion. "The Chinese have the right social idea, Judge; only a royal belch would do justice to this feast of Mrs. Burleigh's . . . No, no, Inspector, you wrong us. If you go floppo on this case it will be despite our best combined efforts. As a matter of fact, it's not the least interesting problem in the world. That note of nudism . . . "

"You got an angle?"

"All God's chillun got an angle, Inspector. This chile has a half-dozen angles. That's what piques me. And I have the feeling that not one of 'em is the correct one."

Moley grunted. "Well, now you take that note—"

"I'd much rather," remarked the Judge, putting down his coffee-cup, "take a nap."

"Then why," asked a cool voice from the Moorish archway, "don't you, Judge?"

They rose hastily as Rosa Godfrey came in. She had changed to shorts, and her firm golden skin was visible to the middle of her thighs. Only the bruise on her temple remained to remind them of her experience in Waring's bungalow the night before.

"Splendid idea, my child," said the Judge sheepishly. "If you could have me taken back to the bungalow in one of the cars . . . I'm sure you won't mind, my boy. I'm feeling a little—"

"I've already had one of the cars," retorted Rosa with a little toss of her head, "go to your bungalow—under trooper escort—and bring your bags and things back here. You're both putting up with us, you know."

"Now, really—" began the old gentleman.

"Kindness incarnate," said Ellery cheerfully. "Miss Godfrey, that was noble of you. I hadn't looked forward to scrambling eggs with too much enthusiasm. Not after *this* repast. My dear

Solon, you look properly peaked; shoo! Mr. Moley and I will carry on."

"Might be better at that," mused the detective, "having some one on the premises. Good idea. Go on, Judge—git."

Judge Macklin rubbed his chin and blinked his bleared eyes. "And all those victuals in the car . . . Well, I can't conscientiously refuse."

"Indeed you can't," said Rosa firmly. "Tiller!" The little valet popped in from somewhere. "Show Judge Macklin to the blue room in the east wing. Mr. Queen will occupy the adjoining bedroom. I've already spoken to Mrs. Burleigh about it."

When the Judge had disappeared after Tiller Inspector Moley said: "Now that you've been nice to the old gent, Miss Godfrey, suppose you be nice to me."

"What do you mean?"

"Show us where that library of your father's is."

She preceded them through a confusion of overwhelming rooms to a jewel of a library. It had the odor as well as the appearance of bookishness, and Ellery sucked in his breath with admiration. Here, as elsewhere, the Spanish motif had been carried out; and Morocco bindings prevailed. It was a tall room filled with shadows, as is proper in any self-respecting library, and was possessed of unexpected nooks and alcoves in which one might bury himself waist-deep in cushions and find peace between pasteboards and leathers.

But Inspector Moley's outraged soul held no room for aesthetics. His hard little eyes probed the corners, and he said gruffly: "Now where's the typewriter?"

Rosa was surprised. "The typewriter? I don't—Over there." She led them to an alcove in which stood a desk, a typewriter, a few filing-cabinets, and the like. "This is father's 'office'—if you

could dignify it by such a name. At least, this is where he potters about with his business affairs while on the Cape."

"He does his own typing?" demanded Moley, skeptical.

"Rarely has to. He detests correspondence. He transacts
most of his business over that telephone there. It's a direct wire
to his New York office."

"But he *can* type?"

"After a fashion." Rosa accepted one of Ellery's cigarets and
flung herself on a leather divan. "Why all this interest in father,
Inspector?"

"Does he use this place much? This alcove?" asked Moley
coldly.

"For an hour or so a day." She was regarding him with an intent curiosity.

"Ever do any typing for your father yourself?"

"I?" She laughed. "Indeed not, Inspector. I'm the drone of
this family. I can't do *anything*."

Moley caught himself up. He placed his cheroot on an ashtray and said casually: "Oh, so you can't type?"

"Sorry I can't oblige. Mr. Queen, what in heaven's name is
all this about? Have you found a new clue? Something—" She
sat up suddenly, uncrossing her legs. There was the strangest
glitter in her blue eyes.

Ellery spread his hands. "This is Inspector Moley's nut, Miss
Godfrey. First rights at cracking it belong to him."

"'Scuse me a second," said Moley, and he stalked out of the
library.

Rosa leaned back, smoking. Her brown throat was naked to
Ellery's gaze as she dreamily regarded the ceiling. He studied
it with half a smile. The girl was a good actress. To outward
appearance she was cool, self-possessed, a normal young wom-

an. But there was a little nerve at the base of her throat which jumped and cavorted like an imprisoned thing.

He went rather wearily to the desk and sat down in the swivel-chair behind it, feeling his bones. It had been a long grind and he was horribly tired. But he sighed and removed his *pince-nez* and scrubbed their lenses with diligence, preparatory to the work at hand. Rosa regarded him slantwise, without lowering her head.

"Do you know, Mr. Queen," she murmured, "you're almost handsome when you take your glasses off."

"Eh? Oh, certainly; that's why I wear 'em. Keeps off designing females. Pity John Marco didn't employ some such protective device." He continued to scrub.

Rosa was silent for a moment. When she spoke again it was in the same light tone. "I've heard about you, you know. I suppose most of us have. Somehow you aren't at all as formidable-looking as I pictured you. You've caught a good many murderers, haven't you?"

"I can't complain. In my blood, no doubt. There's a chemical something inside me that shoots to the boiling-point at the least approach of criminality. Nothing Freudian about it; it's merely the mathematician in me. And I failed in geometry in high school! Can't understand it, because I love discordant and isolated twos and twos, especially when they're expressed in terms of violence. Marco represents one of the factors in the equation. That man positively fascinates me." He was busy with something on the desk. She peeped secretly; it was to all appearances a translucent envelope filled with little scraps of paper. "For example, his obscene habit of getting himself killed *and* undressed. That's a new wrinkle. It calls for some higher mathematics, I'm sure."

The nerve, he noted without seeming to do so, redoubled its squirmings. Her shoulders quivered a little. "That—that was horrible," she said in a smothered voice.

"No, merely interesting. We can't permit emotions to interfere with our work, you see. Perfectly disastrous." He fell silent, absorbed in what he was doing. She saw him take a curious little kit out of his pocket, open it, select what appeared to be a tiny brush and a vial of grayish powder, and, sprinkling the scraps of paper—which he had arranged into a whole—with the powder, lightly and expertly dust the surface with the brush. He whistled a doleful tune, painstakingly turned each scrap over, and repeated the mysterious process. Something seemed to catch his eye, for he took a small magnifying-glass from the kit and peered intently through it at one of the scraps in the light of a powerful lamp on the desk. This time she saw him shake his head.

"What *are* you doing?" she burst out.

"Nothing startling. I'm looking for fingerprints." He continued to whistle as he stowed the vial and brush away in the kit, pocketed it, and reached for a jar of library paste on the desk. "Your father won't mind a liberty or two, I'm sure." He rummaged in a drawer until he found a sheet of blank yellow paper. Then he calmly proceeded to paste the scraps he had been examining onto the sheet.

"Is that—"

"Suppose," he said with sudden gravity, "we wait for Inspector Moley, eh?" He left the paper on the desk and rose. "Now, Miss Godfrey, indulge a little whim of mine and allow me to hold your hand."

"Hold my hand!" She sat up at that, her eyes wide.

"True," murmured Ellery, seating himself on the divan beside her and taking one of her rigid hands in both of his, "this is a pleasure that doesn't ordinarily accrue to a detective in the course of his—ah—labors. It's a very soft and brown and inviting little hand, I note—that's the Watson in me. Now for the Holmes. Relax, please." She was too surprised to withdraw her hand. He bent over it, holding it palm up, and scrutinized the soft paps of the fingertips with keen eyes. Then he turned her hand over and examined the fingernails, brushing the paps lightly with his own fingertips as he did so. "Hmm. Not necessarily conclusive, but at least it doesn't give you the lie."

She withdrew a little, snatching her hand away; there was a scared look in her eyes. "What on earth *are* you babbling about, Mr. Queen?"

Ellery sighed and lit a cigaret. "So soon. Just proves once more that the authentic pleasures of life are of tantalizingly short duration . . . Now, now, don't mind my little insanities, Miss Godfrey. I was merely trying to satisfy myself as to your veracity."

"Are you calling me a liar?" gasped Rosa.

"Perish the thought. You see, physical habits leave—very often—visible marks on the impressionable human carcass. Dr. Bell taught that to Doyle, and Doyle passed it obligingly on to Holmes; it was the secret of most of Sherlock's prestidigitating deductions, as it were. Typing hardens the fingertips; and feminine typists usually trim their nails short. Your fingertips are as soft as the breast of a bird, to quote the convenient poet; and your nails are even longer than your curious feminine *toiletterie* demands. In fine, it proves nothing, since you wouldn't be a habitual typist anyway. But it gave me the opportunity to hold your hand."

"Needn't bother," said Inspector Moley, striding into the library. He nodded at Rosa with a very friendly air. "That was an old gag when I was a cub in trainin', Mr. Queen. The young lady's okay."

"'Thus conscience does make cowards of us all,'" said Ellery, sheepishly feeling a guilty warmth in his cheeks. "But I never doubted it, Inspector."

Rosa stood up, her little chin hardening. "Was I under suspicion—after all I went through?"

"My dear young woman," grinned Moley, "everything and everybody are under suspicion till they're cleared. Now you, you're cleared. You never wrote that note."

Rosa laughed rather desperately. "What *are* you men talking about? What note?"

Ellery and the Inspector exchanged glances, and then Ellery rose and picked up from the desk the sheet of paper on which he had pasted the scraps of charred note found in Marco's bathroom. He passed it to the girl without comment and she read it with a puzzled frown. But she gasped over the signature.

"Why, I never wrote this! Who—"

"I just checked up on your statement," said Moley, losing his grin, "that you can't type. It's true, Mr. Queen—she can't. That doesn't mean she couldn't have pecked out a message on a machine with one finger, but the typing on this note is too even for that. It was done by somebody who's used to typing. So, combined with that kidnaping yarn and the fact that you were in Waring's shack all last night tied up, I guess you're cleared. This thing's a plant."

Rosa sank onto the divan. "No prints," said Ellery to Moley, "worth a tinker's dam. Just smudges."

"I—this is all beyond me. When—where—I don't even know what it *means*."

"This was a note," explained Ellery patiently, "sent circuitously to John Marco late last night. It purports to come from you, as you see, and—rather freely interpreted—makes an appointment with him for one o'clock in the morning on the terrace." He went around the desk, uncovered the typewriter, slipped a sheet of the heavy cream-colored Godfrey stationery into the carriage, and began quickly to manipulate the keys.

The girl was deathly pale in the dim light of the library. "Then that note," she whispered, "sent him to his death? I—I can't believe it!"

"Well, that's what happened," said Moley. "How's it stack up, Mr. Queen?"

Ellery ripped the sheet out of the machine and laid it on the desk side by side with the sheet on which the original scraps had been pasted. Moley trod heavily to a position behind him and the two men studied the adjacent sheets. Ellery had written precisely what appeared on the paste-up.

"Same type," murmured Ellery, taking out his glass and examining individual characters. "Hmm. Clear case, Inspector. Have a look at the capital I's. Notice the slight fading of the right-hand side of the lower serif; worn metal. And the upper right serif of the capital T is gone altogether in both. As a matter of fact, even the consistency of the ribbon seems to be the same; there's the identical muck in the lower case e's and o's." He passed the lens to Moley, who squinted through it for a moment and then nodded. "Yes, this is the machine, all right. Whoever typed the original of this message sat in this very chair."

There was silence as Ellery covered the machine and stowed his kit away. Moley paced up and down, a feral glitter in his eyes. Suddenly a thought struck him and he dashed away without explanation. Rosa sat limply on the divan with a stricken expression. When Moley returned he was hoarse with triumph.

"Just thought I'd make sure this machine has never left the house. By God, it hasn't! We've got somethin' at last."

"What you have," said Ellery, "is concrete evidence that the murderer is associated with this house, Inspector. Before it might have been any one. Yes, yes, that's a cosmic discovery. I think it clarifies certain issues, although . . . Miss Godfrey, perhaps you wouldn't care to listen to a bit of professional theorizing?"

"Perhaps I would!" Rosa's blue eyes were blazing. "I want to hear all about it. If it concerns any one in this house—Murder's despicable under any circumstances. Please talk. I want to help if I can."

"You may get your fingers burned, you know," said Ellery gently. But her mouth only hardened. "Very well, then. What have we? An emissary of a potential murderer whom we shall call X is hired to kidnap John Marco, take him out to sea, kill him, and dump his body overside. This emissary, the formidable Captain Kidd, stupidly mistakes David Kummer, your uncle, for Marco. Your part in the plot is purely incidental Miss Godfrey; X informed Kidd that Marco would be with you, and you were tied up in Waring's cottage merely to keep you from sounding a premature alarm. Before Kidd took your uncle off in Waring's cruiser he telephoned X . . . from all indications, in this very house. He told X that he had 'Marco.' So far, X's plan was successful."

"Go on!"

"But Kidd's stupid blunder," drawled Ellery, "upset X's plans. Very soon after Kidd's telephone-call to him X got the shock of his life. In this house he came face to face with the man who, he thought, was dead and fathoms under out at sea. In a flash he saw what must have happened. The merest inquiry or personal observation would have convinced him that it was Kummer whom Captain Kidd had abducted. Marco was still alive. Kummer was almost certainly dead—I'm sorry, Miss Godfrey— and there was nothing X could do about it; there was no way of reaching Kidd. And yet X's original motive against Marco still remained; obviously he couldn't have been less desirous of killing Marco then than he had been when he originally laid his plans."

"Poor, poor David," whispered Rosa.

The Inspector grunted. "So?"

"X is an unscrupulous and clever criminal," continued Ellery gravely. "All his actions show that, if I'm putting the correct interpretation on them. He recovered quickly from the shock of seeing Marco alive. He laid a new scheme. He knew that you, Miss Godfrey, were trussed up in Waring's shack, helpless until some one should come to release you. He also knew that— forgive me again—a message from you would probably sway Marco more than any other summons. And so he stole in here and typed a note, signing it with your name, making an appointment with Marco in an isolated place on the estate for an early hour of the morning. Then he pinned the note to Tiller's coat in Tiller's room, with specific instructions as to the time of delivery."

"Why Tiller?" muttered Moley.

"Tiller's room is on the ground floor; more accessible, then. Also he would prefer not to risk being seen entering Marco's room. It was a sound plan, and it worked. Marco kept the appointment at one, the killer came down and found him there, stunned him from behind, strangled him . . . " He stopped, the most curious expression of annoyance flitting over his face.

"And undressed him," said the Inspector sarcastically.

"That's the screwy part. That's the part that's got me up a tree. Cripes, *why?*"

Ellery rose and began a stiff-legged strut up and down before the desk. His forehead was furrowed painfully. "Yes, yes, you're right, Inspector. No matter where we start we always come back to that. Nothing fits until we learn why he undressed Marco. It's the only piece that refuses to fall snugly into place."

But Rosa inexplicably was crying, her sturdy shoulders shaking. "What's the matter?" asked Ellery with concern.

"I—I never thought," she choked between sobs, "that any one could be so *vindictive* as to implicate *me* . . . "

Ellery chuckled, and she was so surprised that she stopped crying. "Now, now, Miss Godfrey, that's where you're wrong. That isn't true at all. On the surface, I'll admit, it looks as if you were being framed for the murder—with the note that led Marco to his death having been signed by you, presumably. But examine it, and it becomes a totally different story."

She looked up at him anxiously, still sniffling a little. "You see, X couldn't possibly have meant to frame you for the killing. He knew you would have a powerful alibi—being found tied up in Waring's cottage that way, especially after a mysterious outsider apparently had telephoned young Cort of your whereabouts. As for the note, the murderer probably expected Marco to destroy it. If Marco destroyed it, the existence of the note with your name on it would never even be suspected, and you wouldn't be implicated at all. But even if Marco didn't destroy the note and it was found, X knew that your alibi, plus the fact that you can't type and the signature was suspiciously a typewritten one, would point to a frame-up. As a matter of fact, I suspect X didn't care a whoop if the police *did* discover that it was a frame-up. Such a discovery wouldn't imperil his own safety, and Marco would be dead by the time it was made. No, no, Miss Godfrey, I think X has been quite considerate of you. Much more considerate than he has been of Kummer and Marco."

She digested this in silence, nibbling at the corner of her handkerchief. "I suppose that's so," she said at last in a low voice. Then she looked up at him queerly. "But why do you say 'he,' Mr. Queen?"

"Why do I say 'he'?" repeated Ellery blankly. "Convenience, I suppose."

"You don't *know* anything, do you, Miss Godfrey?" snapped Moley.

"No," she said, still looking at Ellery; then she lowered her eyes. "No, I don't know anything."

Ellery rose and took off his glasses to rub his eyes. "Well," he said wearily, "at least we've learned something. The murderer of Marco typed this note. Since the typewriter hasn't left the house, the murderer typed it *in* the house. You're nursing a viper to your collective bosoms, Miss Godfrey. And that's not as funny as it sounds."

A bored detective said from the door: "The old guy wants to talk to you, Inspector. And Godfrey's been hammerin' our ears off out here."

Moley spun about. "Who? What old guy?"

"The gardener. This Jorum. He says he's got somethin' import—"

"Jorum!" repeated Moley in a startled way, as if he were conscious of the name for the first time. "Bring him in, Joe."

. . . .

But it was Walter Godfrey who entered first, in his dirty

slacks, his tattered sombrero on the back of his head. There were earth-stains on his knees and his fingernails were black with soil. He glanced piercingly at Ellery and the Inspector with his ophidian eyes, permitted himself to look surprised at the presence of his daughter, and then turned back to the door.

"Come on in, Jorum. Nobody's going to bite you," he said in a gentle voice—a gentler voice than Ellery had ever heard him use with Rosa or his wife. The old man shambled in, the soles of his broad shapeless shoes leaving a trail of earth on the floor. At close range his skin was even more amazing than it had been from afar. It was lined with hundreds of wrinkles, the color of soiled rock. His hands, which were twisting his hat, were huge and starkly veined. He looked like an animated mummy.

"Jorum's got something on his mind, Inspector," said the millionaire abruptly. "He's told me about it and, while I've no interest in your success or failure, you understand, I thought you should know about it, too."

"That's white of you," said Moley, tight-lipped. "And why the hell didn't you come to me direct, Jorum, if you had something of interest to say?"

The gardener shrugged his gaunt shoulders. "I ain't buttin' in anywhere. I'm a man minds my own business, I am."

"Well, well? Speak up."

Jorum caressed his gray-stubbled jaw. "Wouldn't have said nothin', only Mr. Godfrey said I should. Nob'dy asked me; so I says to m'self: 'Why should I talk?' It's your job to ask questions, ain't it?" He looked hostilely at Moley's stormy face. "I saw 'em on the terrace."

"Saw whom?" asked Ellery, coming forward. "And when?"

"Answer the gentleman, Jorum," said Godfrey in the same gentle tone.

"Yes, sir," replied the old man respectfully. "I saw Mr. Marco on th' terrace last night with this here, now, Pitts woman. They—"

"Pitts!" exclaimed the Inspector. "That's Mrs. Godfrey's maid, isn't it?"

"Yep, that's the one." Jorum took out a blue handkerchief and blew his nose on a note of contempt. "Pitts, the snippy one. Old hen, b'gee! Ain't no better'n she ought to be, I'll tell ye that. Not that I wa'n't su'prised, y'understand, when she said—"

"Look here," said Ellery patiently. "Let's get this straight, Jorum. You saw Mr. Marco and the lady's-maid Pitts on the terrace last night. Very well. What time was this?"

Jorum scratched a mossy ear. "Can't tell ye to the minute," he said plausibly. "Don't carry no watch. But it must 'a' been roun' one o'clock in the mornin', mebbe a mite after. I was comin' down th' path too-wards the terrace, see, takin' a look aroun' 'fore turnin' in—"

"Jorum's something of a watchman," explained Godfrey curtly. "Not a regular part of his duties, but he keeps his eyes open."

"Terrace was bright enough under th' moon," continued the old man, "and Mr. Marco, he was settin' by a table with his back to me, all dressed up like a playin' actor—"

"He had a cloak on, Jorum?" asked Ellery swiftly.

"Yes, sir. I seen him wear that there thing 'fore. Made'm look like that there, now, Me-fist-o-feels I once see in an op'ry up Maartens way." Jorum chuckled lasciviously. "Pitts, she was standin' up next to him all togged out in 'er maid's uniform; I could see her face plain. She was sore. 'Fore I hove into sight I heard like a slap, y'understand, an' when I sees her standin' there, sore-like, I says to m'self, I says: 'Oho, Jorum, there's monkey-business!' 'N I hears 'er say, angry-like: 'Ye can't talk to *me* like that, Mr. Marco; I'm a respectable woman!' an' then she comes on up the steps too-wards me, in a huff, an' I dodged into a shadder. Mr. Marco, he just sets there like nothin' happened. He was a cool hand, Mr. Marco, when it come to th' wimmen. I once see him pesterin' Tessie, who helps out in th' kitchen. But this Pitts gal, *she* put'm in his place. Queer . . . "

Rosa clenched her hands and ran from the library.

.   .   .   .

"Get Pitts," said Moley laconically to the detective on duty at the door.

When Godfrey and Jorum had gone, the millionaire prodding his gardener like a proud shepherd, Inspector Moley threw up his hands. "Another complication. A damned maid!"

"Not necessarily a complication. If Jorum's time-sense is to be relied on, our original reconstruction still stands. The coroner said Marco died between one and half-past, and this Pitts woman was being coy with Marco within that period. And Jorum actually saw her leave."

"Well, we'll soon enough find out if this Pitts business is just nothing, or what." Moley lowered himself into a chair and stretched his thick legs. "God, I'm tired! Must be pretty tuckered yourself."

Ellery smiled ruefully. "Don't mention that word. All I can think of is Judge Macklin snoring beatifically away somewhere over my head. I'll simply have to get some shut-eye soon, or drop in my tracks." He sat down limply. "By the way, here's the murder-note. Your local district attorney may find it valuable when—and if—this case ever reaches the prosecuting stage."

Moley tucked the pasted sheet carefully away. They sat relaxed, facing each other, minds emptied. The library was hushed, a cloister in a land of pandemonium. Ellery's lids began to droop.

But they came alive at the sound of clattering feet. The Inspector swung about, tense. It was the detective he had sent, followed by Mrs. Godfrey.

"What's the matter, Joe? Where's that maid?"

"Can't find her," panted the man. "Mrs. Godfrey says—"

They sprang to their feet. "So she's gone, eh?" muttered Ellery. "I *thought* I heard you say something about that to your daughter this morning, Mrs. Godfrey."

"Yes." Her dark features were worried. "As a matter of fact, when I went upstairs before to tell you about luncheon, I had in mind mentioning Pitts's absence. I forgot in what happened." She passed her slender hand over her forehead. "I didn't think it important—"

"You didn't think it important!" howled Inspector Moley, dancing up and down. "Nobody thinks anything important! Jorum keeps his mouth shut. You won't talk. Everybody . . . Where is she? When'd you see her last? For God's sake, haven't you a tongue, Mrs. Godfrey?"

"Don't shout, please," said the dark woman coldly. "I'm not a servant. If you'll keep your temper, Inspector, I'll tell you what I know about it. We've been so upset here today that a thing like that didn't make much impression on me, at first. I don't generally see Pitts until I return from my morning dip to dress for breakfast. Naturally, with everything that—that happened, you see . . . It wasn't until I returned to the house this morning, after I—I found the body, that I asked for her. Nobody seemed to know where she was, and I was too dazed and harassed about other things to push the matter. One of the other maids helped me. All day at various times it's come back to me that she wasn't anywhere about . . . "

"Where's she sleep?" said Moley with bitterness.

"In the servants' wing on the main floor here."

"Did you look there?" he barked at the detective.

"Sure, Chief." The man was frightened. "We never thought— But she's gone. Skipped clean. Took all her duds, her bag, everything. How should we know that—"

"If she took a powder under your noses," said Moley savagely, "I'll have your shields, the pack o' you!"

"Now, now, Inspector," frowned Ellery, "that's not credible. Not with all those troopers on guard. When was the last time you saw her yesterday, Mrs. Godfrey?"

"When I returned to my own quarters after—after—"

"After you left Marco's room. Yes, yes. And?"

"She usually helps me prepare for bed, combs my hair. I rang for her, but she didn't appear for a long time."

"Was that unusual?"

"Yes. When she did show up she complained of feeling ill and asked if she might be excused. She was very flushed and her eyes did look feverish. Of course, I permitted her to go at once."

"Just a gag," snarled the Inspector. "What time was it when she left your room?"

"I don't know exactly. Around one o'clock, I suppose."

Ellery murmured: "By the way, Mrs. Godfrey, how long has this woman been working for you?"

"Not very long. My former maid quit rather unexpectedly in the spring, and Pitts came to me soon after."

Moley said irritable: "I suppose you didn't see where she went. This is a fine kettle of fish—"

A brute in trooper's uniform said from the doorway: "Lieutenant Corcoran sent me to report, Inspector, that there's a yellow roadster missing from the garage. He's just checked up with that man Jorum and the two chauffeurs."

"Yellow roadster!" gasped Stella Godfrey. "Why, that was John Marco's!"

Moley glared out of red-rimmed eyes. Then he sprang at his detective with a yell. "Well, what are you standin' there for, like a damn' dummy? Get busy! Trace that car! This Pitts woman must have run out durin' the night! Get the dope on it, you dumbbell!"

Mr. Ellery Queen sighed. "By the way, Mrs. Godfrey, you say your former maid left you rather precipitately? Did she have any reason for doing so, to your knowledge?"

"Why, no," said the dark woman slowly. "I've often wondered about that. She was a good girl and I paid her well. She'd often expressed herself as delighted with her job Then—she just left. No reason at all."

"Maybe," shouted Moley, "she was a Communist!"

"Ha, ha," said Ellery. "And you secured the ailing Miss Pitts from an agency, of course, Mrs. Godfrey?"

"No. She was recommended to me. I—" Mrs. Godfrey stopped so suddenly that even Moley paused in his stamping about the room to stare at her.

"Recommended to you," said Ellery. "And who performed this friendly service, Mrs. Godfrey?"

She bit the back of her hand. "It's the oddest thing," she whispered. "I just remembered . . . John Marco did. He said she was a girl he knew who needed a job—"

"No doubt," said Ellery in a dry tone. "Respectable woman, eh, Inspector? Hmm. Now, that business on the terrace

couldn't have been a bit of an act for Jorum's benefit, could it?
. . . Well, sir, while you're taking arms against your local sea
of troubles, I give notice that I'm perishing for slumber. Mrs.
Godfrey, *could* you have some one guide me to that sanctuary
your daughter was so kind as to offer my outraged bones?"

VIII
OF HOSPITALITY

A SHIP was sinking at sea. It was a sea of red waves tumbling deep, and the ship was a toy. Colossus stood astride the prow, boldly naked, leering at the dark moon inches above his head. The ship sank and the giant vanished. An instant later his head was small and floating on quiet water, turned blindly to the black heavens. The moon shone brightly on his face; it was John Marco. Then the sea vanished and John Marco was a tiny chinaware man swimming in a glass of water. He was very stiff and dead. The clear liquid kept bathing his white enamelled body, lifting his curly hair, bumping him idly against the sides of the glass, which gradually grew opaque with a dyeing scarlet which looked like . . .

Mr. Ellery Queen opened his eyes in darkness, feeling thirsty.

For a moment his brain was a dizzy vacuum groping toward memory. Then memory flooded back and he sat up, licking his chops and fumbling for the lamp beside his bed.

"Can't say that vaunted subconscious of mine has been of any assistance," he muttered as his fingers touched the switch. The room sprang alive. His throat was parched. He pressed the but-

167

ton beside his bed, lit a cigaret from his case on the night-table, and lay back smoking.

He had dreamed of men and women and seas and forests and strangely animate busts of Columbus and bloody coils of wire and forging cruisers and one-eyed monsters and . . . John Marco. Marco in a cloak, Marco naked, Marco in white drills, Marco in tails, Marco with horns sprouting from his forehead, Marco making Hollywood love to fat women, Marco dancing *adagio* in tights, Marco singing in doublet and hose, Marco shouting blasphemies. But nowhere in the turbulent career of his dream had he even glimpsed a rational answer to the problem of Marco murdered. His head ached and he did not feel at all rested.

He grunted at a knock on his door and Tiller glided in with a tray bearing glasses and bottles. Tiller was smiling paternally.

"You've had a nice nap, I trust, sir?" he said as he set the tray down on the night-table.

"Miserable." Ellery grimaced at the contents of the bottles. "Plain water, Tiller. I'm thirsty as the very devil."

"Yes, sir," said Tiller with a raising of his precise little brows, and he took the tray away and returned instanter with a carafe. "You'll be hungry, too, sir, no doubt," he murmured as Ellery drained his third glass. "I'll have a tray sent up at once."

"Good lord! What time is it?"

"Long past dinner, sir. Mrs. Godfrey said you weren't to be disturbed—you and Judge Macklin. It's almost ten o'clock, sir."

"Good for Mrs. Godfrey. Tray, eh? By George, I am hungry. Is the Judge still sleeping?"

"I fancy so, sir. He hasn't rung."

"'Thou sleepest, Brutus, and yet Rome is in chains,'" said Ellery sadly. "Well, well, that's the greatest boon of senescence.

We'll let the old gentleman have his rest; he's earned it. Now fetch me that tray, Tiller, like a good fellow, while I wash some of this grime off my body. We must pay due reverence to God, to society, and to ourselves, you know."

"Yes, sir," said Tiller, blinking. "And if you'll pardon my saying so, sir, this is the first time any gentleman in this house has quoted both Voltaire and Bacon in the same breath." And he pattered imperturbably away, leaving Ellery staring.

Incredible Tiller! Ellery chuckled, jumped out of bed, and made for the bathroom.

When he emerged, freshly bathed and shaved, he found Tiller arranging a table with creamy napery. A huge tray filled with covered silver dishes and giving off a delicate aroma of hot food made his mouth water. He got hastily into a dressing-gown (the admirable Tiller had unpacked his bag in the lavatory interval and put away his things) and sat down to stupefy his appetite. Tiller presided with a deftness and self-effacement that proclaimed butlerage still another of his infinitely variegated accomplishments.

"Uh—not that I'm casting aspersions, you understand, Tiller, at your perfect conduct," said Ellery at last, setting down his cup, "but isn't this the proper function of the butler?"

"Indeed it is, sir," murmured Tiller, busy with the dishes, "but you see, sir, the butler has given notice."

"Notice! What's happened?"

"Funk, I fancy, sir. He's a reactionary, sir, and murders and such things are a little out of his line. He's offended, too, at what he terms the 'shockin' coarse manners' of Inspector Moley's men."

"If I know Inspector Moley," grinned Ellery, "his notice won't get him out of here—not until this case is cleared up.

By the way, has anything special happened since my dip into oblivion?"

"Nothing, sir. Inspector Moley has gone, leaving a few of his men on duty. He asked me to tell you, sir, that he would be back in the morning."

"Hmm. Thanks awfully. And now, Tiller, if you'll clear this mess out . . . No, no, I'm perfectly capable of dressing myself! I've done it for some years now, and in my own way I'm as hostile to change as that butler of yours."

When Tiller had gone, Ellery rapidly dressed himself in fresh whites and stole into the adjoining room, after a futile knock on the communicating door. Judge Macklin lay peacefully snoring in a chamber resplendent in royal blue. He was wearing rather flamboyant pajamas and his white hair stuck innocently up from his head like a halo. The old gentleman, Ellery saw, was probably good for the rest of the night; and so he stole out and went downstairs.

.   .   .   .

When Regan out of the sweetness of her nature plucked aged Gloucester's beard, he said rather plaintively: "I am your host. With robbers' hands my hospitable favours you should not ruffle thus." It is not recorded that this admonishment awoke repentance in the breast of Lear's daughter.

Mr. Ellery Queen found himself in a quandary; and not for the first time in his career. Walter Godfrey fell short of being the perfect host, and he was the type of fat little man whose facial follicles are infertile; nevertheless Ellery had eaten his food and slept, so to speak, in his bed; and to pluck—in a continuation of the figure—hairs from Godfrey's beard was an act of sheer effrontery to the laws of hospitality.

In short, Ellery found himself perched on the horns of the usual dilemma: to eavesdrop or not to eavesdrop. Now, while eavesdropping is an affront to hospitality, it is an essential to the business of detection; and the great question in Ellery's mind was: Was he first a guest, or was he first a detective? He decided very shortly after the opportunity presented itself that he was a guest by sufferance only, and in the face of special circumstances; wherefore he owed it to himself and to the cause of truth in which he was enlisted to listen with all the power of his keen ears. And listen he did, with enlightening result; realizing that the quest for the Holy Grail itself is not more beset with difficulties than the merest seeking after one true, unvarnished word.

It had happened quite unexpectedly, and he had had to wrestle with his conscience on the instant. He had descended into an apparently empty house; the vast cavern of the living-room was untenanted; the library, into which he poked his head, was dark; the patio was deserted. Wondering where every one was, he strolled out into the fragrant gardens, alone under a tepid moon.

At least, he thought he was alone. He thought he was alone until he came upon a bend of the shell-garnished path and heard a woman sob. The garden was luxuriant here, the bushes tall; he was quite invisible in their shadows. Then a man spoke, and Ellery knew that the unpredictable Godfreys, husband and wife, were beyond the bend.

Godfrey was saying in a low voice from which, even now, he could not banish the whip-note: "Stella, I must talk to you. It's high time some one laid the law down. You're going to give me the truth of this business or I'll know the reason why; d'ye understand?"

Ellery was perched on the horns for a trice only; and then he was listening very closely indeed.

"Oh, Walter," Stella Godfrey was sobbing, "I—I'm so glad. I've got to talk to somebody. I never thought you . . . "

It was a time for confession: the moon was melting and the gardens an invitation to burdened souls.

The millionaire grunted, but it was a softer grunt than usual. "By God, Stella, I can't make you out. What are you crying for? It seems to me that you've done nothing but cry ever since I married you. The Lord knows I've given you everything you've wanted; and you know that there's never been another woman with me. Is it this Marco tripe?"

Her voice was muffled and unsteady. "You've given me everything but attention, Walter. You've ignored me. You were romantic enough when I married you and you—you weren't so fat. A woman wants romance, Walter . . . "

"Romance!" he snorted. "Poppycock. You're not a child any more, Stella. That stuff is all right for Rosa and this Cort boy. But you and I—we're past that. *I* am. And you ought to be. Trouble with you is that you've never grown up. Do you realize that you might very easily be a grandmother by now?" But there was an uncertain note in his voice.

"I'll never be past that," cried Stella Godfrey. "That's what you can't seem to understand. And it isn't only that." Her voice became calmer. "It's not merely that you've stopped loving me. It's that you've put me out of your life altogether. Walter, if you paid me one-tenth the attention you pay that dirty old man Jorum, I—I'd be happy!"

"Don't talk nonsense, Stella!"

"I've never known why you . . . Walter, I swear! You—you drove me to it—"

"To *what?*"

"To—all this. This terrible mess. Marco . . . "

He was silent for so long that Ellery began to wonder if he had not gone away. But then Godfrey said hoarsely: "I see it now. Just a fool. I'm supposed to be smart. You mean to tell me—Stella, I could kill you!"

She whispered: "I could kill myself."

A rising wind slithered through the gardens, leaving a trail of curious music. Ellery stood still in the midst of it and thanked the fates which had awakened him in time. There were revelations in the air. And one never knew—

The millionaire asked quietly: "How long, Stella?"

"Walter, don't *look* at me that way . . . Since—since spring."

"Just after you met him, eh? What a sucker I've been. Didn't have much trouble picking Walter Godfrey's prize plum, did he? Just a sucker. Blind as a damn bat. Under my nose . . . "

"It—it wouldn't have happened at all, I think," she choked, "if he hadn't . . . Oh, Walter, that night you'd been beastly to me—so cold, so indifferent. I—He took me home. He began to take me home. He—he made love to me. I tried to resist, but . . . Somehow, he got me to take a drink from his flask. And another. And after that—I don't know. Oh, Walter—he took me to his apartment . . . I came to there. I—"

"How many others have there been, Stella?" The little man's voice was like chilled steel.

"Walter!" The tone rose in alarm. "I swear . . . He was the first! The only one. I just couldn't stand it any longer. Oh, I had to tell you, now that he's—he's . . . " Ellery could almost see her youthful shoulders quiver.

The fat little man was apparently pacing up and down in the path; his shoes crunched against the gravel in short, quick bursts of sound. Ellery started; the Napoleonic little creature was actually sighing! "Well, Stella, I suppose it was as much my fault as yours. I've often wondered how a man feels when he learns that his wife has been unfaithful to him. You read about it in the papers—he takes a revolver, he beats her head in, he commits suicide . . . " Godfrey paused. "But it hurts. Damn it all, it hurts, Stella."

She whispered: "I tell you, Walter, I never really loved him. It was just—you know what I mean. As soon as I'd done it I could have killed myself, even though he—he'd got me drunk. I was sorrier than you'll ever know. But I was trapped and he— oh, he was horrible."

"So that's how you came to invite him here," muttered God-frey. "I did wonder, in my dumb-animal way. You've asked crumby people in your time, but he was unique. And your lover!"

"No. Walter, I didn't want him! It was all over for me long before then. But he—he *forced* himself on me, made me accept him as my guest . . . "

The crunching on the gravel stopped. "You mean to sit there and say *he invited himself?*"

"Yes. Oh, Walter . . . "

"Lovely." His voice was bitter. "He invited himself, he ate my food, he rode my horses, he picked my flowers, drank my liquor, made love to my wife. Pretty soft for him! . . . And those others? That Munn couple, that blowsy old Constable frump—where do they come in? The usual scenery, or what? You may as well tell me, Stella. Maybe you don't realize it, but you've got us into one hell of a jam. If the police find out that you and he—"

There was a swish of feminine clothing, sharp and precipi-tate, and Ellery knew that she had flung herself into her hus-band's arms.

He winced. It was decidedly unpleasant. It was like sitting in at the dissection of a cadaver. But he set his lips and listened even more intently.

"Walter," she whispered, "hold me tight. I'm afraid."

"All right, Stella, all right, all right," said Godfrey, over and over, softly and mechanically. "I'll see you through. But you've got to tell me the whole truth. How about the others? Where do they come in?"

She was silent for a long time. A cricket chirped maddeningly in the bushes. Then she said, so huskily that the words were deep breaths: "Walter, I never saw any of them in my life before they came here."

Ellery could feel Godfrey's astonishment. It filled the sweet air in impalpable gusts. Godfrey was choking; it took him some time to utter coherent words. "Stella!" he spluttered at last. "How can that be? Does Rosa know them? Or did David?"

"No," she moaned. "No."

"But how did they—"

"I invited them."

"Stella, talk sense! Get your chin up, now. This is damned serious. How could you invite them if you didn't—" Even then he did not see the truth.

"Marco told me to invite them," she said drearily.

"He *told* you—! He gave you their names, their addresses out of a clear sky?"

"Yes, Walter."

"No explanations?"

"No."

"What happened when they came? After all, they couldn't have taken it for granted that an invitation—"

"I don't know," she said slowly. "I really don't. It's been so

strange—such an awful, awful nightmare. Mrs. Constable's
been the strangest of all. From the very beginning she *pretended*.
Just as if I'd known her all my life . . . "

The old crackle came into Godfrey's voice. "From the very
beginning? She saw Marco here at once?"

"Yes. I thought she'd—she'd faint when she first saw him.
And yet it wasn't as if she hadn't known. I got the definite
feeling that she had known—that she'd been steeling herself
against the meeting—but that with all that she couldn't help
being shocked. Marco was cool and—and mocking. He accepted the introduction as if he'd never met her . . . But she
fell into the deception instantly. Afraid—she's been deathly
afraid."

Afraid, thought Ellery grimly, of the same thing that has
frightened you, Stella Godfrey. And you're keeping something
back even now. At this moment there is something else which
so frightens you, Stella Godfrey, that you daren't tell—

"That fat old hag," said the millionaire thoughtfully. "Of
course, it's possible that . . . And the Munns?"

There was appalling weariness in her reply. "They're queer,
too. Mrs. Munn especially. She's—funny. She's just a cheap,
pushing creature, Walter, the kind you read about in the tabloids, the grasping chorus-girl type. You wouldn't think a woman like that would be afraid of anything. And yet from the first
moment she saw *him* she was scared to death, too. We—we've
been three women walking on the edge of an abyss, blindfold-
ed. Each of us has been afraid, afraid to talk, afraid to breathe,
afraid to confide in the others—"

"And Munn?" asked Godfrey curtly.

"I—I don't understand him at all. You can't make him out,
Walter. He's so crude and coarse, and yet he has strength. And

he never shows what he's thinking about. He's really acted very nicely up here for a man of his sort. He's been trying hard to be 'society.' Society!"

"How did he treat Marco?"

She laughed a little hysterically. "Oh, Walter, this is almost humorous. *I* have to tell *you* how a man living in the same house with you . . . With contempt. He didn't like him at all. Never paid any attention to him. Only when the other night Marco took Mrs. Munn for a stroll in the gardens I—I saw something in Mr. Munn's eyes. It made me shiver."

There was another interval of silence. Then Godfrey said quietly: "Well, it seems open and shut to me. You're three women he's made love to at various times. He had a hold on you, saw a chance to combine a sponging summer with some good, clean, honest fun. The filthy rat! He made you ask the others here . . . If I'd known. If I'd only known. When I think of what Rosa has escaped. He was making love to Rosa, too, damn his soul! How could a daughter of mine—"

"Walter, no!" Stella Godfrey cried in anguish. "He may have flirted with her . . . I'm sure the other thing—Not Rosa. Not Rosa, Walter. I was so tied up in knots myself I was blind to what was going on. Earle's attitude should have told me. The poor boy's been frantic—"

Ellery heard her sudden sharp intake of breath. He parted the bushes cautiously. A twig snapped, but they did not hear. In the light of the moon they were standing close together in the path, the woman taller than the man. But the man was grasping her wrists, and on his ugly masterful face there was the oddest expression.

"I said I'd help you," he said clearly. "But you still haven't told me everything. Was it just fear that I'd find out that made you such a willing tool of that damned gigolo? Just fear—or something else? The same thing that's petrified the other two?"

But there is a higher power that protects the rights of violated hosts. And eavesdropping is an uncertain business at best.

Some one was coming up the path. Coming slowly, with heavy feet whose drag expressed the most profound and deadly weariness.

Ellery was in the thick of the bushes in a flash. He was destined never to hear Stella Godfrey's reply that night. He crouched under cover, holding his breath, his eyes fixed on the path he had left so hastily.

The Godfreys heard, too. They became incredibly still.

It was Mrs. Constable. She loomed into view, a pale large ghost dressed in grotesquely jutting organdie, her bare arms fat and marbly in the moonlight. Her feet were still dragging, scuffing the noisy gravel, and her huge face was blank with the blankness of somnambulism. She was alone.

Her vast haunches passed within inches of Ellery's head as she rounded the curve in the path.

There was a simultaneous outburst of exclamations, as false in its twitterings as the mechanical song of toy birds.

"Mrs. Constable! Where *have* you been?"

"Good evening, Mrs. Constable."

"Hello. I—I was just taking a walk . . . What a horrible day . . . "

"Yes. We all feel—"

Ellery snarled to himself with bitterness at the vengeful spirit of the fates, crawled out to the path, and very quietly stole away.

IX
NIGHT, THE DARK-BLUE HUNTER

JUDGE MACKLIN came awake. One moment he had been struggling upward through a black turgid fog; but now he was vitally awake, awake in every sense, listening before he was conscious that he was listening, straining to see through the darkness before even his eyes were open. His old heart, he was startled to feel, was pounding away like a piston. He lay very still, aware of danger.

Some one, he knew, was in his room.

Out of the corner of his eye he glanced at the floor-windows which gave upon the Spanish balcony. The curtains were only half-drawn, and he could make out a star-pricked sky. It must be late, then. How late? He shivered involuntarily, causing the bed-clothes to rustle. He did not care for nocturnal visitors, much less for nocturnal visitors in a house in which murder had been committed.

But gradually his pulse slowed down to normal as nothing happened and common-sense repelled the invader. Whoever it is, he thought grimly, is due for the surprise of his life. He gathered his aged muscles for a leap out of bed. He was not so de-crept that he couldn't still give a rousing good account of himself in a tussle . . .

His door clicked suddenly and—his eyes now accustomed to the darkness—he was positive he had seen something white flick out the door. His visitor, then, had left.

"Whew," he said aloud, swinging his bare feet to the floor.

A cool dry voice said from somewhere nearby: "Oh, so you're up at last, are you?"

The Judge jumped. "For heaven's sake! Ellery?"

"In the flesh. I take it you heard our perambulating friend, too? No, no, don't turn on the lights."

"Then you were the one," gasped the Judge, "who just—?"

"Left? By no means. Isn't it Bode's Law that two material bodies cannot occupy the same position in space at the same time? Well, no matter; I was always weak on science. No, that was the prowler I've been expecting."

"Expecting!"

"I'll confess I didn't anticipate that she'd try this room, but I think that can be easily explained—"

"*She?*"

"Oh, yes, that was a female. Didn't you smell the powder? Sorry I can't give you the maker's name and *odeur*; I've never been Vance-ish in that direction. As a matter of fact, she was dressed in something long, flowing, and white. I've been watching here and there for an hour or more."

The old gentleman choked. "From here?"

"No. From my room chiefly. But when I saw her try this door I thought I'd slip in through the communicating door in case of—er—emergency. You're such a sublime old angel. She might have bopped you before you stopped dreaming of that languorous *houri*."

"Don't be ribald!" snapped the Judge, but he kept his voice down. "Why should any one try to assault me? I don't know any of these people and I certainly haven't done anything to any of 'em. It must have been a mistake. She got into the wrong room, that's all."

"Oh, undoubtedly. I was just ribbing you." The Judge, still on the bed, heard nothing at all, and yet when Ellery's voice came again it proceeded from a different part of the chamber—from the door. "Hmm. She's beaten a strategic retreat temporarily. I'm afraid we'll have to wait. Your noisy preparations for getting out of bed scared her off. What were you going to do," chuckled Ellery, "leap at her throat like Tarzan?"

"Didn't know it was a woman," said the Judge sheepishly. "But I wasn't going to lie here and be made mincemeat of. Who the devil was the creature?"

"Blessed if I know. Might have been any of 'em."

Judge Macklin lay back, propped on one elbow. He kept his eyes fixed on the spot where he knew the door to be; he could just make out Ellery's motionless figure. "Well," he snapped at last, "aren't you going to talk? What's been happening here? Why were you waiting? How'd you come to suspect? How long have I slept? You're the most exasperating young—"

"Whoa. One at a time. By my wrist-watch it's almost two-thirty. You must have a singularly easy conscience."

"I'd be sleeping yet if not for that confounded woman. Just beginning to feel the ache in my bones again. Well, well?"

"It's a long story." Ellery opened the door to pop his head out; it was back and the door closed in an instant. "Nothing doing yet. I didn't wake up until ten myself. You must be hungry, eh? Tiller fetched the most delicious—"

"Bother Tiller! And I'm not hungry. Answer me, you idiot! What made you suspect some one would go prowling tonight, and what are you watching for?"

"I'm watching," said Ellery, "for some one to go into the room next door."

"The room next—! That's yours, isn't it?"

"On the other side. The end-room."

"Marco's," said the old gentleman, and he was silent for a moment. "But isn't it under guard? I thought that Roush boy—"

"Oddly enough, that Roush boy is stretched out on a cot in Tiller's bedroom taking a well-earned nap."

"But Moley will be furious!"

"I think not. At least, not with Roush. You see, Roush left the room unguarded on orders. Er—mine."

The Judge stared into the darkness with open mouth. "Yours! It's beyond me. Or is it a trap?"

Ellery peered out into the corridor again. "She must have been properly scared. I suppose she thought you were a ghost . . . Quite so; a trap. Most of them turned in before midnight. Poor souls! They were very tired. Nevertheless, I carelessly let them know—*en masse*—that there wasn't any sense in keeping watch by a dead man's door, especially since we'd already looked the place over; and I informed them that Roush was off in slumberland."

"I see," muttered the Judge. "And what made you think some one would fall into your trap?"

"That," said Ellery softly, "is another story . . . *Quiet!*"

The Judge held his breath, his scalp prickling. Then Ellery's mouth was at his ear. "She's back. Don't make a sound. I'm off on a little spying expedition. For God's sake, Solon, don't crab this act!" And he was gone. The curtains of the floor-window fluttered a little, soundlessly, and a shadow drifted out and vanished. The Judge saw the stars again, cold and remote.

He shivered.

．　　．　　．　　．　　．　　．　　．

When fifteen minutes had passed and his ears had told him nothing except that waves were breaking against rock below and that a frosty wind blew in from the sea through his windows, Judge Macklin crept noiselessly out of bed, wrapped his gaunt pajama-clad body in a silk quilt from the bed, dug his toes into carpet-slippers, and stole to the window. With his hair standing on end at the top of his head, forming a tuft resembling a scalplock, and the quilt draped about his shoulders, he was grotesquely like an ancient Indian scout on the warpath. Nevertheless, his humorous appearance did not prevent him from stealing out onto the long shallow iron-grilled balcony in the best Indian tradition and gaining Ellery's side at a window several yards away . . . one of the windows of the late John Marco's bed-chamber.

Ellery was sprawled on his side in an uncomfortable position, his eyes glued to a plinth of light. The Venetian blind had not been completely drawn—a careless oversight on the marauder's part, since the space left unguarded at the bottom afforded a complete view of the room. Ellery saw the Judge coming, shook his head in warning, moved a little.

The old gentleman calmly spread his quilt, squatted on his lean hams, and peered into the room by Ellery's side, almost doubled over.

The huge Spanish bedroom was in violent disorder. The door of the closet stood open and every one of the dead man's garments lay on the floor outside, tumbled and in some cases torn.

A trunk had been lugged into the center of the room; its drawers sagged, empty. Several valises and suitcases had been hurled away by a disappointed hand. The bed had been attacked in ruthless fashion; a knife had slashed at the mattress, which lay exposed and half of the box-spring. The spring itself had been assailed. The drapes had been jerked off the tester. All the drawers in the room had been pulled out and their contents strewed the floor in a tangle of confusion. Even the paintings on the wall had been examined, for they hung awry.

The Judge felt his cheeks grow hot. "Where's the damned ghoul," he growled *sotto voce*, "responsible for this desecration? I'd cheerfully throttle her!"

"No irreparable harm done," murmured Ellery, without removing his eyes from the plinth of light. "Looks worse than it is. She's in the bathroom now, no doubt making kindred whoopee. Has a knife with her. You should have seen her fly at the walls! Just as if she thought there was one of those secret passageways here you read about in Oppenheim and Wallace . . . Silence. The lady enters. Beauty, isn't she?"

The Judge glared. It was Cecilia Munn.

It was Cecilia Munn standing in the doorway from the lavatory, her mask peeled off. Apparently the countenance she presented to the everyday world was only as deep as her cosmetics. Beneath it lay something appallingly different, now shamelessly revealed. Something raw and naked and nasty, a thing of writhing lips, taut blue skin, and tigrish eyes. One of her hands was clawing empty air, the other brandished a common breadknife which she had probably filched from the kitchens. Her robe lay open, half-revealing small panting breasts.

She made the most sharply etched picture of human rage, bafflement, despair and terror that either man had ever seen.

Even her blonde hair was infected by it, standing hideously on end like a dried mop. The bristling, vivid un-loveliness of her made them both feel sick.

"Good lord," breathed the old gentleman. "She's—she's *animal*. I've never seen . . . "

"She's afraid," muttered Ellery. "Afraid. They're all afraid. In his own way that man must have been Machiavelli and Beelzebub rolled into one. He hammered the fear of—"

The blonde woman soared like a cat—straight for the light-switch. Then there was only blackest darkness.

They lay frozen. Only one thing could have caused such an instantaneous muscular reflex. She had heard some one coming.

It seemed an age. In reality it was only a few ticks of Ellery's wrist-watch. Then light flooded on again. The door was closed once more and Mrs. Constable stood with her back to it, one hand still on the switch near the jamb. Mrs. Munn had vanished.

The stout woman was all jellied, hanging flesh and eyes. Her eyes bulged; her bosom bulged; she bulged all over. But it was her eyes that fascinated them, taking in the mutilation of the bed, the untidy mess on the floor, the sagging drawers. It was like watching a slow-motion film. They could detect every thought as it was reflected in her eyes and on her slack features. She was no longer wooden and expressionless. Beneath her satin wrapper she was trembling violently, shaking in every cell of her fat flesh. Amazement. Horror. Realization. Disappointment. And finally fear, the solvent. She melted into fear like an enormous candle into hot tallow.

She sank to the floor in a tumble of wrapper and flesh, weeping as if her heart were breaking. She wept soundlessly, which made her grief even more hideous. They could see the red cavern of her throat as she opened her mouth, the large beads of tears snaking down her face. On her knees, her huge wattled legs nakedly protruding from the wrapper, she rocked to and fro in a very ecstasy of bitter sorrow.

Mrs. Munn stepped cat-like from behind the bed and looked down at the gross, sobbing creature on the floor. The bestial expression had vanished from her hard, beautiful face. There was almost pity in her contemptuous gaze. The knife was still clutched, forgotten, in her hand.

"You poor slob," she said to the woman on the floor.

They heard clearly.

Mrs. Constable stopped rocking. Very slowly she raised her eyes. And on the instant she scrambled to her feet, all swirling satin, holding her vast breast and staring at the blonde woman.

"I—I—" Then her stricken gaze went to the knife in Mrs. Munn's hand and what color there was in her flabby cheeks ebbed away. She tried twice to speak; twice her vocal cords failed her. Then she babbled: "You . . . knife . . . "

Mrs. Munn looked startled. But when she saw what was frightening the fat woman she smiled and tossed the knife on the bed. "That! You needn't be scared, Mrs. Constable. I'd forgotten I still had it."

"Oh." It was half a groan. Mrs. Constable began to fumble with the hem of her wrapper, her eyes nearly closed. "I guess I—must have walked . . . in my sleep."

"You can cut the baloney with little Cecilia, dearie," said Mrs. Munn dryly. "I'm one of the girls, too. So he took you over the hurdles, did he? Who'd have thought it?"

The fat woman moistened her lips. "I—What do you mean?"

"I should have known. You're no more in *her* class than I am. Did he write to you, too?" Her hard eyes swept over the ugly, misshapen, middle-aged figure with the same mingled pity and contempt.

Mrs. Constable drew her wrapper more tightly about her. Their eyes clashed. Then she said with a sob: "Yes."

"Told you to come up here pronto, hey? Pronto. That's one of my dear husband's favorite words." Unaccountably, she shivered. "Said you'd get an invitation from Mrs. Godfrey, I'll bet, and then sure enough it came. Just like that. Just as if she'd known you all her life, just as if you'd lapped charlotte russes together in pigtails . . . I know. That's what happened to me, too. And you came. Boy, how you came! You were afraid not to."

"Yes," whispered Mrs. Constable. "I was afraid—not to."

Mrs. Munn's lips curled, her eyes flaming. "The damned . . . "

"You," began Mrs. Constable, and paused. Her hand described an arc, mutely. "Did you do—all this?"

"Sure I did!" snarled the blonde. "Did you think I'd take it layin' down? He made me suffer enough, the oily son-of-a-bitch! I figured it was my only chance. The copper'd gone to sleep . . . " Her shoulders sagged. "But it's no use. They're not here."

"Oh," whispered Mrs. Constable. "They're not? I thought— But they must be! Oh, it's unthinkable that they shouldn't be! I couldn't live—I thought at first you'd come and found them." She seized Mrs. Munn's shoulders, her eyes glazed with ferocity. "You're not lying?" she croaked. "You're not holding out on me? Please, please. I have a daughter of marriageable age. My son's just been married. My children are grown. I've always been respectable. I—I don't know what happened. I'd always dreamed of some one like—like him . . . Please tell me . . . Tell me you found them—tell me, tell me!" Her voice rose to a scream.

Mrs. Munn slapped the woman's face, sharply. Her scream choked off and she staggered back, holding her cheek. "Sorry," said Mrs. Munn. "You'd be raising the dead with that squeal of yours. The old guy is sleeping just next door—I got into his bedroom by mistake a while ago . . . Come on, sister, pull yourself together. We're getting out of here."

Mrs. Constable permitted her arm to be taken. She was crying naturally now. "But what am I going to do?" she moaned. "What am I going to do?"

"Sit tight and keep your trap shut." Mrs. Munn surveyed the wreck, shrugging. "There'll be hell to pay tomorrow morning when that copper comes up here and finds this mess. We don't know anything about it; understand? Not a thing. We slept like little lambs."

"But your husband—"

"Yeah. My husband." The blonde woman's eyes hardened. Then she said abruptly: "He's snoring his head off down the hall. Come on, Mrs. Constable. This room ain't—isn't healthy."

She reached for the switch. The lights blinked out. A moment later the men at the window heard the door click.

"Show's over," said Ellery, getting to his feet with some difficulty. "Here, you get back to that bed of yours, young man. Do you want to catch pneumonia?"

Judge Macklin picked up his quilt and without a word made his way along the narrow balcony to the window of his room. Ellery followed him through and went directly to the door, which he opened a little. Then he closed it and unconcernedly turned on the lights.

The old gentleman was perched on the edge of his bed, deep in thought. Ellery lit a cigaret and with relief sank into a chair.

"Well," he murmured at last, eying the still figure of his companion quizzically, "what's the verdict, your honor?"

The judge stirred. "If you'll tell me what's happened since

I've been out of circulation, my son, I'll be able to rationalize a little more clearly."

"Very little. The big news is that Mrs. Godfrey has told all."

"I don't understand."

"Wife confesses infidelity to husband in moonlit garden. Detective gets sore ears listening in." Ellery shrugged. "At that, it was illuminating. I knew she'd crack eventually, but I didn't think it would be to Godfrey. Amazing chap, Godfrey; he's got something. Took the news beautifully, all things considered . . . She confirmed what we had discussed earlier—had never met either Mrs. Constable or the Munns, she said, before inviting them to Spanish Cape. Moreover, it appears that it was Marco who forced her to tender the invitations."

"Ah," said the Judge.

"And Mrs. Constable and the Munns—at least Mrs. Munn—were apparently as embarrassed by the situation as she."

The old gentleman nodded absently. "Yes, yes. I see."

"However, the really critical revelation was cut off by the unexpected intrusion of Mrs. Constable. Not," sighed Ellery, "that it mattered. But I should have enjoyed hearing it from Mrs. Godfrey's own lips."

"Hmm. You mean that she had been holding something back above and beyond these other revelations?"

"Undoubtedly."

"But you know what she meant to tell Godfrey?"

"I believe," said Ellery, "I do."

The Judge unwound his long legs and went into the bathroom. When he emerged his face was buried in a towel. "Now," he said in a muffled voice, "that I've witnessed that little drama next door, I believe I do, too."

"Bully! Let's collaborate. Your diagnosis?"

"I think I understand Stella Godfrey's type." Judge Macklin hurled the towel away and lay down on the bed. "No matter what Godfrey may be as a sociological specimen, his wife at least is a victim of that well-known disease of the bluer blood known as 'pride of caste.' She's a Ruysdael, you know, by birth. You've never read any scandal about one of *them*. First-family-of-Manhattan business; the genuine article. Not especially favored in worldly goods, modern economic conditions being what they are, but veritable nabobs when it comes to Rembrandts, Van Dycks, Dutch antiques, and tradition. It's in her blood."

"And all this spells what?"

"To the Ruysdaels there is only one cardinal sin: getting into the clutches of the yellow press. If you must have a scandal, have it quietly. That's all there is to it. Her fears have been dominated by something tangible, my boy. She tangled with a scoundrel. *The scoundrel possessed proofs.* I believe it's as simple as that."

"*Bravo*," chuckled Ellery. "A wabbly dissertation in social psychology. And not especially original. Conclusion doesn't follow naturally from the facts. However, the scoundrel did have proofs. Once you visualized him as a scoundrel, you see, it almost inevitably followed that he *would* have proofs. I tackled it that way and saved myself a lot of fancy-work. Working on the theory that he had proofs, everything fell patly into place. Mrs. Godfrey's frantic perturbation and stubborn unwillingness to talk—that, I grant you, is probably a sign of her inheritance— Mrs. Constable's frozen funk, Mrs. Munn's watchfulness and crude deceptions . . . When I realized that both Mrs. Constable and Mrs. Munn had been commanded to come here—that was an elementary deduction—it followed that they, too, had somewhere along the line fallen prey to Marco's genius for feminine entanglements. And if they were so prompt in obeying his commands, they were afraid, too. Afraid, obviously, of his proofs. All three of them were afraid of his proofs."

"Letters, of course," muttered the Judge.

Ellery waved his hand. "It doesn't matter. Whatever they are, these women consider them frightfully important. But there's something even more interesting about the situation. Has it occurred to you to wonder *why* Marco wanted Mrs. Constable and Mrs. Munn here?"

"The sadistic impulse, I suppose. But no—With a man of Marco's calibre . . . "

"There, you see?" said Ellery sadly. "That's the sort of mess psychology gets you into. Sadism! No, no, Solon; something much less subtle than that . . . Blackmail."

Judge Macklin stared. "Thunder, yes! I'm fogged tonight. Love-letters—blackmail. They go together, true enough."

"Precisely. And getting the three victims together suggests that the gentleman was setting himself for—what?"

"The 'clean-up' he began to write about to Penfield in that letter when he was murdered!"

Ellery frowned. "From that point, it was child's play. These women have been desperate, the three of them. Marco would not be a piker; not he, from what we've been able to piece together about him. If he demanded blackmail, it must have run into money. He may have been too greedy; probably was. The result was a temporary stalemate, during which some one obligingly snuffed out his worthless life. But the proofs—the letters, whatever they are—still existed. Where were they?" Ellery lit another cigaret. "I saw then that these women would take any chance to get them back. They would move heaven and earth to find them. The most logical place to search would be Marco's room. Consequently," he sighed, "I suggested that friend Roush indulge his need for slumber."

"I hadn't thought of blackmail," confessed the old gentleman, "but I did see—after the event—what these women must have been looking for in Marco's room. Good heavens!" He sat up suddenly in bed.

"What's the matter?"

"Mrs. Godfrey! Certainly *she* wouldn't allow an opportunity like this one, tonight, to pass! Was she present when you dropped the hint about the room's being left unguarded?"

"She was."

"Then she'll be looking—"

"She has, Oscar, she has," said Ellery mildly. He rose and, stretched his arms. "Lord, I'm fagged! I believe I'll go back to bed. And you'd better do the same."

"You mean," cried the Judge, "that Mrs. Godfrey has already searched the room next door tonight?"

"At exactly one o'clock this morning, my dear sir. Odd— just twenty-four hours after her most prominent guest departed this life. Oh, well, that's just a delicate touch of Mother Coincidence's. I was at that convenient balcony-window. I will say that she was more scrupulous about it than the impetuous Mrs. Munn. Left the place neat as whisky."

"Then she's found them!"

"No," said Ellery, going to the communicating door, "she has not."

"But that means—"

"That means they aren't there."

The Judge gnawed his upper lip in exasperation. "But how in the name of the thousand devils can you know that so positively?"

"Because," said Ellery with a sweet smile, opening the door, "at twelve-thirty precisely I searched the room myself. Now, now, Solon, you'll work yourself into a fever. Off to sleep with you! You'll need all the rest you can get. I have the feeling that tomorrow will bring a celestial display of fireworks."

X
THE GENTLEMAN FROM
NEW YORK

"Well, Mr. Queen," growled Inspector Moley the next morning, as the three men sat in his office at Police Headquarters in Poinsett, the county seat—a short drive of fifteen miles or so inland from Spanish Cape, "that was a fine mess you got Roush into last night. I got his report by 'phone this morning. By rights I ought to put him back in uniform."

"Don't blame Roush," said Ellery quickly. "The whole thing was done on my responsibility, Inspector. The man's not in any way been remiss in his duty."

"Yeah, he told me that. And he also told me that Marco's room looks as if a herd of wildcats were let loose in there. You responsible for that, too?"

"Only in a negative way." And Ellery told the story of the night before, beginning with the conversation he had overheard in the gardens between the Godfreys and concluding with the nocturnal visit of the three women to the dead man's bedroom.

"Hmm. Now, that's damned interesting. Good work, Mr. Queen. Only why didn't you let me in on it?"

"You don't know this young man," remarked Judge Macklin dryly. "He's the loneliest wolf in captivity. I daresay he kept his mouth shut because he hadn't worked the thing out by his blasted logic. It wasn't a mathematical 'certainty'; merely a probability."

"How well you read my motives," chuckled Ellery. "Something like that, Inspector. What do you think of my little tale?"

Moley rose and looked out his iron-barred window at the placid Main Street of the little town. "I think," he said gruffly, "it's hot. I don't believe there can be any doubt about what it was those three dames were lookin' for. Marco took the three of 'em over—three silly women hankering for a little old-fashioned lovin'. Then he got the goods on them, turned on the screws, and made 'em pay through the nose. The old story. Sure they were looking for the goods. . . . I'm convinced of it now, anyway. Y'see, I've been getting some dope on Marco."

"Already?" exclaimed the Judge. "That's fast work, Inspector."

"Oh, it wasn't so tough," said Moley modestly. "Got a peach of a report in this morning's mail. Reason it wasn't so tough is that he's been looked up before."

"Oh," said Ellery. "Then he had a record?"

Inspector Moley flipped over a bulky envelope on his desk. "Not exactly. There's a pal of mine runs a private agency in New York, see. I got to thinking yesterday afternoon about this Marco scum. And the more I thought the more it seemed to me I'd heard that name before. It's not a common handle at all. Then I knew where—this friend of mine had mentioned it to me only about six months ago, when I was on a visit to the big city. So I wired him, and it turned out I was right. He sent me all the dope airmail special delivery."

"Private investigator, eh?" said the Judge thoughtfully. "That sounds suspiciously like a jealous husband."

"You're right. Leonard—that's my pal—was hired by some guy to get something on Marco. Seems this bird's wife and Marco had become too friendly. Well, Leonard knows his business. He got enough on Marco to make that smooth weasel turn tail and fork over the letters and photo involved. Naturally, Leonard's information doesn't go any further than the settlement of his particular case, so I can't tell you how or when Marco tied up with this Munn dame. But I can tell you how he tied up with Mrs. Constable, because that was one of the things Leonard found out about him under cover."

"Then his affair with Mrs. Constable preceded these others. Hmm. By how long?"

"Only a few months. Before that there was a long list of victims. Leonard didn't get any too much real information, you understand—all Marco's ex-ladyfriends kept their lips buttoned pretty tight. But he had enough to make Marco fade out on Leonard's client."

"The man must have a history of some sort," mused Judge Macklin. "These rascals generally have."

"Well, yes and no. He just popped out of nowhere, Leonard says, about six years ago. Leonard thinks he was Spanish, of good family, but gone to seed. He seems to have had a swell education, anyway; spoke English like a native, spouted poetry all the time—Shelley and Keats and Bryan and the rest of the love-mongers . . . "

"Byron, no doubt," said Ellery. "But I applaud, Inspector. Who'd ever have suspected you of acquaintance with the amorous?"

"I know what it's all about," winked Moley. "As I was sayin', he talked about rich and famous people as if he'd licked honey with 'em out of the same trough, was on familiar terms with Cannes and Monte Carlo and the Swiss Alps, and all the rest of that hooey. He showed up presumably with a lot of dough, although I think that was just part of the act. Didn't take him long before he got into society, and after that it was easy sailin'. Liked to work the resorts—Florida, the California beaches, Bermuda. He's left a trail behind him like a scared skunk. But try and prove anything."

"That's the trouble with blackmail based on adultery," growled the Judge. "The willingness to pay is an insurance to the blackmailer of his victim's continued silence."

"Leonard says here," frowned Moley, "that there was something else, but he never could put his finger on it."

"Something else?" said Ellery alertly.

"Well . . . a faint trail to an accomplice. Just a suspicion. As if Marco had been working with somebody. But who or in what way he never found out."

"Heavens, that may be immensely important," cried Judge Macklin.

"I'm workin' on it. To make it worse," added the Inspector, "he was tangled up with a finagler."

"Eh?"

"Oh, his official name is 'lawyer,'" retorted Moley.

"Penfield!" both men cried.

"Go to the head of the class. Maybe I oughtn't to do the gentleman an injustice. I think he's a crook because I'm convinced no honest lawyer would have tied up with a mug like Marco. It wasn't as if the guy was ever up on charges, or on trial, and needed counsel. Only it was this Penfield bird who smoothed matters out for Marco with Leonard. The Spaniard didn't even appear. Penfield called on Leonard and they had a nice chat, and Penfield said that 'a client' of his was being shadowed and found it all very annoying, and wouldn't Leonard please call his dogs off? And Leonard looked at his fingernails and said there was a little matter of some letters and photos and things that were botherin' *his* client, and Penfield said: 'Dear, dear. Now isn't that distressing!' And then they shook hands and the next morning Leonard got all the letters and pictures back in the first mail, no sender's address—although the package had been mailed from the Park Row post-office. And you remember Penfield's address. Slick, hey?"

During this remarkable monologue Ellery and the Judge had glanced at each other frequently. The instant Moley paused both of them opened their mouths.

"I know, I know," said Moley. "You're going to say that maybe Marco didn't have his Constable-Munn-Godfrey letters in the Godfrey house at all, and that maybe this Penfield bird has been keepin' 'em for him." He jabbed a button on his desk. "Well, we'll know in a minute."

"You mean you've got Penfield outside?" cried the Judge.

"This office works fast, your honor . . . Ah, there, Charlie. Show the gentleman in. And remember, Charlie, no rough stuff. He's marked 'fragile.'"

Mr. Lucius Penfield beamed from the doorway. He did not look at all fragile. He was, in fact, a very solid and chunky little man with a massive Websterian head almost entirely bald, a neat close-cropped gray mustache, and the most innocent eyes Ellery had ever seen in the face of a human being. They were large, infantile, and angelic—melting brown eyes of a beautiful luster. They twinkled merrily, as if their owner were indulging inwardly a serial jest. There was something

THE SPANISH CAPE MYSTERY · 199

Dickensian about him, for he was dressed very quaintly in a baggy and decrepit sack-suit that was olive-green with age and he wore a high collar and a wide cravat with a horseshoe diamond stick-pin. He looked, indeed, as if he would have shrunk from stepping on a beetle. Apparently Judge Macklin, however, entertained no such conception of him. The Judge's long face was set in implacable lines and his eyes were as cold as twin floes.

"Well, if it isn't Judge Alva Macklin!" exclaimed Mr. Lucius Penfield, advancing with outstretched hand. "Fancy meeting you here! Dear, dear, it's been years, hasn't it, Judge? How time flies."

"Nasty habit it has," said the Judge dryly, ignoring the hand.

"Ha, ha! Still the stormy petrel of the profession, I see. I always did say that the bar lost one of its most truly juridical minds when you retired."

"I doubt if I shall be able conscientiously to say the same about you when *you* retire. That is, if you ever do. It's likelier you'll be disbarred first."

"Sharp as ever, I see, Judge, ha, ha! I was saying just the other day to Judge Kinsey of General Sessions—"

"Spare the details, Penfield. This is Mr. Ellery Queen, of whom you've perhaps heard. I warn you to keep out of his way. And this—"

"Not *the* Ellery Queen?" cried the bald-headed little man; and he turned his sweet, droll eyes upon Ellery. "Dear, dear, this is an honor indeed. Quite worth the trip. I know your father very well, Mr. Queen. Most valuable man in Centre Street . . . And this, you were going to say, Judge, is Inspector Moley, the gentleman who's whisked me away from my very pressing practice?"

He stood there bowing, a beaming little gentleman survey-ing them all with swift, laughing, jovial glances.

"Sit down, Penfield," said Moley pleasantly enough. "I want to talk to you."

"So your man gave me to understand," said Penfield, promptly accepting the chair. "Something to do with a former client of mine, I believe? Mr. John Marco. Most unfortunate case. I've been reading about his demise in the New York pa-pers. You see—"

"Oh, so Marco *was* a client of yours?"

"Dear, dear, this is all very distressing to me, Inspector. I trust we're—so to speak—*in camera*? I may talk freely?"

"And," said the Inspector grimly, "how. That's why I've had you brought down to Poinsett."

"Had me brought down?" Penfield's arching brows arched just a trifle more than usual. "That sounds most unpleasant, In-spector. I take it I'm not under arrest—ha, ha? For I assure you the moment your detective explained—"

"Let's cut the soft soap, Penfield," said Moley curtly. "There's a connection between you and this dead man, and I want to know what it is."

"But I was about to explain," said the little man indul-gently. "You police officers are so precipitate! An attorney, as Judge Macklin can tell you, is a servant of his clients. I've had many clients in my—ah—rather extensive practice, Inspec-tor; I haven't been able to choose as carefully as I should have preferred, perhaps. Consequently, it's my sad duty to relate that John Marco wasn't the—ah—most desirable of charac-ters. Rather an odorous person, in fact. But that's really all I can tell you about him."

"Oh, so that's your angle, is it?" growled the Inspector. "In just what way was he your client?"

Penfield's pudgy hand, adorned with two diamond rings, described a vague arc. "In various ways. He—ah—called upon me from time to time for advice on business matters."

"What business matters?"

"That," said the little man regretfully, "I'm afraid I'm not at liberty to state, Inspector. An attorney's duty to his client, you know . . . Even death—"

"But he's been murdered!"

"That," sighed Penfield, "is most unfortunate for him."

There was a silence. Then Judge Macklin remarked: "I thought you were a criminal lawyer, Penfield. What's this about business?"

"Times have changed, Judge," replied Penfield sadly, "since you retired. And a man must live, mustn't he? You can't imagine what a struggle it is these days."

"I think with a great effort I can. In your case, I mean. And you seem to have developed an extraordinary streak of ethics, Penfield, since the last time we met."

"Development, Judge, sheer development," smiled the little man. "Who am I to be uninfluenced by the trend of the times? A new deal in the profession . . . "

"Rats," said the Judge.

Ellery did not take his eyes off the man's mobile face. It was in constant motion—the eyes, the lips, the brows, the wrinkling skin. A beam of sunlight striking through the window illuminated the shiny top of his head with the effect of a halo. Remarkable creature! thought Ellery. And a dangerous adversary.

"When'd you see this Marco last?" barked Moley.

Penfield placed the tips of his fingers together. "Let me see, now . . . Oh, yes! It was in April, Inspector. And now he's dead. Well, sir, that's just another token of the incorruptibility of the fates; eh, Mr. Queen? A bad actor . . . death. Very pat. The murderous criminal slips through the fingers of our courts for twenty years on technicalities, and then one day he steps on a banana-peel and breaks his neck. It's a sad commentary on our juridical system."

"What about?"

"Eh? Oh, I beg your pardon, Inspector. What did he come to see me about in April? Yes, yes, to be sure. One of our—ah— business conferences. I gave him the best possible advice."

"And that was?"

"To change his ways, Inspector. I was always lecturing him; a likable chap, really, despite his weaknesses. But he wouldn't listen, poor fellow, and now look at him."

"How did you know he was a bad actor, Penfield? If your re- lationship with him was so damned innocent?"

"Intuition, my dear Inspector," sighed the lawyer. "One can't practise criminal law in the courts of New York State for thir- ty years without developing an uncanny sixth sense, as it were, about the criminal mind. I assure you it was no more—"

"You'll never get anywhere this way with friend Penfield," said Judge Macklin with a grim smile. "He can keep this up for hours, I've heard him do it myself, Inspector. I suggest you come to the point."

Moley glared at his visitor, jerked open a drawer, snatched something out of it, and slammed it down across his desk in front of the little man's chair. "Read that."

Mr. Lucius Penfield permitted himself to look surprised, smiled deprecatingly, took a pair of horn-rimmed spectacles out of his breast-pocket, set them on the tip of his nose, picked up the paper gingerly, and scanned it. He scanned it very carefully. Then he set it down, removed his spectacles, returned them to his pocket, and leaned back in the chair.

"Well?"

"This is apparently," murmured Penfield, "a letter begun by the deceased and addressed to me. I deduce, from the abrupt manner in which it is interrupted, that death intervened and that therefore his last living thoughts were of me. Dear, dear, that's most touching, Inspector. A tender tribute, and I thank you for having permitted me to see it. What can I say? I'm too moved for words." He actually dug into his trousers for a handkerchief and blew his nose.

"Buffoon," said Judge Macklin softly.

Inspector Moley's fist crashed on his desk; he sprang to his feet. "You're not going to get out of this as easily as all that!" he roared. "I know that you and Marco corresponded regularly this summer! I know that you fixed at least one attempted extortion case when the going got too hot for both of you. I know—"

"You seem to know a good deal," said Penfield gently. "Elucidate,"

"My friend Dave Leonard of the Metropolitan Agency has written me all about you; see? So don't think you're pulling the wool over my eyes with all this confidential business-matter talk!"

"Hmm. You haven't been idle, I see," murmured the little man with a beaming glance of admiration. "Yes, Marco and I did correspond this summer, that's true. And I did call on Leonard—charming fellow—a few months ago in the interests of my client. But . . . "

"What's this clean-up Marco started to write you about?" shouted Moley.

"Dear, dear, Inspector, there's no cause for violence. And I really can't hope to interpret Marco's thoughts. *I* don't know what he meant. He was quite mad, poor chap."

The Inspector opened his mouth, closed it again, glared at Penfield, and then turned and stamped savagely to the window, fighting for self-control. Penfield sat with a sad expectant smile.

"Uh—tell me, Mr. Penfield," drawled Ellery. The lawyer's head swung about, a trifle warily. But he was still smiling. "Did John Marco leave a will?"

Penfield blinked. "Will? I wouldn't know, Mr. Queen. I never drew up such a document for him. Of course, some other attorney may have. I don't bother with such things."

"Did he own any property? Would you say he has left an estate?"

The smile faded, and for the first time the man's urbanity deserted him. He seemed to feel that a trap lurked somewhere in Ellery's question. He eyed Ellery closely before replying. "Estate? I don't know. As I say, our relationship was not—ah—" He paused, at a loss for words.

"The reason I ask," murmured Ellery, toying with his *pince-nez*, "is that I had a notion he might have consigned certain documents of value to your care. After all, as you say, the lawyer-client relationship is more or less sacred."

"More or less," remarked the Judge.

"Documents of value?" echoed Penfield slowly. "I'm afraid I don't quite understand, Mr. Queen. You mean bonds, stock certificates, things like that?"

Ellery did not reply at once. He breathed on the lenses, scrubbed them thoughtfully, and then placed the glasses on his nose. During the entire operation Lucius Penfield watched with respectful absorption. Then Ellery said lightly: "Do you know a Mrs. Laura Constable?"

"Constable? Constable? I don't believe I do."

"Joseph A. Munn? Mrs. Munn, the former Cecilia Ball, actress?"

"Oh, oh!" said Penfield. "You mean the people staying at the Godfrey house currently? I thought I'd heard their names before. No, I can't say I've had the pleasure, ha, ha!"

"Marco didn't write you about them?"

Penfield pursed his red lips. It was evident that he was struggling with several doubts, engendered by the fact that he did not know how much Ellery knew. His angelic eyes flicked over Ellery's face three times before he replied: "I've a shockingly bad memory, Mr. Queen. I can't recall whether he did or not."

"Hmm. By the way, to your knowledge did Marco cultivate the hobby of amateur photography? Quite the thing these days. I just wondered . . . "

The lawyer blinked, and Moley turned around with a frown. But Judge Macklin kept his frosty gaze steadily upon the little lawyer's face.

"You do jump about so, don't you, Mr. Queen?" murmured Penfield at last with a wry smile. "Photography? He may have. I wouldn't know."

"At least he left no photographs with you?"

"Certainly not," said the little man instantly. "Certainly not."

Ellery glanced at Inspector Moley. "I believe, Inspector, that there's no point in detaining Mr. Penfield further. He obviously—ah—can't help us. Very nice of you to have taken the trouble of coming down here, Mr. Penfield."

"No trouble at all," cried Penfield, his good humor returning

206 · ELLERY QUEEN

in a twinkling. He bounced out of the chair. "Is there anything else, Inspector?"

Moley grunted helplessly: "Beat it."

A thin watch popped into Penfield's hand. "Dear, dear, I'll have to hurry if I want to catch the next 'plane out of Crossley Field. Well, gentlemen, sorry I couldn't have been of service." He shook hands with Ellery, bowed to the Judge, tactfully ignored Inspector Moley, and backed to the door. "Nice to have seen you again, Judge Macklin. I'll be sure to send your regards to Kinsey. And, of course, I shall be glad to tell Inspector Queen, Mr. Queen, that I saw—"

He was still talking and beaming and bowing when the door closed upon his sweet, angelic eyes.

"That man," said Judge Macklin grimly, still looking at the door, "has talked juries out of convicting at least a hundred professional murderers. He has bribed witnesses and intimidated others who were honest. He has commanded judges. He has deliberately destroyed evidence. He once smashed the promising career of a young assistant district attorney by involving him in a patently framed scandal with a notorious woman of the underworld on the eve of a murder-trial . . . And you expected to get something out of him!" Moley's lips moved soundlessly. "My advice to you, Inspector, is to forget the man ever existed. He's much too slick for an honest policeman. And if he is involved in Marco's death somewhere you may be sure you'll never discover the connection or get proof."

Inspector Moley clumped out to his deskman's office to see that his orders had been executed. Mr. Lucius Penfield, whether he anticipated it or not, was returning to New York with what is professionally known as a "tail."

.   .   .   .

As they were driving back to Spanish Cape, the Judge said suddenly: "I don't believe it, Ellery. The man's too clever for that."

Ellery, who had been steering the Duesenberg abstractedly, said: "What *are* you talking about?" Penfield's departure seemed to have infected Moley's office with the virus of newslessness. Reports had come pouring in which told precisely nothing. The coroner had inspected John Marco's lifeless clay inside and out and sent word that he had nothing to add to his original opinion concerning the cause of Marco's death. There had been a bulletin from the Coast Guard, and numerous reports of "progress" from local officers all along the coast: to the effect that no one had yet even glimpsed Hollis Waring's stolen cruiser, that no man of Captain Kidd's unusual description had been seen anywhere along the seaboard since the night of the murder, and that David Kummer's body had not yet been washed ashore. It had all been very depressing, and the two men had left Moley fuming in a stew of impotence.

"I mean the notion that Penfield is in possession of those letters," muttered the Judge.

"Oh, is that worrying you?"

"He's too smooth to touch anything like that with his own fair hands, Ellery."

"On the contrary, I should think he'd have got his hands on the documents the very first thing if he'd been able."

"No, no. Not Penfield. He might advise, instruct, but he wouldn't handle personally. His knowledge of Marco's criminality would be sufficient hold for him—and that's a power over Marco he could carry about in his head."

Ellery said nothing.

He brought the Duesenberg to a halt before the Grecian pillars opposite the entrance to Spanish Cape. Harry Stebbins's belly pushed open the door of the gasoline establishment.

"If it ain't the Judge! *And* Mr. Queen." Stebbins rested his arms confidentially on the door of the Duesenberg. "I see ye scootin' in and out o' Spanish Cape yesterday. Ain't it awful about that murder? One o' th' troopers was tellin' me . . . "

"Quite horrible," said the Judge absently.

"Think they'll find the critter that did it? I hear this Marco was all naked when they found him. What's the world comin' to, that's what *I* want to know. But I always said—"

"We're staying at the Cape now, Harry, so you needn't bother about a housekeeper for us. Thank you just the same."

"Stayin' with the Godfreys?" gasped Stebbins. "Lord-a-mighty!" He stared as if at demigods. "Well, now," he said, wiping his oily hands on his overalls. "Well, now if that don't beat all hell. And I was just talkin' to Annie last night about a woman. She said—"

"We'd love to stay and hear the opinions of Mrs. Stebbins," said Ellery hastily, "which I've no doubt are fascinating, but we're in something of a hurry, Stebbins. Stopped to ask you a question or two. How late were you open Saturday night?"

The Judge glanced at him, puzzled. Stebbins scratched his head. "Why, I'm open all night Saturdays, Mr. Queen. That's our big night. All that traffic comin' up from Wayland—the amusement park ten mile' or so south, ye know—and all."

"You mean you don't close at all?"

"That's the ticket, sir. I take my snooze Saturday afternoons, when I get a lad from Wye to relieve me—I live on'y a couple hundred yards away from here. But I'm back around eight an' keep the old place runnin' through the night. The boy'll be back any time now to give me a breather. Annie'll be waitin' with a nice hot—"

"No doubt, Mr. Stebbins; that's one of the delights of married life, I hear. But tell me—is it generally known that this gasoline station remains open all Saturday night?"

"Weil, sir, there's that sign right on the post there. An' since I been doin' it nigh on twelve years," chuckled Stebbins, "I guess folks sort o' come to know it."

"Hmm. And were you here yourself Saturday night?"

"Oh, sure. I just told ye that. See, I—"

"Were you outside here around one o'clock in the morning?"

The pot-bellied man looked blank. "One o'clock? Well, now . . . Hard to say. Matter o' fact, Mr. Queen, I had a busy night Saturday night. Caught me sort of unaware. Don't know where all the cars come from all of a sudden, but they all seemed to run out o' gas at the same time. Took in a good bit o' change . . ."

"But *were* you?"

"Guess I must 'a' been. I was runnin' in and out of the office all night. Why?"

Ellery sent his thumb whistling over his shoulder. "Do you think you would have noticed any one coming out of the Spanish Cape road there across the way?"

"Oh!" Stebbins regarded them shrewdly. "So that's the ticket. Well, sir, I guess I would of an ordinary night. My lights here are pretty bright an' they shine right on those two stone things. But Saturday night . . . " He shook his head. "Rush didn't let up till near three in the mornin'. My oil-rack's inside, I had to keep on goin' in to make change . . . Some one might have come out, sir."

"You're sure," muttered Ellery, "you didn't actually *see* somebody?"

Stebbins shook his head. "Can't say one way or t'other. Might 'a' been."

Ellery sighed. "Too bad. I'd more or less hoped for something definite." He reached for his brake, thought better of it, and twisted about again. "By the way, where do the Godfrey chauffeurs get their gas and oil, Stebbins? Here?"

"Yes, *sir.* I carry just about the finest grade of—"

"Oh, to be sure. Many thanks, Stebbins." He released his brake and yanked on the wheel, heading the car for the stone pylons across the road.

"Now why," demanded the Judge as they purred along the road through the park in the cool shade, "did you ask those questions?"

Ellery shrugged. "Nothing cosmic. Too bad Stebbins didn't notice. If he had, he would have clinched matters. We proved yesterday that the killer made his escape by the land side. Where could he have gone if he didn't come out by this road? Unless he threw himself off the cliffs it wouldn't be possible to get out any other way but from the main-road exit back there. Couldn't even dodge through the park here—that high wire fence would be unscalable to any creature but a cat. Had Stebbins said no one emerged opposite his station, we should have proved more or less satisfactorily that the killer had escaped—to the house."

"I don't see why you even questioned it," said the old gentleman. "You go to the most unconscionable lengths to 'prove' a virtual fact! Certainly now we know enough about the basic situation to make it highly improbable that this was an outside job."

"You never know anything until you've proved it right."

"Nonsense. You can't order life mathematically," retorted the Judge. "Most of the time you 'know' things without factual evidence."

"I'm Coleridge's 'thought-benighted skeptic,'" said Ellery unhappily. "I question everything. Sometimes I even question the results of my own thinking. My mental life is very involved." He sighed again.

The Judge snorted, and neither man spoke again until the Duesenberg rolled to a stop before the mansion.

Young Cort was lounging in the doorway to the patio, looking sullen. Beyond him they could see Rosa lying in a deckchair, in an abbreviated bathing-suit, sunning herself. No one else was about.

"'Lo," said Cort without conviction. "Any news?"

"Not yet," murmured the Judge.

"Martial law still, eh?" A scowl darkened the young man's brown face. "This is beginning to get on my nerves. I'm a working man, did you know that? Can't get out of this damned place. Those detectives are all over the scenery, blast 'em. I'll swear one of them wanted to follow me into the bathroom this morning; I could see the yearning in his eyes . . . There was a call for you a couple of minutes ago, Queen."

"There was?" Ellery jumped out of the car, followed by the old gentleman. A uniformed chauffeur ran up and drove the car off. "From whom?"

"I think it was Inspector Moley on the wire . . . Oh, Mrs. Burleigh!" The ancient little housekeeper was passing on the balcony above. "Wasn't that Moley calling Mr. Queen a while ago?"

"Yes, sir. He said to call right back, too, as soon as you got here, Mr. Queen."

"Back in a jiffy," cried Ellery, and he dashed across the patio to vanish under the Moorish archway. The Judge went slowly into the flagged court and sat down beside Rosa with a thankful groan. Young Cort rubbed his back against the stucco wall of the patio, watching with an expression of the most sulky stubbornness.

"Well?" Rosa asked in a low voice.

"Nothing, my dear."

They sat in silence for a while, soaking up the sun. The tall powerful figure of Joseph Munn sauntered out of the house, followed a moment later by a bored detective. Munn was in bathing-trunks; his massive torso was burned a deep brown. The Judge examined the man's face through half-closed eyes. He had never seen a face, he thought, so perfectly controlled, and with so little effort. Suddenly he was reminded of another face, seen hazily through the dusty windows of many years. There was no similarity of feature, but a startling similarity of expression. The face had belonged to a notorious criminal, a man wanted in a dozen States for rape, murder, bank-robbery, and a score of lesser crimes. The Judge had studied that face while a vitriolic district attorney excoriated its owner before a hostile jury; he had watched it when the angry verdict had come in; he had watched it while he pronounced sentence of death. It had never once changed expression . . . Joseph A. Munn possessed the same gift of smoothly frozen imperturbability. Not even his eyes were an index to his thoughts; they were hard and half-concealed in screwing wrinkles developed through a lifetime of peering through vast distances in the glare of a torrid sun.

"Mornin', Judge," said Munn in his deep voice, very pleasantly. Then he grinned for an instant. "That's a good one. 'Mornin', Judge!' Well, what's doing, sir?"

"Very little," murmured the old gentleman. "From the way things are going, Mr. Munn, I should say the killer has an excellent chance of remaining a free and unknown agent."

"Too bad. I didn't like this Marco *hombre*, but that's no call for murder. Live and let live is my motto. Down where I come from they settle things in the open when they do want action."

"The Argentine, eh?"

"And vicinity. Great country, Judge. Think I'm goin' back there. Never thought I would, but I realize now there's nothing in this big-city stuff. I'll take the wife down there with me soon as I can get away. She'll go over big," he chuckled, "with the *vaqueros*."

"Do you think Mrs. Munn would care for that sort of life?" asked the Judge in a dry tone.

The chuckle died. "Mrs. Munn," said the big man, "is going to have a chance to learn to like it." Then he lit a cigaret and said: "Be seein' you. Don't take it so hard, Miss Godfrey. No man's worth it—to a girl like you . . . Well! Guess I'll go down for a swim." He waved his muscular hand in a friendly way and strolled toward the exit from the patio. The sun gleamed on his bronzed torso, Rosa and the Judge stared after him. He paused to say something to young Cort, who still stood sullen guard at the doorway, shrugged his big shoulders, and stepped out of the patio. The detective sauntered after him, yawning.

"He gives me the creeps," said Rosa, wincing. "There's something about that American Firpo that—"

Ellery came striding into the court, his heels ringing against the flags. His eyes were bright and there was unusual color in his lean cheeks. The Judge half-rose from the chair.

"Have they found—?"

"Eh? Oh, Moley called to say that he'd just had the latest report on Pitts."

"Pitts!" exclaimed Rosa. "They've caught her?"

"Nothing quite so exciting. She's vanished very expertly, that lady's-maid of your mother's, Miss Godfrey. But they *have* found the car she escaped in. Fifty miles or so north. Near the railway station in Maartens."

"Marco's roadster!"

"Yes. Abandoned. No clue in the car itself, but its location gives them something to work on." He lit a cigaret and gazed at it with burning eyes.

"Is that all?" said the Judge, sinking back.

"It's enough," murmured Ellery, "to give me the most astounding thought. Irrelevant as the very devil. And," his face darkened, "disturbing. Mark my words, Judge, we're in for it now with a vengeance!"

"In for what?"

"That," said Ellery, "remains to be seen."

XI
OBOLUS TO CHARON

Mr. Ellery Queen had once observed: "Crime, Ducamier or somebody has said, is a cancer on the social body. That's true, but peculiarly. For despite the fact that cancer is an organism run wild, it nevertheless must possess pattern. Science concedes as much even while research men are trying to recognize it in their laboratories. That they've failed is neither here nor there; the pattern must exist. It's the same story in detection: recognize the pattern and you're within shooting distance of the ultimate truth."

His chief difficulty, he reflected soberly as he sat smoking and thinking in his room after an early, rather strained luncheon with the others in the main dining-room, was that thus far the pattern had eluded him. True, he had glimpsed it vaguely from time to time, but in the end it always swirled away, a dancing and provocative mote.

There was something wrong. What it was he did not know, but he was sure that somewhere either he himself had erred or a deception had been practised upon him which had cleverly achieved the same result. That the murder of John Marco had been a brilliant coup, the logical end of a logical plan, he was more and more convinced. It had all the earmarks of cool, precise deliberation and—so to speak—malice aforethought. It was this that troubled him. The more logical the plan, the more easily he should be able to recognize it. A bookkeeper goes through a complicated but correctly calculated account with ease; it is only when a mistake has occurred somewhere that he runs into misadventure. And yet the intricate design of John Marco's murder remained alien. It was apparently unsymmetrical somewhere. He realized suddenly that his strange mental impotence might have been caused not so much by the predetermined ingenuity of the criminal or his own error as by a pure accident . . .

Accident! he thought with a rising tide of excitement. That might very well be the answer after all. Experience had taught him that the best-laid plans more often than not went awry; that the better laid they were, in fact, the more likely it was that they *would* go awry. Plans depend for success upon a multitude of factors which the planner relies upon to operate in perfect co-ordination; this was especially true, he knew, in the plan of a murderer. Let one factor fail to function properly and the whole scheme was imperilled. The planner might patch it up on the instant, but a chain of circumstances over which he no longer had control would have been started . . . It was here that the discordant note would creep in to muddle logic, to put the design off-balance, to spread a haze over the eyes of the investigator.

Yes, yes, the more he thought about it the clearer it became to him that John Marco's murderer had run afoul of sheer mischance. What the devil could the accident have been? He jumped out of his chair and began to stride about the room.

He had no hope that application of gray cells to this baffling problem would bring immediate results. But there were possi-

THE SPANISH CAPE MYSTERY · 217

bilities. John Marco's nakedness . . . his eternal, confounded nakedness. Surely there was the barrier, the haze-producer! It de-
fied sanity. It simply could not have been part of the murderer's
original plan; Ellery felt that, knew it. And yet—what did it
mean? What could it mean?

He pounded the floor, frowning and chewing his lip. Then
there was the business of Captain Kidd's error . . . *Error!* Here
he had been thinking along lines of mischance, and the blunder
of the clumsy sailor had not once occurred to him! David Kummer had inadvertently stepped within the focus of the murderer's plan. Perhaps Kummer was the key to the whole problem!—not the unfortunate chap himself so much as the fact he
represented: that Captain Kidd had mistaken him for Marco.
Surely this had upset the plot. Had it caused the murderer to act
prematurely? Was the whole answer merely an offshoot of the
blunder-through-haste? More vexing than that: was there a connection between Kidd's error and the fact that the murderer had
undressed the dead man?

Ellery sighed, shaking his head. There was a paucity of facts;
or something intervened to prevent him from seeing clearly
if all the facts were there. He shut his mind to what he was
rapidly coming to believe was the most invidious problem in
crime-detection he had ever had the misfortune to encounter;
and he began to think of other things.

For there were other things to think about. He thought he
envisioned with sufficient intelligibility what might be in the
wind.

The last he had seen of Judge Macklin the venerable jurist
had been making with enthusiastic anticipation for the other
side of Spanish Cape, where the golf course lay, for a stretch of
his long legs. The others were in their rooms or scattered about

the estate, rather nervously pursuing the commonplace in an effort to flee from John Marco's ghost. The detectives were lolling about, enjoying themselves. This, he realized, was an opportunity. If his stab in the dark had hit the mark, the thing should happen at any moment now.

He put on his white coat, threw his cigaret into an ashtray, and quietly made his way downstairs.

.　　.　　.　　.　　.　　.　　.

It came at precisely two-thirty.

Ellery had spent more than an hour patiently patrolling the cubicle in the main hail downstairs in which stood the miniature switchboard controlling the various telephone lines and extensions. By custom the board was tended by an under-butler; he had promptly sent the man packing. A neatly made chart on the board indicated by name the occupants of all the rooms, and the particular extension running to each room. There had been nothing to do except wait; and wait Ellery did with an indefatigability tempered by expectation of the unknown. For over an hour the buzzer on the board remained mute.

But when it burst into raucous sound he was seated before the board in a flash, clamping the head-set about his ears and manipulating the main-line plug.

"Yes?" he said, striving to make his voice sound pompously menial. "This is the residence of Mr. Walter Godfrey. To whom did you wish to speak?"

He listened intently. The voice which vibrated in his ears was odd. It was hoarse and muffled, as if its owner had stuffed something into his mouth or were speaking through cheese-cloth. The tones were forced, artificial; obviously a determined effort was being made to disguise it.

"I want to talk," said the odd voice, "to Mrs. Laura Constable. Will you connect me, please?"

Connect! Ellery's mouth tightened. The speaker knew, then, that there was a switchboard. He was positive this was the call he had anticipated. "One moment, please," he replied in the same aloof voice; and he depressed the lever under the tab indicating Mrs. Constable's room and rang. There was no answer and he rang again, and again. Finally he heard the click of her instrument and her voice, husky and slurred, as if she had been roused from sleep. "There is a call, Madam," he intoned, and instantly connected the two lines.

He crouched in the chair, hands over his earphones, in furious concentration.

Mrs. Constable, still half in the arms of her siesta, said: "Yes, yes? This is Mrs. Constable. Who is it?"

The muffled voice said: "Never mind who this is. Are you alone? Can you speak freely?"

The stout woman's exhalation of breath roared against Ellery's eardrums. In an instant all trace of sleep had fled from her voice. "Yes! Yes! Who—"

"Listen to me. You don't know me. You never saw me. When I hang up you'll make no effort to trace this call. You also won't tell the police about it. This is a little business deal just between you and me."

"Business deal?" gasped Mrs. Constable. "What—what do you mean?"

"You know what I mean. Right now I am looking at a photo. It shows you and a certain man who is dead in bed together in a hotel-room in Atlantic City; and he wasn't dead *then*. It was a flashlight picture taken during the night; you were asleep and didn't know about it until long after. I also have a roll of eight-millimeter motion-picture film. It shows you and this same man kissing, making love. It was taken in Central Park without your knowledge last fall. I also have a signed statement by a lady's-maid who was in your employ last fall and winter, testifying to compromising things she saw and heard in your Central Park West apartment during that time when your family was away—things between you and this dead man. I also have six letters written by you to—"

"God in heaven," said Mrs. Constable queerly. "Who are you? Where did you get them? *He* had them. I can't—"

"Listen to me," said the vague voice. "And never mind who I am or where I got them. The point is they're in my possession. You'd like to have them, wouldn't you?"

"Yes. Yes," whispered Mrs. Constable.

"Well, you can. For a price."

The woman was silent for so long that Ellery wondered what had happened to her. But then she replied; in a tone so weary and broken and hopeless that Ellery's heart contracted in a spasm of pity. "I can't . . . pay your price."

The blackmailer hesitated, as if surprised. "What do you mean—you can't pay my price? If you've any idea that I'm bluffing, Mrs. Constable, that I haven't got those films and letters—"

"I suppose you have," muttered the stout woman. "They aren't here. So some one must have got them—"

"You bet! I have. Maybe you're afraid I won't give up the stuff when you pay me? Listen, Mrs. Constable—"

Unusual blackmailer! thought Ellery grimly. It was the first time he had ever heard one stoop to argument. Could this be a false trail after all?

"He got thousands out of me," croaked Mrs. Constable. "Thousands. All I had. Each time he promised me . . . But he didn't. He didn't! He fooled me. He was a cheat as well as a—a . . . "

"Not me," said the muffled voice eagerly. "I'm on the level in this thing. I want my cut and I won't bother you any more. I know just how you feel. You can take my word I'll turn the stuff over on payment. Just you send me five thousand dollars by the route I'll tell you, and you'll have them back in the next mail."

"Five thousand dollars!" Mrs. Constable laughed—such an eerie laugh that Ellery's scalp prickled. "Is that all? I haven't got five thousand cents. He milked me dry, damn him. I have no money, do you hear? Not a cent!"

"Oh, so that's your angle, is it?" snarled the anonymous caller. "Pleading poverty! *He* got enough out of you. You're a rich woman, Mrs. Constable. You're not going to get out of this so easily, I tell you! I want that five thousand and you're going to give it to me, or—"

"Please," Ellery heard the woman whisper in agony.

"—or I'll make you wish you had! What's the matter with your husband? He made a fortune only two years ago. Can't you get it from him?"

"No!" she shouted suddenly. "No! I'll never ask him!" Her voice broke. "Please, don't you understand? I've been married so long. I—I am really an old woman. I have grown children, nice children. He—my husband would die if he knew. He's a very sick man. He's always trusted me and we've always been happy together. I'd rather—die myself than tell him!"

"Mrs. Constable," said the blackmailer with a note of desperation in his voice, "you evidently don't realize what you're up against. I'll do anything, I tell you! This pig-headedness won't get you anywhere. I'll get that money out of you if I have to go to your husband myself!"

"You won't find him. You don't know where he is," said Mrs. Constable hoarsely.

"I'll go to your children!"

"It won't do you any good. Neither of them has any money in their own right. Their money is tied up."

"All right, damn you!" Even through the muffled tones Ellery detected the sheer, lashing fury. "Don't say I didn't warn you. I'll teach you a lesson. You think I'm fooling around. That photo, the film, the statement, and the letters will be in the hands of Inspector Moley so damn' quick—"

"No, please, please!" cried Mrs. Constable. "Don't! I tell you I'm helpless, haven't got the money—"

"Then get it!"

"But I can't, I tell you," sobbed the woman. "I've no one to go to that I'd—Oh, don't you understand? Can't you get money from some one else? I've paid for my sin—oh, I've paid a thousand times with—with tears, with blood, with all the money I had. How can you be so heartless, so—so . . . "

"Maybe," screamed the voice, "you'll wish you'd scraped up that five thousand when Inspector Moley gets that stuff and turns it over to the newspapers! You damned fat, stupid cow!" And there was the crash of a slammed receiver.

Ellery's fingers raced over the board, working feverishly. He barely made out Mrs. Constable's whimper of pure despair as he broke the connection and dialed the operator.

"Operator! Trace that call. Just hung up. This is the police—the Godfrey house. Quick!"

He waited, chewing his fingernails. "Fat stupid cow." The other things, the intimate knowledge apparently of Marco's affairs. This was some one who knew more than mere chance possession of incriminating photographs and documents might indicate. Some one vitally involved. He felt sure of that. What he had learned crystallized his suspicions. When the time came his judgment would be vindicated. Meanwhile, if he could speed matters along . . .

"I'm sorry, sir," sang the operator. "The call was made from a dial telephone. I have no way of tracing it. *Thank* you," and there was a little click in Ellery's ear.

Ellery sat back, frowning, and lit a cigaret. He sat there for some time in silence. Then he called Inspector Moley's office in Poinsett. But Moley's deskman informed him that the Inspector was out; and after leaving word for Moley to call him back Ellery put down the headset and wandered off.

In the main hall a thought struck him, for he ground out his cigaret in a cast-iron pot filled with sand and made his way upstairs to the door of Mrs. Constable's room. He shamelessly put his ear against the center panel and listened. It seemed to him that the sound he heard was the choked result of sobbing.

He rapped. The sobbing ceased. Then Mrs. Constable's voice said strangely: "Who is it?"

"May I see you a moment, Mrs. Constable?" called Ellery in a friendly tone.

Silence. Then: "Is that Mr. Queen?"

"Yes, it is."

"No," she said in the same strange voice. "No, I don't want to talk to you, Mr. Queen. I—I don't feel well. Please go away. Some other time, perhaps."

"But I wanted to tell you—"

"Please, Mr. Queen. I'm really not at all well."

Ellery stared at the door, shrugged, said: "Quite all right. I'm sorry," and strolled off.

He went to his room, changed into bathing-trunks, slipped

into canvas shoes and robe, and went down to the Cove. He would have at least one swim in the Atlantic Ocean, he thought grimly as he nodded to the trooper on guard at the terrace, before this accursed case was polished off. He felt sure that there was nothing to be gained by haunting the switchboard any longer that day. This was to be a lesson . . . to the others. He would hear from Inspector Moley soon enough.

The tide was fairly high. He dropped his things on the sand, plunged into the water, and with powerful strokes headed out to sea.

. . . .

He opened his eyes to a blunt touch on his shoulder. Inspector Moley was leaning over him. On the Inspector's massive red features there was an expression so peculiar that Ellery snapped into wakefulness and sat up in the sand abruptly. The sun was very low on the horizon.

"This," said Inspector Moley, "is a hell of a time to sleep."

"What time is it?" Ellery shivered; the breeze against his naked chest was chilly.

"After seven."

"Hmm. I had a long swim and when I got back to the Cove I couldn't resist this soft white sand. What's happened, Inspector? Your face is eloquent. I left a message with your deskman, you know, to have you call me back. That was early this afternoon. Haven't you been to your office since two-thirty?"

Moley compressed his lips and turned his head in an exploratory way. But the terrace was deserted except for the trooper on duty, and the rims of the cliffs on both sides were blank and stark against the sky. He squatted down in the sand beside Ellery and dug into his pocket, which bulged.

"Take a look," he said quietly, "at this." His hand emerged with a flat small packet.

Ellery rubbed his nose with the back of his hand, sighed: "So soon?" and took the packet.

"Eh?"

"I beg your pardon, Inspector. I was thinking aloud."

It had been done up in plain brown wrapping-paper and tied with cheap, rather soiled white string. Inspector Moley's name and the address of his Poinsett office had been block-lettered on one face of the packet in watery blue ink that had a suspiciously post-office look. Ellery removed paper and string; out tumbled a thin bundle of envelopes, a small photograph, and a tiny reel of what appeared to be motion-picture film. He opened one of the letters, glanced briefly at the signature, inspected the photograph with a flickering annoyance, unwound a few feet of the film and held the celluloid strip up to the light . . . Then he restored everything to its original state and returned the packet to Moley.

"Well?" growled Moley after a moment. "You don't seem very surprised. Aren't you even interested?"

"To number one—I'm not. To number two—profoundly. Have you a cigaret? I've forgotten mine." Ellery nodded as the Inspector held a match for him. "I was going to tell you about this, Inspector, when I called."

Moley spluttered: "You knew?"

Patiently Ellery recited the details of the conversation he had overheard between Mrs. Constable and the mysterious caller. Moley listened with a thoughtful frown. "Hmm," he said when Ellery had finished. "So this bird, whoever it is, made good his threat to send the stuff to me. But tell me, Mr. Queen." He stared directly into Ellery's eyes. "How'd you know there was going to be a call?"

"I didn't *know*; it seemed, however, a likely happenstance. Let's defer discussion of the actual thought-process; I'll tell you about it some day. Now suppose you tell *me* what's happened."

Moley balanced the packet in his paw. "I was out checking up on what looked like a hot trail to this Pitts woman. Took me to Maartens. But it fizzled out, and when I got back to my office my man told me you'd called. I was about to call you back—this was more than an hour ago—when the messenger came."

"Messenger?"

"Yeah. Boy about nineteen. Came in an old Ford he told me he'd picked up for twenty bucks last year. Just a kid. We've checked up on him and he's absolutely all right."

"How did he happen to have the packet?"

"He's a Maartens boy. Well-known in town; lives with a widowed mother. We worked fast by 'phone with the Maartens police. But the kid's story checked with his mother's. Around three o'clock or so this afternoon the boy and his mother were in the house when they heard a thud on their front porch. They went out and found this package. Attached to it was a note in a faked handwriting and a ten-dollar bill. The note simply said the package was to be delivered to me in Poinsett immediately. And the boy took out his old Ford and delivered it. They needed that ten bucks."

"And they didn't see the person who threw the package on their porch?"

"By the time they got out he was gone."

"Too bad." Ellery smoked thoughtfully, eyes on the purpling sea.

"And that's not the worst of it," muttered Moley, scooping a fistful of sand from the beach and letting the grains cascade through his big fingers. "The minute I got these things and had a look at 'em I called up Mrs. Constable—"

"You *what*?" Ellery came to life with a start, the cigaret slipping from his fingers.

"What else could I do? I didn't know that you'd listened in and heard the whole story. I wanted information. When I spoke to her I thought she sounded funny. I told her—"

"Don't tell me," groaned Ellery, "you said anything about having received these letters and things!"

"Well . . . " The Inspector looked miserable. "I suppose I did sort of hint at it. And, since I expected to be busy at the office keeping in touch with the Maartens police on the trail of the one who'd sent this stuff, I asked her to jump into her car and come down to my office for a chat—told one of my boys over the 'phone it would be all right. She—well, she said she would, right away. Then I got busy on the 'phone and by the time I woke up almost an hour had passed. And the fat dame hadn't come. She should have been there by that time. Doesn't take more than a half-hour slow driving to get to Poinsett from here. I called one of my men here and he said she hadn't left the estate. So—well, here I am." A note of desperation crept into his voice, born of conscience. "I'm going to find out what the hell changed her mind."

Ellery blinked at the sea, his eyes stormy; and then he grabbed his robe and canvas shoes and sprang to his feet. "You've messed this business horribly, Inspector," he snapped, struggling into his shoes and robe. "Come along!"

Inspector Moley rose docilely, brushed himself off, and followed like a lamb.

They found Jorum transplanting a bed of flowers in the patio. "Have you seen Mrs. Constable?" panted Ellery. He was breathing hard after their swift climb from the terrace.

"Th' fat one?" The old man shook his head. "Nope." He continued stolidly with his work without looking up.

They made directly for Mrs. Constable's room. There was no answer to Ellery's knock and he pushed the door open and they went in. It was untidy—bedclothes crushed and wrinkled, a dressing-gown lying in a heap on the floor, an ashtray on the night-table overflowing with acrid butts . . . Silently they looked at each other and went out.

"Where the deuce is she?" growled Moley, refusing to meet Ellery's eyes.

"Where the deuce is who?" asked a mild baritone, and they turned to find Judge Macklin in the middle of the corridor, opposite the staircase.

"Mrs. Constable! Have you seen her?" asked Ellery sharply.

"Certainly. Is anything wrong?"

"I trust not. Where?"

The old gentleman looked at them. "On the other side of the Cape. Just a few minutes ago. I'd been over there on the links, you know, strolling about and enjoying myself. I saw her sitting on the very edge of the cliff—feet hanging over—staring at the sea. North side. I walked over that way and said something to her. Poor soul, she looked desperately lonely. She didn't even turn her head; just as if she hadn't heard me. Kept staring down at the water. So I left her to her thoughts and—"

But Ellery was already racing down the corridor toward the stairs.

.   .   .   .

They sped up the steep steps cut out of the naked rock wall,

Ellery in the van, Inspector Moley puffing behind them, and old Judge Macklin laboring with stern features in the rear. The north segment of Spanish Cape presented the same flat surface, but here the trees and shrubbery were much sparser than on the southern side and the ground had a finished, smoothly grassed appearance that betrayed the workmanship of man. Judge Macklin pointed straight ahead of him as they reached the top of the stairs. They ran that way, thrashed through a clump of trees, burst into the open again—and stopped.

There was no one there.

"Strange," said the Judge. "Perhaps she's wandered off—"

"Separate," said Ellery quickly. "We've got to find her."

"But—"

"Do as I say!"

.   .   .   .

There were violet streaks in the sky; it was growing darker.

They beat their way separately through the middle of the northern segment, which was its most thickly wooded part. Occasionally one of them darted out into the open, looked about, and plunged back into the woods again.

.   .   .   .

Rosa Godfrey trudged seaward from the links, her golf-bag hanging from one shoulder. She was tired, and her hair was blowing about in a careless way.

She paused suddenly. It seemed to her that she had caught a glimpse of something glimmer-white in the distance, near the edge of the cliff. Without thinking she turned away and made for the shelter of the copse nearby. She felt like being alone. There was something about the evening sky and the approaching wrinkles of the sea that gave her a distaste for human company.

. . . .

Earle Cort wandered over the sixth tee, his eyes roving.

. . . .

Mrs. Constable sat on the grassy edge of the cliff, her thick legs hanging over space. Her head was low, her chin almost on her breast. She gazed with glassy eyes at what lay below her.

After a while she placed both her pudgy hands on the very edge and pushed toward the sea, wriggling backward. Her rump scraped against the rubble in the roots of the grass; she almost tumbled in a sidewise fall. Then she drew her legs up and on the very verge of the abyss got to her feet.

Her eyes still looked out to sea.

She stood facing the ruffled water, the tips of her slippers an inch past the edge. The skirt of her gown whipped about in the wind. She did not move, did not stir. Only her gown fluttered about in the wind. She stood black and still against the sky.

. . . .

Mr. Ellery Queen slipped out of the woods for the tenth time. His eyes were weary with strained looking. And his heart was beginning to feel heavier, with the leaden feeling that seems to drag it into the pit of the stomach. He quickened his pace.

. . . .

One moment Mrs. Constable was standing on the edge of the cliff, staring out to sea. The next she was gone.

It was difficult to say what had happened. She had flung up her arms and something hoarse and elemental had pushed past the clogged muscles in her throat and split the evening air. Then she was gone without a trace, as if the earth itself had swallowed her.

In the half-light of dusk there was something magical about it. Magical and dreadful. If the sun had come speeding up again from below the horizon and the sea had vanished in a twinkling it could not have been more dreadful. To vanish like a puff of smoke . . .

    .   .   .   .

Ellery pushed out of the woods. And he stopped.

A woman lay in the grass almost at the edge of the cliff, prone. Her hands were cupped under her face and her shoulders were shaking. A man in knickerbockers stood a foot from the edge, hands clenched at his sides. A bag filled with golf clubs lay nearby.

There was a rustle behind him, and Ellery turned to see Inspector Moley burst out of the woods.

"Did you hear that?" cried Moley hoarsely. "That scream?"

"I heard it," said Ellery with a curious sigh.

"Who—" Moley caught sight of the man and woman, frowned, and began a bull-like charge. "Hey!" he shouted. The man did not turn, nor did the woman look up.

"Too late?" asked a shaking voice. Judge Macklin touched Ellery's shoulder. "What happened?"

"Poor fool," said Ellery softly, and without replying made his way toward the edge of the cliff.

Moley was staring down at the woman; it was Rosa Godfrey. The man's head was blond and bare; it was Earle Cort.

"Who was that screamed?"

Neither gave any sign of recognition.

"Where's Mrs. Constable?" asked Moley in a hacking croak.

Cort shivered suddenly and turned about. His face was gray and wet with perspiration. He sank to his knees beside Rosa and patted her dark hair. "All right, Rosa," he said dully, over and over. "All right, Rosa."

The three older men stepped to the edge of the cliff. Something white swayed gently about sixty feet below; they could just make out one side of it. Ellery fell on his stomach and wriggled forward, thrusting his face over the verge.

Mrs. Constable lay spread-eagled in the churning wafer at the foot of the cliff, face up, on one of the knife-like rocks sprouting from the base. Her long hair had come loose and trailed in the water, with her gown and legs. The water was tinted red around her. She looked for all the world like a fat oyster which has been dropped from a height to split itself upon a rock.

XII
IN WHICH A BLACKMAILER
ENCOUNTERS DIFFICULTIES

THE PRIVILEGE of dying quietly is reserved to nonentities. Death by violence automatically turns a *peu de chose* into a torn figure of importance, making a vital symbol out of the commonplace. In death Laura Constable found the very notoriety she had tried so hard to escape in life. Her broken body became a focal point for all the prying eyes of authority. In one brief swoop through space from grass-grown clifftop to gray rock in blackened water she achieved the significance that passes for immortality in the modern world of news.

Men came. Women came. Camera lenses stared at her unlovely shape, rendered infinitely unlovelier by the impaling it had gone through in the process of extinction. Pencils scribbled smoking words. Telephones jarred to monosyllabic messages. The bony coroner violated her fat blued flesh with impersonal, faintly bored fingers. Mysteriously a scrap of her gown disappeared, torn away by some one whose hunger transcended the ethics of special privilege.

In all this madness of activity Inspector Moley stalked silently, his lowering visage masking his thoughts. He let the reporters have their way with the corpse and the northern slice of Spanish Cape and the bloodstained rock. His men scurried about like headless chickens, plainly bewildered by the turn of events. The Godfreys, Cort, the Munns huddled together in the patio, posed in a daze for the avid photographers, answered questions mechanically. One of Moley's men had already discovered Mrs. Constable's city address and had wired to her son; it was Ellery who, with a poignant recollection of the dead woman's voice, advised against tracing her husband. Everything happened, and nothing happened. It was a nightmare.

The scribblers surrounded Moley. "What's the dope, Inspector?" He grunted. "Who did it? Think it was this Cort guy? Suicide or murder, Chief? What's the connection between this Constable dame and Marco? Somebody says she was his mistress; is that right, Inspector? Come on, give us a break. You haven't told us a thing in this merry-go-round!"

When it was all over and the last reporter had been forcibly ejected, the Inspector motioned one of his men to the door of the lantern-lighted patio, rubbed his forehead wearily, and said in the most conversational of voices: "Well, Cort, how about it?"

The young man glared at Moley out of red-rimmed eyes. "She didn't do it. She didn't!"

"Who didn't do what?"

It was deep night now, and the flaring Spanish torches, cunningly electrical, cast long splashes of light over the flagstones. Rosa cowered in a chair.

"Rosa. She didn't push her over. I swear, Inspector!"

"Push—" Moley stared, and then burst into a guffaw. "Who said anything about Mrs. Constable's being pushed over, Cort? I want the straight of it, just for the record. I've got to make a report, you know."

"You mean," muttered the young man, "you don't believe it was—murder?"

"Now, now, never mind what I believe. What happened? Were you with Miss Godfrey when—"

"Yes!" said Cort eagerly. "All the time. That's why I say—"

"He was not," said Rosa in a tired voice. "Stop it, Earle. You'll only make matters worse. I was alone when it—it happened."

"For God's sake, Earle," growled Walter Godfrey, his ugly face a gargoyle of worry, "tell the truth. This is getting—getting . . ." He wiped his face, although it was quite chilly.

Cort gulped. "As long as she—I'd been looking for her, you see."

"Again?" smiled the Inspector.

"Yes. I didn't feel much like—well, anything. Somebody—I think it was Munn there—told me he'd seen her strolling about on the links, so I went there. When I came out of that patch of brush near the—the spot, I saw Rosa."

"Well?"

"She was leaning over the edge. I couldn't understand. I yelled to her and she didn't even hear me. Then she threw herself back and fell on the grass and began to cry. When I got there I looked over and saw the body lying on the rocks below. That's all."

"And you, Miss Godfrey?" Moley smiled again. "This is, as I say, just for the record."

"It's as Earle says." She rubbed her lips with the back of her hand and stared down at her rouged skin. "That's the way he found me. I heard him shout, but I was . . . petrified." She shuddered and continued quickly: "I'd been out hitting a few golf balls about by myself. It's been so—so deadly around here since . . . Then I grew tired and thought I'd stroll out to the cliff to lie down and just—well, lie down. I wanted to be alone. But I'd no sooner stepped out of the tangle of woods and brush that's one of the hazards when I . . . saw her."

"Yes, yes," said Judge Macklin eagerly. "That's most important, my dear. Was she alone? What did you see?"

"I suppose she was alone. I didn't notice anything—else. Just her. She was standing with her back to me, facing the sea. She was so close to the edge of the cliff that I—I became frightened. I was afraid to move, to shout, to do anything. I was afraid that if I made a sudden sound she'd be startled and lose her balance. So I just stood there, watching her. She seemed like a—oh, I know all this is silly and hysterical!"

"No, Miss Godfrey," said Ellery gravely. "Go on. Tell us everything you saw and felt."

She plucked at her tweed skirt. "It was uncanny. It was! It was getting darker. She stood there so still and black against the sky she looked like a—well," cried Rosa, "a stone statue! Then I suppose I must have gone a little cuckoo myself, because I remember thinking that she—the whole scene—looked like something out of a movie, as if it had been . . . well, *planned*. You know, with an eye to effects of light and shade. Of course, that was merely hysteria."

"Now, Miss G.," said Inspector Moley genially, "that's all very well, but how about Mrs. Constable? Exactly what happened to her?"

Rosa sat very still. "Then . . . She just disappeared. She was standing there like a statue, as I said. The next thing I knew she had thrown up her arms and, with a sort of—of scream, fell forward over the edge. Vanished. I—I heard the thud when she struck the . . . Oh, I'll never forget that as long as I live!"

She twisted about in her chair, her mouth working, and blindly groped for her mother's hand.

Mrs. Godfrey, who seemed frozen, patted her stiffly. There was a silence. Then Moley said: "Anybody else see anything? Hear anything?"

"No," said Cort. "I mean," he muttered, "I didn't."

No one else replied. Moley turned on his heel and said to Ellery and the Judge out of the corner of his mouth: "Let's go, gents."

·　　·　　·　　·　　·　　·　　·

They went upstairs in a straggling line, each occupied with his own thoughts. In the corridor outside Mrs. Constable's room they found two men waiting in the uniform of the Department of Public Welfare, with the familiar and slightly macabre-looking crate at their feet. Moley opened the door with a grunt and the others followed.

The coroner was just replacing the sheet. He straightened and turned with a sour glance. The body made a mountainous heap on the bed. There were blots of blood on the sheet.

"Well, Blackie?" said Moley.

The thin bony man went to the door and said something to the men outside. They trooped in, set the basket down, and turned to the bed. Ellery and the Judge instinctively looked away; when they looked back the bed was empty, the crate full, and the two uniformed men were wiping their brows. No one spoke until they left.

"Well," said the coroner. He was angry; red spots glowed in his cadaverous cheeks. "What the hell do you think I am, a magician? Well! She's dead, that's all. Died as a result of her fall.

Broke her back in two, as a matter of fact, besides doing a little damage to her skull and legs. Well! You birds make me sick."

"What's eatin' you?" grumbled Moley. "No bullet-wound, no knife-cut—nothing like that?"

"No!"

"That's good," said Moley slowly, rubbing his hands. "That's swell. Clear case, gentlemen. Mrs. Constable faced ruin—her particular brand of hell, what with a dying husband, a middle-class laced-up-the-back background, and the rest of it. She wouldn't go to her hubby for the hush-hush, and she didn't have the dough herself. So, as soon as she heard from me that the letters and stuff had been delivered to me—too bad, but what the devil!—she took the only way out she could see."

"You mean she committed suicide?" demanded the Judge.

"Smack on the button, your honor."

"For once," snarled the coroner, snapping his bag shut with a vicious gesture, "you're talking sense. That's just what I figure. There's no physical evidence of foul play."

"Possible," murmured Judge Macklin. "Emotionally unstable, her world crashing about her ears, in the dangerous age for a female . . . yes, yes, quite possible."

"Besides," said Moley with an odd accent of satisfaction, "If this Rosa girl is telling the truth—and certainly she's clear on all counts—it just couldn't have been anything else but suicide."

"Oh, yes, it could," drawled Ellery.

"Hey?" Moley started.

"If you want to start an argument, Inspector . . . and speaking theoretically, I repeat: Yes, it could."

"Why, man, there wasn't a soul within fifty feet of that woman when she took the dive! She wasn't shot at, that's a cinch, and there isn't any knife-wound. So there you are. Cripe, it's a pleasure to write it off with so little trouble!" But he continued to eye Ellery with a broad doubt on his face.

"Pleasures differ. Doctor, the woman landed on her back, did she not?"

The coroner picked up his bag and scowled. "Do I have to answer this fella?" he asked complainingly of Moley. "All he does is ask fool questions. Didn't like him the minute I saw him."

"Come on, Blackie, don't be cute," growled the Inspector.

"Well, mister," sneered the coroner, "she did."

"You don't take kindly to the Socratic method, I see," grinned Ellery; then his grin vanished and he said: "And just before she went over the cliff she was standing on the edge, wasn't she? Quite so. It wouldn't have taken much to make her lose her balance, would it? Of course not."

"What *are* you driving at, Ellery?" asked the Judge.

"Inspector Moley, my dear Solon, believes with Cæsar that *fere lamenter hominess id, quod volute, creodont.* You find Mrs. Constable's suicide very convenient, don't you, Inspector?"

"What the devil do you mean?"

"Wish fathering the thought business, eh?"

"Listen here—"

"Now, now," drawled Ellery, "I'm not saying she didn't commit suicide. I merely wish to point out that it would have been possible even under the circumstances for Mrs. Constable to have been murdered."

"How?" exploded Moley. "How? You can't keep on pullin' rabbits out of your hat! You tell me—"

"I was about to do so. Oh, by a very primitive method, to be sure, but in this case vastly to be preferred over some modern gimcrack. I suggest that it is theoretically possible someone stood in the brush nearby, out of sight of Miss Godfrey and ourselves, and merely *threw a stone* at Mrs. Constable's back—a very broad target, if you will recall the general construction of her anatomy."

They greeted this with dead silence. The coroner glared at him in a gnawed and defeated way. Moley sucked a fingernail.

Then Judge Macklin said: "Granted that Rosa would not have heard a sound nor seen the assailant. But she was looking straight at Mrs. Constable. Wouldn't she have noticed the stone striking?"

"Yeah," said Moley at once, his frown vanishing. "That's right, Judge! Wouldn't she have, Mr. Queen?"

"I don't believe she would," shrugged Ellery, "but then that's only an opinion. Mind you, I'm not saying that's what happened. I'm just pointing out the danger of leaping to conclusions."

"Well!" said Moley, wiping his face with a limp handkerchief. "I guess there really can't be any question about the suicide. This is all swell-soundin' chatter, but it doesn't get you anywhere. Besides, I've got this whole thing figured out in my mind now. It's a theory you can't blast, Mr. Queen."

"A theory covering the entire set of facts?" murmured Ellery, visibly surprised. "If that's true, Inspector, I owe you an apology, for you will have seen something that so far has escaped me." There was no sarcasm in his tone. "Well, let's have it!"

"You think you know who killed Marco?" said the Judge. "I sincerely hope you do. This is scarcely a vacation and, in all conscience, I'd as life get away from here today as not!"

"Sure, I know," said Inspector Moley, taking out a twisted cheroot and sticking it into his mouth. "Mrs. Constable."

.   .   .   .

Ellery kept eying him during the entire time in which they

left the bedroom, escorted the coroner downstairs and to his car, and strolled out through the patio into the moon-drenched gardens. The patio was deserted. Moley had a wrestler's jaw, and he did not seem especially gifted in intellectual attainments; but Ellery had learned through hard-won experience never to judge a man on appearances or even superficial acquaintance. It was possible that Moley had struck something nutritious. Ellery had felt all along that his own thinking had been sterile in this case; and so he waited impatiently for Moley, who seemed to be enjoying himself, to explain.

The detective did not speak until they had reached a quiet spot under a dark roof of leaves. He devoted himself for a full minute to drawing upon his cheroot and watching the breeze whisk the acrid smoke away.

"Y'see," he said at last, in a provocative drawl, "it's open and shut, now that she's dead by her own hand. I'll admit," he continued with magnificent modesty, "that I hadn't specially thought of her before. But that's the way it goes in this business. You're in a fog, but you bide your time and then, whango!— something pops and it's all over but the shouting. All you need is patience."

"Which, as Syros said," sighed Ellery, "'when too often outraged is converted into madness.' Talk, man, talk!"

Moley chuckled. "Marco played his usual game with this Constable woman, made love to her, smashed down her defenses, became her lover. She was probably easy pickin's—just at the age when a handsome phiz is something to moon at in the movies and dream about at home. Well, she soon woke up. Soon as he had his letters and photo and roll of film, he laid his cards on the table: Pay up, sweet sucker. She paid up, scared to death. She was sick at heart, I suppose, but she figured she'd pay him what he asked, get back the proofs, and bury the whole business. Just a fling that didn't work out."

"So far," murmured Ellery, "nothing startling, to be sure, and probably correct. Proceed."

"But we know from the conversation you yourself overheard this afternoon," continued the Inspector equably, "that she was fooled. She paid and *didn't* get back the proofs. And she paid again, and again, until . . . what?" He leaned forward, brandishing his cigar. "Until she was cleaned out; until she didn't have any more dough to stuff into that skunk's craw. What could she do? She was desperate. She couldn't or wouldn't go to her husband, she had no further sources of funds. And yet Marco didn't believe her, because it was through Marco that she came up here. He wouldn't have finagled it so that she'd be invited here unless he thought he could still squeeze a few grand out of her. Now, would he?"

"No, that's perfectly true," said Ellery with a nod.

"Now, Marco was settin' the stage for one last cleanup. He figured it would be easier if he got all his victims together, cracked down on 'em at one time, collected, took Rosa away with him—maybe he did intend to marry her, for all I know— and in that way set himself up for life. Godfrey would have paid plenty to get rid of such a son-in-law and have his daughter back. What happens? Mrs. Constable comes up here, because he ordered her to and she can't help herself, he demands more dough, she pleads poverty, he gets tough and says if she doesn't quit stalling and come across he'll either send his proofs to some tab or to her husband. But she is telling the truth; she's got her back to the wall. What's she do?"

"Oh," said Ellery oddly, "I see." He looked disappointed. "Well, what *does* she do?"

"She plans to kill him," said Moley with triumph. "She plans to have him killed, rather; and on the chance that he's got the letters and things with him, steal them back and destroy them. So she hunts up this Captain Kidd that she's heard about while she's here, hires him to bump Marco off, Kidd picks up Kummer by mistake, she finds out almost immediately, types the note off making the fake appointment with Marco that night on the terrace, goes down, picks up that bust of Columbus and socks Marco, then strangles him with the wire she's brought with her, and—"

"Undresses the corpse?" asked Ellery quietly.

Moley looked annoyed. "That's just pink candy!" he exploded. "Just smoke in our eyes. Doesn't mean a thing. Or if it does, she just got a kick out of—well, you know what I mean."

Judge Macklin shook his head. "My dear Inspector, I can't say I agree with you on any specific count."

"Go on," said Ellery. "The Inspector isn't finished, Judge. I want to hear this out to the bitter end."

"Well, it suits me," snapped Moley, nettled. "She thought she was safe, then. No clue left, the note was either destroyed or, if not, pointed to Rosa. Then she goes lookin' for those letters of hers and those photos. Well, she can't find them. In fact, she goes back with the idea of lookin' again the next night—last night, when you caught her and this Munn doll and Mrs. Godfrey. Then she gets the call from the one who's really got the proofs and sees she's in for the whole damned business of blackmail all over again. She's killed a man for nothing. This time she doesn't even know who's hitting her up. So the game's up and she commits suicide. That's all. Her suicide was a confession of guilt."

"Just like that, eh?" murmured Judge Macklin.

"Just like that."

The old gentleman shook his head. "Aside," he said mildly, "from a number of inconsistencies in your theory, Inspector, surely you must see that the woman doesn't fit as the criminal psychologically? She was petrified with fear from the moment of her arrival at Spanish Cape. She was a middle-aged woman of the bourgeois type—the family woman pure and simple; good clean stock, narrow in her moral viewpoint, attached to home, husband, and children. The Marco incident was an emotional explosion, over as soon as it set off. Now a woman like that, Inspector, may commit murder on impulse when she's pushed far enough, but not an ingenious murder deliberately planned in advance. Her mind couldn't have been clear enough. Besides, I doubt whether she possessed sufficient intelligence." He shook his fine old head. "No, no, Inspector, it doesn't ring true."

"If you gentlemen are through heckling each other," drawled Ellery, "perhaps you, Inspector, will be kind enough to answer a few questions? You'll have to answer them to the press eventually, you know; they're sharp lads and lassies; and you don't want to be caught, as they say in our robuster literature, with your pants down."

"Shoot," said Moley, no longer triumphant or annoyed. If anything, he was worried. He sat biting his fingernails, head cocked on one side as if he were fearful of losing the merest word.

"In the first place," said Ellery abruptly, shifting on the rustic bench, "you say Mrs. Constable, unable to pay blackmail to Marco, planned to kill him. But in planning to kill him, you maintain, she *hired* Captain Kidd to do the dirty work! I rise to ask: Where did she get the money to pay Kidd?"

The Inspector was silent, fretting over his nails. Then he

muttered: "Well, I admit that's a sticker, but maybe she just promised to pay him when his job was done."

The Judge smiled, and Ellery shook his head. "And run the risk of having Cyclops on her neck as a result of welching? I think not, Inspector. Besides, it doesn't strike me that Kidd is the type of scoundrel who would commit murder without payment in advance. You see, there's at least one weakness in your theory, and a very basic one. In the second place, how did Mrs. Constable know about the Marco-Rosa connection—so well as to be certain that the bait of the note would work?"

"That's easy. She kept her eyes open and found out."

"But Rosa," smiled Ellery, "has apparently been very secretive about it. You see, if there's anything in my objection, it's weakness number two."

Moley was silent. "But those things—" he began after a moment.

"And in the third place," continued Ellery regretfully, "you haven't explained that business of Marco's nudity. Most important omission of all, Inspector."

"Damn Marco's nudity!" roared Moley, jumping to his feet.

Ellery rose, shrugging. "Unfortunately, we can't dispose of this case so easily, Inspector. I tell you we shan't have a satisfactory theory until we've discovered one that explains sanely why—"

"Hush," said the Judge in a whisper.

They all heard it at the same instant. It was a woman's voice, choked and faint, but she had screamed somewhere nearby in the gardens.

·　　·　　·　　·　　·　　·　　·

They made their way rapidly toward the source of the cry,

running noiselessly on the thick grass. The cry was not repeated. But the sound of a queer feminine mumbling came to their ears, growing louder as they advanced. Instinctively they felt the need for stealth.

Then they were peering through a yew-hedge into a grove set in a circle of blue spruce. One look, and Inspector Moley set his muscles to spring through the hedge. Ellery's hand tightened on the detective's arm, and Moley sank back.

Mr. Joseph A. Munn, the South American millionaire with the poker face, stood tensed and furious in the girdle of trees, his big brown hand clamped over the mouth of his wife.

The hand covered most of her face; only her eyes, frantic with fear, showed. She was struggling in a mad panic, and it was from her mouth that the mumbling issued, choked and distorted by his hand. Her hands beat backward over her head at his face, and she was kicking him with her sharp heels. He paid no more attention to her blows and kicks than he would have paid to the thrashings of a bug.

Mr. Joseph A. Munn looked neither like millionaire nor poker-faced gambler at the moment. The little veneer he had so carefully cultivated had curled off in a flash of passion, and the cold mask he wore had been dropped at last to reveal a terrifying rage. The muscles of his powerful jaws were drawn back in a brutish snarl. They could see the fierce humps of muscle on his shoulders and the iron bulk of his biceps through the taut coat.

"First lesson," muttered Ellery, "in how to treat your wife. This is truly educational . . . "

The Judge poked a sharp elbow in his ribs.

"If you'll shut that trap of yours," rasped Munn, "I'll let you go."

She redoubled her efforts, the mumble mounting shrilly.

His black eyes flashed; he lifted her from the ground. Her head snapped back and her breath was shut off. The mumble ceased.

He flung her from him to the grass, wiping his hands on his coat as if they were dirtied from the contact with her. She fell in a heap and began to cry in short, gasping sobs, almost inaudible.

"Now you listen to me," said Munn in a tone so strangled that the words were blurred. "And you answer my questions straight. Don't think that forked snake's tongue o' yours is going to get you out of this one." He glared down at her balefully.

"Joe," she moaned. "Joe, don't. Don't kill me. Joe—"

"Killin's too good for you! You ought to be staked down on an ant-hill, you two-timing, rotten little bitch!"

"J-Joe . . ."

"Don't 'Joe' me! Spill it! Quick!"

"What . . . I don't know—" She was quaking with fear, looking up at him as if to ward off a blow, her bare arms raised.

He stooped suddenly, thrust his hand in one of her armpits, heaved effortlessly, and she flew backward to a bench, landing with a thud. He took one stride, raised his hand, and slapped her cheek three times in the same spot. The slaps sounded like revolver-shots. They jarred her to the spine, her head flying back and her blonde hair coming loose. She was too frightened to cry out, to protest. She slumped on the bench, holding her cheek and staring up at him out of her darting eyes as if she had never seen him before.

Both men were muttering in rebellion to either side of Ellery. He said: "No!" in a sharp whisper, and dug his fingers into their arms.

"Now talk, damn you," said Munn evenly, stepping back. He jammed his big hands into the pockets of his sack-coat. "When did this happen between you and that crawling scum?"

Her teeth chattered, and for an instant she could not speak. Then she said in an unnatural voice: "When—you were—off on that business trip to Arizona. Right after we—got married."

"Where'd you meet him?"

"At a party."

"How long did you let him—" He choked and finished with a vile, blistering phrase.

"Two—two weeks. While you were away."

He slapped her again. She buried her reddened face in her hands. "In *my* apartment?" They could scarcely hear his voice.

"Y-yes . . ."

His hands bunched in his pockets. She looked up and at their concealed bulk with slow horror. "Did you write him letters?"

"One." She was whispering now.

"Love stuff?"

"Yes . . ."

"You changed maids while I was away, didn't you?"

"Yes." There was the strangest note in her whisper, and he looked at her sharply. Ellery's eyes narrowed.

Munn stepped back and strode about the grove like a leashed animal, his face a thundercloud. She watched him with almost panting anxiety. Then he paused.

"You're getting a break," he said with a snarl. "I'm not going to kill you, see? Not because I'm softenin', understand, but because there are too many bulls around here. If this was out West, or down in Rio, I'd have wrung your neck instead of slappin' you around like a nance."

"Oh, Joe, I didn't mean to do anything wrong—"

"Don't yap! I'm liable to change my mind. How much did that Marco bastard suck out of you?"

She shrank away. "D-don't hit me again, Joe! Most-most of that money you put . . . in my account."

"I gave you ten thousand dollars for spendin' money while I was away. How much did he get out of you?"

"Eight." She looked at her hands.

"Was it this gig that got us the invite to come up here to Spanish Cape?"

"Y-yes."

"I thought it was the bunk. What a sucker I've been!" he said bitterly. "I s'pose that Constable dame and this Godfrey woman were both in the same boat. Why the hell *else* should the fat one commit suicide? You didn't get that letter back from him, did you?"

"No. No, Joe, I didn't. He fooled me. He wouldn't sell. When we got here he asked me for—more. He wanted five thousand. I—I didn't have it. He said I should get it from you, or he'd turn the letter and—and the maid's statement over to you. I told him I didn't dare and he said I'd better. Then—somebody killed him."

"And a good clean job, too. Only thing is he didn't get the right kind of killin'. They handle those things better down in South America. They can do wonders with a knife. Did *you* bump him?"

"No, no, Joe, I swear I didn't! I—I'd thought about it, but—"

"Naw, I guess you didn't. You haven't got the guts of a louse when it comes to the real thing. Not that I give a damn. Hell, that crooked mouth o' yours couldn't tell the truth if it tried. Did you find that letter?"

"I looked for it, but"—she shivered—"it wasn't there."

"So it's on the level. Somebody beat you to it." Munn scowled thoughtfully. "That's why the Constable critter threw herself over that cliff. Couldn't stand the gaff."

"Joe. How did you—know?" whispered the blonde woman.

"Got a call a couple of hours ago from somebody with a voice that smelled bad. Told me all about it. Offered the letter and the maid's written story for sale. Ten grand. Sounded kind of hard up. I said I'd think it over—and here I am." He slowly tilted his wife's face upward. "Only that horse-thief doesn't know Joe Munn. He'd 'a' done better to go to you direct and have you steal some dough." His fingers were biting cruelly into her flesh. "Cele, you and I are through."

"Yes, Joe . . ."

"As soon as this murder stink blows over, I'm goin' to get me a divorce."

"Yes, Joe . . ."

"I'm goin' to take that jewelry away from you—all the stuff I gave you that you loved so damn much."

"Yes, Joe . . ."

"The La Salle roadster goes to the boneyard. I'm goin' to burn that mink coat you bought for winter and that you haven't worn. I'm goin' to make a bonfire out of every stitch of clothes you've got, Cele."

"Joe . . ."

"I'm goin' to take your last cent away from you, Cele. And d'ye know what I'm goin' to do after that?"

"Joe . . . !"

"I'm goin' to kick you out into the gutter where you can play in the manure with all the rest of the—" For some time his voice went dispassionately on, in a catalogue of American and Spanish obscenity that made the listening men writhe. And all the time Munn's fingers dug into those stricken cheeks, and his black eyes burned into hers.

Then he stopped and pushed her face back gently, and he turned on his heel and marched off down the path toward the house. She sat crouched on the bench, shivering as if she were cold. There were blackish welts on her face; they looked black in the moonlight. But in her attitude they sensed a queer and extraordinary gratification, as if she were also incredibly surprised to find herself still alive.

.   .   .   .

"My fault," frowned Ellery as they made their way rapidly but cautiously back toward the house in Munn's footsteps. "I should have anticipated that call. But so soon! How could I? The creature must be in the last stages of desperation."

"He'll call again," panted Moley. "Munn practically said so. Munn'll tell him to go to hell—*he* won't pay—but then maybe we'll get a line on where this guy is callin' from. For all we know it may be from the house itself. Those extensions—"

"No," snapped Ellery. "Let Munn alone. There's no reason to expect that the call will be any more traceable than the first. And we might spoil everything. We have one card left to play— if it's not too late." He quickened his stride.

"Mrs. Godfrey?" muttered Judge Macklin.

But Ellery was already lost under the Moorish archway.

XIII
FOUL DEEDS WILL RISE

He knocked insistently on the door of Mrs. Godfrey's sitting-room. To their astonishment it was opened by the millionaire himself, who thrust his ugly face pugnaciously up at them and scowled.

"Well?"

"We must speak with Mrs. Godfrey," said Ellery. "It's on a matter of the utmost importance—"

"These are my wife's private quarters," snapped Godfrey. "We've been hounded from pillar to post until my patience is exhausted. As far as I can see all you've accomplished is a lot of talking and running about. Can't this 'important' matter wait until morning?"

"No, it can't," said Inspector Moley rudely, although he had no idea what was in Ellery's mind; and he pushed past the millionaire into the room.

Stella Godfrey rose slowly from a wide couch. She was dressed in something both voluminous and thin, and her mules were on bare feet. She drew her négligé about her with a queer light in her eyes that puzzled them—a soft, dreamy, almost peaceful expression.

Godfrey marched himself in his brocaded dressing-gown to her side, standing a little before her in a protective attitude. The three men exchanged startled glances. Peace had come at last to the house of Godfrey—a peace and understanding that had not existed before. The little man, then, was even more amazingly unpredictable than his reputation . . . They could not help visualizing at this moment the convulsed fury on the face of Joseph Munn as he loomed over his wife in the gardens. Munn was the beast, the primitive man with a simple psychology—a savage sense of possession, a blind agony venting itself in the impulse to hurt, to batter, to crush when that sense of possession was outraged. But Walter Godfrey's was a civilized, almost an effete, psychology. For more than a score of years his wife, while faithful to her marriage vows, had virtually not existed for him; and yet when he discovered that at last she had violated those vows, he recognized her existence, apparently forgave her, and began once more to devote himself to her! Of course, it might have been the unfortunate fate of Laura Constable that drew him to her; the stout woman had been a tragic figure, even in silence, and her shocking end had cast a pall over the household. Or perhaps it was the proximity of danger, the overhanging threat of the law, the fusing property of common fears. At any rate, the Godfreys were as tenderly reconciled as the Munns were irremediably ruptured; that much was evident.

"Mrs. Constable," began Stella Godfrey; the shadows under her eyes had deepened. "She's—they've taken her away?"

"Yes," said Moley gravely. "She's committed suicide. At least you ought to be thankful that there's not another murder to complicate matters."

"How horrible," shuddered Mrs. Godfrey. "She was so—so *lonely*."

"Frightfully sorry to intrude at such a time," murmured Ellery. "Violence breeds violence, and no doubt you're all heartily sick of the whole lot of us. Nevertheless, Mrs. Godfrey, we have a certain duty to perform; and as a matter of fact the more co-operation we get from you the sooner you'll be rid of us."

"What do you mean?" she said slowly.

"We believe the time has come to put our cards plainly and openly on the table. Your silence has put us to considerable trouble, but fortunately we've been able to learn nearly all the truth in other ways. Please believe me when I say that it's no longer necessary for you to keep silent."

The dark woman's hand groped for her husband's. "All right," said Godfrey suddenly. "That's fair enough. How much do you know?"

"As far as Marco and Mrs. Godfrey are concerned," said Ellery regretfully, "everything."

Mrs. Godfrey put her other hand to her throat. "How did you—?"

"We overheard you confess your indiscretion to Mr. Godfrey. A painful breach of hospitality, but we had no choice."

Her eyes fell; dark color dyed her face. Godfrey said coldly: "We won't discuss the ethics of the situation. I hope this isn't for public consumption?"

"Reporters haven't been told anything," said Moley. "Come on, Mr. Queen. What's on your mind?"

"Naturally," said Ellery, "this is strictly among the five of us . . . Mrs. Godfrey."

"Yes?" Then she flung her head up and returned his gaze.

"That's better," smiled Ellery. "John Marco was blackmailing you, was he not?"

He watched husband and wife intently. If he had expected Mrs. Godfrey to react with fear, and the millionaire with shock or anger, he was disappointed. It was plain that since the confessional scene in the garden the night before the woman had unburdened herself completely. In a way, he was glad; it simplified matters.

She said: "Yes," at once, and Walter Godfrey snapped: "Mrs. Godfrey has told me everything, Queen. What's the point?"

"How many times did you pay him money, Mrs. Godfrey?"

"Five, six. I don't remember. First in the city, then here."

"Substantial sums?"

"Quite." They could hardly hear her voice.

"Come to the point!" rasped Walter Godfrey.

"But your personal bank-accounts are still not exhausted?"

"My wife has a considerable fortune in her own name! *Will* you come to the point?" shouted Godfrey.

"Please, Mr. Godfrey; I'm asking these questions out of no morbid curiosity, I assure you. Now, Mrs. Godfrey, have you ever told any one—excepting your husband, of course—of this connection between you and Marco, of the money you've been paying over to him?"

She whispered, "No."

"Just a minute, Mr. Queen." The Inspector leaned forward, and Ellery looked vaguely irritated. "Mrs. Godfrey, I want you to clear up that business of your visit to Marco's room Saturday night."

"Oh," she said faintly. "I—"

"Mrs. Godfrey has told me all about that," snarled Godfrey. "She went there to plead with him. Earlier in the day he had given her an ultimatum; she was to pay him a very large sum on Monday. She went to his room Saturday night to beg him to stop his demands. She was afraid she could not touch any more money without my discovering it."

"Yes," whispered the dark woman. "I—I almost went on my knees to him, begged him . . . He was cruel. Then I—I asked him about Mrs. Constable, Mrs. Munn. He told me to mind my own business. In *my* house!" Her face flamed. "And he called me . . . "

"Yes, yes," said Ellery hurriedly. "That's quite satisfactory, eh, Inspector? Now, Mrs. Godfrey, you're sure no one else knows that you've been paying Marco hush-money?"

"No one. Oh, I'm sure no one—"

Rosa said tightly from the open door to Mrs. Godfrey's boudoir: "I'm sorry, mother, I couldn't help hearing . . . That's not true, Mr. Queen. Mother isn't telling a lie; she just doesn't realize how transparent she's been. To everyone but father, who's been blind."

"Oh, Rosa," moaned Stella Godfrey, and the girl went swiftly to her and caught her in brown arms. Godfrey winced and muttered as he turned away a little.

"What is this?" exploded Moley. "We are learnin' things! You mean *you* knew all this was going on between your mother and Marco, Miss Godfrey?"

Rosa murmured: "There, darling," to her sobbing mother and said quietly: "Yes. No one had to tell me. I'm a woman, and I have eyes. Besides, mother is a poor actress. Every hour of torture she's gone through since that beast came up here I've shared in secret. Of course I knew. We all knew. I'm positive David saw it clearly. I think even Earle—Earle!—knows. And of course all the servants . . . Oh, mother, mother, why didn't you confide in me?"

"Then—but—" gasped Stella Godfrey, "that affair between you and—"

"Rosa!" cried the millionaire.

Rosa whispered: "I had to do something. Distract his attention. Anything . . . I didn't even dare confide in David, and I've always told him everything. It—it was just a job I felt I had to do alone. Oh, I know I was silly and wrong; I should have gone to mother, to father, made every one face the issue squarely. But like a fool I tried—"

"A gallant fool, at any rate," said Judge Macklin softly. His eyes were shining.

"Well!" said Ellery, drawing a deep breath. "I'll wager this will be comforting news to young Mr. Cort . . . To proceed, for we may not have as much time as we think. Mrs. Godfrey, have you been approached by a mysterious person since the murder of Marco—approached to pay further blackmail for the surrender of whatever tangible evidence Marco possessed of your relationship with him?"

"No!" She was obviously terrified at the mere thought, and she clung to Rosa's hand as if she were a child.

"What would you do if such a demand should suddenly be made of you?"

"Fight!" thundered Godfrey. "Fight it out." His sharp little eyes glittered. "Look here, Queen, you've something up your sleeve. I've been watching you, and I like your style. Is this a request for co-operation?"

"It is."

"Then you've got it. Stella, please calm yourself. We're going to be sensible about this. These people know more about such things than we do and I'm sure they'll be discreet."

"Excellent," said Ellery heartily. "Now, some one has secured possession of the proofs of Mrs. Godfrey's affair with the dead man. That person will unquestionably get in touch with you, Mrs. Godfrey, at any moment, demanding a lump settlement in return for those proofs. If you do exactly as we tell you, it's quite possible we may catch your blackmailer and clear away an important obstruction to the solution of this case."

"Very well, Mr. Queen! I'll do my best."

"That's the spirit; much better this way, you see, Mrs. Godfrey. There's a strength in unity that our blackmailer won't suspect—"

"Do you mean," demanded Godfrey shrewdly, "that this blackmailer is the murderer of Marco?"

Ellery smiled. "Inspector Moley believes—Well, one thing at a time, Mr. Godfrey. Now, Inspector, if you'll put that experienced brain of yours to work—"

.   .   .   .

By ten the next morning the anticipated telephone-call to Mrs. Godfrey had not come through. The three men haunted the house, increasingly anxious and silent. Ellery especially was worried. The blackmailer could not possibly have suspected a trap. The creature had called at ten-thirty the previous night, asking for Munn; and Munn, apparently believing himself secure from surveillance, had briefly damned him and hung up. The detective eavesdropping on Moley's order at the switchboard—despite Ellery's admonition—had been unable to trace the call. But Ellery knew that nothing the detective had done could have made the caller suspect he was being overheard.

Some of the mystery was dispelled with the arrival of the morning newspapers. The local county sheet and the leading tabloid of the city of Maartens both roared headlines which told substantially the same story: the story of Cecilia Ball Munn's illicit affair with the late John Marco. Since both papers were under the same ownership, both printed identical proofs—letters and photographs.

"Should have anticipated this, too," muttered Ellery, throwing the papers down in disgust. "Of course that worm wouldn't have tried the same stunt twice. This time the proofs were sent to the papers. I must be getting rusty."

"Not taking the chance," said the Judge thoughtfully, "that the thing would be hushed up again. Unquestionably his chief motive in sending the Constable documents to Moley and now the Munn documents to the press was not so much the punishment of Mrs. Constable and the Munns as a warning to Mrs. Godfrey. I should say the call will come soon."

"Sooner the better. I'm getting fidgety. Poor Moley! He'll never emerge alive from that press conference. Roush tells me they're all on his neck." The editorial pages of both papers had speculated openly on the possibility that at last the "dilatory" police had found the motive for Marco's murder. The suicide of Mrs. Constable was also played up as the alternative theory— the tacit confession of a murderess. But of official confirmation there was no sign. Apparently the Inspector had thought better of his "solution." With the Munns now the center of interest, Moley had them whisked out of sight and range of the reporters—the woman on the verge of hysteria, the man wary, silent, and dangerous.

The Inspector stamped back, weariness and rage battling for possession of his face. Without speech the three men retired to the alcove in which the switchboard stood. There was nothing to do but wait. The Godfreys were in Mrs. Godfrey's boudoir; a detective sat at the board with earphones clamped about his head and a stenographic notebook open before him. Extra 'phones had been plugged into the main line; there were earpieces about the heads of all of them.

The alarm buzzed in their ears at ten-forty-five. At the first syllable Ellery nodded eagerly. There was no mistaking that queer, muffled voice. The voice asked for Mrs. Godfrey; the detective calmly connected the two, picked up his pencil, and waited. Ellery muttered a prayer that the woman would play her part well.

He might have spared his fears. She acted the role of stupefied, submissive victim to perfection—almost with enthusiasm, born out of the surging relief in her heart.

"Mrs. Stella Godfrey?" said the voice with an undercurrent of urgency.

"Yes?"

"Are you alone?"

"Alo—Who are you? What do you want?"

"Are you?"

"Yes. Who—"

"Never mind. I'm in a hurry. Did you see this morning's *Maartens Daily News*?"

"Yes! But—"

"Did you read about Cecilia Munn and John Marco?"

Stella Godfrey was silent. When she replied her voice had become cracked and weary. "Yes. What do you want?"

The voice recounted a list of facts, at each one of which Stella Godfrey moaned . . . It had become strident now, insistent, almost hysterical. It was the oddest thing, and both Inspector Moley and Judge Macklin looked puzzled. "Do you want me to send those things to the papers?"

THE SPANISH CAPE MYSTERY · 261

"No, oh, no!"

"Or to your husband?"

"No! I'll do anything if you won't—"

"That's better. You're acting sensibly now. I want twenty-five thousand dollars, Mrs. Godfrey. You're a wealthy woman. You can pay it out of your own pocket, and no one will be the wiser."

"But I've already paid—so many times—"

"This will be the last time," said the voice eagerly. "I'm not a fool, like Marco. I'm playing square on this. You pay me that money and you'll have the photographs and documents back in the next mail. I mean this. I'm not double-crossing you—"

"I'll do anything to get them back," sobbed Mrs. Godfrey. "Ever since they . . . oh, my life's been miserable!"

"Sure it has," said the voice; it was stronger now, confident. "I understand just how you feel. Marco was a rotten dog and he got what he deserved. But I'm up against it and need money . . . How soon can you get hold of the twenty-five thousand?"

"Today!" she cried. "I can't give it to you in cash, but I have in my private safe here . . . "

"Oh," said the voice strangely. "That's no good, Mrs. God-frey. I want cash in small bills. I'm not taking any chances—"

"But it's as good as cash!" Mrs. Godfrey had been instructed in this very carefully. "They're negotiable bonds. Besides, how could I get cash in small bills? It would be suspicious. The police are all over my house. I cannot even leave the grounds."

"There's something in that," muttered the voice. "But if you think you're going to put one over on me—"

"And have the police find out? Do you think I'm insane? The last thing I want is for any one to—to know. Besides, you don't have to turn the—the proofs over to me until you've cashed the bonds. Oh, please—give me my chance!"

The caller kept quiet, apparently weighing the risks. Then the voice said with a note of desperation: "All right. Let's leave it that way. I wouldn't want you to come yourself anyway. And I can't come to you—not with all those police at your place. Can you mail me the bonds? Can you mail a package without having them find out?"

"I'm sure I can. Oh, I know I can! Where—"

"Don't write this down. You don't want anybody finding a note. Remember this address." The voice stopped, and for a moment the house of Godfrey was a tomb. "J. P. Marcus, care of General Delivery, Central Post Office, Maartens. Repeat that." Mrs. Godfrey in a trembling voice obeyed. "Right. Send the bonds to that address. Use plain brown paper, sealed. Send it first-class mail. Right away. If you do it now, it should get to the Maartens post office before closing tonight."

"Yes. Yes!"

"Remember, if you pull a trick those photos and things will be in the hands of the *Maartens Daily News* editor, and nothing you can do will stop that story from being smeared all over the front page."

"No! I'm not—"

"See that you don't. If you're on the level with me, you'll have the proofs back in a few days. As soon as I can cash the bonds."

There was a click and the line went dead. Upstairs, Mrs. Godfrey swayed into the arms of her husband, whose face was strangely tender. At the switchboard the four men removed their earphones and looked at one another.

"Well," said Moley in a hushed voice, "this looks good, Mr. Queen."

Mr. Queen said nothing for some time; he was frowning and

tapping his lips with the edge of his *pince-nez*. Then he murmured: "I believe we should enlist the services of Tiller."

"Tiller!"

"Oh, it's almost mandatory, if this turns out as I anticipate it will. If it doesn't there's no harm done. You needn't tell him anything vital. Tiller's one of those rare birds of passage who can exist on the minutest crumb of information."

Moley stroked his chin. "Well, this is your party, and I s'pose you know what you're doing." He gave brusque orders and went upstairs to supervise the now all-important mailing operation.

. . . .

"There's only one thing that worries me," confessed Inspector Moley as they sat back in the tonneau of the big black police car late that afternoon speeding toward Maartens. He glanced at the neat, bowler-topped head of Tiller, who was seated beside the driver before them, and instinctively lowered his voice. "And that's the photos, deposition, letters, or whatever the hell this blackmailer's got on Mrs. G. How do we know he hasn't cached 'em somewhere? We may nab him, but then the proofs may slip through our fingers."

"Conscience?" said Ellery over his cigaret. "I thought, Inspector, that you rather anticipated catching Marco's murderer this afternoon. On the plausible theory that—if he was killed for the papers—the present possessor of the papers is the murderer. Don't tell me you're suddenly distressed about the feelings of our hostess."

"Well," grumbled Moley, "it *is* a nasty mess for her, and she's a nice woman underneath. I wouldn't want to give her any unnecessary heartache."

"There isn't much danger of missing those documents,"

said Judge Macklin, shaking his head. "They're much too valuable to that creature to leave lying about. Besides, he knows that if this is a trap—which I greatly doubt, judging from his reactions over the telephone—he has no hope of collecting, anyway. He's utterly desperate now, now that the Constable and Munn attacks failed. No, no, that threat was for effect only. If you catch him, Inspector, you'll find the documents on his person."

They had slipped out of Spanish Cape unobtrusively, on the Inspector's insistence, and at his orders all vigilance there had apparently been relaxed. A drab-colored but powerful car followed them, filled with men in plain clothes, but another just as drab and quite as powerful lurked in the main road outside Spanish Cape, ready for any contingency. Conversations with the Maartens police had insured instant surveillance of the general post-office building in that city. The clerks had been put on their guard and carefully instructed. The package, filled with dummy bonds, but externally faithful to the blackmailer's instructions, had been ostentatiously posted in Wye, the nearest town, with other mail by a servant, and permitted to go through the post in the ordinary course. Inspector Moley had left nothing whatever to chance.

The two cars unloaded their passengers several blocks from the Maartens post office. The detectives in the second car made their way singly toward the big marble building, in ten minutes surrounding it with an invisible cordon. Inspector Moley and his companions entered the building secretly through a rear entrance. Tiller, his bright little eyes inquisitive, was stationed in a corner of the large general-delivery cage and given precise instructions.

"The instant you see any one you *recognize*," concluded Ellery, "give the clerk the signal. He'll do the rest. Or give it to us. The clerk will know from the name."

"Yes, sir," murmured Tiller. "You mean some one connected with the case?"

"Verily. And don't slip, Tiller; not if you value your life. Inspector Moley is setting enormous store by this afternoon. Keep out of sight but where you can see the faces of the people coming to the window. Our quarry might run like hell on seeing you."

"You may rely on me," said Tiller gravely; and he took up his position in the cage. Moley, the Judge, and Ellery concealed themselves behind a partition near a door, set chairs for themselves, and kept their eyes glued upon three unused slots in the wall. Several detectives were stationed in the large room, scribbling at the tables, making out interminable and meaningless money-order blanks. Occasionally one of them walked out into the street, to be replaced instantly by another detective from the outside. Moley inspected his forces with a critical eye, but he could find nothing wrong. The trap was set, it looked perfectly innocent, and there was nothing to do but wait for the victim.

They waited for an hour and twenty minutes, growing tenser with each jerk of the big clock's hand on the wall. The ordinary business of the post office went on, people passed in and out, stamps and money-orders and parcels passed through the windows, the Postal Savings window was in constant use, long queues of customers formed and vanished and formed again.

Moley's cheroot had long since gone out; it stuck between his jaws like a snag at low tide. There was no conversation.

And yet, when the moment came, for all their tension and alertness it almost passed them by. The deception was so nearly perfect. Had it not been for the clerk and Tiller—precautions for which Inspector Moley was heartily thankful afterward—precious time would have been wasted during which considerable confusion might have ensued, permitting the intended victim's escape.

At only ten minutes before the closing hour, when the post office was thronged with homegoing business people, a small thin dark-faced man walked in from the street and made for the General Delivery window. He was dressed quietly; he had a tiny black mustache and a mole under his left eye on the most prominent part of his cheekbone. He took his place in the long line and moved up from time to time like a mouse. If there was anything noticeable about him it was his gait: he walked with a slight hip-swaying motion that was very odd. But otherwise he was a colorless creature who would be swallowed in any crowd.

When the man before him had stepped away from the window he advanced, placed one small dark hand on the ledge, and said in a husky voice, as if he had a cold in his throat: "Anything for J. P. Marcus?"

The three men, peering through the slots, saw the clerk scratch his right ear and turn aside. At the same instant Tiller's head appeared from around the corner and he whispered: "No mistake. Disguised, sir! But that's the one."

The clerk's signal and Tiller's whisper brought them to their feet, galvanized. Moley strode to the door, whipped it open noiselessly, and raised his right arm. He was visible to passersby in the street through the huge plate-glass windows. At the same instant the clerk turned back to the window with a small flattish package done up in brown paper, addressed in ink and its stamps properly canceled. The small dark man grasped the package in his thin hand and, stepping aside from the window, half-turned.

He looked up, belatedly warned by a sixth sense, to find himself in a room filled with silent, staring people. He was surrounded by a solid wall of grim men, slowly closing in on him. A curious pallor spread over his face.

"What's in that package, Mr. Marcus?" asked Inspector Moley pleasantly, clamping his left hand on the man's shoulder, the right buried deep in his coat-pocket.

The brown parcel slipped out of the thin hand and fell to the floor. The dark man swayed and followed it, crumpling almost in sections. Moley stooped swiftly and slapped at the breast-pocket. A comical expression of stupefaction spread over his face.

"Why, he's fainted!" exclaimed Judge Macklin.

"Not 'he,' sir," said the soft voice of Tiller from behind. "The mustache is false. In a manner of speaking, sir, he's a she—as I believe the Inspector, sir, has just discovered." He tittered decorously behind his hand.

"A woman?" gasped the Judge.

"Had me fooled, all right," said the Inspector triumphantly, rising. "But here's the goods in her pocket, by God. We've done it!"

"Good make-up," muttered Ellery. "But the characteristic movement of the hips gave her away. This is Mrs. Godfrey's ex-maid, Tiller?"

"I knew her by the mole, sir," murmured Tiller. "Dear, dear, how easily some persons stoop to sin! Yes, sir, this is Pitts."

XIV
EXTRAORDINARY CONFESSIONS
OF A SELF-MADE MAID

AT POLICE headquarters in Poinsett, for the first time in days, there was jubilation. The place buzzed with rumors, reporters clamored at deaf doors, members of other departments looked in upon Inspector Moley's office where a police surgeon was ministering to the captured woman, and telephones clanged in a mad chorus. The Inspector had brushed aside a sheaf of reports which Ellery, who was the calmest person in the building, took the liberty of examining, but they contained nothing new: there was still no trace of Hollis Waring's cruiser, or Captain Kidd and David Kummer, or—Ellery chuckled—of Pitts; and nothing to report on Lucius Penfield, despite the most careful investigation by detectives working in shifts.

When a semblance of order had been restored to the office and the surgeon had signified by an elevation of his brows that the woman was in condition to be examined, they turned their undivided attention upon her.

She was seated in a big leather chair, tightly grasping the arms. Her skin was gray and muddy. She had cropped her black curly hair close, man-fashion, but with her hat off and the false mustache removed she was very much the woman—a small and frightened woman with bleak brown eyes and little, knife-like features. She might have been thirty, or a year or so older. Even now there was a pixy beauty about her, although it was essentially hard and soiled.

"Well, Pitts, old gal," began Moley genially, "you're caught good and proper, aren't you?" She said nothing, stared at the floor. "You don't deny that you're Pitts, Mrs. Walter Godfrey's maid, do you?" A police stenographer was sitting at the desk, book open.

"No," she replied in the same husky tones they had heard in the post office, "I don't deny it."

"Sensible! You were the one who telephoned Mrs. Laura Constable at Spanish Cape? Mr. Munn twice? And this morning Mrs. Godfrey?"

"So you tapped the wire." She laughed. "Serves me right. Yes, I was the one."

"You sent the Constable papers and things to me by boy from Maartens?"

"Yes."

"You sent that stuff about Mrs. Munn to the papers?"

"Yes."

"That's the girl. We'll get along fine. Now I want you to tell me what happened last Saturday night and the early hours of Sunday morning. Everything."

For the first time she raised her bleak brown eyes to his. "And suppose I won't?"

Moley's jaw hardened. "Oh, but you will. You will, young lady. You're in a tough spot. Do you know what the rap for blackmail is in this State?"

"I'm very much afraid," said Ellery gently, "that Miss

Pitts is considerably more concerned with the rap for murder, Inspector."

Moley glared at him. The woman moistened her dry lips and her eyes slithered to Ellery's face and down to the floor. "Let me handle this, Mr. Queen," said Moley angrily.

"I'm sorry," murmured Ellery, lighting a cigaret. "But perhaps I'd better clarify the situation for Miss Pitts. I'm sure she'll see the futility of silence.

"I might begin by pointing out that I was morally certain Mrs. Godfrey's vanished maid was your blackmailer, Inspector. It struck me when I began to realize that there was a too felicitous juxtaposition of coincidences. Pitts was seen with John Marco—by Jorum—some time during the general period of Marco's murder. Shortly before that some one had stolen into Marco's room, found the fragments of the false note making an appointment on the terrace, pieced them together. Coincidence? When Mrs. Godfrey rang for her maid directly after she returned to her rooms Saturday night, the maid did not respond for a long time. When she did, she pleaded illness; she seemed excited. Coincidence? This maid vanished some time during the murder-period. She took Marco's car for her getaway. Coincidence?" The woman's eyes flickered. "The trail to Pitts ended at Maartens. The packet of proofs sent to you, Inspector, was sent from Maartens. Coincidence? The whole blackmailing business began, as a matter of fact, directly after the disappearance of Pitts. Coincidence? John Marco had recommended Pitts to Mrs. Godfrey when Mrs. Godfrey's former maid, for no apparent reason, suddenly left. Coincidence? But most significant of all—in all three cases involving Mrs. Constable, Mrs. Munn, and Mrs. Godfrey, one of the vital pieces of evidence against the unfortunate women was . . . *the signed deposition of a lady's maid!*"

Ellery smiled sadly. "Coincidence? Most improbable. I was sure that Pitts was the blackmailer."

"You think you're smart, don't you?" snarled the woman, twisting her thin lips.

"I have an appreciation," said Ellery with a little bow, "of my own talents, Miss Pitts. And not only that, but I was also sure that I had struck a fundamental connection between Pitts and Marco. You yourself, Inspector, told me the other day that your friend Leonard of the New York private agency had scented the possibility of an accomplice working with Marco in snaring his victims. A prying lady's-maid in three separate cases willing to testify against her mistress—naturally the different names signed to the depositions are to be construed as merely aliases— fitted perfectly with the conception of such an accomplice as a man like Marco would employ. To visualize Mrs. Godfrey's blackmailing maid as this accomplice required no great effort of the imagination."

"I want a lawyer," said Pitts suddenly, half-rising.

"Sit down," began Moley with a scowl.

"Certainly you're entitled to the constitutional protection of legal advice, Miss Pitts," nodded Ellery. "Have you any particular attorney in mind?"

Hope leaped into her eyes. "Yes! Lucius Penfield of New York!"

There was a shocked silence. Ellery spread his hands. "And there you are. What further proof could any one ask, Inspector? John Marco's rascally attorney is sought by Pitts. Another coincidence?"

The woman sank back, visibly alarmed, biting her lips. "I—"

"The game's up, my dear," said Ellery in a kindly tone. "You may as well make a clean breast of everything."

She kept gnawing her lips; there was a desperately calculating glitter in her brown eyes. Then she said: "I'll make a deal with you."

"Why, you—" Moley exploded.

Ellery placed his arm across the Inspector's chest. "And why not, indeed? We may as well act like business people. At least there's no harm in listening to a proposal."

"Listen," she said eagerly. "I'm stuck and I know it. But I can still be damned nasty. You don't want this Godfrey scandal to come out, do you?"

"Well?" barked Moley.

"Well, you treat me right and I won't talk. You can't keep me from talking if I have a mind to! I'll do it direct to the newspaper boys, or through my lawyer. You can't stop me. Give me a break and I'll keep quiet."

Moley eyed her sourly, glanced at Ellery, rubbed his lips and paced up and down for a moment. "Well," he growled at last, "I've got nothin' against the Godfreys and I wouldn't want to see them get hurt. But I'm not promising, d'ye hear? I'll speak to the D.A. and see if we can't get a lesser plea, or something."

"If," prompted Ellery gently, "you come, as they say, clean."

"All right," she muttered. There was a sullen look on her sharp face. "I don't know how you knew all that, but it's right. I was planted by Marco first with Mrs. Constable, then with Mrs. Munn, then with Mrs. Godfrey. I worked the flash-photo on the fat dame in Atlantic City during the night. I got all the dope, seeing and listening. When Mrs. Constable and Mrs. Munn came up to Spanish Cape, they recognized me at once. They knew what Mrs. Godfrey was in for, I guess, but Marco told 'em to keep their traps shut about me. I suppose they're still afraid to spill it. Now I've told you the whole thing. For God's sake, I want Luke Penfield!"

The Inspector's eyes were shining. But he said shrewdly: "Just a tool, hey? Turned the tables on your boss. Stole those papers and things from his room early Sunday mornin' and lit out to make a little hay for yourself. Is that it?"

The woman's dark face contorted with passion. "And why not?" she screamed. "Sure I did! They were as much mine as his! I always *played* stooge to him, but I held the whip-hand, and damn well he knew it!" She paused for breath, and then cried with a morbid sort of triumph: "Tool, eh? Like hell I was. I was his *wife!*"

.   .   .   .

They were stunned. Marco's wife! The full extent of the man's perfidy spread itself before them on the instant. They all thought with nausea of the danger Rosa Godfrey had escaped, and for the dozenth time there passed through their minds a fierce satisfaction that the man was gone, a menace removed from the world.

"His wife, huh?" said Moley thickly when he had recovered sufficiently to speak.

"Yes, his wife," she said in a bitter voice. "Not much to look at now, maybe, but once I had my girlish figure and a face that wouldn't stop a clock. We were married four years ago in Miami. He was down there playing gig to some millionaire widow and I was on the make myself. We hooked up right away. He liked my style. He liked my style so damned well I made him marry me to enjoy it. I guess I'm the only woman he's ever met that got the best of him . . . We've played lots of games since. This lady's-maid racket was his idea, a recent development. I never did like it. But we made some dough . . . " They let her talk. She was gripping the arms of the chair now, staring into space. "One little deal, then we'd knock off for a vacation and shoot the works. Then another deal when the money was gone. That's the way it went. With Marco dead I was in a hole. No funds, and a tight spot. I have to live, don't I? If he hadn't been so lousy greedy he'd probably be alive today. Whoever bumped him off did a good job. God knows I'm no angel, but he was the worst skunk ever lived. I'd come to hate his guts. And, low as I am, no woman likes to see her own husband making love to other women. He always said it was business, but he enjoyed himself, damn his soul!"

Moley went to her, stood before her. She broke off and looked up at him, startled. "So you twisted that wire around his neck," he said harshly, "to get rid of him and cash in for yourself!"

She sprang to her feet, shrieking. "I didn't! I knew you'd think that! That was what I was afraid of. I couldn't hope to make a dumb cop understand." She seized Ellery's arm, clawing at his sleeve. "Listen. You seem to have a brain. Tell him he's wrong! I may have wanted to—to kill Marco, but I didn't. I swear I didn't! But I couldn't stay there and be found out. If I'd forgotten about money I'd have made it. Oh, I don't know what I'm saying . . . "

She was utterly unnerved. Ellery took her gently by the arm and forced her back in the chair. She cowered in a corner, sobbing. "I think," he said in a soothing voice, "we can guarantee you at least a fighting chance to prove your innocence—if you *are* innocent, Mrs. Marco."

"Oh, I am . . . "

"That remains to be seen. What made you go to his room Saturday night?"

She said in the choked muffled voice they had heard over the telephone: "I saw Mrs. Godfrey go in. Maybe I was a little jealous. And then, too, I hadn't had a chance to talk to—to Marco in private for a couple of days and I wanted to know how he was making out with the three women. He was supposed to be all set for the big clean-up."

She paused, sniffling, and the Judge muttered to Ellery: "Apparently she didn't know of Marco's intention to run away with Rosa. Could he really have been contemplating bigamy? The scoundrel!"

"I don't think so," said Ellery *sotto voce*. "He wouldn't have taken the risk. Marriage wasn't what he was thinking of . . . Go on, Mrs. Marco!"

"Anyway, I watched and a few minutes before one I saw Mrs. Godfrey come out." She took her hands from her face and sat up, staring dully at Ellery. "I was just going to slip into his room when I saw him come out. I was afraid to stop him, talk to him, because I thought some one might see us. He looked as if he were going somewhere. All dressed up. I couldn't understand it . . . I went into his room to wait for him to come back. Then I saw the scraps of paper in the fireplace and fished them out. I went into the bathroom with them so that if somebody came in I wouldn't be caught. When I read what the note said I guess I saw red. I hadn't known anything about this Rosa girl. There wasn't supposed to be any monkey-business with her. I saw that he must have been mixing pleasure with business . . . " Her hands clenched.

"Yes?" said Inspector Moley with sudden kindliness. "We understand how you must have felt, catching him two-timin' you. So you went down to the terrace to spy on him, hey?"

"Yes," she whispered. "After I got Mrs. Godfrey to let me

off—I said I was sick. I wanted to see with my own eyes. The house was quiet—it was pretty late . . . "

"What time was this?"

"When I got down to the terrace near the head of the steps it was just about twenty minutes after one. I—" She gulped. "He was dead. I saw that right away. He was sitting so still, with his back to me. The moon was shining on his neck; I saw the red line below his hair." She shuddered. "But it wasn't that, it wasn't that. He—he was naked. *Naked!*" She began to sob again.

Ellery started. "What do you mean? When you saw him? Quick! What do you mean?"

But she continued as if she had not heard. "I went down the steps to the terrace, to the table. I guess I was in a daze. I seem to remember that there was a sheet of paper in front of him and that one of his hands hung down toward the floor with a pen in it. But I was too scared to—to . . . Then all of a sudden I heard footsteps. On the gravel coming down. I saw what I was in for. I couldn't get out without being seen by whoever was coming toward the terrace. I had to think fast. In the moonlight I had a chance . . . I put the stick in' the other hand and the hat on his head, and I put the cloak around his shoulders and snapped it at the neck, to hide the—the red line." She was gazing with fascinated horror through them at the moonlit scene. "The cloak would hide the fact that he was undressed, I was sure. I waited until the footsteps were near and then I began to talk—anything that came to my head—tried to make believe he'd made a pass at me and acting modest and sore. I knew whoever it was was listening. Then I ran up the steps . . . I saw him hiding near the head of the stairs but made out I didn't notice. It was Jorum. I knew Jorum wouldn't go down after hearing that, but I wasn't taking any chances. I ran back to the house, got the bundle of papers and photos out of Marco's room—he kept them hidden in the wardrobe closet—went to my own room, packed my bag and things, and then I stole down to the garage and took his car and went away. I had a key to the ignition. Why shouldn't I have? I was . . . his wife, wasn't I?"

"If you were innocent," said Moley sternly, "didn't you realize that by running away you were making it look bad for yourself?"

"I had to get away," she said desperately. "I was afraid they'd find out. I went right away because if Jorum saw he was dead he'd have raised an alarm and I wouldn't have been able to get out of the grounds. And then there were those papers."

Moley scratched his ear, frowning. There was the unmistakable ring of truth in the woman's voice and story. True, he had an excellent circumstantial case against her, the stenographic report of her story safely made, but . . . He glanced at Ellery's face as that lean young man turned away for an instant, and he was startled.

Ellery whirled about, sprang to the woman's side, grasped her arm. She cried out, shrinking back. "You've *got* to be more explicit!" he said fiercely. "You say that when you first saw Marco on the terrace he was stark naked?"

"Yes," she quavered.

"Where was his hat?"

"Why, on the table. His cane, too."

"And the cloak?"

"Cloak?" The woman's eyes widened with genuine surprise. "I didn't say his cape was on the table. Or did I? I'm so mixed up—"

Ellery slowly released her arm. There was an agony of hope in his gray eyes. "Oh, it wasn't on the table," he said in a strangled voice. "Where was it—on the flagstones of the terrace? But of course. That's where it must have been when the murderer threw it down to undress him." His eyes were glassy now, glaring in their concentration on her lips.

She was bewildered. "No. It wasn't on the terrace at all. I mean—what's all the fuss about? Oh, I didn't mean anything by it! I didn't mean anything! I see you think—" Her voice had risen to a scream again.

"Never mind what I think," panted Ellery, gripping her arm again. He shook her so violently that she gasped and her head flopped back. "Tell me! Where was it? How did it get there?"

"When I read the note upstairs, in his room," she muttered, her face grayer than before, "I didn't want to take the chance of going down to the terrace empty-handed. I wanted an excuse for being there if somebody caught me. I saw his cape lying on the bed; he'd forgotten to take it with him, I guess." Something hotly fierce flared into Ellery's face. "I picked it up and took it down with me, to say that he had sent me for it—if somebody should stop me. Nobody did. When I saw he was naked I was—was glad I had it to put over him . . . "

But Ellery had flung her arm from him and stepped back, drawing a breath from his toes. Moley, the Judge, the stenographer looked at him with puzzled, almost frightened, eyes. He seemed to be swelling, to have filled out suddenly.

He stood very still, gazing over the woman's head at the blank wall of Moley's office. Then, very slowly, his fingers dipped into his pocket and came out with a cigaret.

"The cape," he said, so low they barely heard the words. "Yes, the cape . . . The missing piece." He crushed the cigaret in his hand and spun about, eyes shining madly. "By God, gentlemen, I've got it!"

CHALLENGE
TO THE READER

"In the mountains of truth," quoth Nietzsche, "you never climb in vain."

No one outside the realm of fairy tales ever scaled a mountain by standing at its foot and wishing himself over its crest. This is a hard world, and in it achievement requires effort. It has always been my feeling that to garner the fullest enjoyment from detective fiction the reader must to some degree endeavor to retrace the detective's steps. The more painstakingly the trail back is scrutinized, the closer the reader comes to the ultimate truth, and the deeper his enjoyment is apt to be.

For years now I have been challenging my readers to solve my cases by the exercise of close observation, the application of logic to the winnowed facts, and a final correlation of the individual conclusions. I have been encouraged to persist in this practice by the warm testimonials of many correspondents. To those of you who have never tried it, I earnestly recommend that you do. You may run afoul of a snag somewhere along the line, or you may indeed after much thinking get nowhere at all; but it has been the experience of thousands that, successful or not, the effort is amply repaid by the heightened pleasure.

Technically there are no snags. The facts are all here at this point in the story of John Marco's death. Can you put them together and logically place your finger on the one and only possible murderer?

—ELLERY QUEEN

XV
OF AN INTERRUPTION

THE DRIVE back to Spanish Cape was accomplished in an electric silence. Mr. Ellery Queen sat hunched in the tonneau of the big car, nursing his lower lip and buried miles deep in thought. Judge Macklin glanced at his frowning face from time to time with curiosity; and Tiller, in the front seat, could not refrain from turning his head at periodic intervals. No one said anything, and the only sound was the rather menacing whine of a rising wind.

Ellery had been impervious to all of Inspector Moley's frantic questions. The poor Inspector was beside himself with nervous excitement.

"Too soon," Ellery had said. "I'm sorry if I've given you the impression that I had the whole answer to this extraordinary problem. That story Pitts told about Marco's cape . . . it points the way. Very definitely. I see now where I was wrong, and where the murderer's plan went awry; and in this case that's more than half the battle. But I haven't thought it out, Inspector. I need time. Time to think."

They had left Moley in a state of apoplectic frenzy, with an exhausted and bewildered prisoner on his hands. Mrs. Marco,

alias Pitts, was formally booked on a charge of attempted blackmail and placed in the county jail. There had been a sad inter-
lude when two young people, their eyes swollen with weeping,
had arrived to visit the county morgue and take legal possession
of the body of Laura Constable. Detectives and reporters had
harried Ellery with questions. But in the midst of pandemonium he maintained unsmiling peace, and at the first opportunity
they had slipped out of Poinsett.

It was only when the car swung off the main highway at
Harry Stebbins's establishment and entered the park-road leading to Spanish Cape that the silence was broken.

"Bad storm comin' up," remarked the police driver uneasily.
"I've seen these winds up here before. Look at that sky."

The trees of the park were in violent agitation, swaying to a
steadily increasing gale. They emerged from the parkland and
began to traverse the neck of rock from the mainland, and they
saw the evening sky. It was the color of smudgy lead and was
filled with huge swollen black clouds racing toward them from
the heaving horizon. On the neck they took the full force of the
wind and the driver wrestled with the wheel to keep the car on
the road.

But no one replied, and they reached the shelter of the cliff-
walls on the Cape without mishap.

Ellery leaned forward and tapped the driver's shoulder.
"Stop, please. Before you climb to the house." The car braked to
a halt.

"Where on earth—" began the Judge, raising his shaggy
brows.

Ellery opened the door and stepped out into the road. His
forehead was still wrinkled, but there was a feverish gleam in his
eye. "I'll be up soon. I think I've got my canines into this thing

properly. On the scene itself . . . " He shrugged, smiled in adieu, and sauntered down the path leading toward the terrace.

The sky was rapidly darkening. A flash of lightning lit up the path; they saw Ellery reach the head of the terrace stairs and begin the descent.

Judge Macklin sighed. "We may as well go up to the house. It will rain soon, and he'll come running back in a hurry."

They drove on up to the house.

·   ·   ·   ·   ·   ·   ·

Mr. Ellery Queen slowly descended the terrace steps, paused on the gay flags for a moment, and then went to the round table at which John Marco had died and sat down. Buried between sheer walls of stone at a depth of more than forty feet, the terrace was a haven from the worst of the wind; and he relaxed comfortably in the chair, slumping on his spine in his favorite position for reflection, and staring out through the entrance to the Cove at the sea. Within the limits of his vision there was no craft to be seen; the storm had made them scurry for shelter. The sea boiled now in the Cove, raising a constant spume.

It faded before his eyes as he looked at more distant and immaterial things.

The terrace grew darker as he sat there; until finally, aroused by the blackness, he sighed and rose and went to the stairhead and switched on the overhead lamp. The umbrellas were swaying and fluttering. He sat down again and took up paper and pen and dipped the pen in the inkpot and began to write.

·   ·   ·   ·   ·   ·   ·

A gigantic drop, from the sound it made, plopped on one of the umbrellas. He stopped writing and twisted about. Then, with a speculative look in his eye, he rose and went to the enormous Spanish jar standing to the left of the lowest step and peered around it. After a moment he stepped behind it. Nodding, he came out and repeated the operation with the jar standing at the right of the stairs. Finally he returned to the table, sat down, and with his hair blowing about in the wind resumed his writing.

He wrote for a long time. The drops increased in size, ferocity, and frequency. One spattered on the sheet before him, blotting a word. He wrote more rapidly.

He finished with the first gust of solid rain. Stuffing the sheets in his pocket he jumped up, turned out the light, and hurried up the path toward the stone steps ascending to the plateau on which the house stood. By the time he had reached the shelter of the patio his shoulders were sopping.

The portly butler met him in the main corridor. "Dinner has been kept hot for you, sir. Mrs. Godfrey has ordered—"

"Thank you," Ellery replied absently, and waved his hand. He hurried toward the alcove where the switchboard stood, dialled a number, and waited with a serene expression.

"Inspector Moley . . . Ah, Inspector, I thought I'd catch you in . . . Yes. Quite. In fact, if you'll come down to Spanish Cape at once I think we can settle this sad business to your satisfaction tonight!"

·   ·   ·   ·   ·   ·   ·

The insular interior of the living-room glowed with isolated lights. Outside in the patio, on the roofs, rain hissed and roared. A furious wind battered the windows. Even above the splash of the rain they could hear the trumpeting surf as it lashed at the cliffs of the Cape. It was a good night to be indoors and they all glanced gratefully at the blaze in the fireplace.

"We're all here," said Ellery in a soft voice, "but Tiller. I especially want Tiller. If you don't mind, Mr. Godfrey? He's been the one bright spot in this case and he deserves a reward."

Walter Godfrey shrugged; he was for the first time dressed in something like a decent costume, as if with the recovery of his wife he had also recovered his sense of social responsibility. He tugged a bell-rope, said something curtly to the butler, and sank back beside Stella Godfrey.

They were all there—the three Godfreys, the two Munns, and Earle Cort. Judge Macklin and Inspector Moley, curiously subdued, sat a little away from the others; and it was significant that, although nothing of the sort had been discussed, Moley's chair was nearest the door. Of the nine the only one who looked happy was young Cort. There was an almost fatuous expression of contentment on his face as he squatted at the knees of Rosa Godfrey; and from the dreamy look in Rosa's blue eyes it was evident that the shadow of John Marco had lifted from both of them. Munn was smoking a long brown cigar, tearing it with his teeth; and Mrs. Munn was deathly quiet. Stella Godfrey, calm but taut, twisted her handkerchief in her hands; and the little millionaire was watchful. The atmosphere was distinctly oppressive.

"You called for me, sir?" asked Tiller politely, from the door.

"Come in, come in, Tiller," said Ellery. "Sit down; this is no time to stand on ceremony." Tiller rather timidly sat down on the very edge of a chair, to the rear, glancing at Godfrey's face; but the millionaire was gazing at Ellery with a cautious alertness.

Ellery stepped to the fireplace and set his back against it so that his face was in shadow and his figure a black unrelieved mass against the flames. The light fell eerily on their faces. He took the sheaf of papers from his pocket and placed them to one side on a taboret, where he could glance at them. Then he applied a match to a cigaret and began.

"In many ways," he murmured, "this has been a very sad affair. On more than one occasion this evening I have been prompted to shut my mind to the facts and go away. John Marco was a scoundrel of the deepest dye. Apparently in his case there was no middle ground between *mala mens* and *malus animus*. Unquestionably he possessed the criminal mind—unembarrassed by the slightest restraint of conscience. To our circumscribed knowledge alone he endangered the happiness of one woman, planned the ruin of another, blasted the life of a third, and caused the death of a fourth. Undoubtedly his ledger, if we only had entrée to it, shows many similar cases. In a word, a villain who richly deserved extermination. As you said the other day, Mr. Godfrey, whoever killed him was a benefactor of mankind." He paused, puffing thoughtfully.

Godfrey said in a harsh tone: "Then why don't you let well enough alone? Apparently you've arrived at a conclusion. The man needed killing; the world's a better place without him. Instead of—"

"Because," sighed Ellery, "my work is done with symbols, Mr. Godfrey, not with human beings. And I owe a duty to Inspector Moley, who has been kind enough to let me run wild in his bailiwick. I believe, when all the facts are known, that the murderer of Marco stands an excellent chance of gaining the sympathy of a jury. This was a deliberate crime, but it was a crime which—in a sense, as you imply—had to be done. I choose to close my mind to the human elements, and treat it as a problem in mathematics. The fate of the murderer I leave to those who decide such things."

A pall of hushed tension fell as he picked up the top sheet from the taboret, scanned it briefly in the flickering fire-light, and set it down again. "I can't tell you how confused and baffled I was until this very evening. There was something in the way of a lucid interpretation of the facts. I felt it, I knew it, and yet I couldn't put my finger on it. And then, too, I had made one very glaring error in my previous calculations. Until the woman Pitts—who you now know is Mrs. Marco—revealed a certain fact, I was literally in a fog. But when she told me that the cape which Marco wore when he was found had been brought down to the terrace by her after Marco's death—in other words, that *the cape had not been on the scene of the crime at all during the murder*—I saw daylight very clearly indeed, and the rest was merely a matter of time, application, and correlation."

"What the devil can the cape have to do with it?" muttered Inspector Moley.

"Everything, Inspector, as you shall see. But now that we know Marco was not in possession of his cape at the time he was murdered, let us start from our knowledge of what he actually *did* possess. He was wearing a complete suit of clothes, with all the fixings. Now, we know that the murderer undressed Marco and took away the complete outfit—or almost complete: that is, coat, trousers, shoes, socks, underclothes, shirt, necktie, and whatever may have been in the pockets. The first problem that must be solved, then, is: *Why* did the murderer undress the dead man and take away his clothes? That there was a sane, an overwhelmingly sane, reason for this act of apparent insanity I knew; and that the whole solution depended upon its answer I felt instinctively.

"I turned the problem over in my mind until I wore it down to its component fibers. And finally I concluded that there were

288 · ELLERY QUEEN

only five possible theories which would account for the theft of the garments of a murder-victim—any murder-victim, in the most general sense.

"The first," continued Ellery, after a glance at his notes, "was the possible explanation that the murderer had done it for the *contents* of the clothes. This was especially important in the light of the existence of certain papers threatening the peace of mind of a number of persons connected with Marco. And, for all we knew, these papers might have been on Marco's person. But if it were the papers the murderer was after, and they were in the clothes, why hadn't he taken the papers and left the clothes, intact, behind? For that matter, if it were *anything* in the clothes, the murderer could have emptied the pockets or torn open linings and secured what he was after without taking the clothes from the body. So that was wrong, obviously.

"The second was an inevitable thought. Inspector Moley will tell you that very often a body is fished out of a river or is found in the woods with the clothes either damaged or missing altogether. In a large percentage of these cases the reason is simple: to conceal the identity of the victim, the destruction or theft of the clothing preventing identification. But this was quite plainly wrong in the case of Marco; he was Marco, no one ever questioned his identity as Marco, and surely his clothing could not have indicated that he was any one else. There never was and cannot be any question of the identity of the corpse in this case, with or without clothes.

"Conversely, there was always the third possibility that in some way the theft of Marco's clothes tended to conceal the identity of Marco's *murderer*. I see blank looks. By that I mean simply that Marco may have been wearing something—or everything—belonging to his murderer, the discovery of which the murderer felt would be fatal to his own safety. But this, too, was clearly wide of the mark, for our invaluable Tiller—" Tiller folded his hands and looked down modestly, although his tiny ears were cocked like a terrier's—"testified that the specific garments he laid out for Marco just before Marco redressed Saturday night were Marco's own. Besides, these were the only garments missing from Marco's wardrobe. Therefore Marco wore them that night and they could not have belonged to the criminal."

They were so quiet that the crackling of the resinous logs sounded like pistol-shots in the room, and the noise of the rain outside had the overwhelming quality of a cataract's thunder.

"Fourth," said Ellery, "because the clothes were blood-stained and in some way the stains were dangerous to the criminal or his plan." A startled look crept over Moley's heavy face. "No, no, Inspector, it's not as elementary as that. If the 'blood' was Marco's, the theory is wrong on two counts: *All* the clothes of Marco's which the criminal took away couldn't have been bloodstained—socks, underwear, shoes?—and even more important, there *was* no blood as far as the victim of this crime is concerned Marco was struck over the head and stunned, shedding no blood in the process; and then he was strangled, another bloodless operation.

"But suppose—I anticipate your question, Judge—it was the *murderer's* blood involved? That is, improbable as it seems from the position of the body, that Marco had engaged his killer in a struggle, in the course of which the killer had been wounded, inadvertently staining Marco's clothes with the killer's blood? Here again there are two objections. The first—again that all of Marco's clothes couldn't have been stained, so why were all taken? The second—on the theory that the only reason the kill-er could want to conceal the fact that he had bled being that he didn't want to have the police look for a wounded person—is simply that no one involved in this case has been injured. Except Rosa, and she has a perfectly sound explanation which does not necessitate such an elaborate deception. So the bloodstain the-ory is out.

"There was really," resumed Ellery quietly after a pause, "*only one last possibility.*"

The rain hissed and the fire cracked. There were knitted brows and puzzled eyes. It was almost certain that none of them—not even Judge Macklin—envisioned the answer. Ellery flipped his cigaret into the fire.

He turned back and opened his mouth . . .

The door burst open, bringing Moley to his feet instantly and jerking their heads around in alarm. Roush, the detective, stood there gasping for breath; he was soaked to the skin. He gulped three times before he was able to utter a comprehensible word.

"Chief! Just—been something . . . Run all the way from the terrace . . . They've cornered this Captain Kidd!"

For a moment they were too stunned to do more than gape.

"Huh?" said Moley in a croaking voice.

"Caught out in the storm!" cried Roush, waving his dripping arms excitedly. "Coast Guard just sighted Waring's cruiser. For some reason the big ape's headin' in for shore—he's makin' for the Cape! Looks like he's in trouble . . . "

"Captain Kidd," muttered Ellery. "I don't—"

"Come *on!*" yelled Moley, bounding through the doorway. "Roush, get—" His voice died away as he pounded off. The peo-ple in the room hesitated, and then with a concerted rush fol-lowed him.

Judge Macklin was left staring at Ellery. "What's the matter, El?"

"I don't know. This is the strangest development—*No!*" And with these cryptic words he sprang after the others.

· · · · · · ·

They made for the terrace, a mad boiling crowd, careless of the downpour—women and men, soaked in a moment, their faces oddly alive and glowing with hope and excitement. Moley was in the van, his shoes squishing on the morass underfoot. Only Judge Macklin was sensible enough to think of protection against the storm; he came last, more slowly, his tall figure draped in a sou'wester he had picked up somewhere in the house.

A group of detectives, their coats gushing rain, were balanced precariously on the white beams of the open terrace roof, struggling with the swivel-joints of the two large brass searchlights. Jorum was there to one side looking on with an indifferent, almost majestic, air. The men's garments whipped madly in the wind.

Moley jumped, shouting orders, onto the terrace. It was a wonder, in all the turmoil raging above his head, that some one did not slip from a wet beam and break his neck on the flags below. But finally the switches were found, and simultaneously two blinding white beams a foot wide leaped into being in the darkness, stabbing at the sky. The flood was gray hell in the path of the beams.

"Straighten 'em out, you clucks!" roared the Inspector, dancing and waving his arms. "Focus 'em through that opening ahead of you!"

Erratically the beams jerked into position. Then they were

horizontal to the terrace, and they fused and crossed each other fifteen feet above the water boiling outside the entrance to the Cove.

They strained and craned, faces streaming, following the rigid paths of the beacons. At first they could make out nothing but the translucent wall of the deluge impinging on the black waters below. But then, as one of the searchlights moved a little, they saw a wildly plunging speck far out to sea. At the same moment a third beam of light swept into view, from the sea-side. It was dancing about the speck.

"Coast Guard," shrieked Mrs. Godfrey. "Oh, catch him, *catch* him!" Her fists were fiercely clenched, her hair hanging in limp strands down her face.

The sharp prow of the Coast Guard boat edged into sight, bearing down on Hollis Waring's cruiser.

The cruiser was in evident distress. It pitched sickeningly, and it seemed dangerously low in the stern. As it came nearer they could discern the pigmy figure of a man staggering about its deck. The figure was too minute for recognition, but that he was in a state of desperation was apparent from his actions. And then, so suddenly that they froze and stopped breathing, the ship's bow upended, it shivered under the impact of a tremendous sea, which momentarily obscured it . . . When the sea tumbled the cruiser was gone.

They groaned in chorus. The beams darted to and fro, searching frantically.

"There he is!" screamed Rosa. "He's swimming!"

One of the beams had touched a dark bobbing head in the water. Arms flashed in and out of the sea. The man was swimming strongly, but he was being buffeted about by the raging seas and he made painful progress toward the Cove. The Coast

Guard ship loomed larger, but it kept off, afraid of running the swimmer down. A lifeline snaked and glittered over the water and fell short. But now they were so close to the cliffs that it was perilous for the ship to come nearer.

"He's making it!" shouted Moley. "Get blankets, somebody! Keep 'em dry!"

In ever-slowing lunges the swimmer inched toward the Cove. He was weakening. Nothing could be seen but the top of his head.

Helpless, they could only watch. And after an age it was over, like the climax of a nightmare. Nearing the entrance to the Cove, he was sucked in suddenly like a sardine. All they could see was a tangle of arms and legs as he hurtled dangerously near the cliff-wall to their right and shot with the resiliency of a cork into the comparative shelter of the Cove.

The detectives could not get the searchlights to focus steadily on the thrashing, half-drowned figure. Three of them dropped to the terrace and bounded across the strip of beach behind Inspector Moley to the water, lunging for the feebly kicking man. Then Moley had the back of the man's neck, and he pulled powerfully, getting the swimmer out of the clutches of the rollers, dragging him backward with the assistance of his men against the suck of the sea.

Standing aloof beside Judge Macklin, Ellery could see nothing of the rescued man. But they could see the faces of the crowding people in front of them, and what they saw on those faces caused Judge Macklin, at least, to narrow his eyes. It was sheer amazement, as if they had all received a stunning shock.

Some one jostled them aside, carrying oilskin-wrapped blankets, and disappeared as he dropped to his knees beside the rescued man. Then Mrs. Godfrey screamed and flung herself forward. They pressed nearer, striving to see.

They heard the man's deep, exhausted voice. "Thank . . . God . . . I—he—kept me—prisoner—somewhere along— coast. I—" The voice stopped. He was panting in huge, terrible, chest-shaking gulps. "Got loose—tonight—fought—boat out of control—I killed—him with a . . . Body overside—boat stove in—by storm . . ."

Ellery shouldered Munn and Walter Godfrey aside. The detective was wrapping the blanket about the recumbent man. He was a tall fellow. His eyes were pink with blood and there was a long dirty stubble on his cheeks and a gaunt look about him, as if he had suffered horribly. His clothes—what remained of a once-white linen suit—were sopping rags.

Rosa and her mother were on their knees beside him, clinging to him, weeping.

Ellery's features wore a pinched look. He stooped and tilted the man's exhausted face upward. It was a good face, strong and resolute for all its gauntness and fatigue.

"You're David Kummer?" he asked in a strangled voice, as if he had difficulty in speaking.

Kummer gasped: "Yes—yes. Who are—" Ellery straightened and jammed his wet hands into his drenched pockets. "I'm frightfully sorry," he said in the same reluctant croak. "It was a good plan and a good fight, David Kummer. But I am compelled to charge you with the murder of John Marco."

XVI
NUDAQUE VERITAS

"Hardest job I've ever had to do," growled Mr. Ellery Queen. He was hunched miserably over the wheel of the Duesenberg, watching the concrete road slip by. They were headed north, for home.

Judge Macklin sighed. "Now you know the problem that often faces a judge. Theoretically in capital crimes a man's fate is decided by a jury of his peers. But so often the court . . . We haven't solved, with all our vaunted civilization, the problem of true equity, my boy."

"What else could I do?" cried Ellery. "I've often boasted that the human equation means nothing to me. But it does, damn it all. It does!"

"If only he hadn't tried to be so infernally clever about it," said the Judge sadly. "He claims that he knew very well how Marco had ruined his sister Stella, what the rascal was doing to her peace of mind. And then he saw—or thought he did—what was happening to his niece Rosa. The trouble with the lot of 'em seems to have been that no one confided in any one else. But granted his righteous feeling of anger at Marco and his determination to kill the scoundrel, why didn't he take a revolver, shoot the man, and be done with it? No jury would have convicted him, especially if he pleaded that it was a crime of impulse, the result of a quarrel. Under the circumstances—"

"That's the trouble with clever men," muttered Ellery. "A crime being necessary, according to their lights, they determine to commit it so ingeniously that it will be insoluble. But the cleverer they are and the more complex their schemes, the more danger they run of something going wrong. The perfect crime!" He shook his head wearily. "The perfect crime is the chance killing of an unknown man in a dark alley with no witnesses. Nothing fancy. There are a hundred perfect crimes every year—committed by so-called submoronic thugs."

They were silent for many miles. Something about the huge rock of Spanish Cape had nauseated the two men; they had almost stolen away, quite as if they had been the criminals. The only word of cheer that had been spoken had come from the lips of Harry Stebbins when they had stopped at his establishment to fill the gasoline tanks.

"I know Mr. Kummer, and he's a good scout," Stebbins had said quietly. "If all I hear about this Marco bird is true, there isn't a jury in this county will convict Mr. Kummer. He's as good as free right now."

David Kummer lay in the county jail at Poinsett, still shaken by his authentic experience during the storm, but quietly grim. Godfrey had retained the most eminent counsel in the East to defend him. Spanish Cape glowered under a blight, cheerless in the sudden raw weather which had fallen. Rosa Godfrey had crept into the arms of young Cort, and her mother into the arms of her father. Only Tiller had remained the same—deferential, discreet, and imperturbable.

·　　·　　·　　·　　·　　·　　·

"You haven't told me yet," said the Judge dryly, as they skimmed along, "how this feat of mental legerdemain was accomplished, Ellery. Or was it just a lucky stab in the dark?" He fixed a shrewd eye on his companion, and chuckled as Ellery glared at him.

"Nothing of the sort!" said Ellery wrathfully, and then he grinned and turned a sheepish glance back at the road. "Psychologist! . . . And they were such pretty notes, too." He sighed. "However, I've gone over them so often in my mind since last night that I know them by heart. Where the deuce was I when that shipwreck intervened?"

"You had come to the conclusion that only the fifth of your five possibilities with regard to the clothes was true."

"Oh, yes!" Ellery kept his eyes on the road. "And that was that the criminal took away Marco's clothes simply *because he wanted them as clothes*." The old gentleman's eyes widened at the simplicity of the conclusion. "But why should the criminal have wanted Marco's clothes as clothes? To clothe himself. Obviously, then, the criminal had no clothes of his own. Startling, but inevitable. Why did the criminal need clothes after the crime? Obviously again—to effect his escape. They were necessary to his getaway."

Ellery waved his hand in a rather bitter gesture. "I originally discarded this possibility because I could not see why the murderer should have taken all the garments on Marco *and left the cape behind*. The cape was, as it were, the most enveloping garment of all. The criminal could hardly have neglected to take this figure-concealing garment—black as the night itself, reaching from throat to ankles—if he had wanted clothes as clothes for the purpose of a getaway. As a matter of fact, with the pressure of haste upon him after a murder, he could easily have dis-

298 · ELLERY QUEEN

pensed with most, if not all, of the things he actually took—the coat, the shirt, the tie surely, perhaps even the trousers—and taken the cape alone; with the shoes, perhaps, for decent under-pinning. Yet he went to the trouble under pressure of taking every stitch of Marco's clothing and left the cape behind! I could only conclude that my fifth explanation was wrong and that still another existed. I didn't come back to that line of thought for a long time—more's the pity; but blundered off into a fog. It was not until Mrs. Marco's testimony late yesterday afternoon, revealing that the cape had not been on Marco's body or on the terrace during the crime, that I saw that the fifth explanation—clothes as clothes for a getaway—must be the correct one after all. There had been no cape for the murderer to take. And so I say that the cape has been the most important factor in this case. For lack of the vital bit of information concerning it this case would never have been solved."

"I see that now," said the Judge, thoughtfully, "although how it gets you to Kummer is still beyond me."

Ellery pressed his klaxon button savagely and shot around a startled Pierce Arrow. "Wait. I pointed out before that the criminal had no clothes of his own. That required clarification. To what extent, I asked myself, did the criminal have no clothes of his own; that is, in what state of undress was he when he came upon the scene of the intended crime? Now we knew precisely what he had filched from the body after the killing. Consequently I was able to say that he couldn't have come in anything corresponding to what he had taken from Marco, otherwise he wouldn't have taken them. That is, when he came he couldn't have been wearing a shirt, a tie, coat, trousers, shoes, socks, or underwear. True, he had left Marco's hat and stick behind. But to say that the criminal came with no clothing of the sort I've described on his body, and yet did come with a hat or stick or both, is of course preposterous. Apparently he had no need of a stick and hat, and simply left these articles behind. At any rate, he had no hat or stick when he came, either. Well, what possible clothing is left in which he might have come to the beach-terrace to commit the crime?"

"Hmm," said the Judge. "It seems to me you can't overlook the possibility that he came in, let us say, a bathing-suit."

"Quite true. I didn't overlook it. As a matter of fact, he might have come in a bathing-suit, a bathing-suit and robe, or a robe alone."

"Well—"

Ellery said wearily: "Now, I've already established that he took Marco's clothing to make his getaway. Could he have made his getaway if he had originally worn a bathing-suit, suit and robe, or robe alone? *Certainly.*"

"I don't see that," protested the old gentleman. "Not if he—"

"I know what you're going to say. But I've analyzed this beyond the possibility of doubt. If he were escaping from the terrace to the house, any one of these classifications—bathing-suit, robe, or both—would have been sufficient for him and he wouldn't have had to take Marco's clothes. There would be nothing remarkable, in the observatory sense, in any one's coming in from a 'swim' in the early hours—if he should be noticed. You were going to ask: What if he had escaped, not to the house, but to some remoter place by way of the highway? The answer to that is that bathing-suit or robe, if he had been wearing either or both during an escape by that route, would have been sufficient. Your friend Harry Stebbins said last Sunday morning, you'll recall, that there's a local ordinance which permits bathers to use the stretch of highway between the beaches—which takes in the exit from Spanish Cape—clad only in bathing costume. In fact, when we saw him he himself had just come walking back from one of the public beaches in a bathing-suit. But if this is common custom the murderer would have been safe to make his escape in such costume no matter at what hour—he could feel sure of not being stopped. Again, I say, had he worn a bathing-suit and escaped by way of the highway he wouldn't have needed Marco's clothes. The only other possible route—besides the house and main highway—is the sea itself. But of course he wouldn't *take clothes* to escape by water, and besides there were no footprints in the sand, proving that escape had not been made by way of the Cove."

"But, if that analysis is correct," began the Judge in a puzzled way, "I don't see—"

"Surely the conclusion is inevitable?" cried Ellery. "If the murderer had originally worn a bathing-suit, or suit and robe, or even robe alone, *he would not have needed Marco's clothes to make his getaway.* But he *did* need Marco's clothes to make his getaway, as I've shown. Therefore I had to conclude that the murderer did *not* originally wear a bathing-suit or robe when he came to the scene of the crime."

"But that means—" said the old gentleman, shocked.

"Precisely. That means," said Ellery calmly, "that he originally wore *nothing.* In other words, when he stole up on Marco and hit him over the head *the murderer was as naked as on the day of his birth.*"

Both men were silent against the roar of the Duesenberg's powerful motor.

The Judge murmured after a moment: "I see. John Marco's nakedness simply became the nakedness of the murderer. Very clever. Very clever indeed! Go on, my boy; this is extraordinary."

Ellery blinked. He was very tired. Hell of a vacation! he thought. But he went on doggedly: "The question naturally followed, if the murderer came naked: Where did he come from? That was the easiest part of all. He didn't come naked from the house, obviously. Certainly not from the highway. He could have come naked only from the third of the three possible routes: *the sea*."

Judge Macklin uncrossed his long legs deliberately and turned his head to stare at Ellery. "Hmm," he said dryly. "We seem to have unearthed a human weakness in the paragon. I can't believe my ears. Here you've proved that the murderer must have come from the sea, and yet only Sunday I heard you prove with just as much conviction that the murderer *couldn't* have come from the sea!"

Ellery blushed. "Go on; heap coals on my head. You'll remember I referred only last night to one vital error in my former reasoning. Yes, that's what I 'proved,' and it will stand in my mind as an eternal monument to a moment of thoughtlessness. It just tends to show that few arguments are impervious to fallacy. We merely hope . . . That was my major slip in this confounded case. You remember my 'proof' was based on two lines of reasoning. The first was that Marco, having begun to write a highly personal letter on the terrace before he was assaulted, dating it at one o'clock and mentioning that he was alone, must therefore have *preceded* his murderer. But if he preceded his murderer, the murderer came *after* one o'clock. But at about one o'clock the tide was very low, the beach was uncovered for at least eighteen feet, and there were no footprints in this sand. So I reasoned that the murderer could not have come from the sea, but had come by land, by the path. Don't you see the fallacy in my reasoning?"

"Frankly, no."

Ellery sighed. "It's simple, but tricky. Didn't see it myself until the final line of reasoning convinced me the first was wrong and caused me to re-examine it. The fallacy is merely *that we took Marco's word for it that he was alone on the terrace at one o'clock.* He said he was alone; but the fact that he said it—even granting that he was not lying, had no motive for lying—doesn't make it true. He simply *thought* he was alone! Either condition—thinking he was alone or being actually alone—would have caused the same effect: his sitting down to write a personal letter. I stupidly neglected to take the illusory condition into account."

"By Judas!"

"Now it was evident why the first 'proof' went wrong. If he merely thought he was alone, it was possible that he *wasn't* alone at the time he wrote the letter; in other words, that he hadn't come first at all, but that his murderer had come first and was hiding on the terrace, unknown to Marco, in ambush."

"But where?"

"Behind one of those enormous Spanish jars, of course. It's the most likely place. Big as a man; you could easily hide behind it. Besides, you'll remember that the weapon employed to stun Marco was a bust of Columbus from a niche in the wall near one of these Arabian Nights' jars. The murderer simply reached over, grabbed it, tiptoed—in bare feet—over to Marco from behind while Marco sat writing, and struck the foul fiend over the head. Then he took a coil of wire which he had been carrying around his own neck, or wrist or ankle, and strangled the unconscious man. The use of wire alone—in preference to a more orthodox weapon—was in a way a confirmation that the murderer had come from the sea. Wire would not hamper swimming; it's light and won't spoil, like a gun; nor is it as awkward to carry as a knife, which would probably have to be carried between the teeth, making breathing difficult. Of course, this last hazard is unimportant. The important thing was that this reconstruction substantially satisfied all the conditions."

"But the sand, my boy," cried the Judge. "It showed no footprints! Then how do you maintain he came—"

"You're usually more perspicacious," murmured Ellery. "For if the murderer came first, he may have come at any time *before* one o'clock, before the tide *got* so low, before the beach *was* uncovered to the extent of eighteen feet!"

"But that note," retorted the old gentleman with a stubborn air. "He couldn't have come much before one o'clock. The false note actually set the appointment with Marco for one. Why should the murderer have done that forcing himself to come so early? He could just as easily have made the time—"

Ellery sighed. "Did the note say *one* o'clock?"

"Of course!"

"Now, now, don't be hasty. If you'll recall, there was a scrap of paper missing immediately after the figure I in the typed note. Unhappy accident, my dear Judge. The actual figure must have been 12. The 2 dropped off with the missing scrap!"

"Hmm. But how do you know it *was* 12?"

"It must have been. Had the figure been 11, or 10, Marco certainly wouldn't have permitted himself to remain involved in a bridge game until half-past eleven. He would have quit early enough to keep his appointment. Obviously, then, the appointment was set for the hour nearest eleven-thirty in point of coming time—which is twelve."

"I see, I see," muttered the Judge. "Misfortune for Kummer. Kummer arrived at the terrace a little before midnight, expecting Marco at once. I suppose he swam in naked for the complet-

304 · ELLERY QUEEN

est freedom of his limbs; and then too the less he had on the less chance there would be, he must have figured, of dropping a clue from his person. But Marco, delayed by Mrs. Godfrey in his room unexpectedly, was held back for a full hour. Imagine having to wait an hour outdoors at night by the sea without clothes on!"

"It was considerably more dreadful than that, from Kummer's standpoint," said Ellery dryly. "Apparently you don't grasp the central implication. *It was that unexpected delay of an hour that caused him to take the clothes!* If Marco had been on time, there would have been no clue at all to Kummer."

"Don't follow," growled the Judge.

"Don't you see," exclaimed Ellery, "that the criminal must have *figured* on the tides? If he came a little before midnight, the tide was high—at its highest. He could almost step from the water to the lowest step of the stairs leading up to the terrace. No footprints to leave in the sand at all. Had Marco been on time, he would have killed the man and returned by way of the sea—still without leaving footprints. For the tide would still have been high enough—*that* crime would have taken only a minute or two—for him to leap over the intervening stretch of sand into the breakers. But he was forced to sit helplessly by on the terrace, watching the tide go out; the beach grew larger, and larger still, and still Marco wasn't there. Yes, yes, a very tough spot for Kummer. He chose to stay and take the hard way out, planning what to do while he waited. I suppose he felt that he wouldn't have an opportunity again to decoy Marco to a place where the man might be murdered with impunity. The inspiration about taking Marco's clothes must have arisen from his realization that he and Marco were of a size.

"At any rate, I knew then that the criminal had come from

the sea, before midnight, naked. Well, was he living at the house of Godfrey during the immediate period of the murder? But if he was, why should he have swum in from the sea—the long, difficult way around—when the route by land over the path from the house itself would have been infinitely easier?"

The old gentleman scraped his jaw. "Why, if he actually was residing in the house at the time and yet chose to come in swimming, it could only be to make it appear that the murderer was an outsider, had been *compelled* to come in from the sea by the outside route. In other words, to cover up the fact that he *was* living at the house."

"Perfectly put," applauded Ellery. "But if this had been his motive, he would have made it *plain* that he had come from the sea, would he not?"

"If that had been his motive—certainly."

"Of course. He would have emphasized the fact, left an open trail from the sea, forced us to believe what he wanted us to believe. Yet, on the contrary, the murderer had made every effort to *conceal* the fact that he had come from the sea!"

"I glimpse that vaguely. How do you mean?"

"Well, for one thing he hadn't taken the obvious escape-route; that is, the way he had come—via beach to water. Had he taken that escape-route he would have left outgoing footprints in the sand, which would have told us the story at a glance. No, no, he wouldn't have minded at all leaving such footprints had he been residing in the house at the time. But what did the murderer do in actuality? He made desperate efforts to *avoid* leaving such footprints! For he undressed the dead man and put on the borrowed clothes—all for the purpose of making his escape by a route *other* than the sea . . . In other words, it was evident that the murderer had gone to great lengths to avoid leaving footprints in the sand, that he wanted to conceal the fact that he *had* come from the sea. But any one living in the Godfrey house during the murder-period would *not* have wanted to conceal the fact that he had come from the sea. Therefore the criminal was not living in the Godfrey house during the immediate period of the murder. Q.E.D."

"But only," chuckled the Judge, "up to a certain point. Where did you go from there?"

"Well," said Ellery gloomily, "when I knew the criminal wasn't in the house during the immediate period of the murder it was child's play. Every one who had been in or about the house on the night of the murder had to be dismissed as the possible murderer. That eliminated Mr. and Mrs. Godfrey, Mrs. Constable, Cecilia Munn and her precious husband, Cort, Tiller, Pitts, Jorum—the whole kit and boodle of 'em with the exception of Rosa Godfrey, Kummer, and Kidd."

"But how did you arrive at Kummer specifically? Or did you select him as the likeliest possibility? Actually, you had no reason to suspect he wasn't dead, you know."

"Peace," intoned Ellery. "It was demonstrable. For what were the characteristics of the criminal—deducible from the phenomena of his crime? They were six in number, and I listed them with care.

"One: He knew Marco and the Marco relationships intimately. Because he knew enough about the supposedly secret connection between Marco and Rosa to frame Marco with the false appointment, ostensibly made by Rosa, by way of the fake note.

"Two: He knew that Mrs. Godfrey came down early every morning to the beach for a swim. Had he not known this, he would have made his escape by the way he had come—over the beach to the water in the Cove and out to sea, leaving foot-prints. For the incoming tide in the late morning would have washed away the prints and left no trace. The fact that he did not choose that route tends to show he foresaw Mrs. Godfrey's appearance before the tide would erase the prints; consequently that he knew she would come.

"Three: He knew the locale so well that he was acquainted with the times of the tides in the Cove.

"Four: He was an excellent swimmer. Since he came from the sea originally, he must have come from a boat anchored off-shore—not too close so that it wouldn't attract attention. But if he came from a boat, then he must have returned to the boat after the crime. He felt compelled, however, to escape by the highway route, as I've shown—"

"Wait—"

"Let me go on. To escape by the highway route he needed clothes, since he had no bathing-suit or robe; Stebbins's place is directly opposite the exit from the Cape—the only spot where he could emerge from the estate by land—and he could take no chance of being seen coming out of that brightly illuminat-ed exit in the nude. So he walked down the highway clothed in Marco's duds, to one of the public beaches. Each beach is a mile or so from the Cove, as we noticed. What did he do? He un-dressed on the public beach—deserted at more than one-thir-ty in the morning—bundled up the clothes (he wouldn't have risked leaving them there)—and swam with the clothes *the min-imum of one mile* back to the boat. Therefore, I say, logic indicat-ed that the murderer was an excellent swimmer."

"There are loopholes," pointed out the Judge as Ellery paused for breath. "You say that if he came from a boat he must have re-turned to the boat. Not necessarily—"

"Most necessarily," retorted Ellery. "He came naked in the first place, didn't he? Did he expect to make an escape by land— in the nude? No, he expected to swim back to his boat. If he had planned to, with his getaway means of transportation waiting for him, then he did. But to go on.

"Five: Physically he must have been built like Marco. Why? In order to have been able to wear Marco's clothes well enough so that had Stebbins seen him or had he met some one on the road during his march to the public beach there would have been nothing incongruous in the fit of the clothing to attract attention to him and probably get him into instant trouble, let alone leaving an indelible impress on a possible witness's memory. A big man, then—certainly about the general build of Marco.

"And six: The criminal had had previous access to the Godfrey house. That was most important."

"You mean the note?"

"Of course. He used the Godfrey typewriter in writing the faked note. But the typewriter had never left the house. Consequently the typist must necessarily have visited the house or been a member of the household to have been able to use the machine."

Ellery slowed down for a red light. "Well," he sighed, "there I was. Rosa Godfrey, even supposing that we doubted the genuineness of her story about having been tied up in Waring's shack all night—could she have been the criminal after all? Impossible. She doesn't swim. She can't type. And while she might have masqueraded in Marco's clothes—theoretically—she would certainly have taken his hat to conceal her woman's hair. But Marco's hat was not taken. Out on at least three counts, then.

"Kidd? Impossible for the reason that, from the descriptions provided, he was a giant of a man, so extraordinary in size that he could never have got into Marco's clothes at all. And shoes—do you remember Rosa's horrified description of the man's enormous feet? No, no, not Kidd.

"There were," continued Ellery with a tired, if reminiscent, smile, "certain whimsical possibilities. Constable, for instance—the unfortunate Laura's invalid husband. But even he could be eliminated on a logical basis. He had never met the Godfreys and so couldn't have known of Mrs. Godfrey's natatorial habits; he had never been in the Godfrey house and so couldn't have typed the 'Rosa' note.

"And Waring. The man who owns the cottage and cruiser. Why not he? Well, because he was, from Rosa's description, a very tiny man; and he had never been—on your own testimony, my dear Solon, within the Godfrey house.

"Only Kummer was left. I didn't *know* he was dead and had to consider him. I was startled to find that he satisfied *all six conditions*. He had intimated to Rosa that he knew about her and Marco. He certainly knew that his sister Stella went for a dip every morning; in fact, she told us he often accompanied her! He was a sportsman—loved the Cape, went sailing; undoubtedly he must have known about the tides. Swim? Very well indeed, according to his sister. Physical ability to wear Marco's clothes? Oh, yes; he was of a size with the dead man, according to Rosa. And last, he certainly had access to the Godfrey typewriter, since he was a permanent resident in the house. So Kummer, the only one satisfying all these conditions, and moreover having been *the only one on the sea* (with the exception of Kidd) during the night of the murder, must have been the criminal. And there I was."

"I suppose," remarked the Judge after an interval of silence, "it's really no feat to reconstruct what must have happened—

after you've arrived at Kummer as the one and only possible criminal."

Ellery depressed the accelerator viciously, and they whizzed by a caterpillar truck. "Of course. It was plain as a pikestaff. If Kummer was the criminal, then it was evident that the whole incident of the kidnaping had been a plant, pure and simple. A plant of Kummer's to get himself out of the way under sympathetic circumstances, to make it look as if he was not only emotionally but physically an impossibility as the criminal. Very clever—much too clever.

"It was evident that he must have secretly hired this Kidd scoundrel to kidnap him—probably telling the monster that it was a practical joke of some sort; or if he told him the truth, paying him sufficient blood-money to insure his temporary silence at least. Kummer involved Rosa because he wanted a witness to what happened—a reliable witness who could tell the police after the event how courageously her uncle had acted, and how helpless he had been in the clutches of the gorilla-like Kidd. Then, too, it was expedient to get Rosa out of the way, where she couldn't spoil the ruse of the false note.

"The whole theatrical business must have been rehearsed between him and Kidd, even to the punch to Kidd's belly and the blow which rendered Kummer 'unconscious.' All for Rosa's benefit. The touch about Kidd's apparently mistaking Kummer for Marco—to the extent of actually addressing him as Marco!—was an inspiration designed to prepare the police for the innocence of Kummer and the murder of Marco apparently by an outsider or some one in the house. Kummer was smart enough to realize that the police wouldn't accept Kidd as the actual murderer of Marco; there was no connection at all between the two. So he had Kidd 'telephone' to some one—in Rosa's hearing, of course; that was very carefully planned, you may be sure—as if Kidd were reporting to an outside employer; as if there were a higher-up (other than Kummer himself, of course). With Kummer lying on the sand 'unconscious' while this call was being made, the deception was perfect. What actually happened, I suppose, was that Kidd dialled one of the Godfrey numbers, waited until he heard the click on the other end which signalled that some one had picked up a receiver or plugged in for a call, instantly pressed his thumb down on his own instrument to break the connection, and then calmly proceeded to conduct a one-sided conversation. No, no, we all erred about this wonderful Captain Kidd, as Kummer sardonically expected us to. He must have been anything but stupid to have followed orders so closely and executed them so flawlessly. Bit of a maritime actor."

"But how did Kummer work the business of the typed note? He was out of the house when it was—"

"Found? Of course. But not when it was planted. He left it in Tiller's closet downstairs just after dinner and just before he asked Rosa to accompany him outside for a chat. He knew Tiller wouldn't find the note until nine-thirty—by the way, another qualification of the murderer, this knowledge of Tiller's habits—when it would be presumed that it had been typed and left *after Kidd's call* to his 'superior.' You will recall, too, that Cort received an anonymous telephone message the morning we blundered on the young lady in Waring's cottage, telling Cort where he might find Rosa. That call, of course, came from Kummer. Wherever he had been hiding out along the coast, he risked making a public appearance just for the sake of that call. I imagine he would rather have given himself up than harmed a hair of that girl's head. He wanted to make sure she was found as quickly as possible."

"Doesn't seem like it, considering the fact that he plunged her into hot water by signing her name to the note."

Ellery shook his head. "He knew she would have a strong alibi: couldn't type and found trussed up in Waring's shack. He didn't mind having the police think the note was framed; in fact, he preferred it for Rosa's sake. And remember, if Marco hadn't been careless about the destruction of the note it never would have been found at all and Rosa wouldn't have been involved in that connection."

They were approaching a large town and the traffic had thickened to an uncomfortable degree. For some time Ellery occupied himself blasphemously with the business of keeping the Duesenberg out of trouble. Judge Macklin sat nursing his chin, deep in thought.

"How much," he demanded suddenly, "do you believe is true in Kummer's confession?"

"Eh? I don't know what you mean."

They crawled into a busy main street. "You know, I've been wondering about what he said concerning this Kidd monster last night. I mean after he explained that he had taken advantage of the storm to make a dramatic re-entrance, deliberately scuttling the cruiser and swimming for his life to shore. He admitted that in his first story—about having killed Kidd in a fight yesterday evening on the boat—he had been mendacious. Then he said that what really happened was that as soon as they got out of sight of Spanish Cape in Waring's cruiser Saturday night—after the 'kidnaping'—he landed the boat in an isolated spot, paid Kidd off, and sent him packing. Gave us the impression deliberately that Kidd is alive and has departed for parts unknown. But somehow it didn't ring true."

"Oh, nonsense," snapped Ellery, honking his klaxon. His face convulsed as he leaned out of the car and yelled to a crowding taxicab with the righteous wrath of all motor-maniacs: "What the hell d'ye think you're doing?" Then he grinned and pulled his head back. "As a matter of fact, when I had evolved Kummer as the murderer of Marco I naturally asked myself what had become of Kidd. He had obviously been the merest tool. The question was: Had he known the truth, or had Kummer deceived him as to the genuine purpose behind the hocus-pocus of the 'kidnaping'? And I saw that two things militated against a *crime en double* . . . You suspect Kummer has murdered Kidd, too?"

"I will confess," murmured the Judge with a frown, "that some such thought had entered my mind."

"No," said Ellery. "I'm sure he didn't. For one thing, it was not necessary for Kummer to tell Kidd what he really intended to do. And for another, Kummer is not what is known as a 'natural' killer. He is a thoroughly sane human being, as law-abiding as the next fellow. He isn't the kind of man who would lose his head. He isn't the kind of man who would deprive a fellow-creature of life merely for the sake of killing or because there was a faint chance mercy would rebound. Kidd, a scoundrel, was no doubt handsomely paid. Even if he has read about the murder somewhere and has considered blackmailing Kummer, he would be deterred by the realization that he himself was an accessory to the crime. This was Kummer's protection against his hireling. No, no, Kummer told the truth."

Neither spoke again until they had left the town behind and were on the open road once more. The air had a bite to it that was a foretaste of autumn, and the old gentleman suddenly shivered.

"What's the matter?" asked Ellery solicitously. "Cold?"

"I don't know," chuckled the Judge, "whether it's a reaction from the murder or the wind, but I believe I am."

Inexplicably, Ellery stopped the car. He sprang out, opened the crowded rumbleseat, rummaged about, and then brought forth something black, soft, and bulky.

"What's that?" asked the old gentleman suspiciously. "Where'd you get it? I don't recall—"

"Drape it around your shoulders, pop," said Ellery, jumping into the car and flinging the thing over the old man's knees. "It's a little memento of our experience."

"What on earth—" began the Judge, astonished, as he shook the garment out.

"The would-be murderer of justice, the detour on the road of logic," cried Ellery in oratorical fashion, releasing the hand-brake. "Couldn't resist it. Matter of plain truth, I swiped it from under Moley's nose this morning!"

Judge Macklin held it up. It was John Marco's black cape.

The old gentleman shivered again, drew a breath, and then with a brave gesture flung the cape over his shoulders. Ellery heeled the accelerator, grinning. And after a while the old gentleman began to sing in a robust baritone the interminable chorus of *Anchors Aweigh*.

AFTERWORD

I REMEMBER sitting down with Judge Macklin and Ellery one autumn night in a Russian place on the East Side, talking to the accompaniment of *balalaika* music and sipping tea out of tall glasses. There was a huge Russian with black whiskers at the next table, noisily guzzling his tea from the saucer, which is the orthodox Russian fashion; and the man's physical proportions rather naturally turned the talk to Captain Kidd and in a moment to the case of John Marco. I had been urging Ellery for some time to whip his notes into shape and write a book around their experiences on Spanish Cape; and I thought I would press the present opportunity while he was in a receptive mood.

"Oh, *all* right," he said at last. "You're the world's cruelest slave-driver, J. J. And I suppose it is as interesting as anything I've been mixed up in lately." He was still morose from the effects of the Tyrolean case he had failed to solve during the summer.

"If you're going to fictionize this thing," remarked Judge Macklin dryly, "I suggest, my son, you plug up one rather gaping hole."

Ellery's head came around like a setter's to point. "Now what," he demanded, "do you mean by that crack?"

"Hole?" I said. "I've heard the whole business, Judge, and I didn't see any."

"Oh, but there is one." The old gentleman chuckled. "Rather personal with me. You mathematicians! But as long as you make a fetish of strict logic, you don't want your adoring public making your life miserable with triumphant letters."

"Now, don't be provoking," snapped Ellery.

"Well," said the Judge dreamily, "you think you eliminated everybody in that analysis, don't you?"

"Of course!"

"But you didn't."

Ellery lit a cigaret rather deliberately. "Oh," he said. "I didn't? Whom did I omit, pray?"

"Judge Macklin."

I choked over my tea at the comical expression of surprise on Ellery's normally nonchalant features. The Judge winked at me and began to hum with the *balalaikas*.

"Dear, dear," murmured Ellery in a distressed way. "I certainly am slipping. There goes your book, J. J. Fallacy. Hmm . . . My dear Solon—as the mother lamb said to the daughter lamb when she left home—don't kid yourself."

The old gentleman stopped humming. "You mean you *did* consider me—? Why, you *pup*! After all I've done for you!"

Ellery was grinning broadly. "And I acknowledge receipt. But, after all, truth is beauty, and beauty truth, and to hell with old friends; eh? I considered you purely as an exercise in logic. I'll admit I was relieved to find that you could be eliminated."

"Thanks," said the Judge; he was considerably crestfallen. "You didn't mention it."

"It—er—isn't the sort of thing you mention to friends."

"But what is the eliminating point, Ellery?" I cried. "There's certainly nothing in what you've told me . . ."

"Perhaps not," laughed Ellery. "But it will be neatly buried in the book. Remember, Solon, our conversation with Stebbins on that Sunday morning?" The old gentleman nodded. "Remember what I told him?" The old gentleman shook his head. "I told him you couldn't swim!"

J. J. McC.

DISCUSSION QUESTIONS

- At the moment of the "Challenge to the Reader," were you able to predict any part of the solution to the case?

- After learning the solution, were there any clues you realized you had missed?

- Did any aspects of the plot date the story? If so, which ones?

- Would the story be different if it were set in the present day? If so, how?

- What role did the setting play in the narrative?

- If you were one of the main characters, would you have acted differently at any point in the story?

- Did you identify with any of the characters? If so, who?

- What sort of detective is Ellery Queen? What qualities make him appealing to readers? What qualities make him an effective crime-solver?

- Did this novel remind you of anything else you've read? If so, what?

- If you've read other Ellery Queen novels, how does this compare with what you've read?

H.F. Heard, *A Taste for Honey*

Dolores Hitchens, *The Cat Saw Murder*
Introduced by Joyce Carol Oates

Dorothy B. Hughes, *Dread Journey*
Introduced by Sarah Weinman
Dorothy B. Hughes, *Ride the Pink Horse*
Introduced by Sara Paretsky
Dorothy B. Hughes, *The So Blue Marble*

W. Bolingbroke Johnson, *The Widening Stain*
Introduced by Nicholas A. Basbanes

Baynard Kendrick, *The Odor of Violets*

Jonathan Latimer, *Headed for a Hearse*
Introduced by Max Allan Collins

Frances and Richard Lockridge, *Death on the Aisle*

John P. Marquand, *Your Turn, Mr. Moto*
Introduced by Lawrence Block

Stuart Palmer, *The Puzzle of the Happy Hooligan*

Otto Penzler, ed., *Golden Age Detective Stories*
Otto Penzler, ed., *Golden Age Locked Room Mysteries*

Ellery Queen, *The American Gun Mystery*
Ellery Queen, *The Chinese Orange Mystery*
Ellery Queen, *The Dutch Shoe Mystery*
Ellery Queen, *The Egyptian Cross Mystery*
Ellery Queen, *The Siamese Twin Mystery*

H.F. Heard, *A Taste for Honey*

Dolores Hitchens, *The Cat Saw Murder*
Introduced by Joyce Carol Oates

Dorothy B. Hughes, *Dread Journey*
Introduced by Sarah Weinman
Dorothy B. Hughes, *Ride the Pink Horse*
Introduced by Sara Paretsky
Dorothy B. Hughes, *The So Blue Marble*

W. Bolingbroke Johnson, *The Widening Stain*
Introduced by Nicholas A. Basbanes

Baynard Kendrick, *The Odor of Violets*

Jonathan Latimer, *Headed for a Hearse*
Introduced by Max Allan Collins

Frances and Richard Lockridge, *Death on the Aisle*

John P. Marquand, *Your Turn, Mr. Moto*
Introduced by Lawrence Block

Stuart Palmer, *The Puzzle of the Happy Hooligan*

Otto Penzler, ed., *Golden Age Detective Stories*
Otto Penzler, ed., *Golden Age Locked Room Mysteries*

Ellery Queen, *The American Gun Mystery*
Ellery Queen, *The Chinese Orange Mystery*
Ellery Queen, *The Dutch Shoe Mystery*
Ellery Queen, *The Egyptian Cross Mystery*
Ellery Queen, *The Siamese Twin Mystery*